RITE OF DARKNESS

ORDER OF THADDEUS
BOOK 7

J. A. BOUMA

EmmausWay Press

An Imprint of EmmausWay Media Group

PO Box 1180 • Grand Rapids, MI 49501

www.emmauswaypress.com

This book is a work of fiction. The characters, organizations, products, incidents, and dialogue are drawn from the author's imagination and experience, and are not to be construed as real. Any reference to historical events, real organizations, real people, or real places are used fictitiously. Any resemblance to actual products, organizations, events, or persons, living or dead, is entirely coincidental.

PROLOGUE

NEWBURY-FALLS, MASSACHUSETTS
BAY COLONY. 1687.

A wicked wind stirred the barren trees in the forest still frozen from the merciless winter, their limbs shaking with indignation at the women below huddled around a fire blazing with the fires of hell itself.

Trying them, passing judgment on them, condemning them, as if possessing providential insight into their impending trespasses.

The coven of suspicious women had stolen themselves away in the dead of night. They were a cross section of young and old, paupers and propers alike.

The rest of the village had occupied itself with the trappings of spring, even as winter held on for dear life—shearing sheep, churning sweet, spring milk into butter, sowing Indian corn for later harvest. So they used the opportunity to gather and complete the task they were given: the task of testifying to an untapped power of the ages, a spiritual force and consciousness permeating the Universe.

The women huddled around the fire atop the stone altar now blazing from the winds whipping off from the bay a half a mile away, waiting with bated breath for the One who would make it all possible. The fire's crackles and pops combined with the wind's whistles and creaking protestations from the surrounding trees was the only soundtrack for the evening.

The woman at the center of them all who had brought them together in the dead of night counted the assembled. Five, plus herself.

Six.

The number of humanity. Of enlightened consciousness.

A smile curled upward at the thought of all she had accomplished, all that she had endured the past few years since plumbing the depths of the power herself. Finding other kindred spirits to share in the bounty had not been easy. For the sort of power leveraging the full depths of human consciousness was not permitted. It was unlawful.

Heretical...

Yet she persisted, making the connections with like-minded souls and assembling the coven of women who would carry forth the plans of the Guardian of the ancient spiritual Order.

Her mouth curled upward as she studied those whom she had chosen, those who had made the decision to walk down this path of higher consciousness offered by the sublime powers gifted by the Ruler of the Power of the Air.

There was Elizabeth How, a woman married to a farmer in her early fifties who had long been particularly adept at leveraging the higher consciousness and preternatural affections of the Ruler.

Forty-year-old Mary English, the daughter of a prominent merchant and husband to an entrepreneur and newly elected councilman, had been hesitant, her soul still clinging to the old ways. But she had made the case and convinced the woman it was in her best interest, as well as her husband's business.

Susannah Martin, a sullen, unkempt, and petite seventy-one-year-old widow had been previously accused of dabbling in such darkness decades before, but was acquitted. Yet she came running at the chance to reconnect with the ground of her being once offered.

Martha Carrier was a late-thirties, abrasive mother of five whom many sisters and not a few brothers in the coven called "Queen of Hell"—both with affection and vilification.

Elizabeth Proctor, a forty-one-year-old mother and the matriarch of the household served by the woman who had orchestrated the evening, stood with protective hands around her swollen belly, knowing all too well the stakes, given her familiar connection with an Accused.

And then herself, a twenty-year-old orphaned servant of Elizabeth and her husband John, two vile people who abused her without mercy. However, given her deep connection to the evening's rite and its various manifestations over the years, and the need to assemble a coterie of the willing, she had tolerated it.

All for the cause, the consciousness, the—

A drum beat interrupted the woman's contemplation.

Dum-ditty-dum-ditty-dum-dum-dum.

Somewhere, the sound pierced through the howling wind, low and hesitant yet growing in surety and intensity. Soon, it was echoed by three or four more, a stereophonic beat surrounding the women from all directions and converging on the altar ablaze with the fires of hell itself.

"He has arrived, my darlings," the woman whispered, her mouth widening into a grin as a ping of adrenaline coursed through her body, all at once making her bosom grow warm and her bowels go weak.

This is the day which the Ruler hath made...I will rejoice and be glad in it!

The women spun toward the sound, their hooded robes rustling and the flames flapping in protest as a wild wind gusted through the trees on the arrival of their guest.

Out from the shadows he appeared. A ghastly, ghostly

being with the face of an ancient god, the ibis Bird-Man. Thoth, the Egyptian god of knowledge, of human consciousness.

Despite the frigid nighttime air, the man who wore the ancient face was bare-chested and tanned to a burnished bronze, his upper shoulders ringed by an intricate weave of gold and turquoise beads at the base of his neck. As he plodded toward the women, a long beak of onyx black, silent and probing, peered down at them from behind a mask of gold, flanked by ribbons of indigo.

A murmuring chorus, a mixture of confusion and anticipation, rippled through the gathered faithful who were about to pledge themselves to the incarnation of all that they held dear.

All at once, the echoing drumbeat ceased from the shadows, as suddenly as it had risen.

A sacred silence enveloped the gathered. Even the trees themselves seemed to have ceased their protestations in honor of what was about to commence, the only sound coming from the elemental, the primal, the archetypal ingredients of the universe: the flapping fire, the pops of earth's wood, the raging river a stone's throw away, and a distant whistling wind.

Bird-Man stood erect, immobile, peering. As if sizing up those who would dare give themselves through this rite of darkness to the Ruler, the Authority, the Cosmic Power, the Spiritual Force.

"So these are the ones, are they?" he finally said, voice deep and gravelly and significant. "Those who have pledged to deed their souls to *Ha-Satan*?"

"Yes, master," the woman said, bowing low with outstretched arms, her knees knocking together under her long skirt—both from the frightful chill and the freighted depth of the moment.

The man said nothing, his onyx beak merely passing over the women again before nodding approvingly.

"Excellent..." he finally muttered with approval. "Have you brought the elements?"

The woman looked to Martha Carrier, who nodded as she raised a large basket covered by a dark cloth for protection. Inside bore the elements of the sacred, secret rite. The elements parodizing another sacred ritual stretching back a millennium plus nearly seven centuries.

"Excellent..." Bird-Man said again. "Then let us begin."

A small wooden table had been brought and set up near the blazing altar. Martha set the basket on the table, then stepped aside as the guest assumed his position behind it.

The man lifted the black veil, dark, angular shadows from the fire nearby dancing across his face and body, making him look menacing, wicked.

Demonic.

Although...perhaps it wasn't the firelight after all.

Bird-Man was chanting something under his breath, his mouth moving with dramatic invocation as he summoned all that the Universe held beneath the surface—the man seeming to grow in size and shape the more he invoked the ancient words summoning the ancient, primal Ruler, the one who was humanity's original Consciousness.

With one hand, the man raised what looked to be a loaf of bread, dark and almost crimson in the light. With another, Bird-Man raised an earthenware chalice.

Bread and wine.

Flesh and blood.

The elements at the heart of the rite, ushering in the light of human consciousness suppressed for generations.

Suddenly, the drumbeat started up again—*dum-ditty, dum-ditty*—in all of its stereophonic glory as the man bearing the elements began the alternative ritual.

"Let us eat this bread and drink this cup in remembrance of the consciousness available to all," he said.

In one motion, Bird-Man tore the loaf of whatever it was in half, something black and liquid draining to the table beneath.

The women assembled a line reminiscent of the Eucharistic ritual performed each Sunday at the village church, the congregants lining the aisle and shuffling forth with outstretched hands for a bite of the bread, a sip of the cup.

The woman at the end of the line couldn't help but let a giggle slip at the display of burlesque sacrilege.

One by one, the women went forth, eating and drinking with abandon. When the one woman arrived, she bit into what she thought was bread. Only to realize it was cold flesh of some sort, slimy and sour, her lips stained crimson.

She forced down the tough meat, swallowing hard as the drumbeat continued its syncopated rhythm and reaching for the earthenware cup, drinking a mouthful. Only to realize it, too, was of somatic origin.

Actual blood.

The woman handed the chalice back to Bird-Man, wiping her mouth and bowing reverently before hastening back to the other women.

Suddenly, the man began to sway. Front to back on the balls of his feet. His head moved in sync: back and forth from side to side.

A growl began to well up within the belly of Bird-Man. At first faint, but growing in intensity until it exploded in a supernatural roar the woman could only describe as a fierce black bear mauling a goat to death.

And then, all at once, it ceased. But in its place was something altogether not of this world.

"Mine you all are," a Voice said, guttural and deep-throated and wholly unlike that of the original Bird-Man. *"Mine I say!"*

The women looked at one another, their faces registering a mixture of shock and fear and intrigue.

"Sign the book that will deed me your soul. In return, I give you

my consciousness, so that you may know both good and evil, the depths of the Universe in all of its fullness."

Bird-Man retrieved a book from his back, a small crimson-colored hardback, along with an athame ceremonial blade. He presented both to the woman.

She took them with shaking hands, but knew what needed to be done. Pressing the knife into her palm, she slit it open. The blood ran black in the dead of night, her life force dribbling across her wrist in hot, steamy rivulets and down onto the frozen ground below.

The woman winced, but taking a small, sharpened stick handed to her by Bird-Man, she dipped it into her blood, then opened the small red book and signed her name.

The drumbeat now picked up pace, and the trees shook their limbs in protest as a wind gusted through the forest upon the signing.

She handed the book and knife back to the man.

Immediately, the woman burst out into a cackle and began flailing about, having been overcome by a force, the promised Cosmic Force, opening the doorway into the primal consciousness. The one first tasted by humanity's original ancestors.

This continued as each of the other five women followed in this one woman's footsteps: slitting their palm with the athame blade, dipping the wood pen into their blood, signing their name to the Bird-Man's red book. All the while being overcome by cackling and writhing.

The drums were hammering away now, stirring the elements of the universe into a frenzied state with their *dum-ditty, dum-ditty* refrain.

When they were finished, Bird-Man led each of them by the hand down to the river. One by one, into the frigid waters he took them, dunking them below its knee-high surface in an unholy parody of the Christian rite of baptism. Sealing the deal and claiming their souls for himself.

When they emerged, the women suddenly fell to the ground and arched their backs. In their own ways, each of their faces transformed into a series of menacing poses. Cheekbones and lips and eyebrows all contorted in ways not thought possible.

And then a Voice, all their own, emerged. Different in tone and timbre from Bird-Man and unique to each woman. All having been overcome by the Ruler of the Power of the Air—their consciousness having been turned over, their eyes having been opened to the knowledge of good.

And Evil.

Then it all ceased, as quickly as it began. The Voice, the arching, the transformation, the drumbeats. Bird-Man had left during it all, retiring back into the shadows.

All that remained were the elements: the crackling fire, a light rain now slapping the women and hissing in the fire, the earth's killjoys waving judgmental branches from above, and the howling wind threatening to spread their secret.

Without word, each woman left her separate way, bearing with them their newfound Voice deep in their bones—the eyes to their consciousness having been opened, the deed to their souls having been sold. All for the power offered by the Ruler.

Over time, it would manifest itself in various ways; they couldn't help themselves. Which would grip the region with a blazing, unrelenting fear lasting for generations.

Many would be accused; all would give their lives for the cause. It was, after all, their upside-down cross to bear, given what they had signed over.

And to whom they had signed it over.

Soon, the consciousness that would usher humanity into the marvelous light of the Ruler of the Republic of Heaven would be unearthed and unleashed.

With nothing to stand in its way.

CHAPTER 1

FAIRFAX, VIRGINIA. PRESENT DAY.

"I'll take one of your large, bottomless buckets of popcorn and a supersize soda."

Silas Grey handed his credit card to the pimply-faced teenage boy looking like he had just rolled out of bed as his date for the matinee movie sidled up next to him.

"I will never understand how you Yanks can handle consuming copious amounts of trans fats and refined sugars whilst filling your mind with rubbish at the cinema," Celeste Bourne moaned, grabbing his hand and resting her head against his arm.

Retrieving his credit card from the teenager, Silas laughed. "It's an American tradition. Besides, I'm not sure our choice of entertainment is much better than our choice of snacks."

"You do realize you made my point for me in one fell swoop, don't you? And if I knew you were such a horror-flick junkie, I'm not sure I would have agreed to this courtship of yours."

Silas shrugged. "What can I say, I'm an onion with untold layers brimming with all kinds of bits of revelation."

"That's what I'm afraid of," she murmured.

The attendant handed Silas an empty, supersize soda cup and a bucket overflowing with popcorn, which Silas handed to

Celeste. "Why don't you go get us a seat and I'll fill up our Coke."

"Coca-Cola?" Celeste said, making a face as they made their way over to the drink station. "It's Dr Pepper or nothing, mate."

Silas opened his mouth and eyes with dramatic flair. "You're a DP gal? I had no idea!"

Celeste shrugged and grinned. "What can I say? I'm an onion with untold layers brimming with all kinds of bits of revelation."

He laughed and gave her a peck on the cheek. "Alright, Dr Pepper it is. But just this once. I'll meet you inside."

Folding his arms, Silas leaned against the drink station and watched the love of his life walk through a crowd of adults dressed in Halloween costumes toward an attendant taking tickets for *Another Nightmare on Maple Creek Road*, her hair perfectly twisted in a brunette braid that stretched the length of her back, black boots snugging her well-toned—

"Yo, dude?" a pasty white guy dressed in black with long greasy hair interrupted, the top corner of his mouth raised with irritation and a hand with black painted nails motioning to the Mello Yellow.

Silas raised a brow and smirked.

Can we get any more cliché?

"Yeah, buddy," Silas said with irritation at having lost his view. "Hold your horses."

He filled up on the DP and headed for a night of horror-flick bliss, feeling like the luckiest guy on the planet.

It had been six months since he and Celeste made their on-again-off-again dating relationship more official, committing to date each other and see where the Spirit led them. After offering his commitment to get more serious about their relationship, in Saint Peter's Square during Easter Mass of all places, Silas grabbed the reins and tried leading them more intentionality than he had given any relationship before.

In the past, he was either too immature as a person or too serious about his work to give any attention to his love life. After making mistakes with women as a teenager and then in college, he vowed to follow Saint Paul's exhortation to do *'everything to the glory of God'* when he rededicated his life to Christ during his tour in Iraq with the Army Rangers. Which included everything he did in the bedroom—or not in the bedroom, as was the case until marriage.

But then Celeste Bourne came along...

It was like he was a teenager again, feeling all twitterpated as Thumper so accurately described the punch-drunk love that had taken over his heart and brain. He found it difficult to concentrate on his research projects with the Order of Thaddeus, ancient defender of the Christian faith. His credit card bill was larger now, going all out to provide tickets to the Kennedy Center, dinners in Georgetown and Adam's Morgan, small gifts here and there to express his love with flowers and books he thought Celeste would like. She kept telling him to stop showering her with such gifts, but he couldn't help it.

He loved her.

This wasn't to say there weren't complications—primarily with their mutual place of employment. Given that she was his superior as director of operations for SEPIO with the Order of Thaddeus and he her subordinate direct report as an agent, it was a delicate dance with the rest of the Order. Rowen Radcliffe, Order Master, couldn't have been more thrilled, dismissing any concerns about fraternization and divulging his secret prayers petitioning the Holy Spirit to work his nuptial magic. And the rest of the crew—Zoe and Abraham, Gapinski and Torres—thought it was about time they tied the knot anyway. Somehow they were making it all work.

Silas just prayed he didn't screw it all up. Because he had a bad habit of sabotaging his relationships. Usually intentionally when things got serious. He vowed things would be different this time around.

He found Celeste seated in the middle eight rows up in the stadium seating section. He pardoned himself as he squeezed past a pair dressed as witches, jostling their Dr Pepper and managing neither to spill it nor step on any toes.

"I have to say," he said, slumping down next to her, "you do know how to pick a good movie theater seat."

"I had some help growing up." She handed him the popcorn and commandeered the Dr Pepper, promptly taking a sip. "Daddy was big into the cinema and showed me a thing or two about how to ensure the best visual and aural experience."

"Well, God bless Daddy," Silas said, popping a few kernels of the buttery goodness into his mouth.

She raised the armrest sitting between them and reached for the popcorn herself. But Silas jerked the bucket away, tossing a large handful onto an oversized man dressed as a warlock sitting next to him.

Silas instantly reddened. "Sorry about that, sir," he apologized.

The man scowled at him and brushed the kernels to the floor, leaving a streak of glistening oil across his black garment. He scowled again but grunted something that communicated, don't worry about it, then went back to eating his own popcorn.

He apologized again then leaned toward Celeste, who was stifling giggles to the point of tears. Silas wasn't too far behind.

Their heads met as they tried to contain themselves like two high schoolers when a familiar voice from behind killed the mood.

"I'm watching you two, Silas and Celeste. Just do us all a solid and keep it G for the kiddos, alright?"

Celeste startled and sank into her seat. "Please, dear God, let it not be so..."

Silas turned around to confirm the truth of it.

He frowned when he saw the familiar six-foot-four man sitting a few rows behind, offering a nod of bro solidarity and grinning as he chewed a mouthful of candy. Jujubes by the look of the extra large green box he was holding.

"Gapinski? What the heck are you doing here?"

"Chaperoning," he said, continuing his full-mouth grin, specks of red and green and yellow candy glistening in between his teeth.

"Seriously, mate, are you creeping up on us or what?" Celeste said, turning around. "I've got half a mind to report you to the authorities on suspicion of stalking."

"Naw, it's not like that. Besides, I was here first. You two lovebirds were so enraptured in your perfect-couple selves that you didn't notice your good SEPIO pal chilling a few rows back."

"Would you shut up back there?" someone bellowed from down below.

"Right back atcha, pal," Gapinski said.

Silas said, "Sorry, man. We'd ask you to join us, but the row is a little full."

Gapinski laughed. "Thanks, but I'd rather get a root canal with all those pheromones floating around down there. And besides, someone needs to make sure there's enough room for the Holy Spirit between you two lovebirds. Much better view from up here."

"Come on!" the same guy yelled from down below.

"Sounds like someone didn't take his meds this morning," Silas said. "We'll catch you after the flick."

"Just remember," Gapinski said, pointing two fingers at his eyes. "I've got my eyes on you. Both of 'em." He pursed his lips and motioned his fingers toward Silas and Celeste down below, then back at his eyes again.

"Thanks, mate," Celeste said. "We owe you one."

The two faced back around as the lights dimmed and the

screen showed the familiar green introduction before a movie trailer played for yet another horror flick began to show.

"I guess we better be on our best behavior with Nurse Ratched back there," Silas said, slumping down in his chair and getting comfortable.

"And best not forget to leave room for the Holy Spirit between us," Celeste said with a giggle.

Silas grinned and leaned in for a kiss. "Not a chance."

After cycling through a few slasher flicks that seemed even more tropey than the main event, the film opened with a return appearance of the actor who had made the original *A Nightmare on Maple Creek Road* shine with his characterization of Kevin Fraser, the psychopath with the razor glove.

He was kneeling before the altar at an abandoned church that looked in severe disrepair from either neglect or abandonment. Dark stains streaked the walls from ceiling to floor. Pews were smashed and overturned. The high altar itself at the front, usually bearing the Eucharistic elements, was barren, the Bread and Cup missing.

Silas wondered about the imagery, what the author was trying to convey about the Church, when a shadow loomed over the psychopath. Mysteriously his skin was no longer pockmarked and scarred as it was in the original film. It glowed with a luminescence that seemed to cast the man in an almost angelic light.

As the shadow came crashing down upon the psycho, enveloping him in its darkness, Silas jumped when a door down below suddenly opened. He grabbed Celeste's leg, and she giggled.

"Got the jumpies, do we? I thought you were a pro at these slasher films?"

Light cut through the darkness at the ground beneath the red *Exit* sign. A shadow rushed inside and took an empty seat in the second row, the door thudding close behind it.

Silas took a breath to calm his strumming heart, then chuckled and grinned at Celeste. "Darn kids these days, sneaking into movie theaters through the emergency exit." He threw a handful of popcorn into his mouth and reached for the Dr Pepper. "What has the world come to?"

"Don't tell me you've never had your fair share of sneaking around the cinema as an adolescent, Agent Grey."

He shrugged. "I cannot tell a lie."

The rest of the movie was basically a recapitulation of the previous one, with some of the original characters now middle-aged and being chased by the same psychopath, but with an update that seemed to be saying something about the evils of capitalism and climate change while trying to pose as a story of redemption through gumption and human ingenuity—as if thousands of years of history hasn't told us a single thing about the capacity of the human heart for evil and its complete inability to rescue itself. Celeste cringed throughout most of it, burying her face in Silas's shoulder. Which he didn't mind one bit.

At the climax, Kevin-the-psychopath made another appearance, surely making Carl Jung proud by having given himself once again fully to his shadow side. He let loose a barrage of bullets into a crowded street of trick-or-treaters, exchanging his original blade-equipped glove for an AR-15—another thinly veiled commentary on recent gun-control debates.

The *rat-a-tat-tat* sound of bullets ricocheted throughout the theater, an impressive display of aural greatness that caused even Silas to tense at the realness of it all. The barrage received the obligatory screams and cries for help from the victims who started fleeing for their lives. Kids and adults fell in the street from the mayhem and writhed before the monster cackling with joy.

Then a screeching roar that sounded like a cross between a strangled sheep and irate mama grizzly bear reverberated around the theater—but from down below, panning from stage left toward the center. It was dark, almost demonic, and crescendoed with a wicked intensity.

Silas craned his head in confusion at the noise, a shiver walking up his spine and a faint warning going off at the back of his lizard brain at the frightening, almost supernatural-sounding noise.

More screams and cries of agony ensued, but there was something different about these ones.

Same menacing reply to the leaden rampage unleashed from a high-powered assault rifle. Different timbre and tone and tenor.

The warlock next to Silas mumbled something to his partner on a shaky breath and leaned forward out of his seat toward the front for a closer look. Silas did the same.

The picture on the screen continued its fictional mayhem, its light casting an eerie glow across people down below yelling with horrifying terror at what they were experiencing and standing to flee for their lives.

Literally.

Another *rat-a-tat-tat* sounded, followed by three more menacing bursts of depravity.

The only problem was that the sounds were wickedly out of sync with what was flashing on the screen.

The on-screen psychopath wasn't shooting. In fact, he had discarded his weapon for his trademark knife-claw glove.

"GUN!" someone shouted down below.

Silas leaped to his feet, trying to discern what had happened.

Then he saw it.

Someone had mowed down the first three rows with an automatic rifle that rang with menacing terror.

Inside the movie theater.

CHAPTER 2

Silas threw Celeste to the floor and pressed himself on top as another barrage of wickedness was hurled out into the theater.

People screamed in agony as they fell to the ground and others thudded into walls and seats in useless escape as the terrorist continued mowing down the movie-going crowd.

No way in hell would he let that bastard take her out. He would die before he'd let that happen!

Unfortunately for the terrorist, Silas had a concealed carry license for the Commonwealth of Virginia. Which he was putting to good use by withdrawing his weapon hidden inside his jacket.

As Gapinski counseled him on his first day on the job with the Order of Thaddeus's Project SEPIO: '*Never leave home without cold, hard steel.*'

Wise words.

"Silas..." a familiar voice said lowly from behind. "Please tell me you came packing heat."

The gunfire came to a sudden halt. Silas chanced a glance above the row in front, figuring it was just the window he needed.

He was right. The man was reloading, holding up a massive weapon, barrel aiming for the ceiling, the sight sending chills skittering up his spine with memory—a mirror image of what he had held for years while fighting for Uncle Sam in the Middle East post-9/11. The effects of which he had tried to medicate but still failed to get under control.

A faint click echoed as the new clip mercilessly filled with more lead slid into place. Another screeching roar escaped past lips curled back at a frightening angle, teeth bared and tongue hanging out like a panting dog.

No way, no how...

Silas closed one eye and aimed for center mass, then let loose *one-two-three-four-five* rounds.

Just as the man dropped to one knee and started opening up again on those fleeing and hiding for their lives.

The bullets bit uselessly into the screen behind him, but they startled the man and drew his attention to the stadium seating.

Silas flattened himself beneath the seats again on top of Celeste as the psychopath refocused his aim and answered with way more lead than Silas thought necessary.

"Glad to know you followed my advice, bro," Gapinski bellowed again behind as the gunfire opened up a new front in its terrorism. "But next time, do us a solid and hit the target!"

Celeste screamed beneath him as the bullets found purchase in the seats in front of her, chewing into more flesh and sending bodies slumping to the concrete. She winced, grabbing her head with both hands and twisting it from side to side, as if injured.

"Are you alright?" Silas asked in a rush.

"I'm fine," she hissed. "We've got to do something!"

Silas knew her tone was borne more out of irritation from an impulse to act and run headlong into the heat of battle than out of fear for what she would face. It was one of the many qualities he liked about her. Her fearlessness and bold resolve was an inspiration that gave him the courage he himself needed.

He said, "Don't worry, sweetheart. Plenty more rounds where that came from."

The barrage stopped again. Silas thought the psycho was ready for yet another refill, but then the gunfire started back up. This time in short *one-two* punch gunshots, followed by yelps and gasps and agonizing cries.

"Oh, God! Please don't—" someone screamed before being cut short by another pair of *pops*.

They were getting closer, and they were followed by a clunking pair of steps, more screeching roars escaping the man in guttural bursts that sounded positively otherworldly.

Pop-pop. Pop-pop.

Clunk, clunk, clunk.

Pop-pop. Pop-pop.

Clunk, clunk, clunk.

"My God..." Silas whispered. "He's going row by row."

The warlock he had been sitting next to was whimpering a foot from his head, his massive body squeezed between the row of chairs and draped by a black cape that bobbed and swayed with each convulsive, stifled sob.

Silas noticed the backside of the man was peeking up above the threshold of the seatback in front of him, and was more pronounced as he shook and whimpered. He motioned for the man to get lower, but he didn't see him.

Pop-pop. Pop-pop.

Clunk, clunk, clunk.

The warlock suddenly yelled with impassioned fright, back arching and hands flying to his ears.

Another barrage was thrown their way, nicking the man in his backside and throwing him up above the parapet of seatbacks.

Which gave the terrorist the kill-shot opening he needed.

A pair of bullets pierced the warlock's face. He instantly crumpled to the concrete floor like a bathrobe in a tangled mess of limbs.

"Bloody hell..." Celeste stifled a scream with her hand. "I've got my 9mm just inside my boot. Give it over and we can take down this bloody psycho together."

"I like the sound of that," he huffed breathlessly, shuffling back over a woman dressed as a princess who had taken one in the head.

Pop-pop. Pop-pop.

Clunk, clunk, clunk.

Pop-pop. Pop-pop.

Clunk, clunk, clunk.

The terrorist was closer now. Only a few rows away. Probably just crossed the main walkway dividing the front section from the stadium seating.

There was another pause in the fire. The sound of a clip slipping out and thudding to the floor was followed by the man reloading another.

Giving the SEPIO pair all the window they needed to end this thing.

Celeste scrambled from the concrete floor slick with the blood of the warlock pooling out from his face. But no time to think about that.

"Ready?" she said, readying on her haunches.

He nodded and did the same, feet pulled underneath and knees bent to spring into action. "Aim..." he whispered.

They popped up from the floor into a defiant stand and fired as one, like any couple should when they tackle life together. Particularly when putting down a psycho on Halloween.

The man jolted from the force of their reply, his eyes rolling back into his head to reveal only white orbs that raged of the demonic. He slammed into a wall leading to the exit with arms splayed out and his own rifle firing on impulse. Just like any great slasher film worth its salt. But a way better ending than anything *Another Nightmare on Maple Creek Road* could have cooked up.

Silence enveloped the space even as the memory of the barrage and screams echoed in their heads.

"Nice shot, kiddos," Gapinski said, standing himself. "I would have joined in the fun but my piece is at the cleaner."

Silas hopped over the seatback in front, feet planted on an armrest. The sudden movement startled a young couple into a spastic screamfest, the man in particular hyperventilating with clenched eyes. He ignored them and ran across the row from armrest to armrest, weapon aimed at the man spread out on the floor.

Celeste was close behind. Gapinski was struggling to extract himself from his row, grunting with complaint.

Silas leaped to the floor, grabbing the butt of his weapon with both hands and padding forward with purpose—the terrorist clearly in his sights.

But he didn't move, didn't make a sound. The psycho was quickly disarmed when Silas padded up to his side and sent his assault rifle sailing down the side aisle with a kick.

He holstered his weapon and knelt beside the man, who didn't at all look right.

There were those eyes again, white and haunting; there were those lips, curled back and mouth open in a perpetual state of raging depravity; there was slick foam running down his chin. But there was more.

The man was Caucasian, with icy blue eyes and blond hair, face badly scarred by what appeared to be acne or some other deep skin blemish, almost scale-like. Around his neck was what Silas could only describe as a necklace made of bones. A shiver walked up his spine at what he saw tattooed just beneath it in crisp black ink.

A pentagram—wait, no: a pentacle, the lines clearly forming a five-point star used as a talisman by neopagans and as a magical object of the occult.

He swallowed and took a breath, then leaned in for a closer look at the man. Tiny burns of some sort, cigarettes maybe, were evident up and down the pasty-white arm that had been holding the rifle, its sleeve having been pulled back in the tumble.

"Really?" Gapinski said, walking up and shaking his head. "A dude sporting a pentagram tattoo shoots up a movie theater watching a slasher film on Halloween. How cliché can you get?"

"But odd, right?" Silas said.

"Odd, I'll give you," Celeste said. She winced again, closing her eyes and shaking her head before taking a breath and nodding toward the man. "Check him out, will you?"

Silas furrowed his brow at the sight, then stepped around to the man's other side, noticing a backpack strapped to his back underneath.

Faded forest green JanSport with a faded brown faux leather bottom. Looked like it had seen some use.

He reached around and wrenched it off the man, then threw it to Gapinski. "See what's in here."

The man let out a scream. The backpack fell to the floor with a thud.

"You check it out, man!" Gapinski complained.

Celeste sighed and reached for the bag. "Apparently, this is a job for the girl in the group."

Before opening it, she hesitated. "Are you sure about this? Shouldn't we leave this to the authorities?"

"There's something about this that feels wrong. Did you both catch the ungodly sounds that psycho made?"

"Sounded like a cross between Godzilla and a velociraptor," said Gapinski.

"What are you saying?" Celeste questioned.

Silas shook his head. "Not sure, exactly. But my gut tells me to open it."

Celeste held his gaze a beat then started unzipping the bag.

"I'm warning you..." Gapinski complained. "If a head pops out, there's no telling what I might do."

She finished unzipping and carefully opened it. The two guys craned over her shoulders.

Gapinski covered his nose and gave a disgusted cry.

A rank, sour smell and a faint buzzing sound escaped the sack. Some sort of animal was missing its head, and white worms the size of rice were inching along the exposed flesh to their hearts' content. Dried leaves of some sort, smelling of lavender and rosemary and sage, were scattered about. Five candles, wicks blackened and base dripping with hardened melted wax were arrayed on top of the animal.

And resting on top of those were two books. Very old books, by the looks of it. Maybe two or three hundred years.

Silas reached inside and retrieved them.

The first was a hardback bound in red cloth, crimson and vibrant and hiding delicate pages scrawled with faded black ink, the pages seemingly singed at its edges and smelling of smoke and peppery incense. Other than that, it was a perfectly preserved volume, though aged.

"What's it about?" Celeste asked.

"Not sure. Looks like just a bunch of handwritten names. Maybe a register of some sort?"

"Or little black book—in red?"

Silas shrugged and reached for the other book, a stiff hardback bound in faded burgundy leather, its pages stained and damaged by mildew.

"This one's not much better..." he mumbled.

He peeled back the cover, its crisp but tender pages whispering to him. Faded black ink was scrawled along the underside and end page. He turned to the title page, glimpsing the word *witchcraft* when Celeste startled.

"Oy, look here!" she exclaimed.

He closed the book as she reached inside, waiting to see what she had found.

She withdrew a jar that had been wedged against the side. Inside was an upside-down crucifix, floating in yellowish-brown liquid.

Gapinski brought a hand to his mouth. "Is that what I think it is?"

She brought the jar up to her nose, then winced. "Sure smells ripe."

"Eww!"

"I heard about a similar photographic exhibit in the 80s," Silas said. "Piss Christ, I think it was called."

"Sure looks like piss to me," Gapinski said, hand still covering his mouth.

"But in this case, the crucifix is upside down."

"Which is thoroughly pagan," Celeste said.

"Occult, even..." Silas added.

She nodded grimly, then set the jar back inside the backpack.

He asked, "Why the heck was this man carrying such a thing inside a movie theater?"

"A more apropos question would be," Celeste offered, "why was this man carrying it along with a slaughtered animal, candles, herbs, and two mysterious books?"

"And before going all psychopathic maniac on the joint?" Gapinski added.

Silas nodded. "Agree."

He stuffed the books back inside, then carefully pried the bone necklace off from the dead man's neck. Looked like the bones were held together by some sort of resin. He slipped it into the backpack then zipped it closed and stood, slinging it around his shoulder.

"Hold up," Celeste said.

Silas turned toward her. "What's up?"

"We can't just take evidence from a crime scene. That opens us up to major criminal liability."

"I'm with her," Gapinski said.

"You saw what was in here. A pagan symbol combined with occult objects and that pagan Piss Christ replica, plus those books and the sounds that dude made I can only describe as... well, supernatural—all of it seems to make this our business, the business of the Order of Thaddeus." He planted his hands on his hips and sighed. "Whatever this business is."

"I don't know about that," Celeste cautioned. "Evidence tampering opens the Order up to way more liability than I care to imagine. And personally, nabbing evidence from a crime scene is not what I'd like to go down in the books for."

"Again, I'm with her," Gapinski said. "But regardless, if we don't get out of Dodge soon, the po-po are liable to think we were the ones who went on a psychopathic rampage."

Celeste turned to Silas who had his head cocked and brows raised with a plea.

She took a breath and sighed. "Fine. We take the backpack and get to work on...whatever this is. But the minute we know anything, we go to the authorities. Deal?"

"Deal," Silas said, grinning as if he got his way. Which he technically did.

"And wipe that grin off your face, as if you just scored a goal, smartie. Or else no loving later."

"Like I said, keep it G for the kiddos!" Gapinski complained.

Silas led them down the aisle to the emergency exit. He hesitated and looked back at Celeste, who nodded him onward. He took a breath and shoved through.

It was early evening now, the sun having begun its descent beneath the horizon, inflaming the darkening sky with the orangish-red fires of hell. Which seemed appropriate.

A tract of rocks, green with algae and stained brown from weathered wear, lined the backside of the building. On the other side stood the theater's parking lot flanking the south side of the mall. Red and blue lights flashed and sirens blared around the edge ahead.

Looking as if they were in the clear, he stepped out, followed quickly by Celeste and Gapinski.

He was wrong.

Rounding the corner was a squad of heavily armed men wearing thick black padded armor and helmets with plastic visors—all bearing menacing assault rifles that put the psychopath left dead inside to shame.

And all pointed at the SEPIO trio.

CHAPTER 3

Silas's heart seized in his chest and his breath faltered at the sight of the heavy police presence. He understood why, given not only the high-alert status of the region but also the recent panic over a rash of mass shootings ricocheting around the country.

Nonetheless, panic flooded his veins, and he knew the night just went from really bad to terrible real quick.

"On the ground! On the ground!" the counterterrorism unit screamed in unison.

Silas complied, raising his palms and flattening himself to the pavement.

Celeste and Gapinski quickly followed.

One of the unit members landed hard on Silas's back. He winced and grunted as the officer wrenched his arms behind him.

"We were victims of the domestic terrorism behind that door!" Silas yelled as the man yanked off the backpack and quickly secured his hands with plastic ties. "I'm a former Army Ranger, and I've got a weapon on the inside of my jacket with a concealed carry permit."

That revelation seemed to activate the men in a way that seeing them flee from the building hadn't before.

Two others quickly apprehended Celeste and Gapinski, throwing their full weight into their backs and securing them with the same plastic ties.

"Hey, dude, be gentle," Gapinski complained. "I'm breakable!"

"My weapon is stowed safely in my boot with the same permit as well," Celeste said as she was dragged up to her feet. Her 9mm was secured, as was Silas's Beretta.

Silas was also brought to his feet, as was Gapinski whose forehead was bleeding.

"The man you're looking for is inside," Silas said. "We were able to incapacitate him before more lives were lost. Unfortunately..." Emotion caught in his throat as the images of the dead and sounds of the dying finally caught up with him.

"Let's go," the lead officer said, grabbing Silas by his bound arms and leading him forward. "We'll sort this out at command."

The parking lot was a mess of rescue and law enforcement vehicles and personnel. A large mass casualty unit the size of a semi was anchored at one end, lights whirling along with the rest. Several acronyms from the full spectrum of federal and state agencies were present in force, taking command, and no doubt jockeying for control, of a domestic terrorist event just outside the nation's capital that added to the year's toll of similar catastrophes.

People were lined up in rows sitting along the sidewalk, some bleeding and most crying from the weight and shock of it all. Stretchers with white sheets, bulging where bodies lay hidden underneath, were being wheeled toward a row of ambulances. News crews were also out in force, their satellite dishes raised high and personalities chattering away bearing the grim news that meant bags of gold in advertising dollars.

And then there were Silas, Celeste, and Gapinski, caught up in what should have been a nice night out on the town. At least for two of them.

The trio were brought outside a command center that looked like a souped-up RV and told to sit on the ground and wait for instructions. Five men surrounded them facing inward with weapons drawn across their bodies and ready to respond to any movement they didn't like.

Silas thought it was overkill, but he understood the need for extreme caution given what the nation had been facing the past few years with homegrown domestic terrorists rampaging from nightclubs to theaters to country music festivals.

The officer who had handled Silas sauntered up the stairs and into the mobile command unit. Inside, he talked with a frantic looking petite blonde whose head was buried in a tablet and cradling a cellphone against her ear. The man gestured outside to the group, and she turned for a look.

"Don't suppose he's giving her our drink order, do you?" Gapinski said, shifting uncomfortably on the ground.

Silas wasn't paying attention. He was too focused on trying to keep his head on straight after what had just happened. Too focused on not letting the event dredge back the painful memories of what he had witnessed—what he himself had perpetuated—while at war with international terrorists overseas.

He closed his eyes and took a deep breath, starting a countdown routine he had developed during his tour with the Rangers to get his head in the game. He hadn't had to use it in a while and was silently cursing himself for his weakness.

He began at 1000 and counted backwards:

999, 998, 997, 996...

He took another breath, the image of his Ranger buddy Colton blown to smithereens by that damn roadside bomb in Iraq seizing his consciousness.

He winced at the memory—from the sounds of the blast

and screams of agony to the smells of the burning flesh; from the taste of blood in his own mouth from hitting his face on the window during the explosion to the sight of Colton missing part of his face.

946, 945, 944—

Silas was jolted from his trance when the counterterrorism unit commander threw open the door to the command center with an echoing thud.

He sauntered back down the stairs along with the woman. She followed him toward the trio—until she stopped short.

"Silas Grey?" she said with surprise.

He snapped his head toward the pair. Furrowing his brow, he narrowed his eyes with concentration at the woman who clearly recognized him. Took him a beat, but then it hit him.

Brittany Armstrong.

Former girlfriend he had dated briefly back at Georgetown. And by briefly, it was all of two weeks. Sort of.

"Saved by the blonde!" Gapinski said, looking to Silas for understanding.

If memory served him right, he ended the relationship with an email. It was for a good reason, but still. Texting hadn't yet been a thing, and serving notice through email wasn't supposed to be a thing. But it was to the immature twenty-year-old who was now nearly two decades older—and now at the mercy of his former girlfriend, sitting next to his now current girlfriend and partner, and other partner.

This could get messy...

"Go ahead, Tom, and get those restraints off. I'll vouch for him. Even though he did dump me. And through email of all things."

"Dude, we're at the mercy of a jilted ex-lover?" Gapinski whispered. "And through email, no less?"

Silas threw him a look as he rubbed his wrists after having been freed.

"Yes, do tell, dear," Celeste said as her ties were cut. "Sounds like a jolly good story behind that one."

Silas stood and offered a limp wave. "Uh, hey there, Brit. Nice to see you again."

"Hey, yourself," Brit said, folding her arms and widening her stance.

Yeah, not good.

He looked to the ground and rubbed the back of his reddening neck. "We, well...we sort of dated back in college."

"Sort of is a good way of putting it."

He chuckled. "Looks like you didn't look back. And clearly you've made a life for yourself with the FBI." He smiled and offered her his hand.

"You could say that." Brit opened up for an embrace instead. "Oh, come on. For old time's sake."

He hesitated, stealing a glance Celeste's way, but opened up as well. They hugged awkwardly before letting go.

Silas threw his partners an embarrassed grin as he pulled away then raked a hand through his thick dark brown hair. The cigarette pack in his pocket was screaming for attention at his heightened state of anxiety. But he had promised Celeste he would quit after picking up the nasty habit again earlier in the year. Now seemed not the time to test that promise.

Brit said, "Last I heard, you had made a pretty good go of life yourself. Professor at Princeton, isn't that right, after playing with the Marines in the Middle East?"

"Rangers," Silas corrected, "and ex-professor. I've, well..." he glanced at his partners, catching Celeste's eye who had folded her arms and widened her stance—mirroring Brit to a T. He took in a breath and continued, "I've moved on to another venture."

"Like shooting up a movie theater?" Brit said with a wry grin.

Silas startled, then started stumbling for words to explain.

"Relax, I'm just kidding. So who are your accomplices?"

Without waiting for an introduction, Celeste announced with extended arm, "Celeste Bourne."

Brit took it. "Bourne? As in the confused CIA Ludlum character?"

Celeste flashed a grin. "I was a Bourne before Bourne was a Bourne."

Silas noted her tone, which was more of a challenge than an explanation. He sensed rising tension between the two women—which he found all at once cute and terrifying.

"Alright then," Brit said. "There you go. And you?" she asked, turning to Gapinski.

"Matt Gapinski," he said with a wave. "And I wasn't a Gapinski before I was a Gapinski—or something." He chuckled; no one else did. "Nevermind..."

"So what the hell happened here?" Brit said, crossing her arms again.

Silas led her through the events in the theater—from the emergency exit door opening, which he figured was when the psycho gained entrance, to him opening up with the AR-15 and finally Celeste and him taking the man down.

"Thank God you two were there. Could have been much worse." She motioned toward the command center then led them forward.

Silas followed, shaking his head and sighing. "Just wish we could have stopped him sooner. So many lives were lost..."

Brit climbed the stairs and smiled. "I do remember liking that about you. The whole superhero quality. You wore it well."

"Thanks," he said, glancing behind at his partners, heat rising up the back of his neck and hearing a stifled giggle from Gapinski. All that mattered was what Celeste was thinking. And he couldn't tell either way.

He hadn't shared much with her about his dating past. Mostly because there wasn't much to share, but also because of the shame it carried. He imagined she would find out sooner than later.

The four settled around a table along the side of the command center. Brit asked a few of the remaining personnel to leave, then hoisted up the JanSport bag that had been leaning against her bench. "Who wants to explain what this is? Tom told me it was found on your person, Silas."

Silas flashed Celeste a glance and shifted uncomfortably on the bench. She offered a slight nod, and he steeled himself for offering an explanation.

"So, you know how I said I had left Princeton for another venture?" he began. "Well, it's with a religious order."

Brit furrowed her brow. "A religious order? You? Like with monks or something, and vows of celibacy and all that?"

He laughed nervously. "No, not really. It's called the Order of Thaddeus."

"Now this takes the cake. Sorry, but you'll have to excuse my disbelief. Silas wasn't all that religious back in college. Quite the partier, and other things..."

Silas shifted again and raked a hand through his hair. "Yes, well, that was a long time ago. And since then, I've devoted my life to my faith in Jesus Christ. But at any rate, all three of us are with the Order, and we thought the contents of the backpack related to our work."

"Which is?"

He hesitated, then said, "Which is protecting and preserving the memory of the Church from nearly the very beginning of her existence, especially from a militant group that has been threatening and attacking the Church since the beginning called Nous."

"Nous..."

The edge to her voice annoyed Silas. Like what he imagined people thinking when someone said they were abducted by aliens or saw Bigfoot.

He let it go and nodded. "In the past, Nous struck at the heart of Christian ideas by propagating heresy and seeking to undermine the essence of the Christian faith by destroying her teachings. Its power and influence has waxed and waned over the centuries and manifested in various ways. But in recent years, they have stepped up their game big time—and with violent results. Remember the attacks against churches across the world earlier this year?"

"Sure," Brit said. "We were running ops with Homeland Security to determine the nature of the threat across the country."

"And so were we," Celeste said. "Us three, with the Order."

"Wait, that was this shadow organization you call Nous?"

"It was," Silas said. "But the point isn't Nous, the point is that there is something about what happened in that theater and what's in that bag that doesn't sit right with me. Something I thought the Order could help solve. Especially because of the sounds we heard."

"The sounds..."

"Yeah, the sounds," Gapinski said, stepping in to help. "Sort of a cross between Godzilla and a velociraptor. Gave me the heebee-jeebees." He shuddered and shifted against a window.

"I'm not sure if any of it's related," Silas continued, "but between the supernatural yelps the man made, combined with the cultish memorabilia—it seemed like a job for the Order of Thaddeus."

Brit sat back and folded her arms. She said nothing for the longest time before the ends of her mouth curled upward and she leaned forward with a guttural laugh, offering a snort for good measure. A quirk Silas remembered had been one of the excuses for the email he had sent dumping her twenty years ago, as immature as it was.

He rolled his eyes and glanced at Gapinski, who shrugged, then turned to Celeste, who looked annoyed.

"I'm sorry," Brit said, recovering. She waved her arms with apology and said again, "I'm sorry, but this all sounds like some cheap airport novel or one of those bargain-bin Kindle deals."

"Brit, come on..."

"I seem to remember an episode of *The X-Files* from the 90s that sounds vaguely familiar."

Silas stood. "Nice seeing you again, Brit. If you're done with us, and we're no longer being detained, I think we'll take off."

"Oh, Silas, I was just playing around."

Celeste slid out as well, followed by Gapinski.

"No, it's fine. You've got a job to do and we shouldn't stand in your way. But, hey, if you see a bird tattoo on the guy, give me a call. If you still have my cell number it hasn't changed since college."

He chuckled, but the look from Celeste told him bad move. Even Gapinski raised a brow.

"Why a bird tattoo?" Brit said.

"Huh?" Silas said, chiding himself. "Oh, it's a Nous calling card. Anyway, good luck with the investigation."

Brit thanked them for the insight and said the FBI would take if from there, but that they should be prepared for follow-up questions. Then she sent them on their way.

"I can see why you sacked her," Celeste said as they walked from the command center, "especially through email."

"Does that mean she's fair game?" Gapinski said, grinning and jabbing Silas in the side.

The two glared at him as they weaved through the law enforcement personnel.

"What it does mean is that date night is over," Celeste said. "Time to fill Radcliffe in on the matter."

"Always something," Gapinski mumbled.

Indeed there was with the Order of Thaddeus.

And Silas suspected whatever had gone down in that theater was just the beginning.

CHAPTER 4

WASHINGTON, DC.

The Order of Thaddeus Master, Rowen Radcliffe, sat in a chapel glowing with orange flickering candlelight deep under the main nave of the Basilica of the National Shrine of the Immaculate Conception, America's largest Roman Catholic church anchored in Northeast DC. He needed the space to reflect, to pray; his soul demanded it. He thirsted for the sacred ritual of evening prayer given what had just transpired across the Potomac River in Northern Virginia.

He sat still on a polished honey-stained wood pew bench, eyes closed and hands folded on his lap. It was his happy place, a sacred space he had come to often the past several months since the former headquarters to the Order at the Washington National Cathedral was brought to its knees in the same persecuting terror that had ravaged the worldwide Church during Holy Week earlier in the year.

Crews were still working around the clock to restore the cathedral to its original grandeur, as well as the former headquarters of the Order of Thaddeus. It would be some time until all the repairs were complete, and the timeline kept being pushed further out each week. Meanwhile, they were making do with an outfitted former outpost of the Order. It was a thorn in his side that challenged every ounce of his spiritual constitution, a bother he had to confess to the Lord almost daily. However, he was quite liking the sacristy. Much more private, quiet, serene than anything at their previous headquarters.

A holy hum filled the space as he sat trying to calm himself after another domestic terror attack—and involving three of his own agents, no less. They had rung him several minutes ago with news of the ordeal. Which had sent him scurrying to the polished bench for spiritual refuge and sustenance until their arrival.

His leg tapped with anxious vibration as he clenched his prayer beads and thanked the Lord for his protection over his agents. Then he mentally walked himself through the evening office of prayer, reciting it by heart.

Whispering an opening stanza to the ritual, he said, '*I will praise the Lord, who counsels me; even at night my heart instructs me. I keep my eyes always on the Lord. With him at my right hand, I will not be shaken.*'

He fell to his knees on a well-worn red velvet prayer pillow and began reciting the confessional:

Most merciful God,
I confess that I have sinned against you in thought,
word, and deed,
by what I have done, and by what I have left
undone.
I have not loved you with my whole heart; I have not
loved my neighbor as myself.
I am truly sorry and I humbly repent.
For the sake of your Son Jesus Christ, have mercy on
me and forgive me;
that I may delight in your will, and walk in your
ways,
to the glory of your Name. Amen.

Radcliffe returned to his pew, murmuring with eyes closed, '*O God, make speed to save us; Lord, make haste to help us.*' He crossed himself and continued: '*Glory to the Father, and to the Son, and to the Holy Spirit: as it was in the beginning, is now, and will be forever. Amen.*'

He continued through the evening prayer ritual, murmuring with holy breath:

> *O gracious Light, pure brightness of the everliving*
> *Father in heaven,*
> *O Jesus Christ, holy and blessed!*
> *Now as we come to the setting of the sun, and our*
> *eyes behold the vesper light, we sing your praises,*
> *O God: Father, Son, and Holy Spirit.*
> *You are worthy at all times to be praised by happy*
> *voices,*
> *O Son of God, O Giver of life, and to be glorified*
> *through all the worlds.*

Then again, the Gloria: '*Glory to the Father, and to the Son, and to the Holy Spirit: as it was in the beginning, is now, and will be forever. Amen.*'

He crossed himself again, from forehead to chest, left shoulder to right, then brought out his Bible, a thick, heavy book with well-used pages from years of study filled with underlines and tiny notations. He turned to a passage the Holy Spirit brought to his attention when he had heard news of yet another mass attack on human civilization: Mark 5, the story of Jesus healing the Gerasenes demoniac.

His fingers trembled as he searched the sacred Scriptures for the passage, both from age and from a deep sense of foreboding at what the world might be facing.

He found it and read it silently to himself:

They came to the other side of the sea, to the country of the Gerasenes. And when he had stepped out of the boat, immediately a man out of the tombs with an unclean spirit met him. He lived among the tombs; and no one could restrain him any more, even with a chain; for he had often been restrained with shackles and chains, but the chains he wrenched apart, and the shackles he broke in pieces; and no one had the strength to subdue him. Night and day among the tombs and on the mountains he was always howling and bruising himself with stones. When he saw Jesus from a distance, he ran and bowed down before him; and he shouted at the top of his voice, "What have you to do with me, Jesus, Son of the Most High God? I adjure you by God, do not torment me." For he had said to him, "Come out of the man, you unclean spirit!" Then Jesus asked him, "What is your name?" He replied, "My name is Legion; for we are many." He begged him earnestly not to send them out of the country. Now there on the hillside a great herd of swine was feeding; and the unclean spirits begged him, "Send us into the swine; let us enter them." So he gave them permission. And the unclean spirits came out and entered the swine; and the herd, numbering about two thousand, rushed down the steep bank into the sea, and were drowned in the sea.

The swineherds ran off and told it in the city and in the country. Then people came to see what it was that had happened. They came to Jesus and saw the demoniac sitting there, clothed and in his right mind, the very man who had had the legion; and they were afraid. Those who had seen what had happened to the demoniac and to the swine reported it. Then they began to beg Jesus to leave their neighborhood.

Radcliffe closed his Bible and sighed, reflecting on a distant memory from a former life, from younger days.

Did they not realize the service Jesus was offering on their behalf?

He shook his head at the ignorance and rashness of those people from the first century chronicled in the passage.

Then one end of his mouth curled upward, his mind recalling a bit of advice from an old friend and colleague in ministry from days long past: *'People would much rather explain away or turn a blind eye to the manifestations of evil than deal with the Devil in their midst.'*

How much more so during these modern times! His adopted nation seemed to be convulsing of late, alongside the rest of the West. Even his homeland of England had seen its fair share of psychotic episodes burst upon the public. Oh, the politicians and princes of the world railed against the prevalence of guns and the violence of video games, blamed it on homespun ideologies spewing violence and on a lack of social mobility. To be sure, those were all sources of the world's evils at one level or another.

But he knew better; knew it in his bones. Knew things and had seen things from firsthand experience that gave him a vastly different perspective on the truth of things. When would the world finally awaken to the deeper realities influencing the human heart, the deeper unseen realities clawing and conspiring beneath the surface of our seen one—the ones that no piece of legislation or prescribed pill or proposed embargo could even hope to touch?

The wickedness of the human heart knows no bounds. As do the schemes of the Devil himself.

"The schemes of the Devil…" he mumbled before sighing and shaking his head. He eased himself back down on his knees once again and recited the Lord's Prayer. He crossed himself, then continued with the final prayer:

> *O God, the life of all who live, the light of the faithful, the strength of those who labor, and the repose of the dead: We thank you for the blessings of the day that is past, and humbly ask for your protection through the coming night. Bring us in safety to the morning hours; through him who died and rose again for us, your Son our Savior Jesus Christ. Amen.*

Protection through the coming night, safety to the morning hour, indeed...

A door clanged opened behind him and the patter of several pairs of shoes tapped softly across the stone floor.

Radcliffe whispered an *'Amen'* and crossed himself one final time for the night before pushing himself up to stand on unsteady legs. He hated growing old, if not for the only reason that it put a strain on his bones and body, making it that the more difficult to see through to the end the mission Lord Christ himself had given him.

"Praise God you're all safe," he said as the trio rushed to greet him.

"Sorry to bother you whilst in the midst of your evening prayers," Celeste apologized. "But we figured you would have wanted us to reach you as soon as we arrived."

"No worries," he said, reaching in for an embrace. "I'm just relieved to know my three favorite people on the planet are still in one piece."

"It'll take more than a possessed psychopath to bring this crew down," Gapinski said proudly.

"Possessed?" Radcliffe exclaimed.

"Well, figuratively speaking."

"I'm not so sure..." Silas said. "But let's wait to discuss all this in more private quarters."

Radcliffe took careful steps as he led them through still-unfamiliar corridors he was attempting to memorize; it was a losing battle. However, they only got lost once, so that was an improvement. He had known the previous headquarters backward and forward, and he quietly cursed his old age for not being able to commit the same floor plans to memory. Alas, another reason that perhaps he should finally retire and pass the baton along to someone younger, someone more capable.

Along the way, Silas and Celeste recounted the horrific events from the evening. He especially listened with bated breath as Silas described the sounds the man made, ones that echoed memories from his former life. He didn't say anything then, but he quietly contemplated the gravity and nature of what they had experienced, muttering a prayer beneath his breath for the Spirit's supernatural protection and guidance.

Soon, they reached a palm-reading keypad that stood guard outside a nondescript door. Radcliffe reached for it, and within a second the door unlocked.

"Now don't be disappointed," he warned. "My new study pales in comparison to what I had before, but it does the job. In we go."

He was right. Where the original study felt as large as a small gymnasium, this was more the size of a generous two-stall garage. The place carried the smell of leather, aged pulp, and smoke, a comforting blanket of familiarity in these fraught times.

Mahogany-wood bookcases lined the walls, filled with the familiar sight of vintage tomes stretching the spectrum of theological topics, biblical commentaries, and the history of the Church. A fire crackled and popped at one end. A collection of barely-worn leather couches and chairs commanded the threshold of the ornately carved marble fireplace. Radcliffe led them to the oasis, but made a detour toward a minibar nestled between two bookcases.

"Anyone care for a nightcap?" he shouted across the room.

"Yes, please," the trio answered in unison as they sauntered over to the couches, promptly slumping down in exhaustion.

He chuckled. "I imagine so."

He poured four generous glasses of Port wine, figuring the richly sweet nectar from Portugal would do their souls good, considering all that had transpired—and all that he feared was to come.

"There we are." He lowered a silver platter and the agents each took a glass, all three promptly taking a mouthful.

He took his own glass and set the tray on a cherry table sitting at the center of the group. He slumped hard into his leather chair and took a sip, humming with pleasure and licking his lips with a satisfying smack.

"Right, now where were we?" Radcliffe asked.

"Telling you about the part when the psychopath started levitating and puking pea soup?" Gapinski said between sips.

"It wasn't like that," Silas corrected. "But, yes, there was an otherworldliness to the whole experience. Which probably goes without saying."

"But you said *possessed*, Matthew," Radcliffe said between his own sips. "Why that descriptor?"

"I'm not sure I would go that far," said Silas.

"I would!" Gapinski said. "The guy was nutso to the maxo. And you heard those sounds!"

Radcliffe leaned forward. "What sounds?"

"Tell him!"

"Well, there was this screeching sort of roar that came from the guy every so often."

"Go on," Radcliffe encouraged.

Silas took another sip and shifted in his seat. "I would

describe it as a cross between a bleating, strangled sheep and an enraged grizzly bear."

Gapinski snapped his fingers and pointed at Silas. "That! Definitely a pissed off mama bear eating a goat. Or, something."

"But then there is the matter of the backpack," Celeste said.

"The backpack?" the Order Master asked.

She nodded. "Inside was a decapitated animal, candles, and herbs."

"Good Lord," he said, rubbing his temple where an ache began to throb.

"And bones. Don't forget the bones," Gapinski said.

Celeste nodded. "Yes, and bones. Made into a necklace and sitting around the man's neck."

Radcliffe drained his Port then stood and sauntered off for more.

"Then there's the matter of the books," Silas added.

"The books?" the Order Master asked from halfway across the room.

"Some volume with hand-scrawled names, the other was unclear. There was some handwriting on the inside cover, and I caught a glimpse of the word *witchcraft* on the title page, but got distracted by Celeste's Piss Christ discovery."

Radcliffe froze mid-step, then spun around. "Witchcraft, you say? And...well, what's this other business?"

Celeste explained, "A replica of the sacrilegious photograph of a crucifix in a jar of human excrement."

"Except in this version," Silas added, "the cross was in the jar upside-down."

Radcliffe went to respond when a phone resting on a side table buzzed with interruption. He rolled his eyes with irritation and sauntered over.

Settling back in his chair, he pressed the *'Speaker'* button and said, "Yes?"

"Sorry to interrupt, Master Radcliffe," Zoe Corbino said, the resident techie and on-site operations coordinator. "We have a...well, someone is here asking for you."

"Zoe, dear, please dispense with the theatrics and just tell me who it is."

She cleared her throat. "He says he's a long-lost friend. A Father Gabriele D'Amante?"

Radcliffe nearly yanked the phone from the table.

"Gabe? Here?" Radcliffe exclaimed, standing and grinning with delight.

"Uh, apparently."

"But what on earth for?"

"He didn't say. Only that he had urgent business that you would understand. Something about your previous life."

Radcliffe's face fell and grew grim. "I understand. I will be right up."

The Order Master ended the call and headed for the door with determination.

Silas stood. "Sir, wait a minute."

The man spun around, face pulled together with worry. "Yes?"

Silas looked to Celeste and then to Gapinski before settling back on Radcliffe. He asked, "Who is that man?"

Radcliffe stood stiff and took a measured breath. "President of the International Association of Exorcists and chief exorcist for the Archdiocese of Detroit."

Now Celeste stood. "And what was Zoe referencing, something about your previous life?"

He hesitated, his eyes roaming toward the ground and searching for words. He took a breath and looked at the trio squarely. "I was a colleague of his, on exchange from the diocese of London."

The Order Master paused, then finally got on with it: "I was an exorcist."

CHAPTER 5

Radcliffe led the group on shakier legs than Silas had remembered, his heart sinking at the sight of the man who had faithfully led the crucial Christian Order beginning to show his age.

At nearly eighty, the Order Master had seemed impervious to the inevitable ailments doled out by Father Time. But recently, it seemed the man had been having a tougher time of it, complaining about his 'sack of bones' not being what they used to be and forgetting things when his mind used to be sharper than his own.

Silas had been spared the heartache of watching his own parents grow old, his mother having died at his and his twin brother's birth and father in the Pentagon during the 9/11 attacks. Now, he was witnessing the deterioration of someone he had grown quite fond of the past year. He said a prayer for the man and hoped it wouldn't interfere with yet another crisis he feared was looming on the horizon.

After making a few wrong turns, the crew finally made it out of the crypt and to the main level of the basilica. They popped up a stairwell at the front of the vast nave to the right of the high altar. Thankfully, it was late and there was no evening Mass.

The Order Master picked up his pace, shuffling down the long aisle past polished honey-stained pews in neat, dutiful rows underneath three massive domes above, the gaze of saints and celestial beings and Christ himself urging them onward. The trio followed close behind, and soon the four reached the narthex, the heavy walnut entrance doors closed tight with no one in sight.

Radcliffe spun around the marble floor searching for his friend, his brow furrowed with a frantic, searching gaze.

"There," Silas said, grabbing his shoulder and pointing down one side of the narthex to a small chapel. A golden glow alighted a statue of pure white marble inside, and standing in front of it was silhouetted a man in black robes.

The Order Master rushed forward. "Gabe?" he said, calling out.

A portly man of average height wearing black vestments spun around, back hunched and neck draped by a purple stole, the kind priests wear for both confession and exorcisms. A sigh of relief escaped through jowly cheeks before rising with a smile.

Father Gabriele D'Amante sauntered out from the chapel with arms outstretched, "Rowen, you old coot!"

The men embraced in a giddy bear hug, all decorum thrown out the window at two old friends, who had clearly gone through the thick of it together, being reunited. They shared a private joke and bent over with laughter, the space echoing with joyous reunion and shared affection.

Leaning over to Silas and Celeste, Gapinski said, "I can't remember the last time I've seen Radcliffe looking so happy, so at peace."

Silas smiled and nodded. It was true. The man had been bearing the weight of the Christian world on his shoulders the past year with the furious, fiery plots Nous had let loose against the Church. It did his soul well to see the man so contented.

But soon, Radcliffe drew his face back into the familiar look of grim determination that had marked the man for the year Silas had known him. Apparently, it was time to get back to work.

Radcliffe offered a grinning sigh and gestured to his companion. "Agents, I am pleased to introduce to you a dear, old—"

"Old? Speak for yourself, Radcliffe," Father D'Amante interrupted, his words tinged with an Italian accent. "I've still got plenty of vim and vigor flowing in these bones."

"Vim and vigor?" He scoffed and rolled his eyes. "Flowing Scotch and Chianti, perhaps! At any rate, as I was saying before you interrupted...I present to you Father Gabriele D'Amante. And this here is Celeste Bourne, director of operations for SEPIO, and then Silas Grey and Matt Gapinski."

"Pleased to make your acquaintance," Gabriele said. "I have watched your exploits from afar for quite some time. And I must say, thank you for the service you offer the Church. Contending for the faith under culture's siege is perhaps as delicate an operation as contending for the souls of men under Satan's siege."

Celeste said, "Rowen mentioned you are an exorcist with the Archdiocese of Detroit, isn't that right, as well as the president of some exorcist association?"

The man nodded. "'Tis true. In fact, it's the reason for my surreptitious arrival this evening."

"Oh?" Radcliffe said, raising a brow. "Do tell."

The man hesitated, eyeing the trio as he turned back to his old friend. "Might we have a word in private, Rowen?"

The Order Master glanced at his companions. "Whatever it is you have to say to me, you can say in front of them. But I do declare, your secretive tone is slightly alarming."

"As it should be." The exorcist stepped closer to his old friend, the trio leaning closer for a listen. He fixed him with serious eyes that betrayed a hint of fear, then whispered, "It is happening again, Rowen. He's back."

"What is happening?" Celeste whispered.

"Who is back?" Silas echoed.

Father D'Amante glanced at the SEPIO agents then back to Rowen, whose eyes had gone wide and face had drained of color.

On a faltering breath, Radcliffe said, "I think it is time we retire down below and have ourselves a little chat."

Silas and Celeste glanced at each other as the Order Master left with Father D'Amante.

"What's this about, Celeste?" Gapinski said. "I didn't know our fearless leader was a former exorcist. Did you?"

Laughter echoed back toward the trio as they continued watching the two men leave down the aisle.

She shook her head. "No, I did not either. But we best get to it. I imagine if the man sought out his long-lost friend in the dead of night, something must be amiss, and darkly so."

"That's what I'm afraid of," Gapinski complained.

Silas led the way following after Radcliffe, who had already descended with his friend down to the crypt. Catching up, the trio followed him back to the modest study where they had been earlier.

"Impressive, Rowen," Father D'Amante said, eyeing the study as he entered.

Radcliffe sighed and shook his head. "You should have seen its previous iteration at the old headquarters."

"Yes, I heard about what happened to the cathedral. Horrid, horrifying news."

"Indeed, it is—and was. But we're making do here at our new accommodations." Radcliffe gestured toward the grouping of chairs and couches. Sitting and making himself comfortable, he said, "Now, what is this business you're bearing in the dead of night?"

The visitor got comfortable himself, shifting uneasily in his overstuffed leather chair still stiff with newness.

He eyed the other three, then took a breath. "There is a darkness descending upon the land, Rowen. One that I have not felt for some time. Not since our days battling the Prince of Darkness together those many years ago."

"What do you mean, Gabriele? You said, it's happening again. By *it* you mean the clusters, don't you?"

Father D'Amante nodded gravely. "I do."

"What clusters?" Celeste asked, turning to Radcliffe. "What's he going on about?"

The Order Master took a breath and shifted in his seat, looking as if he was settling in for the long haul.

"Decades ago, early in my ministry," he started, "I participated in a program put on by the Congregation for the Doctrine of the Faith to train more exorcists in the 1970s. After the infamous *The Exorcist* movie hit the cinemas, there was a surprising rise in the number of those seeking such sacramental rites. So off to Rome I went, where some 500,000 people a year seek an exorcist."

"Half a million possessed peeps?" Gapinski exclaimed.

"Golly..." Celeste echoed.

"That seems unreal," Silas said with agreement.

"Not all of them are actually possessed," explained Father D'Amante. "But it is the truth of the matter that many seek the deliverance rite yearly. And I had the misfortune of being tied to the hip with this one for months on end when I was similarly tapped after leaving my practice."

"Your practice?" Celeste said.

"I was a trained psychotherapist working in Rome, and then I...." The man paused, staring off into the fire and searching for the vestiges of a distant memory. The man smiled and returned.

"Well, during my practice," Father D'Amante went on, "I was positively baffled by what I would witness with several patients during the course of the calendar year. Things that I had very little scientific explanation for from my training in psychotherapy. And I was an early follower of Carl Jung with his new science of psychoanalysis, of all things!"

The man lapsed into a fitful cough, seeming to struggle for breath before dislodging whatever was creating the bother. He swallowed and apologized, then continued.

"At any rate, I was profoundly affected by what I saw through the course of my practice. Which prompted me to search for answers that would ultimately lead me away from modern medicine and its well-worn paths of mental health treatment, and toward the older, more ritualized remedies of the faith I had left behind. So I dropped everything and trained to be a priest. Right alongside this windbag, here."

The man winked and chuckled; Radcliffe smiled and nodded, his eyes seeming to glisten with the unexpected surprise of having his friend back at hand.

"I'm sorry to interrupt the flow of your story, Father D'Amante," Celeste said, "but I sensed there was an urgency to your visit. And you made mention of clusters and a return to something you both had confronted."

The man nodded. "Yes, forgive me. I can get carried away by the travelogue sometimes."

"Sometimes...?" Radcliffe muttered.

Father D'Amante smacked his arm. "Yes, sometimes. At any rate, the two of us were stuck together along with a more seasoned exorcist amongst the hundreds appointed in the city. Over the course of many months, we assisted the man in the sacramental practice, learning the Roman Ritual, or the Rite, as it is known, in order to take up the deliverance ministry amongst a world beginning to...I would say, almost throb with spiritual wickedness."

Radcliffe nodded. "Indeed. Remarkably, and I can only give the Holy Spirit credit for his miraculous intervention, the two of us hit it off, and the rest is history, as they say. We spent the next several years working together, being transferred by the Congregation of Faith and Doctrine to Boston, and that's when we began to formulate a sort of theory about the burgeoning cases of demonic possession."

"The clusters?" Silas said.

"That's right. Possession clusters, we called them. It all started with a woman, do you remember her name?" Radcliffe asked, turning to Father D'Amante.

"Rosa," the priest said.

"That's right. Rosa. She had come to us by way of her grandmama, if I recall correctly, and she recounted to us an episode where she awakened in the middle of the night to find herself paralyzed. She told us there was something holding her down so that she couldn't move, couldn't breathe. She thought she was going to die."

"She tried waking her husband," Father D'Amante went on, "but her body was simply pinned to the mattress. All she could move were her eyes, darting them around in horror. The sensation eventually subsided, but the next night she awoke in the darkness to the sound of someone breathing hot, angry exhalations on the back of her neck."

Gapinski shuddered. "Creepy..."

"That's one way of putting it. Thoughts of evil spirits rushed to Rosa's mind. Her grandmother, who was both an American Indian and a devout Catholic, had warned that if she ever encountered evil spirits, she should ignore them because they feed on attention. Rosa tried, but the breathing wouldn't stop. Then she felt a hand brush her head, whipping up her hair."

Gapinski shuddered again. "Creepy..."

Ignoring the man, Radcliffe picked up the story: "Rosa leaped out of her bed and turned on the lights. When she did, she swore she heard a pack of stray dogs break out in wild howls, almost as if whatever was in her bedroom that night had raced out of the house and into the neighborhood dogs."

Silas said, "Like the pack of pigs Jesus sent those legion of demons into, the ones that ran off the cliff."

Radcliffe nodded. "Indeed. But it didn't stop there. She would often hallucinate, seeing giant spiders crawling around her bedroom. Rosa wouldn't eat, wouldn't sleep for days afterward. She didn't feel safe. She felt utterly violated."

"I imagine so," Celeste said. "And how does this connect to the cluster notion you made mention of?"

Radcliffe glanced at Father D'Amante and nodded. The man said, "Because forty-seven more people reported the exact same phenomenon to us in the span of the next week, people all clustered in the northwest end of Boston."

The room fell silent with the revelation, the crackling pop of the fire offering the only soundtrack.

The phone buzzed with interrupting disturbance.

Radcliffe rolled his eyes and muttered something under his breath. He hit *'Speaker'* and said, "What is it now?"

"Sorry to disturb you again, Master Radcliffe." It was Zoe. "We seem to have ourselves another visitor."

The man huffed. "What is this, a hostel? Who is it now?"

"A woman. And apparently with the FBI."

Silas sat stiff, scooting to the edge of his seat. He glanced at Celeste, who was leaning back with folded arms.

Dear God, please no...

"Why, pray tell, is the FBI visiting us? And in the dead of night of all times?"

Zoe replied, "She's looking for Silas. A one, Special Agent Brittany Armstrong?"

"Yeah, buddy!" Gapinski said, smiling wide at Silas and nodding like a frat boy.

Radcliffe turned to Silas. "Do you know this woman?"

Silas rubbed the back of his reddening neck. He went to reply when Gapinski did it for him.

"Former girlfriend. Who he apparently dumped by email." He shook his head and stifled a giggle.

"What's he talking about?" the Order Master asked.

Silas frowned. "Nothing. But, yes, I knew her at Georgetown, and...well, she was the lead FBI counterterrorism agent on site at the movie theater."

"My, my. The plot thickens. But what does she want, Zoe?" he said back toward the phone.

"Don't know. Want me to send her down?"

"No!" Silas exclaimed, jumping out from his seat. Laughing nervously, he said, "I mean, that's not necessary. Probably some more questions about what happened at the theater. I'll just meet her up top."

"Good idea," Celeste said, standing as well with a smile. "I imagine a second opinion wouldn't hurt."

Silas went to leave when he froze, eyes wide with indecision. "Uh, sure..."

"Definitely, count me in," Gapinski said, joining the couple and rubbing his hands together. "Wouldn't want to miss the fireworks. I mean, a chance to tell my side of the story, of course."

Radcliffe looked at the trio, his forehead creased with a mixture of confusion and amusement. "Jolly good. Knock yourselves out."

CHAPTER 6

Silas hustled through the cathedral crypt, hands in his pockets and growing annoyed at the company.

What the heck were they thinking? They didn't think he could be alone with his ex-girlfriend from two decades ago without, one, his current love getting all jealous like a high schooler, and, two, his friend getting all immature with giddiness like a junior higher?

He took a deep breath and slowed his pace, sighing and cursing himself for his irritation.

Simmer, Silas. Not cool...

So what if there was a twinge of jealousy in Celeste? There was zero reason for it, but he would probably feel the same if someone from her dating past showed up. He'd go to the moon and back to assuage whatever emotions were percolating under the surface. That he vowed, then and there. And besides, she probably wanted to come because she was the director of operations for SEPIO. Totally her right to accompany him, which made whatever it was he was feeling his problem, not hers.

But then there was the Brit factor: What the heck was *she* thinking, coming back into his life like this after all these years? Sure, she was the lead investigator of another domestic terrorist event in a string of them that year. And sure, he was part of said ongoing investigation. So totally had the right and legal obligation to follow up. But still...And showing up at his work like this?

Again: What the heck?

He shook his head, his mind throbbing with the memory of the two of them from two decades ago. One he'd soon forget, and one he'd rather Celeste not know about.

It wasn't just that he dumped her by email two weeks into their official dating relationship. That wasn't the entire truth of it. He had been head over heels for her all through their sophomore year. Had talked for hours over the phone during the summer before their junior year, even fooled around during a visit to her family's lake house—which is when they made their relationship official.

Then three days into the first semester, he found out she had been cheating on him with his best friend and roommate. Totally devastated him. And then 9/11 happened, which sent him reeling with the death of his father. The moment he had needed her the most he couldn't stomach relying on her. Didn't have it in him to forgive her and move on from the betrayal either.

Hence the email.

He clenched his fists in his pockets and swallowed, emotion threatening to rise to the surface.

"Something the matter, love?" Celeste said, coming up to his side.

He took a breath and smiled. "No, I'm good."

"Yeah, buddy, something the matter?" Gapinski said, coming to his other side.

OK, his irritation at his friend's junior high antics were justified; those were definitely warranted.

The trio echoed up the stone stairs that led to the same

entrance into the nave near the high altar Radcliffe had brought them through an hour ago.

"Just totally confused why Brit's back," Silas said. "Thought we had cleared it all up back at the theater. And besides, you heard her. She didn't want our help anyway. Didn't need our help. So why the heck is she back?"

"Didn't want or need *your* help, you mean?" Celeste said with a wry grin as they crested the stairs into the nave.

Boy, was she good.

The truth of it stabbed him in the heart in a way she wouldn't have understood. It must have registered. He faltered a step, then two, but kept walking down the aisle, quickening his pace.

"Just having a play at you, love!" She chuckled and grabbed his arm.

He tensed, but quickly slackened his arm and slowed. He scoffed and said, "Sure, I know. And, yeah, you're probably right. Never was one for rejection."

"Hey, I thought you said you jilted her?" Gapinski said.

Silas went to shoot him a look when he caught Brit sitting in a pew near the back row.

Speaking of which...

Brit stood and stepped into the aisle clutching a tablet. The sight of her in the dim lighting falling from above stole his breath.

He cursed himself for the private indiscretion, but he couldn't help it. Part of his heart was still wounded, part of it was still held by that woman. Even from two freakin' decades ago.

"What's up, doc?" she said, echoing off the domed ceiling and offering that breathy giggle that had made his heart soar.

The trio met her in the middle. She added. "He hated it when I said that. Because even then Silas Grey had his sights on the golden PhD. Although, wasn't it an MD back in the day?"

He laughed nervously. “Something like that.”

“I didn’t know that...” Celeste said from his side.

Silas closed his eyes and took a stabilizing breath. It was going to be a long night.

He said, “Good evening, Brit. Or, perhaps I should say, good morning. Not sure which it is.”

“Yeah, me either.” She folded her arms and leaned back on a leg. “Hey, remember when we used to go on those crazy-late binges during undergrad into the early morning, and then gorge out on pancakes to take the edge off before class?”

Silas’s eyes widened with both embarrassment and fright. He turned to Celeste and Gapinski and offered a sheepish grin. Both looked surprised, but in different ways and probably for different reasons.

“Oh, wait,” she continued. “That’s right, you probably don’t want your religious co-workers to know about those days.” She laughed again, this time sounding far more sour than sweet.

“Anyway...” Silas said. “I assume you’re here about the theater shooting. What’s going on?”

“Now, Silas, you know what they say about assuming.”

“Brit...”

“Oh, alright, sourpuss. It’s just been so long, sometimes I miss our banter.”

He closed his eyes again, mortified.

“You were saying?” Celeste said, arms folded and wearing that no-nonsense glare that showed she meant business. “Something about that theater shooting matter?”

Saved by Celeste.

Brit’s open mouth at being challenged creased into a flattened smile. “Right. The matter about the theater shooting. Well, you were right, Silas.”

“About what?” he asked.

“There was another tattoo.”

The three shifted with collective interest and tensed at what it surely meant.

Silas's blood grew cold, the words he had said about calling him about a bird tattoo burning a menacing hole of fear through his bowels.

"Another tattoo?" he said on a shaky breath.

"Yeah..." Brit said, eyeing the three skeptically. "Here, take a look."

She turned on the tablet, found what she wanted, and spun it around for the three to see.

White light shone faintly off their faces slack with disbelief.

There it was: two intersecting lines bent at each of the four ends, signaling their old foe.

Nous...

"Are you kidding me?" Silas whispered, grabbing the device from Brit with a mixture of confusion and dumbfounded surprise.

"Always something," Gapinski cursed.

Yet there it was in black-and-pale-skin, sitting right there on the underside of the man's wrist.

He shook his head, wondering about the connection between the man and the Church's arch nemesis stretching back to the earliest days of Christianity.

Then his gut clenched wondering whether his twin brother Sebastian was playing a role in it all, knowing he had joined the organization a year ago. He hadn't spoken with the man in several months since letting him go after he had been kidnapped in a deranged scheme cooked up by that maniac Rudolf Borg to revive a pseudo-Jesus through DNA technology rivaling Michael Crichton's bestselling technothrillers.

"No way, dude," Gapinski said, interrupting his thoughts. He folded his arms and shook his head. "Or, I guess, dudette, as the case may be. Total coinkydink tattoo. No way this guy is Nous."

Celeste folded her arms and nodded. "I agree. This doesn't seem like Nous's MO."

"Excuse me?" Brit said, taking the tablet back from Silas. "Nous? Isn't that the organization you mentioned back at the theater?"

"If the theater was showing *God's Not Dead 4* or the fourth iteration of *Left Behind*, then maybe," Gapinski continued, ignoring the question and leaning against a pew.

"You saw the tattoo." Silas turned to Gapinski and Celeste, ignoring Brit's question as well. "And, yes, it doesn't make sense that Nous would suddenly start sending operatives to shoot up movie theaters on Halloween."

Gapinski snorted. "Yeah, sort of seems like they'd want to make Halloween the safest, most wonderful time of the year, given the crazy they're into."

"But if there is a chance this is connected to them..."

"Hold on a second," Brit said, grabbing Silas's arm. "Connected to whom?"

He glanced at it, then at her, their eyes meeting.

She quickly withdrew her hand and said quietly, "You said to call you if I found these markings, which aren't in any known FBI database. And yet you seemed to anticipate them."

"I didn't say that. Had no clue, and really I was joking."

"No, you knew exactly who or what they belong to. And I need to know what you know."

"We tried to tell you, if you recall," Celeste said with narrowed eyes. "They belong to a very ancient enemy of the Church."

"Nous, is that right?" Brit said.

"Yeah, remember, the one you basically wrote off as the ravings of Fox Mulder?" Gapinski added. "Though, truth be told, I thought the same thing when I heard about it all."

She smirked and shook her head. "Well, if that sounded like an episode of *The X-Files*, what we found next surely does."

The FBI agent returned to her tablet and brought up another image. "Recognize this man?"

The trio leaned over and then recoiled with revulsion at a man lying on a gurney with a white sheet pulled up to his chest.

It was the psychopath who had shot up the movie theater, face drained of life and looking more white than he already had been. It was also twisted with a curious, haunting expression—like Edvard Munch's painting popularly dubbed "The Scream," by nature of the central figure's gaping mouth and hollow, bulging eyes, whose hands were up against his head as if expressing the collective anxieties and horrors of modern man.

"I assume you've identified him?" Celeste said.

Brit nodded. "We have."

"How did you get that done so soon?" Silas asked.

"The man was former military, and the on-site blood draw found a match in the government DNA database."

"Which branch?"

She hesitated, then said. "Army Rangers."

Silas folded his arms, shifted uncomfortably, and lowered his gaze at the revelation.

"But he's younger than you, so no crossover."

He shook his head. "Well, then who is it?"

"That's classified," Brit said, "given the nature of the ongoing investigation and all."

"Then why bring it to our attention?" Celeste questioned.

"I brought it to you because of what we recovered from the man's apartment in Grand Rapids, Michigan."

"Grand Rapids?" Celeste said. "That has to be at least six hundred miles away."

"Six hundred and fifty."

"That's a mighty long way to travel just to shoot up a movie theater."

"And from an odd part of the country," Silas added. "Wouldn't have thought a sleepy Midwestern city that's basically an extension of the Bible Belt would produce this kind of fellow."

"That's what many of us thought as well," Brit said. "But from what we can gather, the Devil told him to."

"What, the dead guy went all zombie and told you that?" Gapinski said.

The FBI agent frowned. "No, but his journal did, if you believe such a thing." She advanced to another picture on the tablet showing pages of lined paper filled with messy chicken-scratch handwriting.

Silas whistled and brought a hand up to his chin. "Clearly our mystery man believed it."

"And clearly brought on by schizophrenia or an acute dissociative disorder."

"Maybe, but it sounds like you've already made up your mind on the man's psychological state. So why bring us into it?"

She took a breath and clenched the tablet to her chest again. "Because during an initial autopsy, the man was missing nearly three liters of blood."

"Three liters of blood?" Silas exclaimed.

"What, was the guy a vampire or something?"

"Pretty sure vampires don't suck their own blood, genius."

Brit continued, "What's more, is that his blood was found splattered all over the walls of his apartment in various forms of satanic writings when police conducted an initial raid on his place of residence. They also found upturned crosses and other satanic symbols. However, initial interviews with known associates, family members and co-workers had zero recollection of him belonging to any cult."

The group fell silent, standing still to contemplate the revelation that a man drove over six hundred miles away to a movie theater to unleash a wicked massacre, believing the Devil told him to do it.

Finally, Silas cleared his throat and said, "Brit, I assume you're here because you'd like our help."

Brit smirked. "As loath as I am to admit it, yes, I was thinking along those lines. Not much to go on right now, but with your academic background and...well, newest vocational pursuits, thought I'd go out on a limb to see if you'd have an interest in lending a helping hand."

"Then I'd say it's time to get our Order Master, Rowen Radcliffe, involved. That is," he said, turning to Celeste, "if you agree, director of operations."

Celeste smirked. "Agree. Come along, dear."

"Just wait until you get a load of the other guy," Gapinski said, coming alongside Brit as they walked the aisle back toward the stairwell leading into the crypt.

"And who is that?"

"An exorcist!"

"Good Lord..." she mumbled. "What have I gotten myself into?"

Trailing the group, Silas sighed.

I'm wondering the same thing right about now.

CHAPTER 7

Celeste led the group through the nave, tracing the route back toward the crypt and on toward Radcliffe's study for the second time that evening.

Every one of her bloomin' nerves were set on edge by the events of the past eight hours. The horror flick was bad enough, but she had relented. A small gesture for the sake of love.

Of course, there was the psychopath who had stormed the cinema and slaughtered those poor patrons. She had seen her fair share of horrifying injustice working with MI6. Even was responsible for putting down a few psychopaths herself—resulting in fallout that still haunted her, much like the innocents who had died in that theater. But what had unfolded—from the debauched disregard for human life to the supernatural emanations from the man—had certainly taken the cake above all she had experienced working for Her Majesty.

Then there were the mysterious discoveries bordering on the occult, and the subsequent apprehension by the authorities, and interrogation and dismissal by that dreadful FBI counterterrorism agent who had snogged Silas a time or two—it was all catching up to her.

She just wanted to go to bed, maybe curl up with a glass of

white wine and a gripping crime thriller series she had recently discovered set in the Lincolnshire fens that reminded her of home—if nothing else, definitely white wine to dull the pain still lancing through her head and put her nerves at rest. Maybe add some saltines to put her tummy back in order and pop an Advil to squash her rising temperature.

But she had to put on the face her team expected of her. The steely woman who was always in control. The one who had the right word and just-in-time intuition to untwist the Order's knickers and set the world straight again. Showing no emotion, never letting her guard down, and definitely not revealing the true nature of her inner world—the nature of what she was reeling from that evening in particular.

From the events by some menacing design that had triggered her something fierce—something she thought had long been dealt with but seemed to be raising its ugly head for an encore.

And she didn't know what to do about it.

Then there was that woman...

Her steps echoed through the stone stairwell down toward the crypt with thudding irritation. Not just because the Yank plucked her ever-living nerves. Celeste wanted to slap herself upside her own head for her petty, jealous girlishness and for wanting to cower in the face of Silas's returned lover, as ex as she may be. Yet she also wanted to fight with everything she had to make sure it was clear he was a taken man. That he was hers.

Her Granny would surely be proud of her for breaking out the claws to fight for what she desired, as pathetic as it felt, feeling all needy and girly. The thought made her skin crawl with goose pimples. She brought her arms around her front to massage the chill, coming up to Radcliffe's study.

She shook off the bother and took a steely breath, pressing her palm against the security panel and opening it when the door unlocked. The two men inside were right where they had left them, near the fire but now huddled together over a book.

Standing, Radcliffe said, "Ahh, the cavalry has returned! Come in, come—" he startled when Brit appeared through the doorway. "Who is this?" he asked with a hushed rush, turning with a skeptical eye to Celeste for answers.

"Silas's ex," Gapinski said, adding a chuckle for good measure.

Silas shoved him in the back. He stumbled forward and complained about being breakable.

"No need to be alarmed, Rowen," Celeste said. "I know we're breaking protocol, but I trust you'll be interested in what she has to say. Rowen Radcliffe," she said, turning to the FBI agent, "meet Brittany Armstrong. And Ms. Armstrong, this is the Order Master."

"How do you do, Ms. Armstrong," Radcliffe said.

"Brit is fine," the FBI agent said with an extended hand.

He took it. "Welcome to our humble abode. But I am curious why a visit from the FBI was in order at this late hour."

"I think you'll want to sit down for this one," Silas said.

"And break out another bottle of Port," Gapinski added.

Father D'Amante remained seated, staring contemplatively at the fire without paying them much attention. The five others joined him, Radcliffe resuming his chair across from the other visitor while Celeste and Brit took the couch. Silas and Gapinski remained standing on either side of them.

"So what's this about? I'm beginning to think we've been thrown into a Sherlock Holmes novel with the events of the evening and now a visit from the federal constable!"

Silas said, "Brit is the lead FBI investigator for the mass shooting from earlier, and she thinks the Order might be able to help."

"Oh? Do tell."

He motioned to Brit. "Tell him."

"We've uncovered the identity of the man, who we believe is a resident of Grand Rapids, Michigan."

"Grand Rapids?" Radcliffe exclaimed.

"I had the same response," Silas said.

"Dear me..."

"As I mentioned to your colleagues," Brit continued, "several liters of blood had been drained from the man before the attack, and we found blood splattered about his apartment in satanic writing."

"Satanic, you say?" Father D'Amante said, turning toward her.

She nodded. "The typical pentagrams and 666 numerals, and the like, along with several occult artifacts."

"Such as?" The man was fully engaged now, having moved to the edge of his seat.

Brit glanced at Silas, who nodded her onward.

She said, "Such as tarot cards, amulets, pagan symbols, even healing crystals and birthstones."

"Doorways into the demonic..." Father D'Amante murmured.

"What was that?" Brit asked, looking at the man with a skeptical eye.

"This is Father D'Amante, Brit," Silas explained. "An exorcist with the Archdiocese of Detroit."

"An exorcist? Those things are still around?"

"You'd be surprised, young lady," said Father D'Amante. "While eight years ago there were fewer than fifteen known Catholic exorcists in America, today there are over a hundred."

"A hundred? Clearly I've lapsed for longer than I thought."

"It is indeed remarkable. The Church has reclaimed this traditional ministry that had been set aside. This past year alone I have received 1,700 phone or email requests for the exorcism Rite, by far the most I've ever received in one year. Others get at least a dozen requests each week."

"Remarkable...But what was it you were saying about gateways into demonism?"

Father D'Amante shifted in his seat, seeming to settle in for the long haul.

He said, "Good question. Demons use doorways to take possession of a person."

"Doorways?"

"Things like habitual sin and family curses, which can include sins committed by one generation that carry on in later generations."

Celeste pushed a lock of hair behind her ears and shifted uncomfortably in her seat, the memory of her past burning within her. And the embers of a force she thought had gone long cold seeming to warm from its dormancy.

She glanced at Silas as the priest continued to explain, wondering if he could detect anything within that had seemingly sparked to renewed life in the theater. Closing her eyes, she said a prayer of protection, and forgiveness, from what she had renounced those many years ago.

"However," Father D'Amante went on, "there are two clear doorways that seem to allow demons to gain purchase in people's lives."

"And what are those?" Brit asked, leaning back and folding her arms with clear skepticism.

If you only knew, child... Celeste thought.

The priest explained, "Abuse, particularly sexual abuse, is a major gateway for demonic activity. From my estimation, as many as 80 percent of those who have come to me in my lifetime seeking an exorcism have been victims of sexual abuse."

"Golly..." Celeste said. "And why do you suppose that is?"

The man shifted in his seat again. "Given the nature and trauma of sexual abuse, it creates what I would call a soul wound in a person, making them more vulnerable to demons and susceptible to their affliction. Now, this isn't to say that people are tormented by such abuse so that they *believe* they are possessed. Instead, abuse fosters the conditions for actual demonic possession, given the satanic depravity the victim has experienced at the hands of people."

"But from a secular standpoint," Brit said, "this sort of link you describe here to sexual abuse does help explain why someone might become convinced they are being tormented by some menacing, overpowering evil. And, I have to say, this so-called correlation with abuse strikes me as eerily ironic, given the scandals that have rocked the Church."

"For context," Silas explained, "Brit was a psychology major at Georgetown."

"And went on to earn a PhD in criminal psychology before joining the FBI," she added, "but, yes, that's my context."

"Point taken," Celeste said, "but your conjecture doesn't answer the 'why now?' question behind exorcism's comeback. I have to imagine you know of no evidence that exists to suggest sexual abuse has increased, do you?"

Brit frowned. "No. You're right, it hasn't."

"What is the second doorway, Father D'Amante?" Silas quickly said, trying to play interference between the women.

That hacking cough came back, assaulting the man in a way that sounded like he might pass out from sheer exertion. It soon passed, and he apologized.

"The second doorway," the priest said, "is the occult."

Celeste shifted in her seat, glancing at the others and shoving another stray lock of hair behind her ears.

"That I can buy," Brit said. "At least in theory."

"I believe the root cause in the prevalence and resurgence of demonic possession in our age is due to the reawakening of interest in magic, divination, witchcraft, and attempts to communicate with the dead."

"Sort of goes without saying, but maybe you could spell out the 'why' for us lay people."

Father D'Amante shifted in his seat. "Engaging with the occult involves accessing parts of the spiritual realm inhabited by demonic forces. Those practices become the engine that allows the demon to come into a person's life—into their very person—and take possession over them, their faculties and senses. Plenty of journalistic and academic studies in recent years have documented the renewed interest in magic, astrology, and witchcraft, especially among the Millennial generation."

"In essence, the occult takes the place of God," Radcliffe added. "It is all about power and knowledge, and taking shortcuts into the supernatural apart from God. Even forms that may seem innocent enough can serve as doorways into the demonic realms."

"Please don't put Harry Potter in that camp," Brit moaned.

"Absolutely!" Father D'Amante said, pounding his fist on his armrest.

"Well, there goes my nighttime reading," Gapinski complained. "And here I'm only on book four!"

The exorcist glared at the man. "Such books and films may seem innocent on the surface, but they are far more devious and dangerous. They have disarmed Americans from the reality that all magic is darkness and not of God, regardless if it is conjured by twelve-year-old wizards-in-training or sixty-year-old witches and warlocks from an urban coven."

"So you'd suggest this man opened a doorway for the Devil to gain entrance into his life and possess the man?" Brit asked.

D'Amante shook his head. "I have no idea if your perpetrator was possessed by the Devil. People do horrible things each day that don't require demonic possession. The depths of wickedness within the human heart is unplumbable."

"But you said it yourself: The objects we found at the apartment are doorways to the demonic."

"Indeed, they are."

"And combine this with the sharp rise in possession cases and requests for exorcism," Radcliffe said, "a good case seems to be made for at least the possibility this fellow was possessed. Especially given the ungodly, supernatural emanations from the man you heard, Silas."

Brit leaned back and stared at the fire still crackling and popping away. "I wonder whether these two trends, this belief in the occult and the rising demand in exorcisms, might have the same cause."

"What do you mean?" Radcliffe asked.

She leaned forward. "Think about it. So much of modern life feels dark and wicked and beyond our control. Take the raging opioid epidemic or the hemorrhaging of blue-collar jobs. Add to that urban and even rural communities that breed estrangement and fear, rising anxiety and depression from social media—and maybe these social ills have led people to believe that other more preternatural forces are at work."

"Perhaps..." Father D'Amante said. "But I would suggest it's precisely these times of crises that such preternatural forces gain footing in the first place. Combine this with the clear rise in occult activity in the West and the loss of the Church's footing in society, and the tendency that people seek spiritual fulfillment through the occult as Christianity ebbs—you've got a potent cocktail for the sort of rise in possession we have witnessed."

Brit leaned back again. "Explain."

D'Amante took a breath that led to another coughing fit. He recovered and leaned forward. "As people's participation in orthodox Christianity declines, there has always been a surge of interest in the occult and the demonic. The same was true at the turn of the nineteenth century, with the rise of mediums and other Eastern superstitions coinciding with people's anxieties about the industrialization of the economy and social upheaval it caused."

"What are you talking about?" Silas asked.

"I'm talking about the loss of meaning through work, harsh working conditions, the pollution darkening the sky. All of these social ills led to a deep existential crisis, which coincided with spiritual ones. The same seems to be true today with the rise of the digitalization of the economy and automation, leading to loss of vocational and internal meaning, along with the social upheaval it's caused with immigration and satanic racist ideologies. Just like then, there is a hunger for contact with the supernatural, even as the thirst for Christ's font has waned."

Radcliffe nodded to his old friend. "I agree. As the influence of the Church and institutional religion of Christianity has fallen, people have begun to look for their own answers. At the same time, there has been a resurgence in magical thinking through American culture, with the rise of movies and TV shows touting the supernatural, and other media about demons and the demonic."

"So you're saying," Silas said, "that today's increased willingness to embrace all things paranormal and supernatural outside the confines of the Church seems to have begun as a response to the increased secularization of the American culture specifically and the West broadly."

"Even before spreading through the culture and landing back on the Church's doorstep, as it were," Celeste added, "with people seeking to be rescued from demons. Sort of a self-fulfilling prophecy, isn't it?"

Radcliffe nodded. "Indeed, you're both right."

"I don't know..." Brit said skeptically. "Perhaps it's my academic bias and training in psychotherapy, but going back to your suggestion that sexual abuse is a doorway for the devil, there is also a high prevalence of childhood abuse of different kinds with dissociative disorders. Psychological disfunction brought on by acute psycho-social trauma seems to be a much better explanation than demons for what we're seeing with the rise of mass shootings."

D'Amante nodded. "You are right and I agree. There is a high correlation between such abuse and DIDs."

"DIDs?" Silas asked.

"Dissociative identity disorders," Brit said with a slight grin. "I'm impressed a priest is down on the lingo of popular psychology."

"A priest who was a former psychotherapist," Father D'Amante said with a wink.

"Even better."

"The Church acknowledges all of this, by the way," he went on. "However, the chairman of Columbia's psychiatry department told me that while a great majority of those seeking exorcisms would likely suffer from a known psychiatric condition, even he has seen cases that could not be explained in terms of normal human physiology or natural laws."

"And besides," Celeste added, "Western psychiatry has certainly failed to accommodate widespread spiritual traditions that explicitly acknowledge the demonic. It's really modern Western societies that draw a sharp line between experiences attributed to the spiritual or the supernatural and the material, daily world. Which, by the way, the Church had historically eschewed until the Enlightenment."

"The lines certainly are beginning to blur, I'll give you that," Brit said. Sighing, she added, "I suppose if someone lapses into an alternative, dissociative identity state that declares it is a demon bent on wrenching that person's soul from its body and crushing it like a tomato, I suppose it would be hard to prove otherwise."

"A proper acknowledgement, Agent Armstrong," Radcliffe said. "Psychiatry has only given us the prism through which to aid in our understanding of these symptoms. However, no blood draw or psychological assessment can pinpoint the medical source of these types of splits within a person. And perhaps the science of it all has clouded our judgment of deeper dimensions for too long."

He glanced at his old friend, then continued, "A very good friend of mine once offered me some sage advice that seems apropos once again: '*People would much rather explain away or turn a blind eye to the manifestations of evil than deal with the Devil in their midst.*'"

Silas glanced at D'Amante, who nodded with a slight, knowing smile. He said, "Wise words. But where does that leave us?"

"I wonder if I might have a look at the man," the priest said. "Perhaps you have a photo you took of him for me to see?"

Brit shrugged. "Sure. Knock yourself out."

She turned on her tablet and brought up the crime scene photos of the man and the contents of both the backpack and his apartment the FBI had so far recovered. Then she handed the device to the man.

D'Amante brought a pair of spectacles to his face and took the tablet. Scanning the first picture of the man, he gasped, bringing a hand to his mouth and shaking his head.

"I know this man."

CHAPTER 8

"Roland Vander Molen," Father D'Amante said with a sense of urgency. He looked Brit square in the eyes and pointed at the image on the tablet. "That's who this is, isn't it?"

Silas glanced at Brit, noting her eye twitch with revelation.

She took a breath before answering, then said, "How do you know this man, Father?"

He sat back without answering, his jowly face going slack with disbelief.

"Father?" Brit said rather loudly, bringing the exorcist back to the moment.

The man cleared his throat and sat forward. "You understand, I cannot go into great detail about the man, given the seal of confession."

"Damn your seal!" Brit exclaimed. "We've got a mass casualty event on our hands and a dead psychopath with a pretty messed up, mysterious past that I'd like to get in front of before it leads to something either of us don't want on our conscience."

Father D'Amante wiped his face with both hands and

sighed. Nodding, he said, "I understand. I don't want that either, considering..."

"Considering?" Brit pressed. "Come on, Father. I need your help. The country needs your help."

Silas had to give it to her. She was good at what she did, drawing the man out and getting him to cooperate. It's what he remembered liking about her when they met sophomore year at Georgetown.

"I met Roland Vander Molen as a teenage boy," Father D'Amante began. "When he was sixteen, almost seventeen. He was brought to me by a priest friend of mine in Grand Rapids who didn't know what to make of the lad. But the story goes back further."

He took a breath and shifted in his seat. "The lad was an only child who was strongly attached to his aunt, a spiritualist who had directed him to use a Ouija board at an early age. After she died, Roland and his parents reported witnessing in their household the strangest phenomena they could only describe as supernatural. Back in Maryland, before they moved to Grand Rapids. Anyway, furniture moved from one end of the room to the other, scratching noises sounded from Roland's mattress, various objects were reported to levitate toward the ceiling. All of these paranormal experiences always seemed to happen around Roland, wherever he was. Eventually, the family fled their home in Maryland and stayed with relatives in the West Michigan area. It was there that the boy underwent at least thirty exorcisms over the course of the next few years, nearly every other month. Sometimes more."

"Exorcisms you performed?" Brit asked.

The man nodded.

"What happened?"

Father D'Amante shrugged. "What always happens. With each encounter, Roland spoke in an unrecognizable voice, deep and guttural. He shouted Latin phrases he had never before learned. During one of his final visits, he vomited with such great volume that I had to wear a rain jacket! And during the course of the holy Rite, the boy, who was now a man at nineteen, fought so violently that a dozen people were required to restrain him. At one point, I even saw the word *hell* appear on his forearm, etched right into Roland's very flesh."

He paused, his hand drifting to his mouth and gaze drifting toward the crackling fire.

"And then what happened?" Brit probed.

The priest sighed. "In April earlier this year, after several hours into an exorcism, Roland finally surfaced from his trance-like state a new man. I thought I had finally rid him of the beast that had tormented him for so long."

"But..." Brit pressed.

"But then he disappeared. Haven't heard from him since. Not until this evening."

She slumped back into the couch and folded her arms. "Sounds like a page from the script of *The Exorcist*, if you ask me."

"I assure you, my dear, what transpired over the course of those many months was indeed real. Roland was possessed, by a demon. There is no doubt."

Brit rolled her eyes and slung her leg across the other.

"I understand the skepticism, Ms. Armstrong," Radcliffe added, "but belief in the demonic isn't only a tenet of Christianity. It stretches back as far as the earliest times of human civilization. Babylonian priests would cast wax figurines of demons into a fire during exorcism rites. The ancient Greeks believed in demon-like creatures at the shadowy borderlands of the human world. And within other religions, Hinduism, for instance, refers to basically demons that challenge the gods and frustrate our own lives."

"But demons, in the twenty-first century? Who still believes that stuff, anyhow?"

"You'd be surprised," Father D'Amante said. "Belief in demonic possession is widespread in the United States today. Recent polls suggest that around 70 percent of Americans believe the Devil is real. As I said earlier, demand for exorcisms is growing alongside this swell in the demonic. Our colleagues in the field are receiving more pleas for help every year."

"Alright, fine. People believe in demons," Brit said. "But explain this alleged demonic influence. And I do stress *alleged*."

The man grinned. "Good question. The Church sees the influence of the Devil and his minions existing on a spectrum. On the one hand, there is ordinary demonic activity, in which a person is influenced in their thought life and tempted to sin, often through deception and accusation and doubt and enticement. On the other end is the extraordinary, the most extreme being actual demonic possession, in which one or more demons seize control of a person's body and speak through that person."

"How do you determine which is which?"

"Through a process called discernment, we ascertain whether someone is suffering from a genuine case of possession or simply mental illness. One of the more important steps is for the person requesting the Rite to undergo a psychiatric evaluation with a mental-health professional. Most cases end there, since the majority of those who claim possession are simply suffering from psychiatric disorders like schizophrenia or a dissociative disorder."

Gapinski said, "Must be a relief to know you're just coo-coo for Cocoa Puffs instead of possessed!"

"Actually, it's quite the opposite. It can be a real letdown, I'm afraid."

"I suppose it makes sense to want a diagnosis," Silas said, "to regain back some control over yourself when you feel so out of control with such knowledge."

Radcliffe nodded. "Indeed. If neither a mental-health evaluation nor a physical exam explains the person's affliction, then we take the case more seriously. At this point, an exorcist begins looking for the classic signs of demonic possession."

"Which are?"

Father D'Amante explained, "The ability to speak in a language the person has never before learned; physical strength far beyond their condition, be it age or ability; access to secret knowledge; and a vehement aversion to Jesus Christ and things like crucifixes and holy water."

"And here is what you need to understand," Radcliffe added. "Only a small number of requests for the Rite make it through the discernment process. Through the course of my own decade of experience in the role, I myself only had worked with a handful of individuals who were truly possessioned."

Father D'Amante nodded. "The Church treads lightly here, offering a skeptical eye. We view the Rite as a sort of nuclear option, the final countermeasure that is important to have at the Church's disposal. One that should be used only when no other explanation can be found, but also one that should indeed be used as a way to bring spiritual healing and deliverance."

"And you diagnosed Roland Vander Molen as being possessed?" Brit asked.

"Yes, I did."

She grew quiet, contemplative, seeming to consider this revelation.

"For those few people the Church believes are truly possessed," Radcliffe added again, "a half-dozen or more exorcisms may be carried out before the priest is confident that the demons have been fully expelled. Sometimes more."

"Just as you had performed with Roland Vander Molen, Father?" Brit asked.

Father D'Amante nodded. "That's right. I only wish I had been able to be more successful with the man. Because the demon clearly had a stranglehold on him in a way even I did not discern."

"Which means, what? That Roland wasn't responsibly for his psychopathic rampage? The Devil made him do it is the excuse that gets him off?"

"Not at all, my dear. Clearly, Roland opened himself up to the Devil's influence those many years ago. And the fact remains that the man still possessed a sinner's heart in need of redemption that was clearly capable of—well, a psychopathic rampage, as you said. However, that's not to exclude the work of the Prince of Darkness himself in commandeering the man for his own wicked ends."

Brit went to respond when the familiar phone resting next to Radcliffe beeped with interruption.

As Radcliffe scoffed at yet another call, Brit's phone announced itself with a *purr* as well. Silas felt his own phone buzz in his pocket with an alert. Gapinski and Celeste seemed to have received their own interrupting announcements as their hands went to their pockets in unison to retrieve their phones.

Something had clearly happened.

"Yes, Zoe? What is it now?" Radcliffe said.

Brit was on her phone as well, apparently listening to an earful from Tom, the commanding officer left in charge of the movie theater investigation in her absence.

"Uh, guys..." Gapinski said, face staring at his phone with open mouth.

"It's happened again," Celeste said. "And in Grand Rapids, of all places."

"And it looks like a whole mess of the same mass shooting events," Silas added, "all clustered around the West Michigan area."

"No way that's a coinkydink," Gapinski said.

Silas clenched his jaw and said nothing, only nodding in agreement.

"To the command center, if you would," Celeste ordered, standing and heading to the door.

Silas hustled up to her side as the others quickly fell in behind them.

"So how are you doing?" he asked.

"Sorry?" she said, giving him an inquisitive look that bordered on irritation.

"You know, with the shooting and all. Noticed you wincing before as well."

"I'm fine," she said in a rush. "Why are you asking?"

He smiled and offered a chuckle. "Just trying to do my boyfriendly duty. And, as your partner in crime with SEPIO, checking in on my boss."

Rounding a bend in the hallway, she smiled and said softly, "Really, I'm alright. As much as could be expected of anyone who survived our ordeal, I reckon."

A set of reinforced double doors stood guard to the central nervous system of SEPIO, the muscular outfit of the Order of Thaddeus answering the series of crises that had befallen the Church over the last year. It was charged with guarding and protecting the faith—and using most means necessary. Sitting next to the door was a palm-reading security apparatus that awaited activation.

"Right. In we go," she said.

Silas offered the device his hand. When one door unlocked, he opened it to reveal a space that was nearly the size of a school gymnasium, but paled in comparison to the one that had been destroyed earlier in the year where they had conducted important SEPIO briefings and monitored events affecting the global Church.

"After you," he said, holding the door for Celeste.

She gave a smile and put a stray lock of hair behind her ear, then went inside. The others quickly followed, Brit nodding and smiling while continuing to rattle on with Tom on her mobile. Looked like she was joining the party, which would make things very interesting.

Dimmed recess lighting around the perimeter shone down upon narrow tables lining the dark walls commanded by workstations manned by a few agents normally executing on SEPIO orders. At the center of the room, a raised platform with screens and chairs and direct-line phones to operation centers around the world was awaiting Celeste's control. Massive screens anchoring one wall tracked critical mission updates and news footage from the world's major outlets reporting on issues affecting the Church.

Unfortunately, they were very much not dark that evening.

A CNN news anchor was offering up-to-the-minute updates on the latest developments that had brought the six people scurrying from Radcliffe's study to the command center.

"Right," Celeste said, addressing the SEPIO agents who had been present and were staring at the central screen. "What's happened?"

"A repeat of what went down in Northern Virginia," Brit said, putting her phone away after ending her call. "But on a far larger scale."

"Go on," Celeste said, folding her arms.

"Tom, my guy back in the field, confirmed what CNN is reporting here. Three other movie theaters have been hit by mass shooters in the Grand Rapids area, as well as several churches who were hosting alternative Trunk-or-Treat events to the cultural Halloween one."

"My God," Silas said. A murmur of gasps echoed his disbelief throughout the room.

"The cluster..." Father D'Amante said with a gasp. "It's been activated."

"Cluster?" Brit said, turning to him.

The man hesitated, glancing at Radcliffe who was still staring forward at the CNN report, face slack with shock.

"Father," she said, louder and with command, "what aren't you saying? What cluster?"

"Before you arrived," Silas said, "Father D'Amante and Radcliffe were telling us about their exorcism work ministering to people possessed by demons several decades ago. In one city, Boston, over forty people exhibited the same symptoms in the span of a few weeks."

"Forty people in a week?"

"Tell her, Radcliffe, and about the theory you began to formulate."

Still staring at the screen scrolling with news, Radcliffe blinked and centered his attention. "That's right. But it wasn't in one city; it was one part of the city of Boston."

"Pardon?" Brit said.

"Those forty-seven cases of possession were in the northwest end alone. We discovered several more pockets in the coming year, several more clusters of the possessed."

"Totaling how many?"

"One hundred and twenty-three," Father D'Amante said.

"And what became of them?" Celeste asked.

He took a breath and shrugged. "We lost track of many of them as we moved on years later. However, most found deliverance and went off to lead normal, happy lives, free from the attacks of the Evil One."

"And the rest?" Brit asked.

The priest hesitated, then said, "They have continued to fall under the attacks of the Enemy, seeking regular help from the Rite over the years from other exorcists and their deliverance ministries."

"For four decades?" Silas said.

"That's right. An exorcist isn't like popping a few Advil to make a headache go away, or getting a penicillin treatment for pneumonia. Once and done, like medical treatment. Possession is far different than natural ailments."

He paused and stepped forward, saying with desperation, "Which is why I need to see Roland."

"That's not going to happen, Father," Brit said.

"Why not?" Celeste protested.

She twisted to meet Celeste. "Because the body is part of an ongoing investigation—"

"That has clearly gone off the rails to Hades and back! One that Father D'Amante has clear insight into, given his exorcism ministry with the lad and the depths of what he shared with us earlier."

Brit sighed and raked a hand through her blond hair, clutching the tablet to her chest.

She said, "What do you hope to gain from seeing him, Father?"

Father D'Amante took in a breath through his clenched jaw. "Certain signs of demonic trauma that I dare say could aid in your investigation. I assure you, I will maintain the utmost discretion. I only aim to help."

"Come on, Brit," Silas cajoled. "Given Father D'Amante's connection with the man, and given the sheer wickedness of the events here in Virginia, it can't hurt for him to offer an hour of his time. Maybe it will help your investigation. Especially now that it seems to be expanding beyond the Beltway."

Without letting Brit answer, the priest took another step closer to the woman, fixing her with wide, frightened eyes. "I will say this, that what we have witnessed here this evening in Virginia and now back in my home of Michigan, I fear it is only the beginning. And that is why I wish to help. To stop the contagion from spreading."

The FBI agent furrowed her brow and took a step back,

seeming to clench the tablet closer to her chest and hold her breath with what Silas detected was a hint of fear.

Then it passed. Brit loosened her grip and swallowed. "Fine. Let's go, and I'd love for you to explain more on the way. But you answer to me, understood?"

Father D'Amante nodded.

"When I say go, we go. And none of your hokus-pokus exorcism stuff."

He smiled and gave a bow. "Understood."

She turned to Silas and offered a wry grin. "Looks like we're partnered up again, Sy. And on a demon hunt of all things."

He laughed nervously. "Yeah, I guess so."

"We're all one big happy family, aren't we?" Celeste said, flashing him a frown as she turned to leave. "I've got keys to an SUV we can commandeer for the ride over."

Gapinski said to Silas, "An FBI agent, an exorcist, a religious order Master, a former MI6 agent, former Marine, and a former Princeton professor walk into a morgue. Sounds like the beginnings of a kick-ass funny."

Silas smirked and nodded.

Yeah, real funny. The night just keeps getting better and better.

CHAPTER 9

LOCATION UNKNOWN.

The waters beneath the soaring helicopter churned below with ill intent, a hellish darkness capped by white boiling waves down below that had swallowed ships whole through stormy seas stretching back centuries, taking their cargo of fur pelts and netted fish down to a watery grave on top of crew members young and old. Six-pound cannonballs from the fort anchoring the limestone bluff above the island took care of the rest as it guarded the strait that had been home to various civilizations giving up their dead across time's expanse.

Creating the perfect miasma of souls for Rudolf Borg's purposes. Especially given the haunted happenings that had been rumored for more than a century and the island's history as a burial ground for its aboriginal ancestors.

He had been skeptical when Sebastian Grey recommended the location for his latest operation seeking to expand the minds of humanity and draw the world into a greater depth with its ground of being outside the stuffy, stale, stifling confines of the Church. But his partner had insisted that it was the perfect spot for their experimental project, given both its isolation and its proximity to an American testing ground ripe for transformation.

Then there were the connections the place had with the more arcane partners who they were seeking to leverage in order to foster a greater spiritual awakening. An awakening that would offer the world a spirituality that leveraged the best knowledge from the natural and supernatural worlds.

And then it all went to hell. Literally.

The phone call had come in the dead of night. He was nursing a dreadful fall cold that had laid him out twice over when his new darling phoned, interrupting a deep sleep that had been dreadfully hard to come by.

Normally, he quite enjoyed it when the man rang him, especially at night. That familiar stirring in his belly he had not felt since Jacob had been more than welcomed by the arrival of the newcomer. Especially since the man was the twin brother of his newest rival—Silas Grey, agent with the Order of Thaddeus.

His quickening quickly faded when, on a shaking breath, the man told him to turn on the television.

Borg hated coy; Sebastian discovered his hatred that night.

He threw off his cover and padded naked across the room to an antechamber with a television. The strobing lights from rescue vehicles and the swarm of state and federal agencies playing across multiple channels told him all he needed to know.

In a flashing eruption of rage, Borg lit into the man who quickly confessed to losing one of the subjects earlier in the week. The very man who had torn into an early evening screening of a horror flick at a cinema in Northern Virginia being reported across the world.

Borg's bowels went weak, his heart sank to the cold, stone floor beneath his gilded bed nestled in the castle serving as the headquarters for the entity he had commanded for a decade in the heart of Germany.

The Devil was no longer contained.

The man nearly crushed his mobile device into pieces at the display of incompetence.

Then, as quickly as it spiked, his flash of anger eased, and his face returned to its normal pinkish hue from the crimson rage. He took a breath and ordered Sebastian to explain himself.

The man did, carrying on about how he had wanted to make Borg proud; how the man had overpowered them and fled the compound earlier in the week; how he had wanted to handle the "incident," as he put it, on his own without pestering Borg for a solution; how it had all gotten away from him after losing track of the beast, but that he was handling the fallout in DC; how he was ensuring the project would go forward without further incident in light of the upcoming deadline.

It had taken everything within him not to end the man's life then and there for the jeopardy he had caused Nous and all they were laying for the coming spiritual enlightenment. And then to learn he'd also lost the two books as well during the man's escape—it was all too much.

But then the quickening returned at the sound of the man's sobs and pleas for mercy, and he remembered why he had kept him close to his side—for all he meant for Nous, for SEPIO.

Something about keeping the brother of your enemy close seemed like wise counsel. And the eye candy did him well, too.

Borg forgave Sebastian, but warned the Thirteen and especially the Council of Five might not be as merciful. He thought that was that and he retired back to his covers.

Borg ended the call and hopped on a jet to regain control over the situation. But a few hours later, his phone rang the familiar *purr, purr* assigned to Sebastian's contact. On an even shakier breath, he broke the news of the spreading contagion in the Mitten State.

The situation was spiraling down, down, down. He thought he could trust the man to lead. He was wrong. And now he was paying the price. A price he would exact from Sebastian in due course. Pound for pound.

The shoreline came up quick, waves crashing against boulders brought in to arrest the erosion threatening the island and a red-and-white boxy lighthouse to the right closer to the seaside town guiding ships into harbor. The chopper flew low across a canopy of orange and red and yellow leaves still clinging to deciduous trees on its way toward his destination. Within seconds, the bird crested above the tree line to a clearing of closely mowed grass with a two-story manor anchored north fifty yards away.

Coming down hard, the chopper landed on the lawn, dead, fallen leaves stirring up from the rotors cycling down to a halt.

When Sebastian had approached him earlier in the year with the idea for the project, the man not only outlined the contours of his scheme, he also suggested the location for the experiments and a facility. Apparently, all of it had meant something to him from his childhood. Something about Boy Scouts and family vacations or something or other.

Borg slid open the heavy metal door and stepped out into the crisp night, breathing in the chilly air laced with dead leaves and spicy smoke. It reminded him of his own childhood back in Germany. Before his parents shipped him off to that blasted orphanage.

A wind gusted up the bluff sitting a few yards away carrying the scent of dead, unsalted fish and sending a chill up his spine. He pulled his coat tight against his neck and strode toward the house.

The original owners of the manor-turned-inn, its windows glowing dimly and smoke trailing from a center stone fireplace, had balked at being pursued for the property, insisting that no amount of money could persuade the retired couple who ran the joint to sell.

But Borg knew better.

Money doesn't buy happiness, they say, but it does buy property from old biddies who secretly want to retire to Boca Raton. They folded at the first offer, a far cry from what Sebastian had persuaded Borg to offer them.

Speaking of whom...

The man came out from a covered back porch of red brick wearing a tight black turtleneck and a hesitant grin. He also came bearing gifts: two tumblers of caramel liquid.

"Hello, Rudolf," Sebastian said over the din of the rotor blades still winding down, arm outstretched and offering his *mea culpa.*

"My darling, Sebastian," Borg cooed, opening his arms for an embrace.

He wrapped them around the man who stood holding the tumblers of libation, smelling of coriander and cedar—a heavenly combination that sent his pulse soaring.

"No need to buy me off," he continued in Sebastian's ear. "All is forgiven."

He eased back and snatched the offering and promptly took a swig, the sherry oakiness of the Scotch sliding down fast and hitting his empty stomach with a satisfying burn, alighting his stuffy head with delight.

He smacked his lips and hummed with pleasure. "Macallan 18?"

Sebastian grinned. "Twenty-five."

Borg frowned and began strolling across the lush carpet dampened by the evening dew toward the red-brick porch.

"Look at you," he said with a hint of irritation, "breaking out the good stuff at a time like this."

"A time of celebration," Sebastian corrected, voice edged with an eager giggle.

Borg stopped short and narrowed his eyes. "What do you mean, *celebration*? I'm not sure the escaped subject rampaging in SEPIO's backyard is a call for *celebration*."

Sebastian took a mouthful of the caramel liquid and hung his head. "I understand. But the escapee wasn't the entirety of it."

Look at him, all meek and submissive, yet proud and show-offy. Like a puppy that piddled on the floor only to seek to please his master by rolling over.

Better not roll over in your piss or there will be hell to pay...

Borg took another mouthful of the Scotch and started strolling back toward the manor. "Continue," he said with interest.

Sebastian finished his drink with a grin and took the stairs by two, coming up to the porch door. "Here, let me..."

The man hefted open a walnut door held together by iron ribbings, holding it and motioning for him to enter.

Borg did, coming into a large room lined floor to ceiling with dark mahogany wood, a Persian-style rug patterned with blues and reds and greens atop the same wood flooring, and a crystal chandelier dimmed for the night offering enough glow to guide them inside.

"Impressive accommodations, Seba. Glad my investment will afford us at least a humble abode should the rest of our misadventure prove to net us in the red."

Sebastian ran a hand through his thick blond hair and offered a sheepish smile. Borg loved it when he did that. Loved that he held such power over the man to make him do that.

"Yes, well, consider me humbled at my failings, Rudolf. But the bright side is that the cluster has been forming nicely."

"How much longer?" said Borg.

"Not long."

"And our little excavation project?"

The man hesitated, walking to a minibar nestled next to a pair of french doors that opened into a dining area.

What now...

Borg clenched his fists as Sebastian poured himself another drink.

"And our little excavation project?" Borg repeated with a growl.

Sebastian took a breath then promptly threw back a swig. He spun around to face him and swallowed hard.

He said, "We've hit a snag." He took another drink and waved his arms with reassurance. "But, rest assured, we're working on clearing the way to retrieve the final set of bones."

Borg went to offer a reply when the floor thudded suddenly from beneath, sending his heart soaring into his throat.

He closed his eyes and took a breath, then took a drink. "Sounds like one of our subjects is having trouble sleeping."

"They get like that at this hour. The witching hour they call it, I believe."

Borg took a step forward, draining his Scotch and grinning wide with flared nostrils. "Indeed, they do. The Devil's hour it is. And I'd like to sample the goods."

Sebastian laughed nervously and drained his own Scotch. "I'm not sure that's wise."

"Why not?"

"We tend to leave them to their own devices during this hour, the Devil's hour, as you called it."

"What better time to see them in action than during their most primal, powerful hour?"

The man sighed and nodded. "Alright, then. Come with me."

Sebastian led them down a darkened hallway lined with red and blue stripped wallpaper. At the end stood a steel-reinforced door, an addition to the original century-year-old manor specifically for their project.

To the right, a palm-reading device stood sentry. Sebastian pressed his hand against it and waited for it to register. Within a few seconds, it turned green, and heavy gears thudded behind the wall before the door unlocked and slid open.

"Makes me wonder how the subject escaped," Borg mumbled.

"In we go," Sebastian smiled.

Borg stepped down into the stairwell and went to flip a light switch when Sebastian stayed his hand.

"Best not to disturb the beast lurking below," he said. "We have red lights arranged that seem to lull the subjects into a more acquiescent state of consciousness. But I will warn you, they're not entirely stable."

The Nous leader grinned. "I think I can manage."

The wooden stairs sank under his weight as he descended, a cool updraft of wet earth and mildew delighting his senses with every step. A shiver scurried up his spine—both from the dizzying pleasure of the scents and from the anticipation of what he would find secreted away.

A dirt floor greeted them, splashed in crimson from lights fixed upon the low-hanging rafters above, as did two guards stationed to prevent any further incidents. The basement was long, carrying forward the length of the manor, its space filled with cages along the walls and empty steel tables down the center draped with soiled sheets and heavy shackles hanging loosely to the floor.

The air hung with the aged scent that had greeted them on their descent, but it was now mixed with decay and rot, with human excretions and excrement.

Sebastian handed Borg a white face mask to escape the suffocation, but he held up an arm to pass on the offer. His mouth widened with a lustful grin, relishing the fullness of what had been taking place in those sacred quarters, scents and all.

He took careful, deliberate steps through the chamber, the dirt crunching under his boots and air stirring with a presence that seemed to press in against his very soul—a thick, cold force clawing at him with menacing purpose.

Bodies stirred on either side of the chamber as he inched forward beyond the examination tables. Some slumped against the back bars, others on all fours and reaching for the locked gates keeping them at bay.

He paused his advance, taking in the scene and looking behind him for reassurance. Sebastian was close at his heels, and he offered a reassuring hand at the small of his back to keep going.

Borg nodded and took a step forward, eyeing the subjects with a mixture of fear and intrigue when a guttural snarl deep inside the darkness beyond sent him skipping backward into Sebastian.

"Don't worry," the man whispered, hands squeezing his shoulders with reassurance. "It's all secure."

The scraping of heavy steel chains echoed toward the back from beyond the tables, giving Borg a measure of peace.

Until the being sprang out from the shadows toward him with a screeching cry, a wraith of long, greasy hair somehow standing on end. Eyes wildly bulged matched only by a yawning mouth foaming and snapping for purchase.

Borg stumbled back again just as the chains cinched tight around the woman's wrists, halting her advance but doing nothing about the snarling, screeching fury of flesh scrambling after the man.

He thought she was going to positively rip her manacles out from the stone wall that held her at bay. The walls seemed to creak against her might, the chains frightfully close to snapping, that's how much force she laid against her bindings.

"Do something, you moron!" Borg yelled.

One of the guards walked over with a long rod bearing two

short probs sticking out on one end like the connections of a fluorescent bulb. He held it forth, then shoved it into the woman.

Who instantly recoiled from a jolting electrical shock, slamming against the floor wall and slinking back into the shadows, the supernatural rage receding as quickly as it had arisen.

"Electrical shocks are the only thing that seem to work against the forces," Sebastian explained, helping Borg regain his footing.

Borg sloughed off the man's assistance with an embarrassing yank and stood on his own, taking in a stabilizing breath and smoothing his long greasy hair back into place.

Reveling with a grin in the hell they were unleashing on the world.

And daring anyone to stop them.

CHAPTER 10

NORTHERN VIRGINIA.

Celeste's head continued to throb at the temples as she navigated the black Mercedes G-Class SUV bearing the three SEPIO agents and Order Master plus the two guests. The ache had been chasing her since the encounter at the cinema, joined by a faint, flush feeling that was making her perspire in a way that would make Granny complain was wholly uncouth for a British lady.

All she wanted was to curl up with Silas on the couch back at her flat, sipping mulled wine and watching a chick flick to expunge her of the horrors she had witnessed—both on and off screen. But that annoying Fed had royally screwed things up.

Brit had directed her to drive the group to the Northern Virginia field office in Manassas where the body of the terrorist was being held pending the completion of an autopsy, an hour's drive away. Blessedly, she was in the back yammering on with the crew whilst Silas was playing navigator in the front. She could tell he was trying his best not to pluck her nerves with his exquisite backseat driving skills. So far, he was succeeding in keeping them at bay.

Pain lanced through her head again, chased by a wave of heat up her back and a chilling jolt that spread goose pimples across her flesh. Earlier, she had chalked up her symptoms to the traumatic encounter. The bodily reactions were to be expected, given what they had witnessed at the cinema.

But now she wasn't so sure.

She strummed the steering wheel with her left-hand fingers, pushing a stray lock of her bangs behind her ear, the hair at her temples feeling damp and warm from perspiration. She cracked the window a smidge, the cool October air laced with smoke and decaying leaves offering blessed relief.

As well as the trace signature of a memory that rushed to the fore.

It was her final year of secondary school, and she was out frolicking with her friends, much to the dismay of Mum. It was Halloween, and she was celebrating at a bonfire with her mates. She had come dressed as Margaret Thatcher, which should have put her mum at ease. Except the company she had kept back then gave her a continued fright.

It was her dark phase, when her shadow side began piquing her interest more than the light of Christ. It had all started innocently enough, with a Ouija board during a sleepover at her best mate Hannah's house. It was a vintage thing made of honey wood with black lettering and numbers branded into it, smelling of mothballs and a musty basement. Apparently, it had belonged to Hannah's great granny.

Celeste was skeptical of it all, teasing Hannah for her superstitious beliefs. But sure enough, it performed on cue. The wood heart-shaped planchette moved about the board spelling out answers to their questions about the supposed ghosts that haunted the public housing where Hannah and her family lived.

She had never seen anything like it, and initially chalked up the experience to the pair of joints Hannah had swiped from her brother's stash. But the more the two girls toyed with the device over the coming months, the more she wanted to plumb the depths of its secrets.

Culminating in that fateful Halloween the fall before university.

Amber lighting hanging over I-66 leading outside Washington flashed overhead as Celeste drove onward, the memory of her emerging adult adventures churning in her belly. Looking back, she wondered if the fascination came from her parents' disinterest in organized Christianity. Sure, they were Christian, but they preferred their religion to be of the freelance variety rather than stamped with the imprimatur of the Church of England. Perhaps a more rooted faith experience in the Church could have staved off the horrors she had endured before finally meeting Christ personally.

"You OK?" Silas said with interruption, snapping her out of her memory and back to the road.

"Of course I'm alright," she snapped back, pushing that pesky lock of hair back in place, its dampness feeling more pronounced.

Silas said nothing, turning to look back outside.

She took a shaky breath and sighed. "Sorry, love. I'm OK, really."

He turned and offered her a smile, then went back to watching the world pass by outside.

Truth be told, she wasn't feeling fine. And she feared it was all her fault.

"Since we've got the time, Father," Brit said from the back, "I'd like to get the lowdown on your work as an exorcist."

"Of course," Father D'Amante said. "What more would you like to know?"

"Everything there is to know about the Big Guy Downstairs."

Turning around to face the back, Silas said, "You'll have to excuse my friend, here, but she's a bit of a pagan."

Celeste could see Brit wink at Silas from her rearview mirror, who offered a chuckle and a wink of his own. She gripped the steering wheel, feeling flush again. This time more from irritation than the original trauma.

"Yeah, yeah, yeah," Brit said. "My family wasn't the regular church-going type, though I was raised Catholic and did the whole parochial school thing. I'm not really into all that hocus-pocus religious stuff. No offense."

"None taken, my dear," Father D'Amante said.

"I'm spiritual and practice my spiritual rhythms. Just not religious, if you understand."

The priest nodded. "So what is it you'd like to know?"

"How about taking it from the top, starting with the Big Guy himself?"

Celeste scoffed. "We'll need more than a car ride to Manassas to tackle God."

"I meant the Devil," said Brit, "but thanks, dear."

She gripped the steering wheel tighter. It was going to be a long ride.

"That is certainly taking it from the top!" Father D'Amante chuckled. "Well, the idea of the Devil has evolved over time, mostly as a way to explain why evil exists in a world created by an all-powerful, loving God. The word we use for Devil comes from the Greek *diabolos*, meaning 'adversary' or 'opposer.' We only find the Devil in the Old Testament a few times, and even then he is far from a personified being."

"Appears most prominently in the Book of Job, isn't that right?" Silas added.

"That's right. However, some scholars have pointed out that his name is really just a title."

"Would you look at that," Brit said, "Silas got schooled by an exorcist."

Silas smirked. "Whatever. The Devil still had access to the heavenly court and appeared to be acting as God's agent."

"More a kind of prosecuting attorney," the priest corrected, "but close enough. He convinced God to give him the power to test Job's loyalty and unleash a wave of destruction upon his life."

The two exchanged a look again that Celeste took as flirting. She glanced at Silas and cursed herself for feeling like that petty, juvenile teenager she loathed growing up. But she couldn't help it. That woman coming into their lives this way was bringing it all back.

"Now, in the New Testament," Father D'Amante went on, "things are a bit different. The Devil is far more prominent. At the time of Christ's coming, the whole world was lying under the power of the Evil One, as John wrote in his first letter. Part of the mission of Christ, then, was to destroy the works of the Devil, as the Evangelist wrote. This is clearly evident in the battle lines drawn throughout the Gospels. Two sides, between Satan and Christ. The Devil tempts Christ directly in the desert and attacks him indirectly through tempting his followers, inflicting with bodily harm and even through possession. A major feature of the ministry of Jesus throughout the Gospels was him confronting the Devil head-on through exorcisms."

"Alright, so that's the bits from the Bible," Brit said. "What about the beliefs Christianity holds about Satan and evil and whatever?"

"For Catholics, the catechism teaches *'The devil and the other demons were indeed created naturally good by God, but they became evil by their own doing,'* as it says."

"According to Christian tradition," Silas added, "Satan was the principal fallen angel with the highest rank above all other angels. He was the brightest and most perfect of all God's creatures who fell from grace."

"Matthew the Evangelist writes about *'the Devil and his angels,'*" Father D'Amante continued. "Luke speaks of him as *'the ruler of the demons.'* John the Apostle writes about *'the dragon and his angels'* in his Apocalypse."

"But what does it all have to do with us humans on the ground?" Brit asked.

"After the angels fell from grace, God created the world, including our first human ancestors. After God's crowning creative achievement, investing his very image in his human creatures, Satan turned his rage on humanity, as a sort of proxy in his menacing rebellion against God. As Pope John Paul II described it, Satan *'transplanted into man the insubordination, rivalry and opposition to God, which had become the motivation for his existence.'* The Book of Genesis describes how Satan, in the form of the serpent, tempted Adam and Eve to rebel against God and his authority by sinning against him through disobedience—which had the unfortunate effect of dragging all of the created order into chaos and ruin and death."

"That doesn't seem fair. All of creation is ruined because of one lousy apple bite? All they wanted was to know good and evil. Why fault them for desiring a greater depth of consciousness?"

Father D'Amante chuckled. "You seem to know more about Christianity than you give yourself credit for."

Brit shrugged. "I had a proper Catholic school education. And Sister Helda was a brutal teacher."

"Good to hear the Church still has its standards. At any rate, the consequences of human rebellion make more sense when we understand its severity. It wasn't just that Adam and Eve grasped for the knowledge of good and evil. Or a greater level of human consciousness, as you put it. It was about grasping for *power*—the power to decide what was good and evil, right and wrong. That's God the Creator's role, not ours. But that's a bit outside the scope of our conversation I'd imagine. So back to the task at hand—"

The man was interrupted by another one of his hacking

coughs. Celeste worried he wouldn't recover the way he was carrying on.

"Sorry about that," he finally said. "Now, where were we?"

"A deep dive into all things the Devil," Silas said.

"Ahh yes, before we got sidetracked into a homily on the wickedness of humanity. Which, frankly, does have bearing on our discussion. Because part of the result of this fallen world and fallen humanity is that Satan has been given some degree of dominion over our world, over our lives. The Gospel of John calls him *'the ruler of this world'* and Saint Paul referred to him as *'the god of this world'* in 2 Corinthians."

"I thought God was the ruler of the world," Brit said.

"Yes, and no. Ruler and ultimate authority over the universe and everything in it, yes, including the Devil. But Satan still retains his former angelic stature and powers and rule. Although, as Saint Augustine taught, God does not give Satan free rein and a free hand, otherwise no man would be left alive."

"Theologians argue that the Devil and the fallen angels are limited in their actions, isn't that right?" Silas added again.

"That's right. By their nature as created beings and by the will of God. No matter his superiority to humans, the Devil is still a finite creature, which means he is bound by the limitations of the created order. He cannot perform a miracle, for instance, because a miracle is something that surpasses the power of natural laws and reality. Such a performance requires supernatural power, which Satan does not have. His is preternatural power. However, he can still create the appearance of a miracle given that his powers allow him to surpass human limits. And he certainly exerts himself in a way that appears supernatural, even over the affairs of men, going so far as to impress himself upon individuals."

Celeste nodded along with the exorcist. She certainly understood what he was going on about.

"The Devil is also limited," the priest continued, "by God's own will. Again, the Devil is a created being, not the Creator. Which means his status as a lower being is as a creature, far beneath that of God Almighty. He is often falsely represented as a sort of god of evil, a view held by many satanic cults."

"And Nous, I might add," Radcliffe said. "Which is a view found in plenty of heresies that have plagued the Church."

"Like the heretical Manichaeans," Silas said.

"Indeed."

"The who?" Brit asked.

Silas answered, "A group of heretics in the early decades of the Church, as well as the Gnostics which Nous mirrors, who viewed Satan as a sort of rival god to the one true God."

"Sounds like Star Wars," Brit said.

He nodded. "You're right. The clash of good versus evil in many pop culture phenomenons often pits good against evil, or God against the Devil, as equals."

"Which is fundamentally not true," Father D'Amante said, getting animated now. "Even though the Devil, because of his angelic stature, has more power than humans, he can do nothing unless God allows it. The Book of Job, chapter one, makes that clear: *'The Lord said to Satan, Very well, all that he has is in your power; only do not stretch out your hand against him!'*"

"But why would God allow the Devil to harm us at all?" Brit asked. "Doesn't seem fair."

The priest took a contemplative breath and leaned back in his seat. "While this question is not easy to answer, remember that evil's reign was never God's intent. It stole into the world when Adam and Eve rebelled against God, plunging the entire created order into ruin and opening the floodgates for wickedness—particularly what comes from sinful human hearts. Nothing connected to humanity's fall from grace will make sense, including the demonic. In his sovereignty, God permits evil. However, he is still able to work good from it for his glory."

"Sounds like a bunch of poppycock to me," Brit mumbled. "Again, no offense."

Father D'Amante chuckled. "None taken."

"If you ask me," Gapinski said, "it's not like we humans need a whole lot of arm twisting to partner with the Devil in his schemes, anyway. Have you seen Facebook and Twitter feeds lately?"

"Spoken like a true theologian," Silas said.

Brit smirked. "Yeah, I guess social media pretty well seals the deal that we're not as innocent as we think. But I'm not convinced about all this Devil business. How much farther until we reach Manassas?" she asked Celeste.

"Should be soon," Celeste said.

"Then, yes, one more thing."

"Sure. Go on."

"We never did get to the theory you said you had been cooking up regarding your experience with possessions and the clustering effect. So perhaps you could fill us in on that angle. Could be an important one in the ongoing investigation."

"Ahh, yes. Well, as someone with a PhD in criminal psychology, you are no doubt familiar with behavioral contagions, are you not?"

"Of course."

"What's that?" Silas asked.

"A type of social influence," Brit said, "referring to the propensity for certain behavior exhibited by one person to be copied by others who are either in the vicinity of the original actor, or who have been exposed to media coverage describing the behavior of the original actor."

"How about an example for us back-of-the-row kiddos," Gapinski complained.

"Copycat suicide is probably the most famous. The same behavior contagion will occasionally sweep through a school when a child kills themselves, for example, exerting social pressure and offering social permission to follow suit."

"In other words," Celeste said from the front of the SUV, "suicide clusters."

"That's right."

"I suppose copycat serial killers would fall in the same boat?" Silas said.

Brit offered a smile. "Well done, doc. That would fall into the criminal contagion model, but stems from the same psycho-social behavioral contagion."

Turning to Father D'Amante, she said, "And I assume you believe demonic possession follows the same script, Father?"

"Exactly," the priest said. "I believe where certain social pathologies can bear down on a person's psyche, certain spiritual pathologies can bear down on a person's soul. Particularly the demonic kind, where someone opens themselves up to the dimensions of the supernatural, which then creates a climate for the demonic to operate. Such a spiritual, demonic pathology spreads through a population and influences behavior, manifesting in much the same ways as a social or even biohazard contagion."

A jolting chill ratcheted up Celeste's spine at the thought, wondering whether what she had witnessed and experienced in the theater—what she had witnessed and experienced during those years before she decided to follow Jesus—would manifest itself again.

"Did you make any further headway on your theorizing and research?" Brit asked.

Father D'Amante sighed and face slumped. He looked to Radcliffe, whose face also slumped. "Unfortunately, the initial, official investigation was shut down by the Congregation for the Doctrine of the Faith."

"But what about the *unofficial* one?" Celeste said from the front, eyeing the exorcist from her rearview mirror.

One end of the man's mouth curled upward before flatlining. "Inconclusive," was his only reply.

"Looks like we're about to find out," Brit said.

Celeste exited off I-66 and onto Prince William Parkway, her stomach beginning to churn with dread and heat beginning to swelter up her back again at the thought of confronting the psychotic maniac who very well could be the bearer of an ancient kind of contagion.

As dead as he might be.

Because Celeste knew better.

CHAPTER 11

Silas stared out into the dead of night with an arm propped on his window and hand stroking his chin, the glowing street lights waving at him overhead on their final stretch to the FBI field office in Manassas.

He chanced a glance at Celeste, noting her rubbing her temples again and wincing, but kept his gaze fixed forward, his mind trying to work out what was going on with the woman he loved.

In the year he had known Celeste, there hadn't been much cause to fret over how she was faring. She was a woman who was more than capable and stood solidly on both feet, besting most men at pain tolerance and capacity to hold her own.

This was different. He was worried about her. Had been since they left the theater and returned to SEPIO headquarters. She hadn't been herself since the terrorist event. Couldn't blame her; anyone would be freaked after such an encounter.

But she wasn't anyone.

Celeste was MI6 trained with as many years under her belt as director of operations for SEPIO. She had seen combat, seen people get blown away by terrorists, seen the gore and grimness that comes with such territory up close and personal.

So why had what happened in the movie theater seemed to affect her so differently?

He couldn't make it out. He wanted to talk to her about it, sensing something deeper was going on, but they hadn't been alone long enough to suss it out. Now they were a quarter mile away from returning to the body of the psycho that had set it all in motion.

And that wasn't even touching on the other elephant in the back of the Mercedes G-Class babbling away with Father D'Amante.

Silas scratched his chin and shifted in his seat, stealing another glance at the love of his life.

More rubbing of her temples; more wincing.

He frowned and leaned his head against his window with a worried sigh. All he had wanted was a nice evening out together, giggling like two high schoolers in the dark over a juvenile horror flick, stuffing their faces with artery-clogging popcorn and soda, and enjoying each other's company. Been a long time since they'd had a night to themselves with the pace of the last few months. And it was all interrupted—first by Gapinski, then the psycho, and then Brit.

One evening...just one evening.

Ever since the Easter Massacre and the Knights Templar had showed their ugly mugs again five months ago, they'd been burning the day at both ends. Between her travels and his research work, it had been a maddening time finding time to connect. Then he had to go and waste it on some horror flick he knew she didn't want to see in the first place.

And now she was paying the price for what had happened under his watch.

Whatever that price was.

"Here we are," Brit said from the back, interrupting his contemplation and self-flagellation.

Bright white lights illuminated a driveway entrance into a

nondescript four-story building off University Boulevard that looked more like an office park for start-ups than a bureaucratic bunker for spooks and g-men. Celeste turned into it as Brit unlocked her seatbelt. She crawled to the front as Celeste pulled up to a security checkpoint.

A man wearing black and bearing an assault rifle slung across his chest walked up to the vehicle as it halted at the checkpoint. Celeste rolled down her window as another officer started roaming around the SUV's perimeter with a bomb-sniffing German Shepherd.

"Hey, Hank," Brit said, reaching across Celeste to pass him her ID badge.

"Howdy, Brit. Nice wheels. Not your typical government-issued ride."

She snorted a laugh. "I wish. A Benz would be a nice upgrade from those crappy Suburbans."

"I'd say," said Hank, handing her back the ID. Propping his hands on his weapon and leaning in through the window, he added, "And who are these cool cats? Don't look like government-issued g-men to me."

Another snort, followed by a cackle Silas hadn't remembered before that made his skin crawl—and making him thankful things didn't work out way back when.

"These guys are material witnesses in the theater massacre. Three of them are at least. The other two are experts in...well, I'm not sure what. But something I hope will shed some light on the case."

"Roger that," the man said. "Head on in, Brit. But don't let the Devil get ya in there! I heard he's having a wild time of it tonight."

"So I've heard. Thanks, Hank. Be safe."

Celeste eased the Mercedes through the driveway and pulled around into a visitor's spot near the entrance.

Brit crawled to the back and opened the side door. "Alright, guys and dolls, it's showtime. And I'm expecting you two," she said, pointing to Radcliffe and Father D'Amante, "to especially bring it."

"I'm not sure what that means, dear child," Father D'Amante said, "but if the Devil shall show his face, I shall be sure to break out my holy water and scare the hell out of him."

"That's all a girl can ask."

Gapinski slid out the door and stretched his back. "Can I just say, if heads start spinning and Radcliffe starts levitating off the ground, I may or may not scream like a schoolgirl."

"Now that's a sure-fire way to scare the hell out of the Devil!" Silas said. "Probably more than the holy water."

"Let's save the comedy hour for the after party, shall we?" Celeste said. Turning to Brit, she added, "Can we get to it then, dear?"

Brit smirked and nodded. She led the group to the front door, swiping her ID badge and unlocking it. She instructed them to sign in with an attendant at the front desk in a vestibule that soared the full four floors. A fountain bubbled away surrounded by a few trees and other foliage. The man in black manning the desk, feet propped up and reading a comic book, barely gave them a passing glance.

Silas smirked. Good to know the Feds are still recruiting the brightest and best and most vigilant.

Brit led them across the vestibule, bypassing a door that led to one wing in favor of another one, where she again used her badge to gain entrance before ushering them inside.

Utilitarian, government-issued walls lit by dimmed recessed lighting that reminded Silas of his days with the Rangers led them down a wing that smelled of alcohol and sanitized air. Soon, they reached a door with a keypad, and stretching the wall next to it was a long window that revealed the nature of the room beyond.

"The FBI's morgue?" Gapinski exclaimed.

"Just what the doctor ordered for early morning the day after Halloween, don't you think?" Silas said, clasping the man's shoulder.

He jumped and gave a squeaking yelp. "Not cool man. This place gives me the creeps."

"Boys..." Celeste said, giving them both a look. "Let's dispense with the high-school antics and pull ourselves together, shall we?"

She followed Brit and the two exorcists inside the room, quickly trailed by Silas and Gapinski.

White fluorescent lights flickered to life in a room paved with aqua tiles from floor to mid-wall. A bank of steel freezers gleamed in the light at one end, their doors large enough to accommodate their cargo. The center of the room was empty, and the group congregated around the room waiting for Brit to take lead.

She did by pulling a steel examination table on squeaky wheels resting against the wall over to one of the freezer doors. She opened it, then slid out onto the table a body draped by a white cloth with a tag tied to its big toe.

An overpowering smell of decay and rot bloomed throughout the room, so that the gathered brought a collective arm to their face to shield their noses from the stench.

"I think I'm gonna be sick..." Gapinski moaned.

"Hold it steady, partner," Silas said through his sleeve.

Brit made it a point to check the tag, and nodded with recognition. "That's our guy."

"Sure doesn't smell like it," Celeste said through her own sleeve, wincing and pressing her free hand against her temple again. "He's been dead, what, eight or nine hours?"

"It's not unusual for the rate of body decomposition to accelerate under extreme conditions."

"What conditions? And not like this godawful stench."

"Let us see the body," Father D'Amante said, letting loose

the now-familiar hacking cough before recovering with an apology.

Brit wheeled the examination table over to the group, which reformed itself around its perimeter. She eyed Silas, who nodded her onward, then withdrew the sheet from the man's face.

Gasping at what she saw and dropping it to his chest with a flutter.

"Golly..." Celeste echoed with a gasp of her own.

"Now I *am* gonna be sick," Gapinski said, making a retching sound and holding his stomach.

Father D'Amante started babbling under his breath in Italian, presumably a prayer, and Radcliffe joined in, crossing himself and taking a step back on shaky legs.

Expecting a body still pinkish, the head and neck were a greenish-blue hue, a color more in line with the twenty-four hours after death. His eyes were also open and wide, bulging with horror, and his mouth was wrenched open at an ungodly angle, almost as if surprised by what had happened to him.

And it stank to high heaven! The sour stench of rot, like chicken and pork left outside in the high-noon sun to simmer in the middle of July. As if he had been decomposing for days, not hours.

"This is unreal," Silas said, a hand covering his mouth like the rest.

Brit glanced at him, face registering the same shock and something he had never before seen from her.

Fear.

She recovered, swallowing hard and grabbing the sheet again. She continued dragging it down the man's torso before resting it at his pelvis.

More of the greenish-blue color had spread across the man's body, and parts were already beginning to bloat, which normally didn't occur for days.

The room went quiet as the six stood huddling around the psychopath who was pleading far more questions than giving answers, the ting of the fluorescent lighting and low-level HVAC hum offering the only soundtrack for this horror show.

Brit finally broke the silence: "Best get to it. Is this your guy, Father, or not? Does this look like Roland Vander Molen?"

Father D'Amante swallowed hard, his now-ashen jowls jumping up and down with affirmation as his head nodded.

She sighed and folded her arms. "Well, is there anything you can identify from the...well, body, as sorry a state as it's in?"

The exorcist moved closer to the psychopath's shell, eyeing the man in repose. "There, the tattoo of the pentacle."

"You mean the cliché?" Gapinski snorted.

"What about it?" Brit asked.

"It appeared on Roland's skin a few weeks ago."

"What do you mean, appeared? You mean he got it tattooed?"

Father D'Amante shook his head. "No. I mean, during a session, a particularly fierce session, I might add, it just sort of bubbled to the surface. The skin had sizzled and smoked, giving off a horrid smell of burnt flesh."

"Eww," Gapinski complained.

"It was as if the man had been branded by his demonic tormentor."

"OK..." Brit said with unmasked disbelief. "So the tattoo confirms it's your guy?"

The exorcist nodded.

"Anything else?"

He took another step toward the body, examining it closer. "The color."

"What about it?"

"It's of a man who died days ago, is it not?"

She nodded. "That's right."

"I can only explain it as a sign of possession. The minions of death having taken over the man with completion. As Saint Peter wrote, '*Like a roaring lion your adversary the Devil prowls around, looking for someone to devour.*'"

"Minions of death?" Gapinski said on a shaky breath. "You mean demons? Still, in this man?"

Father D'Amante shrugged. "Whether absent or present I am not sure, but destruction and death are clear hallmarks of the Evil One and his army. As well as these puncture marks here and the disfiguration of the man's skin. He had neither last I saw him."

"Then how do you explain them?" Brit asked.

"The possessed will often exhibit physical manifestations on their outer flesh of the internal possession. And the kind of exsanguination you spoke of earlier, the blood found at the apartment, is a classic result of possession."

"Now here is something..." Celeste said, bending over the man's arms and craning her neck around his wrists.

"What's that?" Brit asked, coming to her side.

"Ligature marks, by the looks of it." She pointed along the base of the man's hands on either side of his body.

The group moved closer for a look and eyed the man's wrists, which were indeed ringed by dark purplish-black bruising marks evident even with the spreading hue.

"So, what, the man was restrained?" Silas asked.

"Was this your doing, Father?" Brit asked the priest with no small amount of accusation.

Father D'Amante shook his head. "This was none of my doing, I assure you. We do not hold our subjects with restraints during healing intervention. A few helpers did hold Roland by the arms at times, but for his and my protection. Restraints are not part of our exorcist protocol."

Brit nodded, seemingly satisfied with his answer. "Well, then where did they come from?"

He shrugged. "They had to have appeared within the week. Again, they were not there during our last intervention."

"Did you know whether the man had any known associations, perhaps some kinky groups that got their jollies off from pain and bondage?"

"No, nothing of that sort that I was aware of."

"Well, it sure looks like he was restrained and I'd wager—"

A sudden bassy rumble intercepted the point she was making, echoing with growing intent from inside the room. A vibration that began crescendoing into a guttural moan that seemed to be coming from the center of the room.

From inside the cadaver of Roland Vander Molen.

CHAPTER 12

"What the hell is that?" Gapinski exclaimed.

"Literally," Silas mumbled, stepping back from the body with wide eyes.

Brit stepped to the open entrance, hand on the sidearm hugging her hips, peering through the opening with back against the door trying to discern the source of the racket and rumble.

"Sorry to break it you," Silas said, "but I don't think what we just heard came from outside these walls."

She threw him a look, the same one he had glimpsed earlier. Fear, laced with something else he couldn't place. A knowing look that made him think she wasn't sharing all her cards.

An aftershock rattled the room again carrying with it another deep moan. Before all at once ceasing into an eerie void.

"I'll say it again," Gapinski said, pressed against the turquoise-tilled wall, "what the heck was that?"

"I can assure you, my boy," Radcliffe said, "nothing from this world."

"What do you mean?" Brit said with biting skepticism.

Before he could answer, the steel examination table holding Roland Vander Molen started shuddering with intensity, vibrating his cadaver and throwing his rigid arms down over the sides so that he looked as if he were crucified.

Gapinski gave a frightened yelp; Silas echoed with his own version.

Father D'Amante was the only one who seemed activated by it all, taking a step toward the supernatural display and saying with a breathy whisper: "The Devil is still with this one..."

Before Brit could interrogate him, the door to the examination room slammed shut with such force that a fluorescent light cover fell to the floor with a crash.

Gapinski jumped with a startled scream. He reddened and chuckled. "Whoa, now that was something straight out of *The Exorcist*."

"Probably just an updraft from the HVAC," Brit said, rejoining the group. "One time—"

A rattling from across the table cut her off. The autopsy instruments, in all of their hardened steel glory, startled on their metal tray. A knife even jumped out and toppled to the floor with a bouncing clang.

Gapinski yelped again. "You think that was caused by an updraft from the HVAC, sister?"

The rattling grew until the table itself shook with an aftershock that jolted the resting body inches from the table.

The room gave a collective scream. But that wasn't even the whole of it.

With sudden, supernatural levitation, Roland's body began moving with a wicked arch, its arms still stiffly outstretched and belly reaching dramatically toward the ceiling, heels and head firmly planted on the table while the rest of it bent like a wishbone.

A crying shudder ricocheted around the room at the sight.

It intensified when the sheet covering the man slipped off to the floor, exposing the man with indecency.

Celeste went to replace it when she stumbled against the table and brought a hand to her head, her face twisting with a dramatic wince and crying out in pain.

"Celeste?" Radcliffe shouted.

"Are you alright?" Silas asked, grabbing her arm and holding her steady.

"Feeling a bit woozy is all. Lack of sleep, I think."

"Feeling it myself, sister," Gapinski said. "About ready to—"

He was cut off by the body falling back to the table with a thud and then flopping down to the floor in a dramatic twisting of limbs.

Before anyone could react, Celeste started screaming a frantic, hysterical howl with eyes bulging from their sockets and mouth wide with horrifying abandon.

"Celeste…?" Silas said, wide-eyed with panic yet frozen with indecision.

Then she pulled at her hair, a clump of her brunette locks coming loose in her hand.

"Jeez Louise!" Gapinski said with a jump.

Silas gasped and jumped himself, then took a step back at the sight.

Brit grabbed his arm, and Radcliffe covered his mouth with a moan.

Father D'Amante was the only one to activate without a thought.

He'd been here before and knew exactly what was needed.

The exorcist stepped forward on cool, cautious steps. "Stand back. All of you."

He spread a commanding arm, pushing Gapinski out of the way while inching closer to Celeste. With his other one, he brought out a gold crucifix from the inside of his garment.

Celeste was jolted backward at the sight. She bowed her

head toward the Christian icon and fixed it with a penetrating gaze Silas had never before seen from her, eyes narrowed and dark with glaring ill intent.

Then a sound emanated from her being. Which sounded eerily familiar.

A cross between a strangled sheep and irate mama grizzly bear.

The same one heard hours ago from the psychopath lying in a jumbled greenish-purple mess on the floor!

She growled and glared at the exorcist, then gnashed her teeth at him.

In a burst of jumbled words, she started muttering on about good and evil, God and the devil.

Father D'Amante stood resolute, arm outstretched with the crucifix and unmoving. "The Lord rebuke you, O Satan!" he said with a commanding voice, taking another step and holding the crucifix with an outstretched arm.

Celeste shuttered backward and lashed out with a wicked gnashing of her teeth again.

"What is going on, Radcliffe?" Silas said with strain, his lips quivering with a mixture of shock and horror and fear at the woman he loved still babbling and gnashing and flailing in the face of the exorcist muttering something in Italian and inching closer with his outstretched crucifix.

He replied with a choking whisper, "I dare say the Devil has shown himself. And in our dearest Celeste..."

Then all at once, she fell silent. No more muttering, no more screaming and pulling. No more writhing and flailing about.

The room went silent, all movement and motion seeming to hang in one dramatic suspension of time.

But then she began talking again. When she did, a new persona emerged. Something rose up within her, guttural and gravelly, like that of a deep-throated man whose voice was being masked from identity on those undercover news shows.

"She is mine, this one," the Voice hissed. "*Mine!*"

Silas brought a hand up to his mouth, mind swimming with confusion at the truth of what it all meant.

Was the love of his life possessed?

By the Devil himself?

She snarled and bared her teeth at Father D'Amante, who thrust the crucifix in her direction again, repeating his command: "The Lord rebuke you, O Satan!"

Then he added a prayer, pleading with the Holy Father, Son, and Spirit for assistance: "Oh God, come to my assistance! Oh Lord, make haste to help me! Oh Everlasting God, who have ordained and created the ministries of angels and men in wonderful order: Mercifully grant that, as your holy angels serve you in heaven, they may help and defend us on earth at your command. Through our Lord Jesus Christ, your son, who lives and reigns with you in the unity of the Holy Spirit, one God, forever and ever. Amen."

Another guttural moan followed by a high-pitched screech echoed throughout the morgue. The grizzly bear strangling the sheep that had come from Roland Vander Molen, the psychopath at the movie theater.

Lord Jesus Christ, Son of God...do something!

All at once, Celeste's head started flailing from side to side, cocking back at odd, inhuman angles.

Silas rushed forward to hold her steady, but he was held back by the exorcist still planted firmly to the floor.

"Stand back, I say!" Father D'Amante commanded.

"But we must do something!"

"We are, my boy."

"But—"

He was cut off by another screech slicing through the confusion, followed by a weak cry.

"Help me!" came a familiar voice, meek and mousy and full of trapped dismay, trailed by wracking sobs that heaved the woman's body up and down with a mournful shudder.

It was Celeste, the real one, in all of her glory. Trying to break free.

Then the Voice returned, the one of demonic intent: *"You humans have your own sense of time,"* it hissed with the same guttural growl. *"I have plenty of time. I have all the time in the world. I've been biding it, saving it, stashing it away with this one..."*

Silas shook his head with wide-eyed confusion. What was it talking about? It made no sense...Celeste had never been involved with the demonic! Never gave her soul over to the Devil!

He was interrupted by the voice shifting into a staccato whisper: *"It's your girlfriend I want,"* Celeste said, staring straight into Silas with those haunting, slitted eyes brimming with a menacing wickedness he recalled from the theater.

The Voice continued, *"Not only her body, but her soul!"*

As the Voice spoke, Celeste jerked her head from side to side, as if carried along on strings by a halting puppeteer until Silas thought her head would pop off.

Then her motions slowed. Her head began swaying from front to back like a viper hypnotized by the fabled wind instrument of a snake charmer.

"God can't save her," the Voice within Celeste screeched. *"Do you understand that? She's mine, Silas Grey!"*

The mention of his name by that hideous voice sent a frigid shudder through his bowels so that he thought he would lose them then and there.

Then she went silent. Just the HVAC hum and electric ting of the fluorescent lights above.

No one moved, no one made a sound, no one thought to breathe lest they crack the truce that seemed to spread between the parties. Even Father D'Amante had ceased his prayers and exorcist mumblings.

Without warning, there was another bassy rumble that shook the room until the rest of the light covers crashed down to the floor and shattered. More metal instruments clattered to the floor as well, followed by glass beakers and vials splintering in cases lining the countertops.

In the middle of the melee, Celeste suddenly arched her back, just as Roland's corpse had moments ago. Her face transformed into a series of menacing poses—her cheekbones and lips and eyebrows contorting in ways not thought possible.

The fluorescent lighting above dimmed and flickered before brightening back again, sending jolting bolts of fear ricocheting up Silas's back.

Even Brit gave a startled scream, followed closely by Gapinski.

The writhing continued. It was almost as if Celeste was fighting within herself. As if something inside of her was fighting for her very soul.

"Radcliffe..." Silas yelled.

"Gabriele..." Radcliffe said, laying a hand on his old friend. "End this!"

Father D'Amante began praying aloud, beseeching Jesus Christ and his blood to combat the very forces of hell.

"Almighty and eternal God," he shouted with all of the authority given him by Jesus Christ himself, "who appointed your only-begotten Son the Redeemer of the world, and willed to be appeased by his blood: Grant, we beseech you, that we may so honor this, the price of our redemption, and by its virtue be so defended from the evils of our present life, so as to enjoy its fruit in heaven forevermore, through the name of Christ Our Lord. Amen."

A cackle broke out from Celeste's lips in response. Which turned into hysterical giggling, almost like a spoiled child.

Soon, her body started heaving with guffawing belly laughs from deep inside her being.

The exorcist, crucifix still held outright, switched to quoting a portion of Scripture, Psalm 27:

The Lord is my light and my salvation;
whom shall I fear?
The Lord is the stronghold of my life;
of whom shall I be afraid?
When evildoers assail me
to devour my flesh—
my adversaries and foes—
they shall stumble and fall.

The cackling continued, but seemed to be more pained, as if the Voice within Celeste was recoiling from the Word of God being proclaimed against it.

Father D'Amante continued, taking a sturdy step forward:

Though an army encamp against me,
my heart shall not fear;
though war rise up against me,
yet I will be confident.
One thing I asked of the Lord,
that will I seek after:
to live in the house of the Lord
all the days of my life,
to behold the beauty of the Lord,
and to inquire in his temple.
For he will hide me in his shelter
in the day of trouble;
he will conceal me under the cover of his tent;
he will set me high on a rock.

As he continued reading, Celeste started calming down. Her flailing diminished and the frenzied, frantic movements of her arms and head started to ebb.

The priest continued taking careful steps forward toward Celeste who was now backed up against the large window, proclaiming the Word of the Lord with clear, annunciated words.

Suddenly, Celeste twisted toward the floor and vomited, letting loose a stream of green and brown liquid that seemed far more than her body could have held. It arced in a climactic splash in the middle of the room, then dribbled down her chest.

Then all at once, she wilted to the floor as if she had fainted.

"Celeste!" Silas said, racing to her side, followed quickly by Gapinski and Radcliffe.

He caught her before her head hit the floor. Her eyes were fluttering open, and she was cold to the touch yet clammy and damp with sweat, her hair matted to her head.

"Wha...where am I?" she moaned. "What have I done?"

She looked as though she had just wrestled an alligator or grizzly bear to the ground. Which, in many ways, she had.

"I am so sorry," she panted, "So sorry..."

"Shh, it's alright," Silas whispered, cradling her and kissing her head. "It wasn't your fault."

"I don't know what came over me."

Face white as a sheet and eyes bloodshot with fearful dread, Silas looked to Radcliffe with worry and over to Gapinski before settling on Father D'Amante who looked as spent as Celeste.

The problem was that they all knew what had come over her. Even Brit seemed positively shaken by the encounter, her face fixed with horror and staring at Celeste as if she were an alien.

Holding the love of his life, he said to the exorcist, "Help her..."

Father D'Amante went to respond when the lights dimmed to sudden darkness.

A beat later, yellow emergency lights from across the room flickered on, casting eerie shadows across the room.

"Crapola, more demons?" Gapinski complained, huffing and planting his hands on his hips.

"That was no work of the Devil," Radcliffe said, stiffening before stepping back with worry.

A sudden muffled cracking of *pop-pop-pop* shots echoed outside through a window with drawn blinds. Then another, a more violent and violating series of spatting shots.

Different tone, different timbre.

"Double crapola..." Gapinski said, hand reaching toward his back for his weapon.

"We've got company," Silas said. "And it's not the demonic kind."

"Always something."

CHAPTER 13

Silas eased Celeste to the tiled floor and withdrew his weapon from his back. A Beretta M6, his weapon of choice. A hold-over from his days with the Rangers, but it still did the trick.

Gapinski joined him with a SIG Sauer P226 built for action. His own weapon of choice Silas couldn't bring himself to use.

Brit sprang into action herself, withdrawing her own Beretta—government-issued. She padded over to the side window and parted a set of blinds for a closer look. A curse slipped her lips. "Looks like my two guys are down out front, and one of those crappy BMWs is responsible."

"Maybe you'll take us seriously now," Gapinski said, chambering a round. "I'll bet you my collection of Derek Jeter baseball cards that those looney-tunes parked outside are the Nous folks we tried warning you about."

"Yeah, yeah, yeah. We can Monday-morning quarterback it if we live to tell about it."

"If?"

She ignored him, checking to make sure the lock on the window was secure before hustling back over to Silas at the entrance. Pointing at Radcliffe and Father D'Amante, she said,

"You two stay here with Celeste and lock the door. The window's jammed, so no worries there."

"I'm coming with," Celeste said with protest, standing before faltering to the ground again on weak legs.

"Like hell you are. No pun intended. Anyway, us three will handle the—"

More weapon fire intercepted her instructions, then an echoing crash down the hall just outside the door followed by another round of *pop-pop-pops*.

"They've breached the entrance. Probably just took out my other guy." She took out her mobile phone and let slip another curse. "No signal? What, are they jamming us?"

"Probably," Silas said.

"Who are these guys?"

"We tried telling you," Gapinski said, "but oh no—"

"Shut it, Hoss. Time to move."

Brit chambered a round and glanced back at Silas. "You got a license for that thing?"

He grinned. "A license to kill."

She shook her head. "Still the cheeseball I remember from Georgetown. I hope you've been target practicing since leaving the Rangers, because it's about to get real."

Silas glanced at Gapinski with a knowing grin. "I've been keeping up well enough the past year." He chambered a round of his own and nodded toward the door. "Shall we?"

"On three..." Brit stood at the door and gripped the handle. "And you take lead, hot stuff. Let's see what you've got."

Silas and Gapinski readied themselves at the threshold of the entrance to sweep into the hallway when she opened the door, gripping their weapons and readying themselves for more action.

It had been a nice change of pace since the spring not having to deal with Nous as they had with their relentless assault the year before. Silas was getting used to his life of reading and research with the Order. Much less headache than dealing with the overly privileged college kids and their helicopter-turned-snowplow parents back at Princeton.

But vacation was over. It was go time.

Brit held up three fingers and began the countdown.

Three...two...one.

Closed fist.

She yanked open the door, and the two men slid inside the darkened hallway, dim yellow light from behind giving them barely enough visibility to make out what was ahead.

Silas took the lead, padding forward with weapon outstretched, his shadow stretching before him down the corridor as they made their way toward the vestibule.

They came up quick to the exit door.

And were met with the sounds of *rat-a-tat-tat* gunfire.

He took some comfort that a solid steel door stood between them and the hostiles. But he figured it wouldn't stop whoever it was from gaining entrance anyway. Just bided them more time to end it on their terms. Or delayed their death in a gunfight. One of the two.

Silas opted for the former, not the latter. Especially now that he was fighting for the woman he loved.

He chanced a look through the small mesh-wire window and counted four hostiles aiming at a man darting backward, his back to a row of ferns while opening fire toward the opposite wing before switching to the entrance.

The attendant reading the comic book who had paid them no mind.

He was earning his keep now, that's for sure.

Without confirming with his ex-girlfriend, Silas used the distracting response the man was offering up as leverage for their own rejoinder.

"Let's back our g-man brother out there on three," Silas said.

"Works for me," Gapinski replied.

"Me too," Brit agreed.

Silas glanced at his partners and nodded.

Then yanked the handle and pressed through, gun blazing an arc of lead toward the hostiles.

Gapinski and Brit were hot on his heels offering their own forceful reply.

Which not only destabilized the poor g-man, throwing him off his aim and sending him to the ground scurrying behind the ferns. But completely flipped the hostiles off balance as well, sending them retreating back outside to regroup.

The two followed Silas along the back of the vestibule to just behind the fountain anchoring the center of the vast space.

When an eruption of angry bullets chewed through the wall behind them.

Apparently the hostiles had regrouped.

"Not bad, Sy," Brit said with panting breath. "You managed to get us wedged between a fountain and a group of ferns. What now?"

The *rat-a-tat-tat* eased some, then burst forth with indecisive spats, as if the hostiles were gauging the turn of events themselves.

Silas replied with a volley of lead to keep them on their toes while he tried to come up with an answer. Then his gun clicked empty.

He let a curse slip before sliding it out and slipping in a new cartridge. His last one.

"I counted four hostiles," Silas said, "which isn't the best odds combined with all that heavy firepower."

"We've had worse," Gapinski said.

Silas nodded and grunted with affirmation. "Our only hope is keeping them outside. We've got the covering advantage here, while they're in the open. We've also got what they want, which will force them to advance."

"And what is that?" Brit asked.

He popped off *one-two-three* shots before answering: "The body."

"The body?"

"Guarantee they're here for Roland."

"But why?"

Return fire from the hostiles intercepted his answer, driving them to the floor below the fountain bed.

Silas nodded toward the entrance. "Why don't you ask them."

Brit went to offer a retort when an agonizing cry echoed from behind.

A geyser of blood blossomed from the front desk agent's neck. He fell sideways then fell silent.

Brit cursed then popped to her knees and opened up with fury; Silas and Gapinski joined her in the avenging reply.

Which quieted the whack jobs outside real quick.

"Come on, boys," she said, standing and popping off another *one-two-three-four* rounds. "Let me show you how us g-men get it done."

Without waiting for a reply, she darted forward to a cement column next to the shattered entrance door.

The boys trailed close behind: Silas joining her and Gapinski squeezing behind another cement column on the other side.

"Now what?" Silas complained as another volley of shots rang out, piercing the night air and filling the vestibule with a hateful beat that threatened to resurface visions from similar firefights in Iraq.

Although he'd had no PTSD-freeze outs this time around. So that had to count for something. A silver lining in a darkened cloud raging with sound and fury.

"Look, there," Brit said, pointing toward the black Beamer parked just outside the entrance ramp.

Gunfire erupted from two separate barrels on both sides of the beast, sending the trio behind their bunkers as the bullets chewed the concrete without mercy.

"I think I've got a shot," Gapinski said, sliding out an empty clip and replacing it with his last reserve.

"What kind of shot, flyboy?" Brit said.

"You'll see. Give me some covering-love will ya?"

"He's your partner," she grumbled to Silas. "Will he deliver?"

Silas nodded, tightening his grip on the butt of his Beretta and readying to come to Gapinski's assistance.

He said, "He'll more than deliver."

"Alright, let's do this then."

The *rat-a-tat-tat* gunfire eased to a trickle as the operatives readied themselves for a reply.

Silas and Brit spun around from their concrete barrier and opened back up on the hostiles. Sending them scurrying behind their black beast.

And giving Gapinski the window to act.

He pivoted toward his target, lined up the shot, and sent *one-two-three* of them aiming for the rear.

Which connected in spades.

The Beamer ignited with a deafening *BOOM!*

And sent the hostiles sailing in a crumpled heap ten feet away.

No more gunfire. No more movement. No more nothing.

"That's one way to put down a firefight," Brit said, stepping forward through the entrance on cautious feet.

Gapinski grinned and blew into his barrel. "What did I tell ya?"

"Lucky shot," Silas retorted, following after Brit.

Gapinski snorted. "Lucky my a—"

Livid gunfire erupted with interruption on their right flank. From their own vehicle.

Sending the trio stumbling back inside for cover.

A guy in black, face masked and bearing a 50-caliber machine gun propped on the hood of their G-Class.

"Just when you think the fat lady has eaten her last donut..." Gapinski complained as they took back up their positions behind the concrete columns.

"She opens up a bag of chips?" Brit deadpanned.

The man laughed. "Good one. Hey, Silas, how d'you let her go? I like this one."

Silas glanced at Brit before glaring at his partner. "Feel free to take her, partner," he mumbled before opening up on the remaining hostile out front.

Within seconds he clicked empty. "I'm out," he said, sliding his last cartridge out to the floor.

"Here," Brit said, handing him a refill.

He slid it in just as the Nousati whack job out front began renewing his assault.

"This isn't working," Gapinski complained from against his concrete column out of range of the metal chewing the entrance to death.

Brit shoved a fresh clip into her own weapon as well. "Why don't you two flyboys make yourselves useful and cover me while I put the dog down."

"What do you have in mind?" Silas asked.

She flashed him a grin. "Watch and learn."

He frowned, but nodded to Gapinski across the entrance threshold to assume a covering position on the other side. He complied and wedged himself against a potted tree as the gunfire continued to rage outside.

Silas inched around to the other side of his column and knelt just out of range of the heat being thrown his way inches from his head. "On five..."

Gapinski nodded. Silas held up a fist of fingers and counted down.

Five...four...three...two...one.

All at once, Silas and Gapinski unloaded on their SEPIO-issued Mercedes G-Class, relentless and with spendthrift abandon.

Which did the trick.

The Nousati stayed his own assault.

Which opened a window for Brit to work her magic.

Stepping behind Silas, she leaped through a shattered window and padded across the yard, weapon outstretched and aiming without any cover between her and the hostile.

Ballsy bravado, that's for sure. Silas had to give her that. Just the girl he remembered from Georgetown.

When the two men halted their assault on cue, she widened her stance and gripped her weapon with aiming purpose.

Planting a shot right between the eyes of the idiot hostile when he showed up to resume his post.

No more firing, no more hostiles—all having dropped to the pavement in slumping heaps like the useless scum they are.

Or were.

"She's, like, a superhero..." Gapinski said with wonder.

Silas smirked. "Whatever, pal. Just wait til you get to know her."

The two men stood and padded to Brit's side.

The trio took a breath, then another as she held her hand in a fist to make one final assessment.

Satisfied the world was back to normal once the dust settled, she lowered her arm and started forward. The other two followed close behind.

The trio crunched across shards of glass and kicked aside still-smoldering debris from the Beamer, weapons still outstretched and more than ready to answer the call of duty. They padded toward the downed hostiles to confirm what they figured to be true.

When they were satisfied, the three breathed a collective sigh of relief.

"Guess we lived to tell about it after all," Silas said.

"Nice shooting, sister," said Gapinski, stuffing his weapon in his waist. "You can have my back anytime."

"Thanks. Not bad shooting yourself, killer. And you, too, Sy," Brit said, turning to Silas who kept walking toward the bodies. "Had I known you were good for such a solid shot, I might not have left you for your—"

"Wait a minute..." he interrupted, shoving his weapon at his back and scanning the vast parking lot in a panic.

"What's wrong?"

He spun back toward the smoldering Beamer and then to their Mercedes, counting the dropped hostiles scattered around the parking lot, from one to the next.

One, two, three bodies.

"How many hostiles were there?" he asked in a rush.

Brit said, "If I recall, four. Why?"

Silas clenched his jaw and whipped out his Beretta again, running back into the beaten and bloodied face of the FBI field office, his partners running after him in confusion.

He swept the vestibule on his arrival, face steely and set for action, his head ringing with panic now.

"Hang on, where's the 10-32?" Brit said, coming up to his side.

"I counted only three bodies!"

She cursed and withdrew her own weapon. "Which means there's one more still out there..."

Gapinski joined them and whipped out his own weapon. "Sonofa—"

"Any other way back to the morgue?" Silas hissed.

"No. Just the hallway."

Damn Nousati must have doubled back around somehow

after their advance. Or they had missed him in the initial melee.

He rushed toward the only open door still available.

Just as a figure, dark and brooding, opened fire on the window into the morgue.

"*Nooo!*" Silas screamed, opening up on the man and emptying his final clip.

But not before the hostile threw something through the maw of splintered glass before slumping to the floor.

A beat later, a fantasmic, blooming show of fire and fury exploded into the hallway, sending the three to their knees as smoke and debris billowed down the corridor.

Consuming the room in a raging inferno.

With Celeste, Radcliffe, and Father D'Amante inside!

CHAPTER 14

"Celeste!" Silas screamed from the floor, a raging hysterical cry until his lungs gave out.

"Silas!" Brit yelled, grabbing him by the collar. "Come on!"

He snapped out of his hysteria and scrambled up on unsteady feet, joining her and Gapinski racing through the settling soot toward the morgue.

Which had transformed into a raging war zone.

Wires sparked from above like livid rattlesnakes. Flames flapped in protest from piles of burning debris expelled during the blast, greedy fingers curling toward the ceiling and threatening gluttonous destruction. Rubble was scattered about—shards of glass, mangled equipment, broken turquoise tiles, jagged pieces of cabinetry.

And no Radcliffe or Father D'Amante.

Or Celeste.

Even Roland Vander Molen had disappeared, his body having been either ripped to shreds or consumed with purpose from the terrorising explosion.

Silas fell to his knees, eyes wide and mouth wrenched open, ready to offer a raging reply to the destruction.

But nothing came. His brain froze with indecision, all visual and aural sensations immobilizing him from action. What was there to do but sink into despair for the loss of his love?

Which is what he did, crumpling into a ball without a care for the inferno raging around him.

"Silas!" Brit shouted, shaking his shoulders and trying to heft him upright.

He ignored her, rocking on his knees and holding his head, letting loose a torrential outpouring of emotion spiraling into rage.

"Silas!" she shouted again, this time yanking him by the shoulders and yelling, "Look!"

He raised his head, mind swirling as if in a dream. He saw her pointing toward the back of the room, but he couldn't make sense of it.

He wiped away the emotion flooding his eyes, trying to follow what she was indicating.

Then it hit him.

An open window.

"They escaped..." he said on a shaky breath.

Hope flooded him from head to toe, infusing him with a burst of energy that sent him scrambling up from the floor and running to the opening.

The smell of dead leaves and a distant fire riding on a frigid breeze slapped him in the face, the tears streaming down his face burning with the cold. But he didn't care.

He scanned the parking lot gleaming from the lighting and full moon above, sighting the burned-out corpse of the terrorists' ride and their dead companions, and then the two downed FBI agents lying like crumbled dolls near their checkpoint.

But no one else.

"Celeste!" he screamed, eyes wide and searching with frantic hope.

And then again, adding Radcliffe's name for good measure.

Come on...Where the heck—

Then he heard it.

"Over here!"

A faint yell a hundred yards away, near a grouping of trees still clinging to their blazing red leaves across the road.

Two elderly men were hobbling back to the field office across the parking lot, a woman propped between their shoulders.

Rowen Radcliffe, Father D'Amante.

Celeste Bourne.

Silas's knees went weak and breath caught in his chest at the sight.

He offered a quick prayer of gratitude to the good Lord above before climbing through the opening. He stumbled forward on desperate feet, then took off running across the pavement. Brit and Gapinski climbed out after him.

Sirens were screaming now in the near distance, and the rotors of a helicopter could be heard approaching with intercepting intent, a white spotlight piercing the darkness from above and coming in fast.

"You're alive!" he said, racing up to the trio, taking Celeste off from the men's shoulders.

The elders were breathing heavy, exhausted, frightened breaths as they handed her over to him. She was faring about the same, having not fully recovered from her ordeal before it all went to hell—again.

They slumped to the pavement to catch their collective breaths. Silas held Celeste alongside them, squeezing her in an embrace and stroking her hair as Brit and Gapinski rushed to his side.

They collapsed with the same exhaustion, embracing the group with joyous, giddy reunion.

"How did you all make it out of there?" Brit asked.

Catching his breath, Gapinski said, "Yeah, I was sure we'd be picking through the rubble for parts after—"

"Gapinski!" Silas said with irritation. "Neither the time nor the place, man..."

"What?" he said with surprise.

Brit flashed him a look and put out a calming hand.

"After the firefight erupted," Radcliffe offered, swallowing hard and heaving another recovering breath, "Celeste kept tabs on your progress through the window. Then when the Suburban exploded—"

"That was me, by the way," Gapinski offered.

Silas threw him a look but went back to stroking Celeste's hair.

"Yes, well, jolly good of you, Matthew. At any rate, after the vehicle erupted in flames, Celeste had the foresight to use the distraction to extract us out from our hiding place and usher us out of harm's way across the street."

"Good thing she did," Brit said. "Otherwise things could have turned out very differently for you three."

The Order Master nodded. "Indeed."

"I must say, Rowen," Father D'Amante said, "you and your people sure know how to show an old man a good time. Who do you suppose those men were, anyhow?"

Silas clenched his jaw then eased Celeste against Radcliffe and stood. "Only one way to find out."

He strode across the pavement towards the downed man Brit had taken out with the kill shot to the face, the helicopter now bearing down upon them, its white searchlight zooming across the parking lot as the sirens grew into a maddening announcement.

Reaching the man lying flat on his back, his face a bloody mess, he grasped his wrist and yanked back his cuff.

There it was.

Two intersecting lines, bent at the ends.

"Nous?" Brit asked, kneeling to his side.

He sighed and nodded. Not that he had any doubts, but it did confirm it all.

"Come to clean up...whatever the hell it is we've stumbled upon?" she asked.

"That's my guess."

She stood and took off into the parking lot as he searched the man's pockets. A smile of victory flashed across his lips as his fingers reached around a device.

Silas retrieved a phone and awakened it. There was a missed call.

From Sebastian Grey.

His veins went cold, his bowels went weak at the sight of his twin brother's name.

He glanced at Brit as she wandered away and then to Gapinski, who had his back to him, then he quickly stuffed the phone in his pocket.

"Find anything?" Gapinski said.

Silas startled. "Uh, not yet." He grabbed for the man's jacket zipper, then pulled it open.

When he did, a book fell out. Then another.

A small red hardback and another bound in burgundy leather.

Both looking eerily like the ones he had glimpsed in Roland's backpack in the theater.

"Egads," Gapinski said. "Is that what I think it is?"

Silas picked up the burgundy hardback. "Looks like the same books our psychopath carried."

"The one who shot up a movie theater and whose corpse then writhed as if it were possessed by the Devil himself at an FBI field office—*that* psychopath of ours?"

Silas said nothing.

Before he could check inside, all at once a herd of dark vehicles flashing reds and blues came barreling into the lot.

Aiming straight for the trio.

"Not this again..." Silas complained, stuffing the books inside his jacket and extending his hands in surrender.

"Don't do anything rash, gentlemen," Brit instructed, coming up to them. "Just comply and follow orders. We'll sort it out soon enough."

On cue, men in black with thick necks bearing seemingly thicker weapons stormed out of the vehicles yelling the now-familiar refrain.

"On the ground! On the ground!" multiple voices commanded, the rotors and sirens deafening, the light from above blinding and adding to the confusion.

"Special Agent Brit Armstrong," she yelled above the din, kneeling as she unfolded her ID that held the credentials she had taken out when the vehicles arrived.

"Always something," Gapinski huffed, throwing his hands in the air in surrender and kneeling as well.

IT DIDN'T TAKE LONG for the confusion to be cleared up with the authorities.

But not before all three were pressed into the pavement and the now-familiar plastic bindings were promptly cinched around their wrists and legs, their weapons confiscated, and they were read the riot act. Took a few minutes to confirm Brit's identity, and then the identities of the other five, but eventually all were released and told to stay for questioning.

"Terribly sorry about this, Brit," Tom said, climbing out of yet another black vehicle that had just pulled up to another command center anchored at the rear of the parking lot.

"Don't worry about it," she said. "I suppose now I know what my friends went through last evening."

Gapinski snorted. "How about we call a truce? Let's agree that you'll never again slam our asses into the ground and bind our limbs like pigs, and we'll never again emerge from buildings assaulted by terrorists. Deal?"

She giggled. "Sounds good to me. How about you, Sy?"

Silas glanced over, an arm draped around Celeste's shoulders, who was nursing a bottle of water. He offered a weak grin and nodded, but said nothing. Wasn't in the mood, and his mind was consumed with far greater things than humoring Gapinski's funny bone.

His mind was a jumble of thoughts trying to puzzle through the past half a day. Beginning with what had happened to Celeste, and what had happened in that room.

Then there was the body of the psychopath himself, a person who Father D'Amante had treated for possession and then seemed to bear the marks of a menacing evil straight out of a Martin Scorsese film.

And then the discoveries from the backpack in the theater and now in the jacket of a dead Nous operative: the mystery books, the pagan and occult objects. Which he'd need to circle back with Brit about, because it seemed like something important, and he wondered if she had the 411 on those detail, especially the books.

All that wasn't even touching on his brother's name appearing on the face of a phone recovered from a Nous agent. Not that he was surprised, given what had happened almost a year ago with the Holy Grail. But the truth of it unnerved him. A detail he'd keep close to his chest for now until gaining clarity.

Silas heaved a stabilizing breath and sighed with dread, his gut telling him something deep and dark was beginning to emerge.

And SEPIO was about to be dragged into it.

"Tom," he heard Brit say lowly, "would you mind giving us thirty?"

He nodded. "Take an hour. Hell, take a year after what

you've been through. I'll be in the command center. Holler if you need anything."

She thanked him, then gathered the group together for a chat.

"I'm sure you all would love to go home and crash," she started, "maybe throw back a few. I know that's pretty much all I want to do after the past eight hours. But we don't have that luxury. The FBI field office was just assaulted by terrorists, and the primary evidence in a mass shooting event just went up in flames, targeted by said terrorists. And let's not forget all the crazy that went down beforehand..."

Brit trailed off, giving Celeste a glance before settling on Silas, whose face was grim and distant.

She sighed and folded her arms, then brought a hand to the bridge of her nose and began massaging it. Waiting a beat, she continued, "Needless to say, there's a helluva lot going on here that I'm not equipped to deal with right now. So I need your help if we've got any chance of stopping the continued attacks roiling—"

"Wait a minute..." Silas said, raising his head. "Continued attacks? There have been more?"

"Afraid so. A man with a machete went on a rampage at a nightclub in Detroit, and a woman drove out onto the Navy Pier in Chicago and mowed down a dozen people. Then there are some reports coming out of Milwaukee and Toronto."

"Toronto?"

She nodded.

"Bearing all the same symptoms of our man, Roland Vander Molen?" Father D'Amante asked.

Brit took a breath and nodded. "Not to pick on Celeste or anything...but, what happened in there? Because although it looked like some kind of dissociative state, her emergent identity believing itself to be other-than human, it seemed like something far more—well, supernatural was going on in there. Something I dare say…"

She could barely spit out the word, but she did: "Demonic."

The word settled in the middle of the group like a leadened weight, a bomb dropped in the middle of a land already suffering from fallout.

"That's because it was," Father D'Amante said matter-of-factly.

"Uh, come again?" Gapinski said, turning to Celeste and taking a subtle step back, probably not even realizing it.

"That's right. It was a demon that manifested itself in that room this night."

"But that's insane!" Silas scoffed with exclamation. "Celeste isn't into Satanism!"

The priest took a breath and smiled. "I never said she was practicing such arts, dear child. Far less people who are afflicted by the demonic are into the darker arts of Satan than are those who engage in such practices."

"How so, Father?" Brit said, intercepting Silas's retort, who was beginning to become visibly irritated at the suggestion.

"First things first," Father D'Amante said.

"And what's that?"

"I'd like to offer you a session of healing, my dear," he said to Celeste.

"You're talking about an exorcism?" Silas said.

He nodded. "I'm afraid that if we don't perform the Rite, what happened in that room is only the beginning of more things to come."

"How is that possible? If I understand it right, the only way for such a thing is if a person creates a doorway for the Devil through dabbling in the occult. As you said yourself, Father. And she doesn't nor has she ever practiced witchcraft or dabbled in the demonic and occult. Tell him, Celeste."

Celeste's eyes went wide, and she bowed her head in

silence, not saying a word. But also saying all she needed to in response.

"Haven't you, darling?" Silas asked, bringing a hand up to the small of her back.

She opened her mouth to reply, then stopped short. Taking a breath, she said, "Let's head back to HQ. We can have ourselves a chat along the way. And, yes, Father D'Amante. I agree the Rite is a necessary step forward."

Celeste paused, her face growing steely, resolute, as all eyes took in her revelation.

Then she added, "Because mark my words: The Prince of Darkness has let slip the dogs of war this past day. Not only with me but across America. And we will beat them back with everything we've got. Which, I dare say, begins with me."

CHAPTER 15

"It all started innocently enough," Celeste began on the drive back to SEPIO headquarters in a government-issued SUV Brit had commandeered.

The early dawn sun was now struggling for attention through threatening clouds hanging low and burdened by rain, the sky blooming with a fire that rivaled Dante's visions of the eternal inferno itself.

A few drops slapped the windshield as Silas drove back to DC on I-66, his mind reeling from the revelation that had stilled the group ever since leaving the FBI field office.

Celeste really had been possessed. And brought on by her own hand.

"In what way, child?" Father D'Amante said, his voice gentle and encouraging, grandfatherly even.

She hesitated, glancing with darting eyes from bowed head around the vehicle and pushing a lock of hair behind her ear.

"It started with a Ouija board, of all things. A perfectly coined cliché, I know. Straight out of some supermarket rag, it is. But that's the truth of it."

"Who introduced you to the practice?"

"My best mate during a sleepover. Was thoroughly skeptical, of course. But..."

She trailed off, her face falling with the memory of what had happened. What it had led to.

"But what?" the priest encouraged.

Celeste sighed and leaned back in her seat as Silas neared the city. "But it had worked, spelling out short answers to questions only I could have known. At the time I didn't understand it all. Thought it was a sort of board game like Monopoly or Parcheesi. You're right though, Father. It was a door. And I stepped through."

"But why? Given that you grew up a Christian, grew up in the Church?" Silas asked from the front, trying not to sound accusatory. He was genuinely dumbfounded at it all, and not a little hurt that she hadn't shared this part of her life with him.

"I have to imagine it was precisely because I hadn't grown up in the Church. Or, at least *a* church—my parents preferring their Christianity to be personal and freelance more than religious and institutional. I wasn't very grounded in my faith, and I was curious with what had occurred that evening at the sleepover. The door had cracked open, and then wider still through more experiences. I purchased some healing crystals and books on magic at a local High Street store. And then..."

Celeste's throat choked with emotion, and her eyes began to brim with tears.

Silas's own eyes began welling with emotion, looking at the broken, beaten woman through his rearview mirror, feeling as if something of himself had been ravaged by the Devil himself.

"Go on, dear," Father D'Amante said quietly, urging her to continue her confession.

"And, well, one Halloween, my final year of school before university, my mates and I went to a Black Mass service put on by a local Wiccan outfit."

The atmosphere in the car seemed to seize with the admission, all time standing still, all air being sucked from the vehicle as if in a vacuum.

A cold ran through Silas at the revelation. Even Father D'Amante seemed taken aback by it all.

"My dear..." the exorcist said, his throat stumbling over itself, not able to finish his thought.

"You have to understand," Celeste said, "this was before I decided to follow Jesus. I wasn't his child then, I wasn't following him with my life or hadn't yet consciously chosen him as Lord of my life and Savior of my soul like I had in university."

"If what you say is true," Father D'Amante said, "that you participated in such an occult service currying the favor of Satan, then I dare say you've needed the sacramental ministry long before today."

"I don't understand," Brit said. "What's a Black Mass? What's the deal?"

"It's the heart of the satanic," Radcliffe said on a shaky breath. "A direct assault against the person and work of Jesus Christ himself, making a mockery of his broken Body and shed Blood that anchors the Christian faith."

"At the time, I didn't know what it was I was participating in," Celeste explained. "Thought it was part of the Halloween pageantry. But I can see it as a moment that created a rift in my life. It healed somewhat when I confessed the name of Jesus as Savior and Lord, after my baptism and confirmation in the Church. And frankly, I'm surprised it had laid dormant until..."

"Until this past evening," Silas said, finishing her thought, "when the demon was activated?"

"I'm not sure I would say activated," Father D'Amante said.

"If that was no activation," Gapinski said, "then I'm not sure what the hey-ho-day we witnessed in there!"

"What I mean to say is, given Celeste's story, perhaps a door had been opened way back when without the invitation for a demon to come reside within. Rather, as I have discovered in my research surrounding possession clusters, the demon residing within Roland jumped from him to you."

"They can do that?" Silas asked.

"Indeed," Radcliffe answered. "It was the more controversial aspect of our research that led to our being shut down, but what seemed to have been confirmed through our ministry."

"And what I suspect very well may have occurred this evening," Father D'Amante added.

"But how can a believer be..." Silas trailed off, his throat choking with the weight of his question.

"Filled with the Devil and his minions?" Radcliffe finished.

Silas closed his eyes and nodded, saying nothing.

"Well, lad, consider Judas Iscariot, one of Jesus' own Twelve Disciples. The Evangelist Luke makes plain that *'Satan entered into Judas'* before he carried out his wicked deeds. And even Peter, the rock upon which the Church was founded, Jesus warned him that *'Satan has demanded to sift all of you as wheat.'* The Devil obtained permission to try and drag them into his dastardly designs. And he did!"

"And don't forget Ananias," Father D'Amante said, "another disciple of Christ whom Luke quotes Peter asking, *'why has Satan filled your heart to lie to the Holy Spirit,'* suggesting a contrast to two possible 'fillings' between Satan and the Spirit of God, even within believers."

Silas considered the biblical theology of it all, but was having a hard time wrapping his mind around it. "I hear what you're saying...but demonic possession doesn't seem possible, at least in the way he can with non-believers."

"Certainly the Devil can *oppress* the people of God, isn't that right?" Radcliffe asked.

He considered this and nodded. "Job seems to make that case pretty clear."

"And believers are certainly *tempted* by the Evil One. Jesus

Christ said as much in the prayer he gave his people, and even he himself was tempted by the Devil."

Again, he nodded.

"Then why can't the same power be exerted on a person from the inside with torturous ends? Experience seems to bear the possibility, given the thousands even millions of Christians who have lived to tell about it. And so does the Bible, with Judas and Ananias."

"Then what do we do about it?" Silas said with urgency, pulling into the headquarters of the Order of Thaddeus.

"What I've been trained and commissioned to perform," Father D'Amante said.

His heart seized in his chest, but he knew it was for the best. But an exorcism, on his love?

"Right, let's get on with it then," Celeste said, climbing out of the parked government SUV.

Lord Jesus Christ, Son of God, Silas prayed silently, *you better deliver her! Or so help me God...Because I can't take much more of this!*

RADCLIFFE LED CELESTE, Silas, and Father D'Amante down to his study in the crypt of the basilica, asking Gapinski and Brit to make themselves comfortable in the command center. Too many cooks in the kitchen would not do Celeste any favors, so it would be him and Silas assisting Father D'Amante in the Rite.

After making a fire and making Celeste comfortable in a wood chair flanking the fireplace at a wall beneath a religious icon of Christ the Giver of Life, Radcliffe opened the evening with a short prayer, beseeching the Holy Trinity for assistance that morning to deliver Celeste from the forces of darkness waging war against her.

And then it began.

Silas stood next to Celeste, ready to assist the exorcist, hands sweating and heart strumming a wicked beat against his ribcage. His lungs felt bereft of air, and his tongue tingled for a stick of nicotine to relieve his jumble of nerves.

Radcliffe stood next to him, ready with the same assistance. He grabbed Silas's hand, squeezing it with reassurance.

Silas glanced at the man and nodded, but it was no use.

He was scared to death. Iraq had nothing on what was about to go down, even that dreaded afternoon when his convoy had been blown to kingdom come by that blasted IED and his friend Colton had been blown to smithereens.

He prayed to the good Lord above this morning would be different.

Father D'Amante put his hand on top of Celeste's head. He invoked the protection of Saint Michael the Archangel, revered by Christians as the leader of God's army. Then, without so much as a pause, he jumped right into the Ritual.

"God, creator and defender of the human race," he prayed, beginning the Rite, "look down on this your servant, whom you formed in your own image and now call to be a partaker in your glory. The old adversary twists her torturously, oppresses her with violent force, and disturbs her with savage terror. Send upon her your Holy Spirit, who strengthens her in the struggle, who teaches her to pray in tribulation, and who fortifies her with his powerful protection."

Celeste was still, unmoving, her head bowed and hands folded in her lap. Which didn't last long.

Soon, she began to whimper and nod her head back and forth. She batted Father D'Amante's hand away, like an irritated toddler sloughing off her parents' hold.

It seemed as if the exorcist's hand was an electric wire possessing a current that was shooting through to Celeste, as if animating the love of his life into activation.

It was surreal. It was unreal.

"Hear, Holy Father, the groanings of your supplicant Church," the man continued, "do not suffer your daughter to be possessed by the father of lies; do not suffer your servant, whom Christ by his blood has redeemed, to be detained in captivity of the devil; do not suffer this temple of your Spirit to be inhabited by this unclean spirit."

Celeste banged her head against the wall with a sudden lurch, startling Silas and Radcliffe. She kept at it until the icon of Christ hanging on the hook above her head began to rattle.

Silas stepped back, worrying she might hurt herself.

Radcliffe slipped a hand behind Celeste's head to protect it, and a struggle ensued between the Order Master and his director of operations as she continued rocking.

Silas wondered whether he should offer help, but he couldn't move. He remained riveted to the floorboards and transfixed with dumfounded immobility at the strange rocking figure that was his girlfriend. He prayed silently that God would come to her aid.

As Father D'Amante continued with his own prayers, a low, familiar guttural growl began to emanate from Celeste, sending a chilling jolt ricocheting up Silas's spine.

He studied her, trying to determine where the sound was coming from.

The growls seemed to be bubbling up from deep within her. If he wasn't mistaken, the sound was coming from her stomach.

"Hear, God," Father D'Amante said, "lover of human salvation, the prayer of your Apostles Peter and Paul and of all the saints, who by your grace emerged as victors over the Evil One who—"

Suddenly, Celeste lashed out at the man, trying to shove his hand away with wild arms.

As she struggled, Radcliffe tried to keep her from hitting Father D'Amante.

Silas came around to Celeste's other side, grabbing hold of one of her arms. He was surprised by her flailing arms, powered by a superhuman strength he could barely match after years with the Army and regularly keeping up his strength training.

He knew she was in shape, but this was otherworldly, supernatural.

Preternatural.

"No, no, *NO*!" Celeste shouted, followed by a ferocious "*Basta!*" Italian for *'Enough.'*

Which Silas was sure she didn't know, because the only other language she said she had studied was French, and only half-heartedly.

His eyes were now transfixed on his love with wide-eyed fright, worrying that he was losing her to the Devil himself.

Her eyes were tightly clenched, her face straining with red blotches and crows-feet growing in strength from the corners of her eyes. It was as if she were conjuring every ounce of otherworldly energy from the preternatural source that had come upon her, ready to unleash it on the exorcist doing his best to keep the situation from spinning out of control.

Silas wondered if he might have to intervene. If things got worse, he didn't think Radcliffe or the exorcist could do enough to stop her from harming either them or herself.

Then Father D'Amante prayed with a sudden shout, "Free this your servant, Lord Christ, from every foreign power and keep her safe, so that, restored to peaceful devotion, she may love you with her heart and may serve you zealously with her works, that she may glorify you with praises and may magnify you with her life."

Celeste let out a low, torturous moan at the prayer, her head swaying from side to side, hair matting to her head now wet with perspiration. She didn't sound like herself. Neither human nor even animalistic.

Again, it was something not of this world.

Silas studied her, discerning a clear change having come over her from even the previous sounds she was making.

Where is she and what has overtaken her?

It didn't seem like she was there anymore. Celeste Bourne had left her body. Again.

Without pause, Father D'Amante moved on: "I adjure you, Satan, enemy of human salvation. Know the justice and goodness of God the Father, who damns your pride and envy with his just judgment."

Celeste pierced the room with an ear-splitting scream, an otherworldly tone that split into a three-chord harmony, chilling Silas's veins with ice. Even Radcliffe shifted, his face drained of color now and slack with what he could only discern was petrified dread.

Then he heard it again, that raspy, growly guttural sound that instantly covered his flesh with goose pimples and sent a ripple of worry flooding his veins.

The Voice. Back from the dead of that hollowed-out FBI field office shell.

"Shut up, you stupid priest!" the Voice erupted from Celeste with the same growling intensity, as if her voice was masked by bassy software.

She let loose another scream, sputtering at Father D'Amante in indecipherable Italian.

"You dirty tosser!" the Voice said, changing back to English and followed by more howling and growling.

Celeste was huffing heavy breaths, her eyes wide and lips curled back with rage. Father D'Amante didn't pay it any mind. It didn't even seem to faze him.

"I adjure you, Satan, prince of this world," he said, "know the power and strength of Jesus Christ, who defeated you in the desert, overcame you in the garden, vanquished you on the cross!"

"Shut up! Shut up! Shut up!" Celeste shouted, seemingly trying to drown out Father D'Amante. *"You have no power over meeeeeeeee!"*

Father D'Amante shouted over the din, "I adjure you, Satan, deceiver of the human race, know the Spirit of truth and of grace, who drives off your snares and confounds your lies, depart from this creature of God."

"Piss off!" the Voice shouted. It continued with a furious string of blasphemies and then more curses in Italian that made Silas's head swim.

He recoiled from the viciousness and thought his darling was gone forever—consumed by the menacing evil that had been unleashed through the encounter with the Prince of Darkness hidden away in that psychopath.

Why did I ever suggest we go see that damn movie?!

Celeste interrupted his self-flagellation by suddenly standing.

Father D'Amante pushed her back down into the chair. He said something to her in Italian, and she hissed and spat at him. He turned to Silas and Radcliffe.

"I have commanded the demon to announce himself," he said. "To tell us his name."

Silas knew that the Rite only allows the exorcist to talk to the demon in trying to find out his name. But still, it was unreal to think the man was speaking to a minion of Satan.

"No, no, no," the growly, guttural voice rasped on repeat within Celeste.

"In the name of Jesus Christ, tell me your name, demon, and your business!"

A shriek burst from Celeste before she clenched her eyes and twisted her face, clearly recoiling from the mention of Jesus and the command enjoining it to respond.

Finally, it did: "*You know our name! For we are many, taking up residence in the bones of the signatories who have covenanted with me. For one day, I will cause breath to enter these bones, and they shall live. I will lay sinews on them, and will cause flesh to come upon them, and cover them with skin. And within all humanity I will put breath in them, and they shall live; and they shall know that I am the Ruler who sets men free!"*

Silas trembled under the weight of the Voice's declaration, seemingly almost prophetic. But what was he talking about? The signatories and those who covenanted with him? And this business about bones coming to life?

There was something familiar about it, and perhaps a clue had slipped through, but his head was swimming with delirium under the Voice's force and he couldn't make sense of it.

The room was stifling, and Father D'Amante's forehead was dripping with sweat.

"Depart, therefore, Satan," he said, "in the name of the Father and of the Son and of the Holy Spirit."

Celeste lashed out at Father D'Amante with that hideous, guttural roar, grunting and growling at him between clenched teeth, foam now blooming from parted lips and dribbling down her chin.

The exorcism continued for another several minutes, as Father D'Amante spoke a few Psalms over Celeste and offered another few prayers.

Silas could tell the man was pulling out all the stops, using every tool at his disposal to help Celeste.

By now, the room had become sweltering, and Silas could tell that Radcliffe and Father D'Amante were at the end of their rope, having expended themselves on behalf of their sister in Christ.

Finally, when it seemed like the exorcism might never end, Father D'Amante smacked Celeste lightly on the forehead, and after a few seconds she gradually came out from her trancelike state, her eyes blinking open with confused weariness, arms limp at her side and face flushed.

For a moment, the room was still. No one moved, no one said a thing.

And, blessedly, there was no more demon sounding forth.

Radcliffe looked as if he might fall to the floor from fatigue, his gray hair matted to his head with sweat and panting as if he had just run a marathon.

Silas was at a loss for words. He had believed there was a definite supernatural realm beyond the natural one we all take for granted. But never in a million years would he have dreamed of seeing it manifested with such honesty, such brazenness, with such ferocious horror.

Was it over? Had the demon been cast out? Lord Jesus Christ, Son of God, let Celeste be released from her tormentor...

"I'm going to hear her confession now," Father D'Amante said.

Silas looked to Radcliffe, who nodded for him to follow him outside. "This gesture is part of the context of liberation," he said.

They went out into the hallway to give them some privacy.

Radcliffe shut the door behind Silas, who leaned against the wall and slid to the floor.

"Now that the demon has been weakened by the exorcism," Radcliffe explained, "Celeste can confess her sins, something the demon would never have allowed her to do otherwise."

"The gesture is rather pastoral, isn't it?"

"An exorcist means more than sprinkling holy water and saying prayers. It's also about bringing the sacraments back into a person's life and rightly ordering their soul around Christ."

A half hour later, the door opened, and Father D'Amante and Celeste emerged. She was still a little dazed from her ordeal, wobbling on unsteady feet.

Silas went to her and immediately thrust his arms around her. She sank gratefully into them, curling herself against his chest and sobbing gently.

"I'm so sorry," she whispered between sobs.

"Shh," Silas said, "Don't say that. This is not your fault."

"But I opened myself up to the principalities and dark forces of this age those many years ago."

"Remember the words of Saint Paul, my dear," Father D'Amante counseled, resting a hand on her back, "'*One thing I do: Forgetting what is behind and straining toward what is ahead, I press on toward the goal to win the prize for which God has called me heavenward in Christ Jesus.*' May the peace of Christ comfort your mind, the grace of Christ overwhelm your heart."

Silas smiled at the man and mouthed '*Thank you*' before the two exorcists left to give them privacy.

As they sauntered down the hallway on exhausted legs, Silas could hear a brief echo of their commentary on what they had all witnessed.

On a frightened breath, unlike Radcliffe, he said, "That was a mighty fierce warrior. I was worried she wouldn't survive."

"Like I said," Father D'Amante replied. "He's back."

Who *he* is, why *he's* back, and what the hell *he* was doing with Celeste would be Silas's priority number one from there on out.

Not merely for the Church, but for Celeste.

CHAPTER 16

After Radcliffe and D'Amante sauntered off to recover from the exorcism experience, Silas urged Celeste to get some sleep in one of the dorm rooms down the hall. She wasn't having anything of it.

Blessedly, she had recovered much of her vim and vigor, brightening and regaining much of her color and spunk. She insisted on jumping back into the fray. Silas just wanted her to take it easy and put the whole nightmare behind them.

"Come on, Celeste," he said, voice laced with restrained irritation. "After all you've been through, I'm sure Brit can take it from here."

"I'm pretty sure this is not a job for the FBI, *Sy*," she said, emphasizing the nickname Brit had for Silas. "With the clear connections to Nous and the hell that has been unleashed, quite literally I might add—there is no way I'm relinquishing command of an investigation of this sort to the likes of the FBI."

"Technically, it's the FBI's investigation. We've only been asked—"

She left without waiting for Silas to finish his protest, turning toward the command center down the hall.

He sighed and raked a hand through his hair, wanting

nothing more than to light up and drink away the past half a day. It would have to wait. Because, as much as he didn't want to admit it, she was right.

Whatever was happening wasn't a job for the FBI. He wasn't so sure it was a job for SEPIO either, but there was something threatening about it all that was surely connected to the Christian faith. And with the revelations that Nous was somehow involved...that meant the Church itself was also squarely in the crosshairs.

Silas jogged after Celeste, catching up just as she pushed through the entrance to the command center.

Walking in, they caught Brit say, "If that sounded like an episode of *The X-Files*, what we found next surely does."

"What does?" Celeste said. "What's she playing at?"

"Good to see you're back from the land of the living," Brit said.

"Or dead," Gapinski mumbled with a chuckle.

Silas threw him a look that sent him back behind Radcliffe, arms raised in apology.

"Enough fun and games, folks," Celeste said, "By now, you probably have all heard of my...well, ordeal. Still a bit woozy from it all, and bearing enough embarrassment for a lifetime. But thanks to Father D'Amante, I do believe we've beaten back the beast. For now, at least. At any rate, time to get back to business. So what else have you discovered, Agent Armstrong?"

The FBI agent returned to a tablet she was holding connected to one of the workstations with a collection of images arrayed on a display overhead. She brought up one of them and pointed.

"Recognize these?" Brit asked.

"The bone necklace," Silas said, folding his arms. "The one ringing the neck of that psychopath. What of it?"

She set the tablet on a desk and took a breath, looking at

the ceiling as if searching for words. "As we do in all such cases where human remains are involved—"

"Wait, those are *human* bones?" Celeste asked.

"And here I thought someone had a Fido fetish," Gapinski mumbled.

Brit sighed with irritation. "Yes. That's right. Human bones. Now, as I was saying, we ran some initial tests on the DNA of the bones, and they've come back with a curious result."

"This isn't like you, Brit," Silas said, "acting all coy. If I didn't know better, I'd say you're mildly shaken?"

"I'm not shaken," she said quickly.

"Then perhaps we could move it along," Celeste said. "Whose are they?"

Brit hesitated, then said, "They came back with a 98.7% accuracy for belonging to a woman from the seventeenth century."

"Seventeenth century?" Silas said, stepping forward with interest.

"And that's not all. The DNA matched that of Roland himself."

"Come again?"

"You're saying," Celeste said, "Roland was a distant relative of the woman whose bones were ringing his neck?"

"That's what I'm saying," Brit said.

Gapinski whistled. "Now that is definitely worthy of an *X-Files* episode."

"So whose bones are they?" Celeste asked.

"A woman named Elizabeth How from…" the agent trailed off and offered another one of those breathy giggles.

Silas's heart wanted to soar at the sound, the memories attached to it sweet, and bitter. But it was strumming a mean beat from the weight of all that had transpired the past night—and with anticipation that the next shoe was about to drop.

"You were saying?" Celeste said with an edge.

Brit held her smile but her right eye offered a small twitch—a tell Silas knew was one of irritation. He could still read her, after all these years.

She said, "Elizabeth How, who was killed in 1692 by hanging." She advanced to another image and pointed with a laser pointer at a bone. "You can see there the crack in the horseshoe-like bone. A classic hyoid bone fracture indicative of neck trauma, especially hanging."

"Well, that's a crappy way to die," Gapinski said.

"Yes, it is. But *how* isn't all that is of interest. *Where* is what matters."

"And where was that?" Silas said.

"Wait a minute..." Celeste said. "1692? Are you saying she was from—"

"Salem, that's right," Brit said with interruption.

The room hung with disbelief at the revelation.

"Salem?" Silas finally asked with a smile, a giggle slipping through. "As in, Salem, Salem—in Massachusetts?"

"Like flying witches and black cats and cursed pumpkins?" Gapinski said.

"That would be the one," Brit said.

He folded his arms in a huff. "Always something."

"But that's not all of it."

"Sonofa—"

"Gapinski..." Silas said. "What else? And what have you been holding back from us?"

She went to say something when she twisted her face. "What makes you think I've been holding something back?"

Silas folded his arms and widened his stance. "Because I know you. And because there was a little red book in that psycho's backpack. With pages scrawled in faded black. Saw it before your FBI g-men confiscated it, along with another book."

She frowned. "I could have you arrested for tampering with evidence."

He shrugged. "So arrest me."

Celeste huffed. "Boys and girls, can we put away the sticks and stones and get back to it, please? Now, what is it you're talking about?"

"What did you find?" Silas said.

Brit returned to her tablet and brought up a series of four images arrayed in a square, all showing browned vintage pages with faded black ink scrawled across them in various hand-writings.

She said, "These are the names of a number of women—all from the Salem area. Bridget Bishop, Mary English, Sarah Good, Mary Warren, Martha Carrier, Elizabeth—"

"How," Celeste said with interruption.

Brit nodded, saying nothing.

Then Celeste gasped and brought a hand up to her mouth, whispering: "The Devil's Book..." She offered a chuckle and shook her head. "Of course! How could I be so daft."

"What was that, my dear?" Radcliffe said, leaning toward her for a better hearing.

She cleared her throat. "The Devil's Book, a phantom book no scholar has taken seriously, bound in a red cover, that the women of Salem accused of witchcraft were purported to have signed, giving their souls over to the Devil for his purpose and pleasure."

"And that's the book that was found in the backpack of the psychopath who shot up the movie theater?" Silas asked, knowing it and the other one was nestled in his jacket.

"That's right," Brit said.

"Along with a creepy bone necklace," Gapinski added, "made from one of those hanged signees ringing Kevin-the-psychopath-Fraser incarnate's neck?"

She nodded. "Like I said, something straight out of *The X-Files*."

"I'd say…"

Celeste said, "This revelation of the Devil's Book combined with the bones purported to have belonged to one of the hanged Salem witches—"

"*Accused* witches," Brit added.

She smiled. "Yes, accused. However, in my studies I believe there is more to the case than meets the eye. At any rate, it appears we have ourselves a connection between these diabolical dealings and the infamous Salem witches."

The FBI agent folded her arms and nodded. "That it does. I'll give you that."

The room settled into quiet contemplation, considering the gravity of the connection. And what it all meant.

"Right," Celeste said, finally breaking the silence. "I'd say we best be off to it then."

"Off to where?" Brit asked.

"Why, Salem, Massachusetts, where else?"

"Oh, no, no, no," she said, waving a dismissive hand.

"Why not, Brit?" Silas asked.

"Because this is an ongoing FBI investigation, with rapidly changing circumstances that's continuing to threaten homeland security. You've lost your mind if you think I'm letting a group of half-baked Mossad operative wannabes near it."

"Hey, who you calling half-baked?" Gapinski complained.

"And it's SEPIO operatives, Ms. Armstrong," Celeste corrected with a wry grin. "We're agents of the Church, not the State of Israel. And I dare say, we jolly well saved your FBI bum back there. You would have been blown to bits had it not been for my half-baked wannabes."

Brit sighed and shook her head. "Whatever."

"And besides," Silas added, "you said it yourself. You can't explain what's been going on. Said you needed our help to make sense of Roland Vander Molen."

"And look where it got me!"

"This is way bigger than something the FBI is equipped to handle. There's an element of faith here, and I dare say the occult, dabbling in principalities and powers way beyond human flesh. Whatever has been unleashed is far from over. I'd wager it's just begun."

He paused, giving his advice room to breathe. Then he added, "We're the experts here, Brit. With Nous, with these powers, with the element of faith. Let us help. Let us do our jobs. To help safeguard the Church but also help save the country from this evil."

The room fell into another contemplative silence, Brit and the rest mulling over what Silas had spelled out in plain.

"Fine, but I'm coming with," Brit finally said.

Celeste held up a hand of protest. "I don't think—"

"You've got no jurisdiction in this matter," the agent said, plowing forward. "This is an FBI investigation, and you were brought in as consultants. Nothing more."

"Nothing more?" Silas said. "I'm not sure that's fair."

"But I cede your point," Celeste said. "Alright, off we go to save the Church."

"And America," Brit added.

"You should use our Boston outpost to prepare for your excursion," Radcliffe said. "The Order has been particularly adept at stocking it with tomes and tidbits on all things occult over the years—given its proximity to the infamous colonial village, among other things..."

"Good idea," Silas said. "Can never have too much research under your belt when battling the Prince of Darkness, I imagine."

"Indeed. In the meantime, Father D'Amante and myself are heading to Michigan."

"What for?" Celeste asked.

He pursed his lips and turned to his old friend. "Following a lead."

"Best be careful, you two. The last thing we need is for our Order Master to find himself in a fit of demonic possession."

"And if so, at least I've got the best bloody exorcist I know of to come to my aid," Radcliffe said with a wink. His priest friend chuckled and nodded.

"Agreed. Right, we'll ring you from Boston with anything we discover, and you do the same."

CHAPTER 17

LOCATION UNKNOWN.

Sebastian Grey woke with a start as a tremor shuddered through the cabin of the well-appointed Gulfstream still smelling of fresh, supple lamb skins and wood stain. It was a recent purchase Borg had sprang for their latest adventure—or misadventure, as it was turning out to be.

He righted himself with a groan, easing his seat back forward, head still smarting from the smack Borg had given it when the mission in Virginia went to hell.

His contact at the FBI confirmed it all, that there had indeed been a terrorist attack on the field office in Manassas, just as Sebastian had ordered. And the body of the subject who had fled the island had indeed been incinerated in a blast that took out the morgue examining the evidence from the earlier attack.

Had it all ended there, the mission would have gone swimmingly.

Except for the wee little fact of losing the Devil's Book. The one containing all of the possibilities for resurrecting the power that would right the world again.

And all because of one man and his merry band of holy warriors.

A one Silas Grey.

Sebastian winced at the name of his twin brother.

Of course, it had to be that mousy little wretch, the man who had become the bane of his existence. It was the third time he had waylaid his carefully laid plans, even more for what Nous designed the past year. Mister Boy Scouts, Mister Walker Texas Ranger, Mister—

A pain pricked his palm along the backside near his wrist.

Sebastian looked down at his hand to find he had been clenching it into a fist.

He relaxed his fingers and peeled them back, noticing four tiny tracts of blood. Right where his fingernails had dug into his skin with clenched rage at his brother.

His heart galloped forward at the sight; his tongue started tingling with intoxicating anticipation.

Glancing around the cabin, he brought his hand up to his mouth and stuck out his tongue, wiping it clean with one stroke.

His head soared with the taste of pennies filling his mouth, his breath catching in his chest from the pleasure of it all.

He went to return his seat back to its resting position when he noticed a book had been jostled out from his satchel lying on the floor.

Sebastian frowned, but picked it up, his fingers tingling and a tremor working through his arms at the touch. He threw it to the floor with a fearful start.

Could it sense that he was a doubter, an unbeliever, a hostile apostatizer who had once embraced it in all of its mystical, mysterious glory—only to finally wrest his soul from its anti-science, hypocritical, homophobic, misogynistic, voodoo clutches?

He eyed it suspiciously while nursing a tumbler of the last few pours of Macallan 25. Then he rolled his eyes at his childish antics and took a mouthful, swallowing hard before picking it back up off the floor.

He held it in his lap, cocking his head to intuit anymore tingly happenings.

Nothing.

Superstitious poppycock, Seba!

Taking a stabilizing breath, Sebastian opened the front cover and fanned the pages of the tattered black book. Its pages were edged with crimson stain, and its backbone was cracked right down the middle when he had tried to rend it in two those many years ago. Etched on its cover in faded gold was the title that had nearly ruined his life.

Holy Bible.

Resting it on his lap, he gently caressed the faux black leather, tracing the faded gold letters with his forefinger. One end of his mouth curled upward before he dove inside, peeling back the cover to find his name still scrawled in faded red teenage handwriting across the presentation page.

The Bible had been given to him the day he was confirmed into the Church at his parish, Saint James Catholic Church in Falls Church, Virginia. He started fanning the Bible again with more deliberate care, its pages whispering their holy secrets and the smell of old paper and even older memories slapping him in the face.

The other end of his mouth curled upward now to complete the grin as he recalled that day—whether from agnostic amusement or childhood nostalgia, he wasn't sure.

Dad had been so proud of him for his step of faith, having made sure the Grey boys received proper catechizing, never missing Sunday Mass. This despite going it alone as a single parent and dragging them from one military base to the next strewn across the world. It was this faithful upbringing that had instilled in him a thirst for the divine, for God, finding satiation through serving in the parish soup kitchen and as an altar boy.

All the while that mousy, mouthy Silas was busy chasing girls and getting into trouble with Father Rafferty, paying mind to neither the Blessed Mary nor her begotten Son.

He, however, had set his heart on other things: the priesthood, believing Christ himself had called him to devote his life in service of the Church.

That is until that damned priest opened up a rift in his soul through years of abuse, apparently completely oblivious to the Good Book's list of no-nos on all things sexual.

Sebastian continued fanning the Good Book, coming to the sudden rift he had tried rending through his childhood Bible somewhere in the Book of Proverbs. He stopped and drained the heady, smokey liquid, a balm for the past twelve hours and the sophomoric memories—sweet and sour, to be sure.

He held the tumbler in his hand as he held the Scotch in his mouth, spinning it and observing the various refractions of light from the rifts of etched crystal. All portals for the sublime rays of consciousness humming through the Universe, recalling how the course of his own enlightened trajectory had been set even way back then. The rift etched in his own life turning into a sort of portal that allowed him to escape the confines of the Church, the Authority, through the light of enlightenment—metamorphosing into what he had become.

Like God himself, knowing good and evil. Conscious of all the divine potential humming in the Universe, light—and darkness—awaiting its refraction through just the right rift.

Sebastian swallowed hard, the Scotch now burning his mouth as it slid into his belly. He held up his empty glass and nodded to a spritely attendant at the head of the Gulfstream. The man saw him and hustled over with the bottle, draining the rest of the expensive Scotch into his glass.

He thanked the attendant then promptly took a drink, considering the spark that had lit the fuse of his faith way back when.

It went without saying that he never would have wanted it to go down the way it had. The abuse was horrific and painful, taking years to undo the damage. But there was a small part of him that was thankful to the wicked priest for what he had opened. For opening the doorway into a new power—darker, but more authentic and sublime than anything Christianity could touch. For rending the portal into new realms of higher consciousness that had freed him from the faith that had overstayed its welcome.

In his life, in the world.

He continued fanning the pages of his well-used Bible when a header caught his attention.

The Temptation of Jesus.

A delightful giggle worked its way up from his belly, warming him in a way the Macallan 25 had not.

He promptly took another mouthful of the liquid and began imbibing the story that had set him on this course to begin with in the Gospel of Matthew, chapter four:

> Then Jesus was led up by the Spirit into the wilderness to be tempted by the devil. He fasted forty days and forty nights, and afterwards he was famished. The tempter came and said to him, "If you are the Son of God, command these stones to become loaves of bread." But he answered, "It is written,
>
> 'One does not live by bread alone,
>
> but by every word that comes from the mouth of God.'"
>
> Then the devil took him to the holy city and placed him on the pinnacle of the temple, saying to him, "If you are the Son of God, throw yourself down; for it is written,
>
> 'He will command his angels concerning you,'
>
> and 'On their hands they will bear you up,

> so that you will not dash your foot against a stone.'"
>
> Jesus said to him, "Again it is written, 'Do not put the Lord your God to the test.'"
>
> Again, the devil took him to a very high mountain and showed him all the kingdoms of the world and their splendor; and he said to him, "All these I will give you, if you will fall down and worship me." Jesus said to him, "Away with you, Satan! for it is written,
>
> 'Worship the Lord your God,
> and serve only him.'"
>
> Then the devil left him, and suddenly angels came and waited on him.

Sebastian scoffed and filled his mouth with more Scotch.

What a sissy.

He recalled the first time he had heard the passage. Father Rafferty gave a homily on the three dangers of the Devil inherent in Jesus' temptation: the lust of the flesh, the lust of the eyes, and the pride of life.

Too bad the old windbag never listened to his own homiletical advice.

The priest went on to say, that had Jesus made a deal with the Devil, he would have lost his perfection and been bound to sin like all of us normal people.

But that's where he got it wrong.

Because instead, Jesus would have discovered what Sebastian himself did, what his original ancestors did, Adam and Eve.

Freedom. Consciousness.

The Devil in the desert offered exactly what the Devil-in-disguise offered our first fully formed human ancestors in the Garden: a conscious awareness of all that the glorious human potential held within the Universe. All of the humming potential in all of its five-senses glory to taste and see, to hear and touch, to speak into existence and decide through free choice, through conscious awareness, how to live in the world—how to shape and mold and *bend* it to our will.

Yes, some people make poor choices. But they are made in freedom, nonetheless. And it is for freedom's sake that the Devil works in the heart of mankind, as mysterious as it might be, showing the way into conscious life.

It's what the Snake had offered Adam and Eve; it's what the Devil had offered Jesus. And it's what the Prince of Darkness had offered himself way back when—and what Rudolf had helped him discover.

The Republic of Heaven, full of all the possibilities and potential of conscious life lived on our terms, and enjoying the glory and the power and authority for all time, now and forever.

Amen.

Sebastian drained his drink and then opened the shade to his window for a look.

The plane was banking right and beginning to descend, a pallet of oranges and reds and yellows gleaming down below, and a lake shimmering under the early morning sun on approach.

Just a few more preparations until this evening...

The plans had originally called for the unveiling on Halloween, but the unfortunate event of the escapees and ensuing fallout had delayed them a day.

No matter. It was a far better auspicious occasion anyway.

For why not unveil the full power and freedom and *consciousness* of the Republic of Heaven for the whole of humanity than on the day celebrating the stupid suckers the Church calls saints who had been conned into dying for a sham?

All Saints' Day.

A hand reached around his shoulder, sending a shiver of erotic delight through his body. A head popped around his seat back and rested against his shoulder.

He breathed her in, the scent of incense laced with lavender sending his pulse soaring. The woman who had opened his mind to the other dimensions throbbing through the universe that those dead saints just didn't grasp—not to mention the scientists who once held his mind equally captivated.

But that others through the centuries had tapped into with primal abandon and intuition through the elements common to mankind.

Earth and fire. Wind and water.

And blood...

"Hello, my precious Helen," Sebastian cooed as she came around and knelt at his feet, that perfect Arian face draped by blond locks.

"We are almost being there, darling," Helen said with giddy glee. "Isn't it being so exciting?"

Sebastian grinned at her every word, his heart soaring high by the guttural accent of her Germanic people. These ones who had been light years ahead of the world in realizing all of the scientific-spiritual potential only now being fully understood. And now fully exploited by Nous, by him...

She was intoxicating, infectious. His head began to swim with all she had meant for him.

"They await our final extraction, my love," he said, "to continue what those women so bravely began over three centuries ago."

"Are you being sure everything is in place?"

He nodded. "Everything is back on track, my love."

"Because we cannot be having another—"

He pressed a finger to her lips with interruption.

"All is in order," he whispered. "Promise."

She took a breath and smiled, sighing before reaching in for a kiss.

He tingled at her touch and offered her back ten-fold of passionate energy.

Helen withdrew, but held her arms around his neck. "Soon, the full measure of what's available from the rulers, the authorities, the cosmic powers, all of the spiritual forces of this present light labeled as darkness by the Authority will be fully realized. All for humanity, my love."

Sebastian breathed in the pleasurable potential of those words and grinned.

Exactly. For humanity.

CHAPTER 18

BOSTON, MASSACHUSETTS.

The Gulfstream landed on the tarmac with a bounce, sending Silas's stomach bounding along with it and hands grasping for his creamy leather armrests. The comforts of plush privilege oozing from the well-appointed aircraft of leather and mahogany did little to assuage his worries and calm his nerves. He was just thankful it was a quick hour flight.

"Why couldn't we have driven the eight hours up I-95," he grumbled under his breath as the jet's engines roared with halting purpose.

"Because then we would have missed out on the Order-issued Goldfish crackers," Gapinski said from behind, jiggling a bag of the baked cheddar snacks over his head.

Silas swiped the bag, then tossed it back at the man as the jet finally slowed.

I think I'm gonna be sick...

Silas hated flying. Hated riding in anything without two or four legs firmly planted on solid ground. It's why he joined the Rangers instead of the Air Force or Navy. Dad probably had something to do with that too. Always went on about God Almighty, Creator of heaven and earth, supplying his image-bearing creatures with neither wings nor gills. So they sure as hell had zero right to go flapping or finning through air or water—nothing but solid land for the man.

Darn right. Though curiously, the man broke the rule with every tour of duty change, dragging his sons from this base to that base every few years as kids. Probably why the man finally settled in his post at the Pentagon during their teenage years. Until those jihadi whack jobs took him out...

The jet continued taxiing to the Order's private hangar, and a curious longing for the man began to well within Silas. Didn't know why, as the memory of Dad had faded from view after all these years to nothing but a few highlights.

Perhaps it was the chaos of the past few days, the childlike part of him wanting to run back into the powerful arms of his childhood hero. The ones that had taught him to tie his shoes and throw a football, the ones that had showed him to hold the door open for the ladies, the ones that had held him when he screamed bloody murder in the dead of night from nightmares about faceless boogeymen hiding under his bed.

Except now they were out in plain sight.

And no longer faceless...

Silas opened his eyes and took a breath, easing his grip some but keeping his hands firmly planted on his security-blanket armrests. He glanced over at Celeste, who was sleeping from the flight, the morning sun catching her face just right through the window. Sending his heart soaring.

Her eyes twinkled in a way he hadn't noticed before, catching one part of her left eye shaded slightly darker in the dawn's light. Always something new to learn about that one. Her long auburn hair was resting over her shoulder and braided to perfection, and she stroked the end of it in her dreamlike state. Her cheekbones looked like perfectly weathered desert plateaus, angular and smooth, curving into the familiar nose and lips he had memorized a thousand times over.

But then his face fell. Because given what had transpired over the past half a day, it was as if he didn't even know the woman.

It wasn't just the frightening beast and the accompanying Voice that had emerged through possession. That was bad enough. It was more than that: A part of her story had laid hidden from him, concealed even. And not an insignificant part, either.

Continuing to take her in, he sighed at the thought. To be expected, he guessed, given they had only known each other for a year and had been dating not even half that long. But still. What else lay hidden within the inner recesses of her story—just waiting to pop out without a moment's notice? Screaming like a banshee and hurling demonic curses like a drunken sailor?

He took a stabilizing breath and eased it out when a hand slapped his left shoulder from across the aisle.

"What's got you on pins and needles, Sy?" Brit said, standing as the plane stopped and powered down.

Gapinski snorted. "Not a flyer, that's what."

Silas frowned. "Thanks, pal."

Brit chuckled. "Really? I didn't know that about you. Probably best you were a Ranger then, huh?"

"Something like that," Silas mumbled, unbuckling as Celeste awoke with a groggy moan and stretched with raised arms.

He smiled, bending down and pecking her on the cheek. "Morning, sleepyhead."

"Get a room, folks," Brit mumbled on her way toward the front of the plane.

Celeste smirked. "She's a ripe one, ain't she?"

"You have no idea."

Celeste stood, then did something unexpected. She reached in for an embrace. And when everyone else had deplaned, she kissed him. A long, passionate kiss that sent his pulse surging with pleasure.

When she was finished, she drew back and said softly, "Thank you."

Silas grinned. "Pretty sure I'm the one who should be thanking you after that one!"

"No, I mean for not giving up on me. After what happened."

He twisted his face up and shook his head. "Of course. But there's nothing to thank me for, because you did nothing wrong."

Her head dropped, and emotion began welling at the corners of her eyes.

"But I opened the door all those years ago," she said, voice quivering now. "I let the beast inside—"

"Shh," he interrupted, bringing a finger to her chin and lifting her head. "This is not your fault, alright? So you dabbled with a Ouija board. Big whoop."

"It was way more than dabbling, Silas. And don't be so cavalier about the door I opened."

"You're right. But you shut the door, remember? You gave your life to Christ, trusting in his payment for your sins on the cross for rescue and forgiveness, submitting to him as Lord of your life, right?"

Celeste took a breath and sighed, folding her arms and nodding.

"Then remember what Saint Paul said."

A corner of her mouth tugged into a hopeful smile. "And what is that?"

He reached around her waist and smiled. "As he says in 2 Corinthians, '*If anyone is in Christ, there is a new creation: everything old has passed away; see, everything has become new!*'"

"But—"

"And in Romans, *'There is therefore now no condemnation for those who are in Christ.'* Which means no more shame and no more guilt for whatever it was you may have dabbled with in the past, for whatever doors you may have opened. Including the things of darkness. All that you once were, all that you might have been in what you were pursuing has been completely obliterated in light of what Christ has done for you and your new life in him. A new creation, Paul says. That's what you are, darling."

Celeste grinned and threw her arms around his neck, her cheeks wet with emotion and his heart melting from her angst.

After pulling away, she wiped her eyes on a sleeve. "You know, Silas Grey, I quite like this side of you."

"Oh, yeah? And what side is that?"

"The preacher man side."

He stepped out into the aisle and scoffed. "Preacher man? What do you mean by that?"

"I'm serious, love. If the whole secret agent thing with SEPIO doesn't pan out, I think you'd make a brilliant priest."

"Ahh, but then I'd be resigned to a life of celibacy. And that wouldn't be good for anybody, now would it?"

"No, it wouldn't." She flashed him a wry grin and motioned toward the front of the plane. "Come along. We best get to it before our companions start asking questions."

The pair thanked the pilots running through the final close-down check then climbed down the awaiting airstairs. Waiting for them was a gunmetal gray Mercedes G-Class SUV, their ride of choice it seemed for SEPIO missions spanning the globe. Gapinski was already in the driver's seat, and Brit was opening the passenger's side door.

"You do realize when I said get a room, I was being facetious, right?" Brit said as she climbed inside.

"Yeah, yeah, yeah," Silas said, walking over to the rear door.

"Save it for Saturday Night Live if the FBI cans your butt for mucking up the biggest case of your career."

"A distinct possibility now that I'm partnered with you clowns."

Silas held the door for Celeste, mumbling, "Now don't you see why I left?"

"Perfectly," she mumbled back.

Gapinski threw the SUV into *Drive* and squealed out of the hangar toward the airport exit. "Salem, here we come."

"First things first, tiger," Celeste said.

"What's that?" Brit said.

"A stop at the old Carmelite monastery north of the city. It's part of the Order of Thaddeus now, serving as a safe house and research outlet for SEPIO."

"For heaven's sake..." the FBI agent complained. "What more do we need to know?"

"Plenty," Silas said. "And this is the way we roll, Brit. So either like it or lump it."

"Fine. But if we lose the lead on this, I'm blaming you."

Silas rolled his eyes and went to offer a retort when Celeste squeezed his knee.

"Not worth it," she mumbled.

The drive was a short forty minutes up I-93 and over to I-95. Traffic was light as the city was only just starting to awaken in the early dawn. Soon, they were nearing the Waters River that empties into the Atlantic.

"Look!" Gapinski shouted, pointing out his windshield.

All six other eyes darted outside, searching for the four-alarm notice.

"What?" Silas exclaimed.

"A 24-hour Dunkin' Donuts, baby," he said with a glutinous giggle. He promptly eased the SUV into the parking lot and pulled behind a black BMW ordering at the drive-thru window.

"You'll have to excuse our friend here, Brit," Silas

complained. “Can always count on Gapinski to sniff out the closest feeding trough.”

“You’re welcome by the way,” he said, twisting around and planting his elbow in the horn and sending the Beamer skipping forward a notch.

“My bad.”

The Beamer offered an irritated reply of its own.

“Yeah, right back atcha. I said, my bad! Anyway, as I was going to say, SEPIO missions haven’t been as well-fed since I came on board. You can bet your sweet bippy on that.”

“I bet…” Silas murmured.

“And you know the drill: Get food when you can, because you never know when it’s coming back again.”

“I’m sure the sisters can rustle up some grub. *Healthier* grub. You know, like apples and carrot sticks.”

“Healthy shmealthy. We’re in Boston, man! When in Rome—”

“Eat a Boston Kreme?” Brit said.

“Exactly! Hey, I like this one.”

The BMW pulled forward, finished with its order.

Gapinski pulled up to the drive-thru window and ordered a dozen donuts—four Long Johns, four glazed, and four chocolates with Halloween-themed sprinkles—and a large box of coffee.

“I don’t know, Celeste,” Silas said. “Is this a SEPIO approved budget item?”

Gapinski threw him a look, whipping out his personal AmEx and displaying it for all to see before handing it over to the attendant. “You’ll thank me once we’re knee-deep in research, pal.”

“Now there’s a generous soul,” Brit said. “You could take some notes, you know, Sy.”

Silas rolled his eyes but said nothing.

"Thanks, Brit." Gapinski handed her the box of coffee and donuts. "No donuts for you, bro, after all that drama."

"Wouldn't think of it," Silas mumbled.

"Alright, you two," Celeste said. "I know nerves are frayed from the past few hours and our irritation threshold is low, and we could all do for a bit of shuteye, but let's not eat each other's heads off. At least until we've solved this bloody case."

"Yes, dear," Silas said as Gapinski pulled out of the drive-thru, sneaking around Brit's seat and flipping the box's lid to snatch a donut.

"Hey, that's my Long John!" Gapinski protested.

Silas took a bite and smiled. "Just doing my part to gear up for the road ahead."

"Why I oughta—"

"Boys, let's put away the swords and get on with it, shall we?" Celeste said.

Gapinski frowned. "Yes, ma'am. But Silas owes me a Long John..."

Soon, the Mercedes pulled into a neighborhood of post-war homes, leaves heaped into confetti-like piles in the front yards lining the streets, before turning into the main circular drive of the monastery. They rounded past a statue of the Virgin Mary and parked in a spot in front of the modest two-story structure of bland beige brick stained by time.

Bells tolled as they walked up to the entrance, the call beckoning them for morning prayer. As much as they might want the peace and stability the ritual would bring their souls, prayers would have to wait. SEPIO had other things on their plate.

Like figuring out what the heck was waging war against the world, against the Church.

Against Celeste...

CHAPTER 19

The entrance door to the SEPIO outpost groaned open on unsteady hinges, echoing through the spartan entryway and startling an attendant sitting at a drift-wood-stained desk straight out of the 70s. The air was old and stale, like an urban high school that lacked funding and enthusiasm. Drab cream tiles lined the floor and uneventful stained pine wood lined cases and doorways, all testaments to the vows of poverty taken by the sisters in devotion to God and stewardship of SEPIO's resources.

A petite woman with silver hair, wearing a traditional black-and-white habit and recovering a kind smile, greeted them.

"Hello, sister," Celeste said, striding across the scuffed floor shining with too much wax and offering the woman her hand.

The woman took it. "Welcome children. Are you here for morning prayers?"

"Sadly, no. We," she said, motioning toward her companions, "are here with the Order of Thaddeus."

"Ahh, yes," the nun said, brightening into a knowing grin. "Master Radcliffe said you would be popping by. I'm Sister Marjorie."

"Celeste Bourne. And this is Silas Grey, Matt Gapinski, and Brit Armstrong with the FBI."

The woman's brows rose at the introduction and she grabbed her chest. "FBI? Dear me. This doesn't have anything to do with the rash of possessions plaguing the nation, does it?"

The group glanced at one another.

"What do you know about that?" Silas asked, stepping forward with interest.

She shook her head. "Nothing specifically. But I cannot imagine it any other way, given the wickedness of what has transpired this past night."

"Yes, well, I understand you all have a collection of resources that may help us on our way to solving what has transpired."

"We do. The largest collection of occult and pagan texts stored away in our vaults underneath the monastery. Given our historic location, it made sense."

"I imagine so," Celeste said. "Can you direct us to those resources, perhaps a room where we might conduct our inquiry?"

"It's already been arranged. Come."

Sister Marjorie led them up an echoey stairwell and down a cramped hallway to a modest room with large windows overlooking naked trees struggling to cling to their red, yellow, and orange leaves. The sun was rising above the horizon now, casting bright and cheery light inside, which would serve them well as they pored over texts for the next several hours in search of answers.

"Reminds me of the Port-Royal Abby outside Versailles, France," Silas said, recalling the first time a spark had been felt between him and Celeste during the super-heated moment researching the lost Ark of the Covenant.

Sister Marjorie nodded. "As it should. All of our research rooms are patterned in the same manner. Something about creating predictable, cozy comforts to aid in the Order's problem-solving operations."

"Makes sense."

A computer terminal with a large monitor sat at one end of the room. Next to it was a cart with hot water and tea bags and a large carafe of coffee, as well as a platter of pastries. In the center of the table sat a large Bible and a few tablets, some looking more like oversized ereaders, along with an assortment of notebooks and pens. A large display anchored one wall at the end of the room.

"I assume you've made your way around a SEPIO research outpost?" said Sister Marjorie.

Celeste grinned. "A time or two, yes."

"I'll leave you to it, then. Tea and coffee and some fuel for the research race ahead are yours to enjoy. Feel free to use the notebooks and pens, which are provided for your convenience. There are some large ereaders that have access to the Order's archives, and also a regular tablet with a connection to the television hanging on the wall, but it's beyond me how to make it work, I'm afraid. The library of resources you might find helpful sits one door down. Give me a ring below if you need anything further."

The four thanked the woman before she left, then they got to work.

"Sweet digs you've got here," Brit said, picking up one of the e-ink tablets.

"We've come into the twenty-first century, that's for sure," Silas said. "The computer gives us access to a catalog of everything housed in the facility. The ereaders offer even more access to an expanded billion-book catalog. You can even send articles from the terminal to the ereader tablets."

Gapinski busied himself with the pastries, having abandoned his donuts for finer fare. Brit sank into a chair with an e-ink tablet and propped her feet up on the table.

Silas walked over to the computer terminal. "Let's see what we've got here in SEPIO's Salem archives..."

He logged onto the powerful Boolean search engine to cross-search databases from hundreds of research institutions around the world, including the Vatican's own secure, digital records. But given what this SEPIO research outpost held, he focused his attention on the outpost's library reserves. He typed in the first obvious search string: *Salem witch trials.*

"Right," Celeste said, filling up a mug with hot water. "Have I ever told you of my master's thesis in the occult?"

"Don't believe so, chief," Gapinski said, biting into a cherry danish.

"And actually, an element of my focus was on the Salem witch trials."

"Really?" Silas said. "I didn't know that."

Celeste shrugged. "You didn't ask."

"So what was it about?" Brit asked.

"My degree was in comparative religion, and I examined the underlying spiritual issues surrounding belief in possession and the demonic with the uniqueness of Puritan doctrine."

"Intriguing. So what did you learn from your studies into the trials?"

"Well, in 1692, the Massachusetts Bay Colony executed fourteen women, five men, and apparently two dogs—all on account of witchcraft."

"Two dogs?" Gapinski said. "How can Fido conjure bad Devil juju?"

"You'd be surprised. The first hanging took place in June and the last of them in September of that same year. And not without reason."

"Not without reason?" Brit exclaimed. "Are you saying the trials, the *hangings* were justified?"

Celeste put up a calming hand. "I'm saying no such thing.

What I mean to say is, the region was a hothouse for activity that could only be described as demonic, even occult."

"In what way?" Silas asked.

"Well, do you recall what you all witnessed in the FBI field office?"

No one answered, instead shifting in their seats and looking at one another, as if neither of them wanted to acknowledge or relive the experience.

"That's what I thought. The same behavior was exhibited throughout the course of the months leading up to, into, and beyond the events of 1692 in Salem. Same afflictions ranging from body strains and violent writhing of arms and legs, to choking and convulsions. And it wasn't just adults who exhibited such symptoms, but children were also afflicted, their arms and legs, neck and back contorting as if twisted from side to side, gabbling nonsense and speaking with hysterical voices—all as if under some preternatural, otherworldly force."

"Sounds familiar..." Gapinski mumbled.

Silas threw him a look, but Celeste agreed. "You're right, Matthew. In total, around fifty-five people confessed to witchcraft. Although it's difficult to know how many of those confessions were coerced under rather suspicious interrogations."

Brit scoffed. "I'd say."

"Another 144 to 185 women and men were named witches and wizards across twenty-five towns and villages in the surrounding regions before the crisis had reached its zenith. Strange happenings were reported—illnesses, bad crops, even deaths. Many of the Puritan Christians believed that the Devil was making an organized, all-out assault on their churches and communities. And this isn't even covering the fact that there were known practitioners of folk magic and the darker arts of witchcraft in the region—all of which was illegal and considered a capital crime."

"For real?" Gapinski said, twisting his face up with disbelief. "As in, like, the death penalty?"

Celeste nodded. "When the colonists of Massachusetts Bay established their legal code, the first capital crime to be rendered was idolatry. The second was witchcraft, inveighing against such practices and saying, and I quote: *'If any man or woman be a witch, that is, has or consults with a familiar spirit, they shall be put to death,'* as the 1641 body of laws so read."

"Egads! That's positively medieval."

"Well, you have to understand that the Puritan Christians took the instructions of God outlined in Exodus, Leviticus, and Deuteronomy seriously. On top of these crimes, blasphemy was included, as was murder, poisoning, and bestiality."

"Well, now, bestiality I can understand."

"So what does the Good Book say about it, anyhow?" Brit asked.

"The Book of Leviticus has some pretty direct commands about consulting mediums and wizards," Silas explained.

He grabbed the Bible at the center of the table and started flipping to the book. "For instance, it's commanded in chapter nineteen: *'You shall not practice augury or witchcraft...Do not turn to mediums or wizards; do not seek them out, to be defiled by them: I am the Lord your God.'* And then the Lord outlines the consequences: *'If any turn to mediums and wizards, prostituting themselves to them, I will set my face against them, and will cut them off from the people.'"*

"But that's not the entirety of it," Celeste said knowingly.

Silas nodded. "True. He follows this with another command: *'A man or a woman who is a medium or a wizard shall be put to death; they shall be stoned to death, their blood is upon them.'"*

"Stoned to death?" Gapinski said. "All for dropping by the local purveyor of Lady Luck?"

Brit smirked. "A good reminder why I left the faith and

never looked back. The same commands were given for wearing garments of different materials and getting tattoos, for crying out loud."

"Yeah, but all of those consequences are just in the Old Testament."

"Well, Saint Paul is pretty clear about it too in Galatians 5," Silas went on, "listing sorcery and witchcraft among the works of the flesh that are opposed to the Spirit, and warning that people who practice such things will not inherit the Kingdom of God. And then Jesus himself was as clear in his vision to the apostle John in the Book of Revelation, saying in chapter 21 that for sorcerers and those who practice magic arts, '*their place will be in the lake that burns with fire and sulfur, which is the second death.*'"

"Better watch out, Celeste," Brit said with a wry grin and wink, "looks like hell might be in store for you yet."

"Are you kidding me, Brit?" Silas said with a flash of anger. "You've got no right to judge her like that!"

Brit threw her hands up in surrender. "Just kidding, alright?"

"She's repented of her past sins and been totally forgiven of what she dabbled with."

"Fine, she's good with the Big Guy Upstairs. Geesh, what's the big deal about it all anyway?"

"Because practicing such things is detestable to the Lord as an affront to his sovereignty and power, especially for his people," Celeste replied. "In the Book of Deuteronomy, the Lord God made it clear that his people were to be separate from the nations, from those who rejected his kingship and rule, and not follow their practices. Magic, sorcery, and witchcraft were such practices. So much so that the Lord called such people abhorrent."

Celeste took the Bible from Silas and searched for a passage. "So when the Lord commands," she went on, "in the

Book of Exodus chapter twenty-two, for instance, *'You shall not permit a female sorcerer to live'* and condemn anyone *'who casts spells, or who consults ghosts or spirits, or who seeks oracles from the dead'* as he does in the Book of Deuteronomy chapter eighteen —these aren't just arbitrary killjoy commands but serious protections around the people of God, separating them from not only the nations, but from that which makes them unholy."

"Great," Brit said with interruption, setting down the tablet and standing. "Now that we're all caught up to speed on the Wikipedia low-down on all things Salem witch trials and Christianity and witchcraft, how about we get back out into the field and, you know, do some actual work."

"Waste not research, want not research, I always say, Brit," Silas said, returning to the computer terminal. "By the way, Celeste, I sent you an article."

"Thanks for the fortune-cookie wisdom, Sy, but when do you people get to it?"

"When we're good and ready," Celeste said, picking up her ereader device and swiping it to life.

Brit rolled her eyes. "Well, can I at least borrow somebody's jacket? It's as cold as Greenland in here."

"Don't you mean Iceland?" Gapinski asked.

All three stared at him, brows raised with amusement.

"What?"

"Iceland is the emerald paradise, genius," Silas said, returning to his search results. "It's Greenland that's colder than, well Greenland."

"You don't say..."

"Go ahead and grab my jacket, Brit. It's over by the window on the chair."

"Thanks."

Hugging her arms and beating some heat into them, she hustled over to the window and lifted his coat.

When she did, two books tumbled out and thudded to the floor, opening with flair.

"Well, now here's something interesting," Brit said.

"What's that?" Silas said, glancing over from the computer terminal.

She was holding two books—a slim burgundy hardcover and a small red hardback—and bearing an accusatory look. "What the heck are these?"

His breath seized in his chest and heart galloped forward.

The books he'd swiped from the downed Nous agent at the FBI field office! Hadn't given them thought since everything had gone down.

"These were the books found in the backpack of the now-deceased Roland Vander Molen," Brit said, eyes narrowing and voice growing thick with irritation.

"Uh oh," Gapinski whispered, biting into one of the glazed donuts now. "Duck for cover, bro."

"Brit..." Silas said, standing and stammering, his chair falling backward with a thud. "I can explain."

"You mean, explain how key pieces of evidence from a mass casualty terrorism event ended up in your jacket?"

Celeste said, "Silas, what's she playing at?"

Silas turned to her and took a breath, then turned back to Brit. "It's not what you think. They're not Roland's hardbacks."

"Don't give me that!" Brit exclaimed, taking a step toward him.

"I didn't get them from his backpack."

"Then where'd you get them?"

Silas opened his mouth to answer, then hesitated, glancing to the floor and searching for words.

"Silas Grey, so help me God...If you don't answer me right now, I'm going to have every FBI agent in the Tri-State area so far up your—"

"I swiped them from one of the Nous agents we took out back in Virginia, alright?"

Now Brit opened her mouth to say something. Instead, she walked over and hit him with the book square in his right shoulder.

"Ouch!" he complained, raising his arms in defense.

"Both of these were in the FBI's custody before that Nous psycho swiped them. Do you know how many criminal codes you broke taking these things? Evidence tampering, obstruction of justice—"

"Oh, come on, don't be so dramatic!"

"She does have a point, Sy," Gapinski said.

"Dramatic?" Brit said with a gasp. "Oh, no you didn't! I've got half a mind—"

A high-pitched whistle finally cut through the pandemonium.

"Folks, let's take it down a notch, shall we?" Celeste said.

Before either could protest, she added, "Silas, bad form. That's not how we do things in SEPIO. The goal is to leverage law enforcement agencies, not antagonize them. But, no use crying over swiped hardbacks, alright? Let's get on with it. Brit, what do we have ourselves here? I assume you've run them through your federal systems to crack their code?"

Brit tossed the book to the table and sighed. Folding her arms, she said, "We were *running* them through our systems. I mentioned the red one back in DC, that we checked the DNA on the signatures scrawled inside. The other was in process, but seems to be a vintage volume of some sort dating back a few centuries."

Silas went to pick up the burgundy hardback when he hesitated.

Looking to Brit, he asked, "Do you mind?"

She waved a dismissive hand. "Have at it, Sticky Finger Bandit."

He carefully picked it up off the table, the binding crackling with stiff irritation as he opened the cover to the title page. He read it and furrowed his brow.

"What's it say?" Brit asked.

"*On Witchcraft*. By—"

"Cotton Mather…." Celeste interrupted. She folded her arms with a laugh. "Of course, I should have known! Jolly good, then."

"Why? You know the name?"

"Yes, don't you?"

Silas frowned. "Can't say that I do."

"What does this Cotton Mather fella mean to you?" Brit asked.

"What the name means to me is what I spent a year of my life studying."

"Which is?"

She took a breath then waited a beat. "Which is, that he was a Puritan minister from the Boston area during the late seventeenth century who was one of the primary witnesses and documentarians of the Salem witch trials."

"Good thing I kept that book in safekeeping, then," Silas said.

Brit frowned, then grabbed it from him and swatted at his shoulder again.

CHAPTER 20

Celeste took the book from Brit, adrenaline coursing through her as she held it, the memories of her work, in response to her own experiences with the dark side of the supernatural, rushing to the surface.

"What is this book you're so familiar with, anyway?" Brit asked.

She snapped back to the moment and cleared her throat. "You might describe it as a handbook for all things witchcraft. It also serves as a historical record of the bewitching of Salem and the surrounding area."

"Such as?" Silas asked.

"Such as, guidelines for how one might discover and uncover witches, explanations for how Christians are tempted by the Devil and how Satan entices them to become witches in the first place, as well as methods for resisting such temptation. Then there is the eyewitness testimony of the Salem witch trials themselves. It's all a rather fascinating glimpse into the Puritan sect of Christianity, as well as a glimpse into an interesting part of American history. Not to mention a theology of evil, the Devil, and the occult."

"By Cotton Mather, right?" Brit asked.

"That's right."

"What kind of name is Cotton?" Gapinski sneered.

Celeste replied, "A veritable twenty-nine-year-old prodigy, that's what. Tall and gifted, he entered Harvard at eleven and preached his first sermon at sixteen. He was a renowned and influential minister of Boston's Old North Church who took an especially keen interest in the cases of witchcraft bedeviling the Salem and surrounding area. He also made a curious observation about witchcraft and demonic possession."

"Why curious?" Silas asked.

"Because many thought them to be separate things in those days. However, he made no distinction, noting their near affinity and conjoining them in his celebrated work on the Salem witch trials: *A Memorable Encounter, Relating to Witchcrafts and Possessions*. He believed one could invite the other, suggesting *'It is an ordinary thing for a possession to be introduced by a bewitching.'* His father, Increase Mather, suggested the same, believing one could simultaneously suffer from both possession and bewitching, as one who dabbled in the occult of witchcraft."

Her face fell as she considered the truth of her own life: bewitching begat possession. Her own dabbling in the dark arts seemed to have opened up a doorway for the minion of Satan to invade her life, leaping with menacing intent from the psychopath to her own person.

A chill ran up her spine at the thought. She prayed that the Lord would be for her the mighty shield she needed to resist the Devil and all of its designs.

"The whole thing is a bunch of malarky, if you ask me. Witches, possessing—the trials and hangings!"

"I get the skepticism, but you have to understand that, while such beliefs, and their ensuing repercussions, sound quaint and rubbish to us, for the New Englander, and for that matter the European, witches were real, playing in sorcerous magic and conjuring spells to disrupt agriculture or suspend natural laws, even kill people for sport or as vindictive measures."

"Europe, and especially England, has strong roots in paganism," Silas added. "Hundreds of Christians were martyred carrying the gospel of Jesus Christ to far-flung reaches of the Roman empire, and then into pagan kingdoms of the Middle Ages. And there had been continued resistance against the Church and Christian faith from such pagan forces, drawing people into occult practices."

"That's right. All of which continued on into the New World in the Colonies. And, given the history of it, there seems to have been something supernatural, something devilish, something occult happening in the Salem area the latter part of the 1600s. Which is why Mather said, in this book here."

She found her place and quoted: "'*I have indeed set myself to countermine the whole plot of the Devil, against New England, in every branch of it, as far as one of my darkness, can comprehend such a work of darkness.'* For him and others, this darkness, this plot of the Devil, as it were, was a matter of life and death."

The room settled into a contemplative silence, considering this history.

"We had been holding that book and the little red one at the FBI field office," Brit said. "Which means those Nous hostiles went to a helluva length to get them back."

"Yeah, but why?" Gapinski asked.

Celeste said, "Let's get cracking on and find out, shall we?"

Silas grinned. "Apply some good ol' fashioned research muscle, eh?"

"Music to my ears."

"Now that's what I'm talking about," Brit said.

"I thought you hated this bit?" Celeste said. "Moaning and groaning your complaints and all."

"No, my complaints were about sitting on our asses while

Nous, or whatever, was out there doing its thing. This is a lead. And leads lead to results. Which is what I'm after."

"And I'd imagine your boss back at the FBI mother ship."

The agent flashed her a grin. "Now, we're on the same page."

"Then let's get on with it. I'll set about Mather's work, and you could load the ebook version on your devices and join in the fun as well. However, perhaps it would be best if you all concentrate on other resources available through the SEPIO archives. Divide and conquer seems like a good strategy."

"Sounds good, chief," Gapinski said.

Brit nodded and Silas echoed Gapinski.

"Right, let's get to it. Heads down until we find something of interest."

Celeste sat down with Cotton Mather's book while the rest grabbed the large ereaders at the center of the table.

Brit slumped in the chair near the window in a huff, clearly not relishing the research aspect of the hunt. Gapinski was fiddling with his device, seemingly lost. Silas sat down next to Celeste and was the only one as engaged with the research as she was, which wasn't surprising given his academic background at Princeton.

The memory of them working alongside each other at the abbey in Versailles and the heat exchanged between them during the excitement discovering clues leading to the Ark of the Covenant bubbled to the surface again. Then there was the one racing around the world tracking down the purported Holy Grail and saving the Church from no uncertain doom.

They made a good pair. Not only as research partners and comrades on the thrill of the chase. But partners in crime, two people suited to spend the rest of their lives together, doing life together and supporting one another, their hopes and dreams and ambitions, till death parts them.

At least, that's what she hoped.

Again, she felt as though she were channeling Granny sitting in that chair in the SEPIO research outpost, flipping pages absentmindedly while her boyfriend studiously combed his ereader next to her. She had never really cared for the typical life expected of women, especially British women, and Christian British women—playing a proper housewife to a husband working on High Street or at the wharf or wherever, arranging dinner and lessons for the kids and hosting parties for work.

But now...nearly forty and approaching the age where children didn't make sense, and feeling as if she was missing out on something, even God-intended. Now something within her longed for something more than the cliché of a haggled, bedraggled schoolmarm, destined to a life of singleness and cats.

She giggled to herself at the thought, and her face felt suddenly flush thinking about what life might be like together—as husband and wife, as parents.

Silas cleared his throat, making her jump.

"Whoa, sorry about that, darling!" he said, brushing a hand against her shoulder as he stood and walking to the carafe of coffee behind them.

She giggled again and put a stray lock of hair behind her ear. "No worries, how's the research coming? I'm sure you're cracking along quite nicely."

Silas scoffed as he filled his mug. "I wish. Nothing but the highlights and pop-culture references to the sordid tale."

He walked over and gave her a peck on the cheek.

Brit cleared her throat loudly from the other side of the room and threw them a glaring glance before returning to her ereader.

"She's a jealous piece of work, isn't she?" Celeste mumbled.

"You have no idea," he whispered.

The two returned to their research.

Celeste flipped several pages, scanning for anything of intrigue from Mather's reports on the happenings in Salem, finally landing on some bits that felt resonant.

"Now this is interesting..." She set the book down and reached for the tablet Sister Marjorie had shown her earlier connecting to the television.

Silas leaned over for a look. "What did you find?"

Ignoring him, she found the ebook version of Mather's work and found the passage she was reading. Then she brought the TV to life, using the wifi-connection function to mirror the tablet to the display.

"Take a look at this passage," Celeste said, throwing up the section on the wall at the far side of the room:

> I believe, that never were more satanical devices used for the unsettling of any people under the sun, than what have been employed for the extirpation of the vine which God has here planted...He has wanted his incarnate legions to persecute us, as the people of God have in the other hemisphere been persecuted: he has therefore drawn forth his more spiritual ones to make an attack upon us.

"Is he saying what I think he's saying?" Gapinski said. "That the New World, America, was basically a God-given destiny for Christians, and that Satan was trying to kill 'em off through spiritual attack?"

"Sounds about right," Silas said. "The whole 'City on a Hill' nationalistic nonsense to a whole different level, isn't it?"

"True, but remember that the Puritans had been a persecuted minority who came to the new world, believing they were establishing the Kingdom of God in a new land when the old land, the Old World, had kicked them out and nearly drove them to extinction. So don't be too harsh. You can see this fear here, as well as the connections between witchcraft."

She brought up another passage on the display:

> We have been advised by some credible Christians yet alive, that a Malefactor, accused of witchcraft as well as murder, and executed in this place more than forty years ago, did then give notice of, a horrible plot against the country by witchcraft, and a foundation of witchcraft then laid, which if it were not seasonally discovered, would probably blow up, and pull down all the churches in the country. And we have now with horror seen the discovery of such a witchcraft!

"Now we're getting somewhere," Brit said.

"Indeed, we are. Here's another. A bit longer, but it begins to get to the heart of what they were dealing with. Or, at least, what Mather thought they were dealing with."

Celeste advanced to another portion from Mather's book:

> An army of Devils is horribly broke in upon the place which is the center, and after a sort, the first-born of our English settlements: and the houses of the good People there are fill'd with the doleful shrieks of their children and servants, tormented by Invisible Hands, with tortures altogether preternatural.
>
> These our poor afflicted neighbors, quickly after they become infected and infested with these demons, arrive to a capacity of discerning those which they conceive the shapes of their troublers; and notwithstanding the great

> and just suspicion, that the demons might impose the shapes of innocent persons in their spectral exhibitions upon the sufferers, (which may perhaps prove no small part of the witch-plot in the issue) yet many of the persons thus represented, being examined, several of them have been convicted of a very damnable witchcraft.

"Infested with demons? Sounds like the possession clusters," Silas noted.

Celeste nodded. "Then there is this."

She advanced to another longer portion:

> Some of them that have been cried out upon as employing evil Spirits to hurt our land, have been known to be most bloody fortunetellers; and some of them have confessed, that when they told fortunes, they would pretend the rules of chiromancy and the like ignorant sciences, but indeed they had no rule (they said) but this, the things were then darted into their minds. Darted! Ye wretches; By whom, I pray? Surely by none but the Devils.
>
> There are others, that have used most wicked sorceries to gratify their unlawful curiosities, or to prevent inconveniences in man and beast; sorceries, which I will not name, lest I should by naming, teach them. Now, some Devil is evermore invited into the service of the person that shall practice these witchcrafts.
>
> The Devil has decoy'd a fearful knot of proud, froward, ignorant, envious and malicious creatures, to lift themselves in his horrid service, by entering their names in a Book by him tendered unto them.

"Wait a minute..." Silas said. "Entering their names in a book?"

Gapinski said, "How many donuts you want to bet he's talking about the Devil's Book?"

"The whole lot of them, I reckon," Celeste said. "Perhaps this was why that Nous agent was so keen to retrieve it. Confirming the truth of what they may have speculated, the existence of the whole Devil's Book nonsense."

"Here's another passage," Brit said, voice rising some with interest. She read: "'*more than one twenty have confessed, that they have signed unto a Book, which the Devil show'd them, and engaged in his hellish design of bewitching, and ruining our land.*'

"And listen to this," Silas said, continuing to read: "'*Who can certainly say, what other degrees or methods of sinning, besides that of a diabolical compact, may give the Devil's advantage to act in the shape of them that have miscarried?*'"

"Diabolical compact?" she exclaimed.

"That's not all. Here's another." He read: '*The Witches which by their covenant with the Devil, are become owners of specters, are oftentimes by their own specters required and compelled to give their consent, for the molestation of some, which they had no mind otherwise to fall upon.*'"

"Covenant with the Devil?" Gapinski said. "Like Devil Went Down to Georgia?"

The three turned to him, faces twisted with confusion.

"You know, Charlie Daniels and the whole Devil pact with the fiddle player who—you know what, never mind."

"I think you're on to something, Matthew," Celeste said. "Well, not about the fiddle player, because I sure haven't a clue what you're playing at with that one—but the deal with the Devil bit. Here's another passage bit."

She brought the text to the display:

> These witches, whereof above a score have now confessed, and shown their deeds, and some are now tormented by the Devils, for confessing, have met in hellish rendezvouses, wherein the confessors do say, they have had their diabolical Sacraments, imitating the Baptism and the Supper of our Lord. In these hellish meetings, these monsters have associated themselves to do no less a thing than, to destroy the Kingdom of our Lord Jesus Christ, in these parts of the world...

"Diabolical sacraments?" Brit said.

"And imitating the baptism and the supper of our Lord," Gapinski said. "Is he talking about what I think he's talking about?"

"Seems that way," Silas said. "Some sort of initiation rite of darkness, like the Christian rite of baptism."

"And the Black Mass..." Celeste whispered.

"Black Mass," Brit exclaimed. "That's a thing?"

Silas turned to her and nodded, face falling grim and losing some color.

"I thought that was just a bunch of pageantry for fratboy antagonizers on university campuses."

"Oh, no, dear," Celeste said. "The Black Mass is as real as it gets. It's the central ritual of Satanism, of the occult. And Mathers is just here confirming it was a feature of the Salem witches."

"Alleged witches," Brit added.

"Fine, alleged. Regardless, there is a definite melding together of the occult and these men and women having been *alleged* witches and wizards."

"And look at the result," Silas mumbled.

"What's that?"

"Here, let me show you." He commandeered the viewer and brought up the relevant passage on the screen:

> They have bewitched some, even so far as to make self-destroyers: and others are in many towns here and there languishing under their evil hands.
>
> The people thus afflicted, are miserably scratched and bitten, so that the marks are most visible to all the World, but the causes utterly invisible; and the same Invisible Furies do most visibly stick pins into the bodies of the afflicted, and scale them, and hideously distort, and disjoint all their members, besides a thousand other sorts of plagues beyond these of any natural diseases which they give unto them.

"That's about right up there with William Peter Blatty's tale," Gapinski said.

"Who?" Silas said.

"Come on, Sy," Brit said. "William Peter Blatty, doesn't ring a bell?"

He furrowed his brow with irritation, then shook his head. "Can't say that it does."

"Maybe your girlfriend recognizes the name."

"Why?"

"Because Blatty was the writer of *The Exorcist*."

Rage flashed across his face. "Really?"

"Oh, come on, I was only joking."

"Brit—"

"Leave it alone, Silas. Sticks and stones and all. Besides we've got more important things than getting into it with an FBI agent."

Brit went to protest when Celeste continued. "Check this

out. Mather says something interesting: '*Nineteen witches have been executed at New England, one of them was a minister, and two ministers more are accused. There is a hundred witches more in prison and about two hundred more are accused, some men of great estates in Boston, have been accused for witchcraft.*'"

"Two hundred?" Silas said. "Did I hear that right?"

"That's a serious infestation problem," Gapinski said.

"But how much of those accused were truly witches or wizards or warlocks or whatever."

"That is a good point," Celeste said. "But apparently, as he writes, '*The Execution of some that have lately died, has been immediately attended, with a strange deliverance of some, that had lain for many years, in a most sad condition, under, they knew not whose evil hands.*' So I guess the upside is that there had been a relief after the convicted were...well, hanged."

"Like Elizabeth How?" Brit said

She nodded. "Among others." She added: "Not that I'm excusing their dastardly executions. Neither Christian nor of Christ. But still. The region seemed to find relief once the witchcraft ended."

Again, the room fell into silence, taking in the first-hand witness from the seventeenth-century minister to the supernatural occurrences swirling in and around Salem.

Celeste closed the hardback that had been retrieved from Roland, and then from the downed Nous agent. She pressed her palm against the burgundy surface, massaging its cloth softened with age.

Then she remembered.

She opened the cover to find messy scrawling in faded black ink. She squinted, trying to read the first line: '*Further revelations and thoughts on Salem by CM.*'

She sucked in a surprised breath. "I think I've found something..."

Three heads cocked toward her, and she read what she had found. All three gasped at the realization.

"How many donuts you want to bet that's our roving Puritan reporter?" Gapinski asked.

"But why would it appear in a hardback of his own work?" Brit asked.

"The work was published in several printings shortly after the events," Celeste said.

"And this must be his personal copy," Silas said, "with added notes after the fact. Here, can I see that?"

Celeste handed it over and he scanned the text. Most of it was degraded and smudged with watery bleed. But one section caught his attention.

"Here, listen to this..." He read:

> *MW confirmed what I had suspected, and there came in the confessions of several other (penitent) witches: affirming How to be one of those, who with them had been baptized by the Devil in the River, at Newbury-Falls: before which he made them there kneel down by the brink of the River and sign their name unto His Book, covenanting with the Devil for ten years, six of them were gone, and four more to come, then worshiped him with whole-hearted devotion.*

"Who's MW?" Brit asked.

Silas shook his head. "Whoever it is confirmed the original bearer of those bones that were wrapped around Roland's neck to be a witch."

"Not to mention one of several who made a deal with the Devil," Gapinski added.

"And in a rite of darkness similar to the rite of Christian

baptism," Celeste said, "before signing their life away in the Devil's Book."

Four heads nodded in silence at the revelation.

Silas said, "So when these witches—"

"*Alleged* witches," Brit corrected.

"I'm not so sure about that anymore. Seems like something satanic was definitely going down in New England with what we've heard so far. Not that it deserved their deaths by any means, but still. Anyway, we have all sorts of symptoms plaguing Salem, sicknesses and convulsions and mysterious voices—and they all seemed to cease when they were, well, executed. Am I right?"

Celeste nodded. "Appears to be the case."

"Which seems to at least reveal a correlation between the manifestation of the sorts of behavior we've witnessed the past day and witchcraft."

Suddenly, Gapinski bolted to his feet, jostling the table with a thud and sloshing coffee and tea to its surface.

"Oy, mate," Celeste said, reaching for a napkin. "Where's the—"

"Quiet!" he said with a rush, taking giant leaps to the door and pressing his ear against its wood surface.

The room instantly silenced at the sudden shift.

And that's when they all heard it.

Faint but there.

A *pop-pop-pop*, followed by high-pitched fright.

Gunfire. Screams.

Which meant SEPIO's four-letter curse word had just showed up.

"Nous?" Brit said, withdrawing her weapon.

Silas glanced at her and nodded.

Who else?

CHAPTER 21

"Always something," Gapinski cursed, withdrawing his weapon from his backside.

Silas had to agree with the guy. It sure seemed like trouble followed them around like a bad habit in constant need of satiating. Couldn't they catch a break?

A spray of *rat-a-tat-tat* gunfire was his reply.

Apparently not.

There it was again, another threatening volley: *rat-a-tat-tat*.

Different timbre, different tone from the first set that had drawn their attention. Sounding all too familiar to his military-trained ears.

Automatic weapons.

Which meant this thing was a whole other thing.

"You've gotta have quite the backwards brain to rob a bunch of nuns," Brit said. "Who would do such a thing?"

Then again: *rat-a-tat-tat...rat-a-tat-tat.*

"This ain't no robbery, g-woman," Gapinski said.

"How the heck did Nous find us?" Silas growled from the door now.

"Nous?" Brit said, coming to Silas's side with weapon drawn. "Again?"

Silas shrugged. "Who else?"

"You folks need a new group of friends."

"That's what I keep telling them," Gapinski said, "but no—"

Screams, followed by more weapon fire, cut him off. This time the *pop-pop-pop* had returned. But that menacing *rat-a-tat-tat* was close behind.

All of it distant, none of it approaching.

At least they had that going for them.

"What's the play?" Brit asked.

"Save our sisters and kick some Nous ass, that's what," Gapinski said.

"Let's go in pairs," Celeste commanded. "Brit and Gapinski, Silas and me. Stairs anchor the hallway at either end. Both lead back down toward the cafeteria that sits in the middle of the compound."

"You know," Silas said, "the one with those apples and carrots I was telling you about."

Gapinski threw him a look but said nothing.

Celeste motioned toward the other side of the room. "If my ears have it right, it sounds like the hostiles are having a go of it from the mess hall. Which should make finding them a bit easier."

"Little early for a snack, wouldn't you say?" Brit said.

"We could always invite them in and offer them a Long John," Gapinski said.

Silas scoffed. "You'd give those Nous whack jobs one and not me?"

"Well they didn't moan and groan to high heaven when—"

"Boys!" Celeste shouted, "Let's get on with it."

She moved to the door opposite Silas and gripped the handle, nodding to Gapinski and Brit.

"On my go, slip out and head to the left. Silas and I will follow through and head right."

"Got it, chief," Gapinski said.

"Why not," Brit replied.

Silas gripped his weapon and raised it close to his chest, heart strumming a mean beat now and breaths growing thick with the anxious rush of combat.

Celeste glanced at him, and he nodded. "Right. Let's do this."

She swung open the door and motioned the agents into the hallway.

Their shoes squeaked on the perfectly polished floor with decades of gathered wax—Silas and Celeste going right, Brit and Gapinski going left.

Game on.

CHEERFUL SUNLIGHT STREAMED through stained glass hallway windows, casting colorful rays across the floor and betraying the urgency and desperation of a moment that was anything but cheerful and colorful.

Silas and Celeste padded through the corridor with deliberation, checking each of the doors along the way to confirm what they had already figured.

None of the hostiles had entered the second floor. At least in that wing.

The gunfire and screams had ceased as Silas and Celeste came up to the stairwell door, arms taut and weapons ready for action.

Silas stole a glance through a small window, holding his breath for an initial assessment.

A lone light behind a faded cover with decades of grime cast a blanket of dim yellow light down into the void of concrete cinder blocks painted over with various layers of mint green and cream paint that was chipping in parts. A railing suffering the same chipping condition led the way down below.

But no Nous hostiles.

Silas licked his lips and gripped his weapon with resolve, then nodded at his partner.

Without a word, Celeste opened the door.

He went to enter when an echo of *pop-pop-pop* gunfire from behind stopped him cold.

Silas spun around on his right foot and aimed back toward the stairwell where Gapinski and Brit had headed off into.

He went to pad forward when Celeste gripped his arm.

"No, we keep going," she instructed.

"Our guys are under fire!"

"And they can handle themselves. Gapinski is a big boy and I have to imagine the Feds trained Brit for just such an occasion."

"But—"

"Those sisters that have been rounded up like cattle, some of them probably wounded or even dead at this point. They need us more than our two friends. We keep going, alright?"

Silas swallowed hard at the thought, but understood Celeste was right. Their objective was to neutralize the hostiles and rescue the sisters. Everything else was ancillary.

Not much different from the Rangers, really. Never left a guy behind in battle, but that didn't mean intervening in a firefight before the main objective was secure and won. They'd circle back to their comrades once the object was complete.

He just prayed it wasn't a recovery mission.

Silas finally nodded and returned to the stairwell. He eased through the open door and peered down to the first level with extended weapon.

All clear.

He breathed with relief and padded forward; Celeste was close behind.

Another volley of *pop-pop-pop* gunfire made him regret that decision.

. . .

"SONOFA—"

Another set of rounds exploded in the wall behind the pair, cutting off Gapinski's curse and sending him back behind the information desk where sweet Sister Marjorie had greeted them earlier.

Even then, it was really only built for Marjorie. Certainly not for the hulking six-foot-four SEPIO agent and definitely didn't include his new partner in the designs.

After the pair had darted from the research room and down the hallway to the stairwell, they had made quick work descending to the first floor to the reception area where they had begun their whole cotton pickin' episode of must-see SEPIO TV.

Seeing no one around and hearing neither gunfire nor screams for mercy, the pair thought they were good to go.

Until a man in black returning from the little boys' room still zipping up his pants caught them flatfooted.

It was one of those proverbial slow-mo moments, where neither of the two parties anticipated the turn of events and both hesitated a split second that seemed like an eternity before activating in reply.

When Brit and Gapinski finally did, they didn't see Mr. Nousman's friend chilling behind a statue of Saint Teresa of Ávila, the saint who helped originally establish the Discalced Carmelites in the sixteenth century.

Must have heard them push through into the vestibule from the stairwell door. Because before they knew it, lead exploded above their heads with rude indifference.

Nearly shot the two dead, then and there, the way he sprang out from behind the statue and all.

But Brit was fast on her feet.

Ms. Twinkle Toes popped off three rounds before the Nousati knew what hit him, sending the hostile to the floor in style.

But the Nous agent's peek-a-boo from behind Saint Theresa threw off their game. Or, rather, Gapinski's game. Which allowed Mr. Bathroom Break the window he needed to not only zip up but saddle up.

Sending them diving for cover behind the aforementioned desk where they were now curled into balls trying their darnedest to stay alive while that damn Nous agent worked his piece like Celine Dion worked a mic.

Brit eased up from her crouch and opened up with a reply of her own.

A cry, followed by a collapsing thud, told him all he needed to know.

Score one for the good guys!

"Nice shot, sister," Gapinski said, chambering a round.

She flashed a grin. "Thanks. But we're not out of the—"

That annoying *rat-a-tat-tat* cut her off, coming up from around the corner ahead with a wicked scream and chewing the poor wood veneer desk straight out of the 70s to bits.

"Sure, why not add an AK-47 to the mix," Gapinski complained. "Seems to be the way SEPIO rolls nowadays."

Without standing, he reached his arm overhead and offered his own rejoinder with unloading abandon to give them cover.

The hostile turned tail back into the hallway, giving the SEPIO agent and his FBI partner a window to act.

But then Gapinski clicked empty.

"Always something," he complained.

Brit tossed him a questioning glance.

"I'm out," he said on a worried breath.

Brit's eyes widened slightly before her face turned steely with resolve and the instinct to survive.

She said, "I hope to God that Silas and his girlfriend are faring better."

. . .

It sure was quiet. Too quiet for Silas's liking.

The kind of quiet that reminded him of a nightmare scenario from back in the day patrolling the edges of Mosul, Iraq, one evening that nearly led to his premature death.

He'd been part of an eleven-man patrol unit with some boys from Texas. Somehow he was the only one of the lot not from the Lone Star State. Or, rather, somehow the whole lot of them were from the Lone Star State.

Although, as they say, everything is bigger in Texas, including the size of their patrol units.

It's where he and Colton had first bonded. Sort of happens when you get pinned down in a shelled-out market by a hornets nest of Republican Guard lackeys who didn't realize Bush had declared "Mission Accomplished."

Of course, Silas and Colton and those boys from Texas knew better than the Commander-in-chief anyhow. And so did the hornets nest of Republic Guard lackeys.

One minute, the only sound to be heard for miles was the crunch of their Uncle Sam-bought boots on gravel and debris, a few drunken teenagers taunting them from up the road and giggling in retreat, and a barking dog that sounded in heat.

The next minute, they were pinned down by a livid band of hostiles taking it out on Silas and his band of merry Texans. Thankfully, they had made it out alive. No such luck for the Iraqis, who had all paid for their surprise attack with their lives. Mostly thanks to a well-placed grenade by Colton, who had plenty of practice growing up as a star high school quarterback before enlisting his senior year a few days after 9/11.

And now there was a growing sense as he and Celeste reached the bottom of the stairs that the pair were about to face a rerun of that featured film that still haunted Silas's dreams.

The door creaked on tired hinges, snapping Silas back to the moment.

It was Celeste, pushing through the door and motioning for him to follow.

He swallowed hard and pushed through after her.

Muffled crying echoed toward them, along with the smell of gunpowder and bleach, chased by boiled cabbage and grease.

So they were in the cafeteria after all.

Raised voices commanding silence gave the pair pause. It was followed by a hard slap and more whimpers.

Which spurred them on and quickened their pace.

The hallway was clear, and the previous weapon fire from behind them before the descent below had ceased.

Lord Jesus Christ, Son of God, Gapinski and Brit better be alright...

As they continued forward, they passed closed faded wood doors, stained that dreadful driftwood up above and shellacked to high heaven. All hiding their intent, and their locks all holding firm as they tried them with each step forward.

Satisfied, Silas and Celeste rushed to double doors cracked open to reveal the cafeteria anchoring part of the compound's center. The scene inside stole their breaths.

Ten or twelve women in black-and-white habits were kneeling on the floor, grouped together with arms raised to the back of their heads. Sister Marjorie, looking even smaller and more frail, knelt at the front of the pack, habit jiggling under the moment freighted with fright. All were whimpering at various degrees and pleading for mercy.

Behind them stood four men in black with menacing rifles.

All pointing at the back of their heads.

Sending a jolt of dread through the SEPIO pair.

"Time to act, darling," said Silas. "Because those bastards aren't waiting much longer before they start picking off our sisters."

Soft footfalls and a click, soon followed by the cold, hard barrel of a gun at the base of Silas's head, told him otherwise.

"On the ground!" a voice commanded from behind.

Boy was he sick and tired of hearing those three words. Heard enough of them to last four lifetimes as far as he was concerned.

Celeste's face fell. She went to glance behind when an arm came down on the side of her head. She slumped hard to the floor, out cold.

"Celeste!" he shouted.

Before he was cold-cocked himself and joined her in a slump.

SILAS WOKE to a slap across his face.

His hands were bound behind his back. Celeste wasn't faring much better, lying still beside him under a similar fate. But no Gapinski or Brit. Which gave him a small measure of hope.

"Who the hell are you?" Silas growled, struggling to his knees to face his attacker.

"Sy, Sy, Sy, Sy, Sy," a voice echoed from behind. All heady and sophisticated and airy.

One he had known intimately since childhood.

Silas's chest seized with a mixture of dumbfounded disbelief and irritated shock at the sound of the man's voice. He eased around for a look, confirming the truth of it.

Sebastian Grey.

His twin brother.

Silas's face fell, then turned red and twisted up with rage.

Hands still bound behind his back, he struggled but managed to push himself up to his feet. He narrowed his eyes and lowered his head, then took an instinctive step toward the man striding across the cafeteria with every intent to tear his brother limb from limb—regardless whether his bound hands agreed with the plot.

Bad idea.

In an instant, he was shoved face first to the floor, the carpet burning his cheek and no less than three-hundred-pounds jabbing into his spine and kidneys.

Sebastian tsked. "Now, Sy, do you really think that was such a good idea?"

"What the hell are you doing?" Silas roared, struggling underneath the Nousati still pressing him against the carpet.

"I could ask you the same thing..."

He continued struggling, craning his neck like a turtle and getting his bearings.

The sisters they had spotted were huddled off to the side—all looking alive and without injury, thank the Lord. Celeste was unconscious next to him, a nasty gash on the side of her head still sticky with blood and matting her hair to the side of her head.

His blood boiled at the sight, and a rage he hadn't known since Mosul burst within him.

Except that damn gorilla with both knees still straddling his back rendered it inert.

"Get your cotton pickin' hands off me!" a woman shouted from behind.

"Yeah, what she said!" someone echoed back.

Brit and Gapinski.

All that rage was suddenly doused by the reality that they had been checked—and by his brother, no less.

But not checkmated. Not by a long shot as far as Silas was concerned. Not while he was still alive.

He held onto the slim hope they had one move left without entirely sure what that might be.

Lord Jesus Christ, Son of God, into your hands we commit our backsides!

"Shut up, you two," a man growled with a guttural,

Germanic accent from behind at the struggling pair being brought to join Silas and Celeste.

"Gapinski?" Silas yelled.

"Yeah, dude. We sorta ran out of bullets."

"Wait, is that Sebastian?" Brit said.

"Would you look at who the cat dragged in," Sebastian said with a snort. "Brit Armstrong herself. FBI agent extraordinaire."

"You're in big trouble, Mister! Do you realize how many federal, state, and local ordinances and regulations you're violating?"

Sebastian giggled. "Ahh, but only if I get caught."

Silas grunted and continued to struggle on the floor. "Would you get King Kong off my ass, baby brother? The least you could do now that you've won the flush."

Sebastian sighed, then nodded toward the Nous hostile. "Let him up. But keep that trusty weapon of yours trained on him. His head, in fact."

The gorilla climbed off from Silas and yanked him to his feet. Then he did as he was told, chambering a round and stretching out his massive arm wielding the Heckler & Koch.

Silas smirked. *A dumb German for a dumb German.*

"How did you find us?" Celeste said with grogginess, having woken to consciousness and righted herself. Her eyes were steely, her face set as flint as much as Silas's.

"Now that is quite the tale," Sebastian said with a grin. He gestured to the men in black holding the gun. "My man, Hans, here, decided we needed an early morning donut run before our escapades. I protested, hating those nasty artery-clogging things with a passion that burns bright and strong. Yet, he persisted, and so did the rest. Then, wouldn't you know, they spotted the meathead over there and the lead FBI agent responsible for investigating the Virginia movie theater shooting in the front seat of a low-class Mercedes after being honked at with such classlessness. Just chilling at a Dunkin' Donuts drive-thru of all things! Can you imagine?"

Silas closed his eyes and clenched his jaw at the revelation.

The Beamer.

He turned to Gapinski and shook his head, mumbling, "You just had to have that Long John, didn't you?"

Gapinski frowned. "My bad. Suppose that means we don't need to offer them one after all..."

"Thanks to your man's weakness," Sebastian went on, "Hans here followed you all the way to this dreadful monastery straight out of my nightmares. Which led us straight to you so we could retrieve the property that properly belongs to us."

"Property?" Brit said.

"Yes, property. Now there's a caper story worth your time, Ms. FBI Thing. Crimes I believe the FBI is generally most interested in pursuing, grand theft larceny and all."

"The books?" Silas said.

Sebastian smiled. "Precisely. They were stolen from my possession by that psychopath. A very resourceful fellow. Surprised he got away, given the water... At any rate, just here to reclaim what's mine."

"By kidnaping a bunch of innocent sisters at gunpoint?" Celeste asked.

"Yeah, bad form, bro," Gapinski said.

Sebastian shrugged. "It was the quickest way to get what I wanted. Knew that John Wayne over here would come riding in on his white horse to save the day. Just didn't count on so many co-conspirators."

A door opened at the back, and another man in black came striding over. He handed Sebastian something.

A pair of books.

Silas's face fell at the sight. "What do you want with those things, anyhow?" he growled.

Sebastian smirked, then held his grin and walked up to his twin. He whispered, "To make magic."

Silas lunged for his brother, head-butting him in the nose and sending him sprawling to the floor, his face bursting with crimson.

But he didn't get much further.

The gorilla intervened and wrestled him back to the floor, his knees going back to those kidneys.

"You very well broke my nose, Sy!" Sebastian roared. "Always were a little prick, weren't you?"

"Serves you right, you little—"

His head was drawn back and slammed into the floor, cutting him off and matching his brother with his own fair share of blood.

Sebastian recovered, pressing a handkerchief to his face and gathering up the two books laid splayed open on the floor.

He stood and straightened his coat then spun around to one of his men. "You know what to do."

Silas struggled underneath the man again. "You sorry excuse for a brother!"

Sebastian dipped to one knee next to his left ear and whispered, "It's been nice knowing you, Sy. Good luck on the other side. Hope it was worth it."

Then out his twin went, leaving two of his goons to clean up the mess.

CHAPTER 22

Did he just hear him right? Sebastian had just bid him *adieu,* sending him to his death?

Silas was too stunned for words at the truth of what had happened. That it had finally come to what they had been avoiding ever since Sebastian joined up with Nous—what he himself had staved off just ten months ago.

Stunned, but not surprised.

It had been a slow burn to this moment for the past year. Ever since that moment on the steps of the Lincoln Memorial and then on that frozen pond in Germany, they had been on a collision course that would have ended in either of them meeting their Maker.

But how had it come to this? That Sebastian almost relished in his demise—even in the power to put him down, like some dog he couldn't bother himself with any longer?

In many ways, this one-way train to fratricide had shoved off from the station shortly after he had given his life to Jesus at that chapel service on that base in Iraq. Really, it was more a rededication to his faith that had been sparked during his Catholic childhood and he had let wither to nothing. But after that moment, when he truly had decided to follow Jesus all on his own—not because of his Dad, not because of some religious label, not because it was the culturally appropriate thing to do at the time—he sort of went all John the Baptist on the world, especially his brother Sebastian, quoting chapter and verse on his need to repent and follow Christ as Lord and Savior.

His overzealousness had driven a deep wedge between the two over the years. He had only done what he thought was best for Sebastian and his soul. But his proselytizing had turned Sebastian off rather than on, and now look where they were.

Cain and Able. Jacob and Esau. Joseph and—

A scream, hysterical and out of control, cut through the cafeteria.

He whipped his head to Celeste. But she was sitting still, hands still bound behind her back and knees up to her chest.

Same for Gapinski, who was looking just as shocked and thrown as much as Silas.

It was Brit, screaming at the top of her lungs and throwing off the entire room's center of balance. Going at it in a way he had never seen her before—screeching till her lungs gave out then heaving a lungful of air before having at it again.

The two goons still left behind after Sebastian had gone recoiled with hesitation, seemingly confused and all at once concerned by the psychotic woman screaming bloody murder.

Which Silas took to be her exact intent. Didn't understand it in the slightest. But whatever. He'd take what he could get.

In one motion, he squeezed his arms still bound behind his back underneath his backside and slid them over his legs.

Then he sprang to his feet and plowed into the gorilla who had jammed his kneecaps into his kidneys with satisfying indignation.

The goon's rifle exploded with livid *rat-a-tat-tat* anger at the turn of events. Which drew the second man in black's attention.

Giving Celeste a window to follow Silas's lead as Brit

continued her hysterics, now echoed from the choir of Carmelite sisters still huddled at the back of the cafeteria—far more out of fear than any cockamamy plan to save their backsides.

She leaned back on her bound wrists then planted a satisfying bucking-bronco kick squarely in the guy's kneecaps.

A sickening crunch followed by a pop told the room all it needed to know.

The guy folded like a dollar bill, but not before unloading with indignation. Coming dangerously close to ending Celeste before she rolled out of the way and sprang to do what Silas had already taken first dibs on.

Cinching her still-bound wrists around the hostile's neck and squeezing like there was no tomorrow.

Because there wasn't one if they didn't finish the job then and there.

A few yards away, the other gorilla flailed his four-by-four arms and swatted at Silas with his catcher's mitt palms as he squeezed the guy's neck. But it was no use.

A sickening gurgling noise followed by a strained screech erupted from the goon before he slumped to the ground into unconsciousness.

Whether dead or just down, Silas didn't care.

He slid off from the man with exhaustion just as Celeste finished putting her own dog down.

He fished through the man's pockets and retrieved a knife, then got to work on his hands, carefully slipping the blade between the plastic and sawing till they snapped.

Brit finally halted her hysterics when the two men lay prone on the floor, the sisters now calming as Celeste snapped herself free from Silas's cut.

"Holybamoly, sister," Gapinski said with breathless surprise as Silas undid his bindings. "What the heck was that?"

The agent grinned. "A little thing I call improvisation."

"Did the FBI teach you to do that?"

"Nope. NOW."

Silas scoffed. "The National Organization for Women taught you how to scream like a banshee?"

"And the Feminist Majority."

"I don't get it?" Gapinski said, rubbing his freed wrists.

Silas slid over to Brit then slipped the blade at the plastic between her wrists.

She shrugged. "A girl's gotta know how to attract attention when she's receiving unwanted advances."

"Either way," Gapinski said, "slap me some serious skin! Because that was a performance worthy of an Oscar!"

Brit snorted one of her giggles. Silas freed her hands and she grabbed Gapinski's extended one. "Glad I still got it in me."

"Oh, I'd say you've got more in you than a Boston Terrier in heat at what you just let loose."

"Playtime's over, mates," Celeste said. "Look alive."

She hustled over to the women who were positively beside themselves now, whimpering and shrieking and mumbling the Hail Mary as the head of SEPIO operations tried calming them.

Brit joined her, but neither of them were making any progress. The adrenaline from the moment gave way to hysterics rivaling the show Brit had put on for the hostiles.

Silas and Gapinski brought over Styrofoam cups of water, which helped some, giving the women something to focus on to calm their frayed nerves.

Brit broke off her work and took out her phone, dialing a contact and pressing it to her ear.

"Wait!" Silas said, snatching it from her and ending the call.

"Hey! What are you doing?"

"No calls until we figure out what the heck is going on here."

"No ca—Give me back my phone!" she shouted, both arms scratching for the device. "I need to call this in to FBI Boston."

"Best not until we get things sorted," Celeste said, coming to Silas's rescue.

"Things get sorted my ass! We just survived a major criminal event by known terrorists trying to disrupt an ongoing FBI investigation and national terroristic emergency. No way I'm waiting to phone this in until we get things sorted!"

She swatted for the phone again, but Silas held it aloft.

"Brit, think this through," he said, trying to keep her back with one arm and the phone our of reach with the other. "You call this in and we've got every FBI agent from the Tri-State area descending on this place, descending on Salem, for that matter."

"Exactly my point! And exactly the right call. You know it."

"No it's not, mate," Celeste said. "We know this group better than anyone. The Feds show up and Nous is liable to get spooked and run. That happens and the trail will run cold. And then, as you Yanks like to say, you're s.o.l."

Silas couldn't help but grin at Celeste's disguised potty mouth. He rarely heard her cuss. When he did, watch out. He could tell his love's fuse was quickly burning to blast off.

Brit folded her arms. "Don't you worry your pretty little head off, dear. We have our ways. We'll find them."

Celeste grinned and matched her pose. "Not bleeding likely —*dear*. And besides. You agreed to do things our way, under my control. So, Ms. Armstrong, I'd kindly appreciate you giving me your word that you'll keep your word and keep your mouth shut so that Silas can give you back your bloomin' mobile and we can get on with it!"

Her words echoed more loudly than she probably intended, but it did the trick.

Brit huffed. "Fine. We do it your way. But the first sign this goes south—again, for the third time—I'm done with the Order or SEPIO or whoever the heck you people are." She held out her hand and said, "Now give me my phone, would you?"

"Suit yourself," Celeste said, nodding to Silas and turning away.

Silas slapped Brit's phone onto her palm. She went to pull it back, but he held tight.

"Give her a break, would you," he said lowly.

"What are you—?"

"Don't 'what are you talking about' with me, Brit. I know what you're doing. Some sort of schoolyard mean girls play to try and show her what's what. It doesn't matter."

She went to protest again when he put up a finger. She huffed, but nodded for him to continue.

"Other than the past day, I've not seen you in action," Silas went on, "From what I can tell, you're a pretty good agent. But in the last year, I've seen Celeste under far more fire than what our asses have gotten into and I'll tell you what, she's one of the best field officers I've worked with. Bar none. That's saying something, given the show of valor I witnessed up close and personal with the Rangers. And I'm not just saying that because I'm dating her."

Brit smirked and rolled her eyes.

"No, I'm serious. I'd put her up against any of those towhead desert rats any day. So, please, do me a solid and just lay off. She's only doing what we all want, and that's to stop Nous and bring this whole mess to a close before anyone else gets hurt, alright?"

Brit narrowed her eyes and pursed her lips. He thought she was going to respond with some snide remark when her face softened and she nodded.

"Alright, we'll do it your way. But I hope you all know what you're doing."

Silas's shoulders slumped, the tension deflating some at her acquiescence. "We do. And we don't. Much of what we've experienced hasn't been in any playbook, at least since I've been around the past year. But we know Nous, their motivations and desires. And we'll make them pay."

"And what are those motivations?"

He shrugged. "To do what any psychopathic organization around the world is motivated to do. Cause havoc and create terror. But instead of in the world, they're motivated to terrorize the Church and bring it to its knees. Especially the Order of Thaddeus."

"Helluva way to wreak havoc and disrupt Christianity. But what's the final play, here? What's the end goal?"

Silas sighed and shook his head. "That's what worries me."

She nodded and turned to leave. Instead, she stopped and said, "She's a keeper, Sy. I can tell. Don't you dare let her get away."

Gobsmacked is the word Celeste would have used to explain what he felt in that moment. He knew from back in the day that Brit put up a front and put on a show of things. But he'd never seen her give up her turf in that way before, even to another woman. And he certainly never thought she would give a compliment to Celeste like that.

He smiled. "Don't plan on it."

"We've had a bit of a go of it ourselves over on our end," Celeste said into her own mobile from the other side of the cafeteria.

She motioned for the other three to join her, then put the device on speaker.

"Radcliffe, you're on speaker now."

"What's happened? I jolly well hope you're getting along."

"Yeah, about that..." Gapinski said.

"Nous showed up," Silas said.

"What?" Radcliffe exclaimed. "How the blazes did they find you?"

Silas shot Gapinski a look, but let it slide. "Not important. What is, is that they took our only leads. The red book that appeared to be the Devil's Book and another. What appears to be Cotton Mather's personal copy of *On Witchcraft* filled with some hand notations that seemed important."

"Good Lord..."

"Scared the sisters pretty darn well. Nearly took us out in the process."

"But we survived to fight another day," Celeste added. "And not a small amount of gratitude should be offered to our newest FBI agent friend for making that happen."

"Yeah, mad props, Brit," Gapinski said.

Brit chuckled. "I'm not sure about that. Happy we landed back on our feet. But what we haven't landed on yet is what we're going to do about it."

"We're bloody well going after them, that's what!" Celeste said.

"But how?"

"I can't imagine their being here was a coincidence."

"I don't follow."

"You're right," Silas said. "Sebastian said they had pulled into the Dunkin Donuts on a whim."

"Or a whiff, in my case..." Gapinski said.

He ignored him, adding, "Which means they weren't here for us—"

"But for something else," Brit said. "Look at you, Silas Grey. Maybe there's an FBI agent hidden away in there."

"I don't know about that. But, yeah, you're right. We weren't the main course."

"Just the donut hors d'oeuvre?" Gapinski said.

"Something like that. Anyway, I have to imagine they were heading where we were heading."

"Salem," Brit said.

Silas nodded.

"And here I was hoping to avoid the epicenter of all things witchcraft," Gapinski moaned.

"At least we've got Long Johns for the road," Silas said.

Gapinski gave a nervous laugh. "Yeah, about that..."

"Don't tell me you ate the last one."

He said nothing.

Silas frowned. "At lease we've got the glazed ones left."

"Yeah, about that..."

"The chocolate ones with Halloween sprinkles?" Brit asked.

Gapinski said nothing.

"Oh, come on!"

"Agents!" Radcliffe exclaimed through the mobile's speaker. "I'm wasting away over here whilst you flitter about arguing over pastries."

"Right. Apologies, Rowen," Celeste said, giving her agents a look. "Before we shove of for Salem, tell them what you were beginning to tell me a moment ago."

"Ahh, yes. For that, I will hand it over to my friend, Father D'Amante."

"Thank you, Rowen," a hesitant, weary voice sounded through the speaker. "I echo your sentiment, the one about having a go of it. The possession clusters are growing, in strength and number."

"In what way?" Celeste asked.

"Haven't you heard?"

The agents glanced at one another and shrugged.

"As I said, Father, we've been having it out over here. Perhaps you could fill us in on the 411?"

"Reports of rabid people, out of control and possessed with devilish intent, have been raging through cities spreading farther now into Canada, reaching Ottawa and Montreal, and on into Fort Wayne, Pittsburg, even both Rochester, New York and Minnesota."

"How frightful."

"That's not even the whole of it. Ranchers in Minnesota discovered several dead bulls, all previously healthy and missing their sex organs and tongues. All dying under mysterious circumstances, as there was no entry wound or sign of a struggle, and the parts were definitely cut out with a sharp blade."

"Why would someone go to such lengths to steal Rocky Mountain oysters?" Gapinski asked. "Can't you just order up a pair at the local butcher?"

"Well, in the 1980s," Radcliffe explained, "a few cows were found dead and mutilated in eastern Oregon in the same manner. It was suspected all were killed to harvest their organs for occult practices stemming from peak lunar activity."

"Like the full moon that's going on right now?" Silas said.

"Indeed."

"That's consistent with what the FBI has found in similar mutilations since the 70s," Brit added. "The animals typically die in the same way with the same body parts removed, usually coinciding with a full moon."

"Which means the occult activity is picking up in pace," Radcliffe went on, "and I fear it will soon climax in the unthinkable, given the level of demonic occurrences of late."

"And what is that?" Silas asked.

Father D'Amante answered, "Animal sacrifices are prominent within occult practices, especially the Black Mass."

"Black Mass?" Brit asked.

"That's right. A ritual characterized by the inversion of the traditional Latin Mass of the Church. Often, animals such as bulls and goats, the sorts once part of the Levitical sacrificial system of the Israelites, are sacrificed before their fresh blood is poured over participants who have pledged their souls to Satan."

"Eww," Gapinski said. "Talk about major salmonella danger."

"Pretty sure salmonella is the least of our worries..." Silas said, his heart beginning to hammer at the thought of where all this was heading. “Which means we best get going.”

Celeste nodded. “We’ll ring you, Radcliffe, when we get a clearer picture of the connection with Salem.”

“Be careful, agents,” the Order Master said. “I don’t mean to sound paternal, but the level of demonic activity combined with human occult activity is the highest we have seen in our lifetime. I dare say the hounds of hell have been loosed upon the world.”

“And with my brother leading the charge,” Silas said.

The group went silent before Celeste ended the call. Silas led the quartet back to the Mercedes out front, feeling the need to take charge and take control over a situation that was going to hell—literally.

Because there’s no chance he would let Sebastian get away with whatever the heck he was planning.

CHAPTER 23

Silas took lead driving the agents to downtown Salem, a quick ten minutes at normal speed, half that with Silas driving toward more than just history's most infamous bewitched town.

Sebastian had a good hour on the crew, but there was no way he was going to let him get away with whatever Nous was plotting. Whatever they were, he knew their plans were pure evil incarnate—not only because of what they had witnessed the past day.

Over the past year, with all that he had endured at the hands of the Church's archenemy—from their plot to destroy evidence of Jesus' resurrection and manufacturing an alternative story to the one found in the Gospels; to creating confusion surrounding the nature of Jesus' saving work and literally destroying the Church by blowing up churches across the globe—through it all, he had understood that an evil was at work in the world coming against the Church in a way he hadn't before appreciated.

In his letter to the Ephesians, Saint Paul had urged the Church in chapter six to *'Put on the whole armor of God, so that you may be able to stand against the wiles of the Devil.'* While he went on to say *'our struggle is not against enemies of blood and flesh, but against the rulers, against the authorities, against the cosmic powers of this present darkness, against the spiritual forces of evil in the heavenly places,'* that didn't preclude the fact plenty of willing participants were partnering with said rulers, authorities, cosmic powers, and spiritual forces to bring the Church to its knees.

Including Nous.

Including his twin brother.

Paul went on to exhort, *'take up the whole armor of God, so that you may be able to withstand on that evil day.'* That evil day had surely arrived in force, and Silas Grey would be damned if he was caught flat-footed without being fully armed to do something about it.

Which included the fully re-loaded Beretta sitting at his back in addition to all the other provisions of the armor of God.

Silas sighed and shook his head at the idea as he banked left at a modest beige brick church on North Street. Rushing past a cemetery covered in bright yellow and orange leaves glistening with dew in the mid-morning sun, he wondered whether what he was prepared to do—what he wanted to do—was the right thing to do, a dialogue he'd had with himself since joining SEPIO after swearing off a life of violence since leaving the Rangers.

Riding in to save the day with guns blazing probably flew in the face of everything Christianity stood for, given Jesus' blessings on the meek and merciful, the pure in heart and peacemakers. Then again, warriors rose up at various times to fight against wickedness and injustice pressing in against the Church, bearing both shield and sword to defend the innocent. The risen Knights Templar reminded them of that earlier in the year.

But still. He knew SEPIO threaded a delicate needle to execute on the Order's mission originally handed down by the apostle Jude Thaddeus: Taking seriously his exhortation *'to contend for the faith that was once for all entrusted to the saints'* was delicate business. He and Celeste had talked at length about it, she more convinced of the need to use more muscular means to secure the Church's ends. He wasn't so sure, preferring his desk job and research to the sorts of rollicking adventures he had been dragged into the past year. For him, the pen was indeed mightier than the sword.

Regardless, it was go time. And Silas prayed to the good Lord above that didn't mean putting someone down in the process. Especially Sebastian.

But he was ready if it came to it.

Salem proper came up quick. Clapboard houses looking like they dated back to the town's founding were arrayed in neat rows butting up against the road. They all seemed to follow some prescribed decorating plan: two-level structures painted indigo or charcoal, crimson or tawny, their windows flanked by shutters in tastefully accented shades, all bearing tiny front porches and nonexistent lawns.

Silas craned forward and glanced from side to side in search of his twin. Didn't know what he expected to find, but he knew he was out there somewhere. Only problem was, how to find the little bugger.

Naked trees lining the street were clinging to their dignity with colored leaves quickly turning dead-brown. Those same leaves blew across the road on a frigid gust as Silas blew through a yellow-turned-red traffic light. Their dead scent, combined with a pile of burning leaves in the near distance, wafted through his window cracked open a touch. The breeze was chased by something smelling of cinnamon and cloves and apples baking close by—sending his mind jumping to childhoods past raking their large Virginia yard then collapsing into a mile-high pile of leaves, followed up by donuts and hot cider.

Oh, to be a teenager again, with all of this nonsense still over a decade out...

He turned down a one-way side street in a frustrated huff, more of the same clapboard houses standing witness to Silas's growing impatience with their search.

Finally, an intersection and a crosswalk of people brought them to a halt. Which was probably a good thing, since it seemed like they were on a fast track to aimlessness.

"Where do you reckon they ran off to?" Celeste asked from the passenger's seat.

Silas shook his head. "Who knows. It's like searching for fly crap in pepper out here. Could be anywhere."

"Salem can't be that big a town," Brit said. "No way they got far, even with their hour head start."

The light turned green, and the traffic picked up its pace.

"But where to begin is the question," Celeste said.

"Uh, guys. That looks as good a place as any," Gapinski said, pointing out the window to a burnt-red brick building that looked like a church.

Anchored to the front was a brown sign, its gold letters a beacon of slim hope.

Salem Witch Museum.

"I'd say that blood well works, don't you, dear?" Celeste said.

Silas flashed a smile and nodded. "Sure does."

HE SPUN the Mercedes SUV around the intersection past a wizard statue that smacked of cliché and parallel parked the beast, sliding into a spot out front and kissing the bumper of a black Ford Focus hatchback.

The four got out and hustled to the front doors. Pumpkins were stacked on bales of hay out front with bright yellow and orange fall mums greeting them, as was a large ornate door of darkly stained walnut.

It was early, but Silas hoped someone was in to help, he went to open the door when it thudded open on its own.

A portly woman with blond hair and wearing a long black dress startled.

"Dear me! You gave my heart a start..." She fanned herself and leaned against the door threshold.

"Sorry about that," Silas said. "But glad you're open we're—"

"Sorry, dear," the woman said with interruption, "but we don't open for another hour. I was just getting things prepared."

"OK..."

"Ma'am," Brit said, "we're in need of your assistance."

She stepped forward and withdrew her FBI credentials. She held them up, and the women took them in.

"FBI? Dear me!" the woman exclaimed. "There wasn't a witch sighting, was there?" She giggled something fierce at her funny, with an annoying, nasally tone that set Silas's teeth on edge.

"Not exactly," he said, "but we were hoping you could help us, maybe let us in and look around your museum. Might help us with our case."

She scrunched her face up with indecision and darted her eyes from agent to agent. "Oh, I don't know. It's only my first week on the job..."

Silas rolled his eyes. Great. A rule follower.

"Look," Brit said, "just up the road, a bunch of terrorists shot up a monastery of nuns in the early morning hours, and we believe they've escaped into the city."

The woman gave a frightful squeak, fanning herself and leaning against the doorway again.

"So if you wouldn't mind," the agent went on, "we'd love

just a few minutes inside your museum and a few minutes of your time."

The woman glanced from Brit to Silas and then on to Celeste and Gapinski before nodding. "If you think it'll help, come on in. But that will be $52.00."

"Excuse me?" Silas said. "For what?"

"For the price of admission."

He raised a brow. *Modern-day patriot, this one is.*

Without complaint, he took out his wallet and handed the woman a crisp Benjamin, telling her to keep the change.

She stuffed the hundred in her bosom and led them in.

The inside was a hollowed-out version of the former church that, according to the woman who had become much freer with divulging information since the hundred-dollar bill, had deep roots in the original colony stretching back to the days of the trials. Depictions of the range of events that 1692 year—from the trials to the interrogations and imprisonments to the actual hangings themselves—were arrayed around the space in campy displays with mannequins.

But nothing that would help them catch Sebastian and the other Nousati.

Silas planted his hands on his hips and sighed with frustration. "There's nothing here that we don't already know," he mumbled.

"We're better off roaming the streets," Celeste said, coming up to his side.

He turned to the woman. Chuckling, he said, "You wouldn't happen to have their remains stashed away in here, would you?"

She laughed with a nervous giggle and that same nasally annoyance. "No...but you could always dig them out yourself, if that's your thing."

He took a step toward the woman, joined by the other three.

"What do you mean?"

"Whoa there, only kidding." Again, the nervous, nasally giggle.

"How would we go about digging up the witches, then?" Celeste asked. "Not that we would, dear, just wondering what you're playing at."

"Well, the actual site of the hangings was recently discovered. Proctor's Ledge, it's called."

"Why only recently discovered?" Silas said, taking a step closer to press the woman.

"Traditionally, it was thought that the victims of the witch trials were hanged on the summit of Gallows Hill. But a few researchers confirmed Proctor's Ledge as the definitive site for the hanging. And since the tradition has long been that the victims were buried together in a shallow pit at the site of execution, given that convicted witches would not be allowed burial in the consecrated ground in the city cemetery, it's thought their remains still, well, remain in Proctor's Ledge."

Silas threw Celeste a hopeful grin. This could be the break they were looking for!

"But you're out of luck," the woman went on, "even if digging up witch corpses was your thing."

His grin quickly faded to a disheartened frown.

"What do you mean, out of luck?" Brit asked.

"A pair of researchers backed by bookoo bucks have been excavating the site the past—hey, where are you going?"

Suddenly, something from the night came rushing back to the fore of Silas's memory. A phrase spoken by that damnable demonic voice earlier in the day that seemed like a clue of intent.

During Celeste's exorcism, the Voice mumbled some nonsense about cause breath to enter some bones, and covering them with skin, and some nonsense. He recalled now it mirroring a prophecy of Scripture, Ezekiel 37—typical of the Evil One to quote and twist the Bible to suit its ends.

But in his pride, the Devil let slip his intentions. Just couldn't help himself. There really was something in the bones that would be unleashed and brought to life.

And Sebastian was about to retrieve them.

Silas rushed toward the entrance before the woman finished.

Hearing all he needed to know and hoping to God they hadn't just wasted another hour.

He was followed by the other three as he shoved through the heavy walnut door.

"How much you want to bet our bookoo-buck backed researchers are Sebastian and his goons?" Gapinski asked.

"Is it really a question?" Brit said as they loaded into the Mercedes.

"But what the bloody hell do they want with a bunch of witch bones?" Celeste asked.

Silas brought the SUV to life and backed it up into the Ford, hitting it with too much oomph. Recompense would have to wait.

"Alleged witch," Brit corrected.

"Right, *alleged*. Either way, what's the endgame here?"

He threw their ride into *Drive* and punched it, climbing up on the curb and thudding back into the intersection, rounding past the wizard statue and speeding toward How's Hill.

Only one way to find out.

CHAPTER 24

The last of them were finally recovered inside the tent of heavy cream canvas, the Universe giving an almost approving nod at what they were finalizing inside by offering a blanket of mid-morning sunlight and warmth as the crew hauled up the last of the bones.

Little did the Universe know what they had in store for these relics imbued with a primal power stretching all the way back to the start of human existence itself.

Symbolizing life and consciousness, death and rebirth, for generations it has been thought that bones hold the fertile potential of all that arises from the earth. They are what's left of human consciousness, carrying within the memory of their original host. And the relics of such memory-markers would soon be reunited to release into the world the last vestiges of that memory.

The one that had been recovered weeks ago in the dead of night and fitted around that blasted Roland character, a distant relative of Elizabeth How, proving his theories right: There was a nascent power still residing in those bones waiting to be released.

And Sebastian Grey would harness it, for humanity.

He stood at the edge of the last of the deep wells his crew had carved on the side of the unsuspecting hillside nestled between two single-family houses in the heart of the birthplace of American witchcraft. Who knew that the original site of execution had been hiding in plain sight, just waiting for him and his merry band of mercenaries to uncover the font of primal power?

When he began researching in earnest at the beginning of the year the trials that had made Salem so infamous, he discerned a secret truth behind the mass hysteria that was far more primal than many acknowledge. And when he stumbled up on a small red book on the dark web with a curious selection of names, scrawled in human blood, he knew he was on to something. That wasn't even touching on the family legend that had piqued his curiosity since childhood and he had noodled on from time to time since college.

Months later, he would read about a momentous discovery by two researchers, Marilynne K. Roach and Professor Emerson "Tad" Baker, who had uncovered new information about the actual site where the nineteen Salem witches were executed for the crime of witchcraft. A memorial had been erected over the site a few years ago, which was all the x-marks-the-spot he needed to put his plan into motion.

Took some doing, but Sebastian was able to convince the mayor that he and his merry band of researchers from George Washington University (his former place of employ he was using as a cover) would add a greater depth of appreciation for the mendacity and hysteria of the trials if they were allowed to exhume the bodies and give them a proper place of appreciation. And given the recent theft—perpetuated by his own hand, of course—retrieving them would also ensure their future safekeeping.

Balk, she did, but she folded like the cheap suit she was wearing when he wrote the sizable seven-figure grant check to the city. All in the interest of historical inquiry and preservation, of course.

LiDAR radar imaging had earlier confirmed that bodies were indeed lying buried on the hillside. But not all of the ones he knew carried the cosmic forces waiting to be unleashed. One in particular he cared most about had been exactly where the family legends had said it would be, back on that island he had visited in childhoods past.

The rest he was finishing exhuming beneath dreadful shrubbery that dreadful mayor had planted herself as memorials to the Nineteen's sacrifices in the face of religious hysteria and bigotry.

But seriously, shrubbery? How does anyone conceive that wintercreepers or boxwoods or arborvitae for the gods' sake could possibly do those women and men justice for resurrecting the original cosmic force that animated our human consciousness?

A shudder of revulsion ran up Sebastian's spine. Then one end of his mouth curled into a smile, and then the other. For soon they would be used to resurrect that primal power again.

Speaking of which...

His breath seized in his chest at the sight of the last of the bones being raised to the surface, the last of the vessels containing the dark memory of what had been unleashed upon the earth those many centuries ago.

And it was now his, all of them. Awaiting their use in the rite to release back into the world the power they hold, for the sake of resurrecting the human consciousness once again.

Yet he was still short one ingredient. He just prayed to the Universe it would be provided before the time was up.

"Marvelous, simply marvelous, Dr. Warren!" an annoying larkish woman cooed from behind.

His face instantly fell, and he wanted to slap her across that overly-makeuped face of hers for ruining his moment. But he closed his eyes and took in a measured breath, stuffing his impulsiveness in abeyance. For now.

But the mention of his *nom de plume* did make him giggle inside, a clever little device he'd conjured to hide his true identity, but all too germane to the task at hand.

Sebastian gathered his wits about him for the final few minutes before he and his crew whisked their prize away for safekeeping and the ceremony that would bring it all to pass.

He smiled broadly and spun around to greet the woman.

"Ah, Mayor Bradly. So good of you to join us on this auspicious occasion," he cooed back. "It is a marvelous feat of historical justice for those poor, innocent souls, isn't it? And no thanks to your generous commitment to historical inquiry, I might add!"

Lips slathered with bright red lipstick parted to offer a giggling reply. "Oh, stop! I was merely a cog in the machinations of government bureaucracy that helped pave the way for your brilliant work of recovery."

And I have to imagine the cool several million helped grease the skids, too...

"Yes, well, soon enough the world will reap the fruits of your machinations, as you put it, right after we prepare the bones for examination and public presentation."

Sebastian brushed past her and nodded to one of his men who had carefully placed the bones in a black case, along with the others.

The man nodded back, latching the case and carrying the precious cargo to the rear of one of the awaiting SUVs.

"Wait, where are you taking them?" Mayor Bradley asked.

"Why, back to my place of employ, naturally."

She gasped. "In DC?"

"Why, yes. Where else? I can't very well examine them here," Sebastian said with a chuckle.

The woman folded her arms and stood stiffly in her cheap

blue pinstripe between him and the van, those slathered lips pursing together with indignation.

"I am sorry, Dr. Warren," the woman said, "but there must be some sort of misunderstanding. This was not at all what we agreed to."

Sebastian's face flooded with a reddened rage. He went to offer a reply when a sound caught his attention from behind.

A door opened then suddenly slammed shut.

Another pair echoed with arrival until one final one sent his heart jolting with confusion.

The memorial park and surrounding Pope Street was supposed to have been a restricted area, open only to him and his men. Part of that damn down payment to that insufferable broad holding him up.

Which meant they had visitors.

He didn't have to venture a guess who.

SILAS SLAMMED his door with more force than was necessary, and probably wise, given the circumstances. His brother himself very well could be holed up behind those canvas tents doing Lord knows what. But still. Stealth was probably what the doctor ordered for such a time as this.

Whatever. To hell with stealth. Given the past few days, stealth was the last thing on his mind.

Three more doors closed behind him as he padded toward the grouping of canvas tents up ahead. The street was blocked from further passage, with a City of Salem police cruiser blocking traffic and an overstuffed cop with too much time on his hands flipping through his mobile. Too bad they were out of Long Johns or they would have had the perfect carrot to smooth their passage.

The man chuckled as Silas hustled closer, probably

laughing at some Facebook meme or cat vid on YouTube. Then he startled and opened his door.

Here we go...

"Hey, you can't pass through here!" the cop squawked, his voice high and almost strained, like air seeping through the end of a cinched balloon.

Cat vid. Definitely a cat vid.

"Howdy, partner," Silas said, extending his hand as the oaf bothered himself to climb out of his vehicle to do the work he imagined the man was paid off to do. Money probably disguised as a grant to the city for Nous to do whatever it was doing inside those tents.

"Sir, this is a restricted area," the cop said, putting up a halting hand.

"Silas Grey, former Army Rangers," Silas introduced himself. Figured name-dropping Uncle Sam might have currency. Although on second thought, it was New England. "I have reason to believe whoever is in those tents over there was part of a major terrorist event north of the city, at the old Cistercen monastery."

The man jolted at the word terrorist. Most cops did nowadays. Last thing they wanted on their watch was the big T disturbing their peace with mountains of paperwork. Plus, the body count was a real bummer, too. Especially for a tourist trap like Salem.

Celeste hustled up to his side, followed by Brit and Gapinski.

"Who are you guys?" the man squawked again, this time his right hand sliding to his holster without much grace.

Silas clenched his jaw with irritation. He didn't have time for this.

But neither did he have time for his ass getting thrown into the slammer either.

So he glanced at Brit and nodded toward the man. Perhaps her FBI creds would still have some mileage left in them.

She stepped forward and reached inside her pants pocket. She withdrew her badge and flashed it at the cop.

"I'm Special Agent Brit Armstrong, officer. And—"

A scream sliced through the street, followed by the revving of an engine, then one more.

And then *pop-pop* gunfire.

The officer threw his hands on his head and ducked, clearly no match for a Long John let alone a criminal conspiracy sitting under his nose this whole time.

The agents did not follow suit.

All four withdrew their weapons and aimed for the circus.

Just as two Beamers looking like the one they had spotted at the Dunkin' Donuts came peeling out from behind the canvas, collapsing the structure and sending a woman with way too much lipstick limping out in a screaming panic and clutching her side.

"Now do you believe me?" Silas mumbled, leaving the sorry excuse for law enforcement and rushing back for their Mercedes.

Silas climbed inside then cranked the beast back to life.

The other three slid inside, but he didn't even wait for their doors to close before he lurched forward after his brother and the abomination they had picked up inside that hillside.

Missed the cop hoisting himself up off the ground by an inch, and then only missed swiping the paint off from his car by a hair. No matter. Soon they were back at it, weaving through the narrow one-way street chasing after his brother.

Again.

"You figure they gathered up the bones of those deceased witches?" Brit asked.

"You mean *alleged* witches?" Celeste said with a wry grin.

"Yeah, yeah, whatever. But what's the deal with that?"

“I have to imagine that’s exactly what they were after. Bones of all sorts are often used in occult rituals.”

“And that’s what this is about, an occult ritual?”

Celeste shrugged. “We’ll need to ask those blokes.”

Horns blared at the intersection up ahead with anger and irritation as the two black BMWs sprinted through it without a care.

Silas was more cautious, slowing enough to make sure all was clear before flooring it after the Beamers banking left at the threshold of a park still full of color.

Soon he was following suit, making the hard left as the escaping SUVs pulled away.

“Would you look at that,” Gapinski said. “Witch Hill Road, how appro—”

“Watch out!” Brit yelled.

Silas braked then swerved to avoid a car backing out of its driveway.

The car honked in irritation, but he ignored it, throwing the SUV into a higher gear and flooring it as the Beamers wound left past red-brick apartments.

He caught up along a stretch that took them back toward another intersection, driving hard and fast through residential streets and weaving past cars surely not accustomed to high-speed chases.

Sirens began to sound in the distance as the caravan opened it up south on Highland Avenue, a four-lane stretch of small businesses pockmarked with more residential homes and the regional hospital system.

About time you all decided to show—

The lead car suddenly smacked into the front end of a minivan good and well while trying to make a sharp left, ripping off its front end and leaving its status questionable.

The one trailing it spun around, not waiting for it to recover.

Silas did a once over as he passed, not seeing his brother inside among the cursing Nousati throwing their hands up in irritation at the turn of events.

He smirked at their luck and pressed on, chasing after the BMW he hoped held his brother.

And whatever the heck they had taken.

The Beamer was pulling away now as they weaved through a road lined with brilliantly colored trees. Not if Silas could help it.

He pushed the Mercedes and closed the gap, just as the hostile SUV shoved into a parking lot. A golf course, by the looks of it.

It kept going without pause, smashing through a metal gate and bounding up onto the green.

"What the heck is that maniac doing?" Brit asked.

Didn't matter one bit to Silas. He followed after and soon the pair were winding across expertly manicured and fertilized fairways toward destiny.

In the distance, a thwapping was heard over the din of the whining engines.

A sound that was all too familiar.

Chopper.

"How is it that whenever we're hot on Nous's ass," Gapinski said, "there's a bird ready to pick them up?"

Silas ignored the man, but had to agree. Old, real old.

Winding through the course, the pair of SUVs kicked up dirt and grass still slick from the dawn's dew. Blazing past the putting green and the first hole, they mounted a path that carried them up to the second hole fairway and on through the fourth hole, weaving past sand traps and splintering the white-and-red hole flagstick.

Halfway through the nine-hole course now, with no end in sight.

Silas wiped his head beading with anxious perspiration

from the chase. "Darling, how about you do me a solid and blow out one of their tires."

"Lord knows she's been around that merry-go-round a time or nine," Gapinski said.

Celeste withdrew her weapon and chambered a round. "Sure thing...darling."

She gave him a wink and rolled down her window. She unbuckled her seatbelt and banged her head on the ceiling on a wicked bump past the fifth hole.

"Sorry! You OK?" Silas said.

Rubbing her forehead, she winced. "I'm alive. But I can't say the same for those blokes up ahead in a few short seconds."

Silas held the Mercedes steady as she leaned out for a shot, the thwapping louder now and the bird growing in their rearview mirror.

Pop-pop-pop Celeste sounded.

Shredding a tire on the first go of it and sending the Beamer skidding sideways on uncertain legs.

She offered a second helping for good measure: *pop-pop-pop.*

This time, blowing out another tire and the back window and sending someone slumping against the steering wheel in a loud whine of injury.

"Nice shot," Brit said, sounding impressed.

Celeste smirked and blew at her barrel. "I'd go up against any of your g-men any day of the week."

The BMW rolled to a halt.

Just as the chopper was coming in for a landing.

Sebastian and another guy, both carrying large black cases, bolted from the slain beast and rushed for the helicopter now resting on the seventh hole green.

Silas slid the Mercedes yards away from the Beamer, and Celeste was out the door before he brought it to a halt.

She took off after Sebastian, firing a warning shot toward the pair that landed with a puff a few feet from him.

He didn't flinch. The men kept running toward the chopper, gaining ground and closing the window for SEPIO to seal the deal.

But Celeste was gaining too, now only a few yards from the man at the rear.

The other three were a few yards behind her and ready to offer back up.

When a *rat-a-tat-tat* with livid intent cut through, shredding the still-dewy lawn.

There it was again: *rat-a-tat-tat.*

Not from the men running away out front but from behind.

Silas spun around for a look.

The injured Beamer they'd left behind, missing its face and coming in hot and heavy.

And the four agents totally exposed with no defense but their sidearms.

Silas raised his weapon and fired with abandon as the Beamer zoomed past, along with Brit and Gapinski who were at his side—blowing out the rear window but doing nothing about the threat.

It spun an arc and made for the escaping pair, sending Silas diving out of the way.

And Celeste.

Who dove forward as it slid behind her.

Planting itself between Silas and the love of his life.

"Noooo!!" he screamed, scrambling from the ground after her with no visual.

The sound of doors clicking open, followed by the *pop-pop-pop* of gunfire made him scramble faster.

He came up to the BMW's rear heaving heavy, hot breaths and bolted into view with his weapon ready for action.

Just as two Nousati grabbed Celeste off the ground by both arms and dragged her toward the chopper up ahead.

His brain froze with indecision. If he fired, he risked hitting his love. They also had a head start by yards, heading straight for the chopper.

Get it together, Grey!

His brain snapped into gear, so did his legs. He screamed a raging cry of indignation and tore off after Celeste, a round of gunfire coming as a reply from the chopper.

His brother.

"Sonofa—" Gapinski sounded breathlessly from behind as Silas left them in the dust.

Sebastian and the one man were now on board the bird.

And now Celeste was dragged on board as well.

"Celeste!" Silas screamed as the helicopter lifted from the ground.

He was still a few yards away, and the window of opportunity was quickly closing.

The bird rose quickly, soaring feet by feet on an updraft of thwapping blades and spitting more lead down below.

One of them connected, jolting Silas's arm back with lancing pain.

He cried out but paid it no mind. Couldn't, not with Celeste's life on the line.

Pumping his arms and tearing after the ascending bird, he launched himself high into the air on a desperate prayer, hoping to latch on to the landing skids in an attempt to save his love.

He stretched his arms out, as if going in for the countdown-to-zero game-winning dunk that would clinch an NBA championship.

And missed by a foot, his arm *whooshing* past the steel skids as the chopper quickly gained height and rushed through the eighth hole fairway.

Silas hit the ground hard, his legs buckling under the sudden drop and sending him into a roll until he crashed into a boulder nestled at the edge of a sand trap.

His head exploded with stars and dimmed into darkness. But it all barely registered. He only had one thing on his mind.

"Celeste!" he cried desperately on shaky legs clawing forward through the sand with purchase.

The bird rose higher and higher, banking north and flying away to freedom, disappearing past the tree line.

"Celeeeeeste!!" Silas screamed until his lungs gave out, his face red with agonized rage and body crumpling onto his knees and into a helpless heap.

All while his brother flew away with the love of his life.

CHAPTER 25

Silas was a spent man.

He'd lost his father, and then mother before that; lost his best friend in combat; lost his passion project, his career; lost his brother to who knows what, the dark side or whatever; and now this.

The love of his life.

Gapinski was at his side, crouched next to him and tying a strip of his shirt around his upper arm. Bullet had grazed it pretty good, and he was bleeding pretty good. But he'd live.

Brit was jabbering into her mobile, having called the local authorities to report the kidnapping.

"We'll get those bastards, buddy," Gapinski said. "Mark my words, we'll get 'em, and get back Celeste. No question about it."

But that's all that it was. A big fat question mark without hope of resolution.

How could this have happened? How could God have allowed this to happen? All of it—from the psychopath shooting up a movie theater and all of the other displays of violence radiating across the Midwest and Canada to his brother terrorizing a bunch of nuns and then kidnapping...

He couldn't bring himself to voice the truth of it, even silently to himself.

But he had to. Had to face the root of this rage that was now consuming him as he sat slumped in the sand trap, a question that had been haunting him since he had seen the unmasked evil in the theater, and then in the morgue.

How could God allow such evil to unfold across the world —much less over his own children?

Where was God in all of this, in the pain and agony, the death and destruction from pure, unadulterated evil? The kind that runs rampant in suburbs and slums alike, all in different forms with different clothes on, but evil still the same?

There's the respectable kind like white lies to spouses and cheating on taxes and mindless consumption in ever-increasing gluttonous, greedy measure. Then the medium kind that does nobody harm but ravages the soul just the same: addictions like porn and opioids. And the systemic evil that ensures minorities are enslaved to generational cycles of poverty, the one-percenters continue hoarding wealth, regimes maintain an iron-grip on power through habitual human rights abuses, gangs consume the fatherless and ravage entire neighborhoods.

Pure, unadulterated evil. All flowing from the hearts of men, stoked by the principalities and powers of this dark age—and apparently now with a level of possession not seen since the days of Jesus, or perhaps Salem circa 1692.

With nary a word from the Lord.

It's like he's gone dark, hiding his face from the world and letting it sink further and further into the shadow of Death's darkest valley, perhaps giving humans exactly what they've always wanted: the power to decide not only what is good and evil, but the power to do it, celebrate it, perpetuate it—all without a care in the world for the consequences for that Devil's bargain.

Literally.

The theological side of Silas's brain knew why it was the way it was. That God had never intended his very good world to be so shredded, so vandalized, by the wickedness that seems to define much of twenty-first-century life. That seems to define twenty-first-century people. Although, it's been this way from the beginning.

Ever since Mama Eve and Papa Adam grasped after that damn fruit, not in the interest of gaining knowledge of good and evil, but grasping after the power to decide what was good and what was bad—ever since then he knew the world has been reeling from that choice. After all, choice is at the heart of any relationship, even with God—the hope of intimate love or possibility of heartbreaking rejection. Of rebellion.

Our ancestors chose the latter.

All in the interest of power. The right to *'be like God,'* as the Devil promised. And we've been paying the price ever since.

But still. While that's what his head told him, his heart just ached for a world that was busting at the seams almost every day to be put back together again. Now his own heart had been rent in two at what had happened in his own world, and he just wanted it to be better.

Wanted Celeste back, to have and to hold, until death parted them. Preferably a half century later.

Silas buried his face in his hands and squeezed, trying to drain away the jumbled bundle of agonizing thoughts and apostatizing doubts ricocheting around his soul, totally oblivious to his still-throbbing arm.

God, where are you? When life goes dark, when evil consumes the good?

Like his precious Celeste...

Again, that blasted theological side of his brain knew that a day would come when all the evil in the world would be obliterated for good. That one day, Jesus Christ himself will return to his broke, busted creation to finally put it back together again. To make all things new, as John the Apostle wrote in the Book of Revelation. But that's not all.

Because not only will God dwell with us, being with his people, *'he will wipe every tear from their eyes. Death will be no more; mourning and crying and pain will be no more, for the first things have passed away.'* Not only that, the Devil himself and all of his minions, even those who actively live in rebellion against God, denying Jesus Christ as singular Lord and Savior, will be done for—thrown into the lake of fire, the second death.

His brain knew this; his heart confirmed it.

But in that moment, sitting ankle deep in the dirty sand of a golf course, he momentarily forgot what was true. All he wanted to know was, what the hell was taking God so long?

"Hey, guys?" Brit said softly, coming up on the other side of Silas and putting away her mobile. "First of all, how are you doing, Silas? Your arm going to be alright?"

He didn't move, didn't speak. Finally, he managed to drop his hands to his lap with a leadened thud and grunt an affirmative.

She said softly, "We'll get her back, Silas. We'll get her back."

He nodded, but held his head with eyes closed, body and mind and soul numb to the world, to Brit's empty promises.

"On the flip side, I've got something you need to hear about."

It hurt to lift his head, every muscle screaming with pain and the goose egg from that damn boulder sending bolts of pain from one side to the other, but he did—raising it to meet Brit's eyes now level with his. He winced at the accompanying pain in his arm, the adrenaline now wearing off.

Crouching next to him, she said, "I called my supervisor back at the field office. Not only to check in and give an update on all the crazy, which I can't say he was all that pleased about, but that's for me to handle. I also called for an update on the main gig that launched us into the crazy in the first place."

"And?" Gapinski said, taking over for Silas, who still found it hard to speak.

"And, well..." she trailed off, folding her arms and bringing a hand to the bridge of her nose.

Silas sat straighter. This wasn't like Brit, all coy and indecisive with a reveal. Straight shooter all the way, she was. Which meant something big was up.

"What happened?" he said.

She shook her head. "It's not what happened, it's what we found."

Silas was growing impatient. The love of his life had been kidnapped and airlifted by psychopaths on a putting green, and here Brit was choking at a time she should be saving Celeste!

He took a breath before he did or said something he'd regret.

"Brit, please," Silas said, "what's—"

"There's a connection here with your family, Silas."

Now he stood. Every bone and ligament and muscle protested, but he made it to his feet.

"What the hell are you talking about, there's a connection with my family?"

She stood herself and hesitated, but plowed forward. "The little red book."

"The Devil's Book?"

"Right. Well, you noted back at the monastery that the ink looked like blood. You were right. It was. We ran it through FBI databases along with our ancillary partners."

Gapinski snorted. "You mean Ancestory.com, right? Yeah, I know about your ancillary partners. You ain't seein' me give my DNA to no ancillary partner, no sir—"

"Gapinski!" Silas said. "And, Brit, spit it out, would you? What are you getting at?"

"What I'm getting at," she said, looking down at her phone, "is that you're a match."

Silas furrowed his brow. "A match? For what?"

"For Mary Warren. One of the Salem witches."

"Far out..." Gapinski said. "Your ancestor was a witch?"

"Alleged witch," Brit said. "But, yes. It's all right here?"

She handed her phone to Silas. He took it, his head swimming with the possibility of it all, that he was somehow related to one of the Salem witches.

"But how did..." He trailed off as he scanned through a PDF report.

"Before the raid on the Manassas field office, our guys ran some tests on parts of the book, concentrating specifically on what we also had discerned was blood—human blood. We took some samples, and, well, your military records threw up a match."

He handed the phone back to Brit, his mind still swirling with it all—that he had a blood connection with someone who had been fingered and tried as one of the Salem witches.

Which meant Sebastian had blood connection with the same witch.

"I know how this might feel," Brit went on, "but plenty of people have been found to have ancestral connections with the alleged Salem witches. American presidents have been related to Susannah Martin and John How, for instance, both tried and hanged. Same for Oliver Wendell Holmes, even Walt Disney and Lucille Ball."

Gapinski snorted a laugh. "Now that's ironic, given she testified before the twentieth century's greatest witch trial, the House Un-American Activities Committee on her ties to the Communist Party."

"Impressive. You know your history."

"Guys, can we get back to it?" Silas said.

He folded his arms and started pacing, his heart

hammering now and chest growing tight. Not only as he contemplated the depth of his family connection to the still-undefined conspiracy. But as the synapses of his brain began to piece together a distant childhood memory told to him and his brother growing up.

But what was it?

Silas spun around. "Who was the woman I was related to again?"

Brit check the PDF on her phone. "Mary Warren. But I'm not sure who that is."

"Warren...Warren...Mary Warr—"

And then memory began to surface.

His eyes widened. "I may have something."

He recalled the story his father had told him and Sebastian as teenagers, then recounted it for Brit and Gapinski:

"THREE HUNDRED YEARS AGO, *your great, great, great, great, great, great—"*

"Dad!" Silas moaned. "Give me a break. How many greats you gonna say?"

"Shut up and let him tell the story!" Sebastian said.

Silas huffed and rolled his eyes.

The boys and Dad had just finished riding around the island when they stopped near a small pool of water on the outskirts of town, setting their bikes in the grass and resting their backs against a fallen tree. They were dripping with sweat from the ride, and the mid-July temperatures didn't help. But it matter. They were together—father and sons, dad and brothers.

Dad took a breath and continued, "As I was saying...your great, great, great, great grandmother came to this here island."

"Really? Mackinac Island, three hundred years ago?" Silas marveled. "No way!"

Dad chuckled and nodded. "Yes, way! Right here on this island she came."

"But why?"

"He's getting to it!" Sebastian said.

Silas went to slug his brother when Dad intervened. "Boys, cut it, the both of you! Now, as I was saying. Her name was Mary Warren. And she was a witch!"

"A witch!" Silas marveled again.

"That's right. Or, well, was fingered as one. No one could be entirely certain on account she raised her hand to accuse others of being witches before she could be convicted of one herself. She herself was fingered, convulsing and muttering abominations. But she escaped the gallows by being the village's star witness against the accused."

"What village?"

There was a hesitation in his voice, and his eyes diverted out to the pool. But then he said it plainly: "Salem."

The boys looked at each other and shrugged.

"At any rate," Dad continued, "The woman, your great, great, great, great," he took a dramatic breath, "great, great, great, great," he took another as the boys giggled, "great, great grandmother Warren had the lowdown on all the other witches and wizards because she led a coven of them in a rite of darkness where they made a deal with the Devil himself."

"A deal with the Devil?" Silas asked.

"That's right. Even wrote their names in his book, handing over their souls."

"Scary," Sebastian said.

Dad nodded, then he went on, "Up and fled when the dust settled back on the East Coast, hitching a ride with French settlers on their way out west to the newly explored territories of the upper Ohio all the way to this here island. And the family's kept her secret all these years."

He leaned back and folded his arms, eyeing the pool again.

"Could have made a new life for herself, she could have, free from the Devil. But nope. Had to keep at it until the Devil tracked her down and she got back in the saddle. Because that's the thing, boys, the Devil will always catch up with you."

Dad sighed before adding, "Soon enough, great, great, great, great," he took the same dramatic breath, "great, great, great, great," he took another as the boys protested with loud 'Stop it!' complaints, "great, great grandmother Warren—oh alright, last time. But it sure is fun. Anyhow, soon enough, people got whiff of her dealings with the Devil and dunked her in that there pool of water until she admitted to being a witch."

The boys' eyes widened like saucers as they stared at the water.

"Never did get to it, because she drowned beforehand. They buried her in Saint Ann's Cemetery and stories have it that her ghost still roams the island, seeking others to sign her deal with the Devil."

Dad went silent, and so did the boys. The only sound to be heard were Lake Huron's waves slapping the shore and a pack of seagulls flying overhead.

Finally, Silas said, "Dad, why are you telling us this?"

Again, that hesitation and that averting eye. But then he turned around and looked them smack-dab in their faces: "Because the Devil runs strong in our family. And I need you to promise to do what Saint Paul instructed, with all of your might listen to the great apostle."

"And what's that, Dad?" Sebastian said, giving Silas a frightened eye.

Dad eyed Sebastian, then settled on him especially, placing both hands on his shoulders and saying: "'Be strong in the Lord and in the strength of his power, so that you may be able to stand against the wiles of the Devil,' as he says. 'Take up the whole armor of God, so that you may be able to withstand on that evil day, having done everything to stand firm.'"

. . .

Silas went silent, then added, "Dad reiterated how messed up our family tree was, that this deal with the Devil or whatever could bring chaos to our lives, given what that woman, Mary Warren, did. Never gave it much thought. But I guess Dad was right..."

Gapinski looked to Brit who shrugged. What was there to say to that?

He sighed and rubbed his face. "I always thought it was just a family tale Dad told to scare us crapless. Had no idea there was any truth to it."

"Remember those initials Celeste found," Brit said, "the ones on the underside of the cover to that book we recovered from Roland? MW. No small chance those belonged to Mary Warren, the woman who ran her mouth."

Silas nodded with exhaustion. At least they connected that dot.

"I wonder..." Gapinski said, staring off toward the tree line.

Silas turned to him. "Wonder what?"

"Well, remember when your bro mumbled something about water?"

"When was this?" Brit asked.

"Back at the SEPIO outpost, after his goons kicked the crap out of us. Said he was surprised Roland escaped because of the water."

Silas sat straighter. "That's right. Now that you mention it."

"You don't think the guy's holed up back on your family vacay spot, do you? Maybe chased after your great, great, great banshee of a grandmammy, no offense, but I—hey what are you doing?"

Silas stood and was running for their Mercedes, phone out and dialing Radcliffe.

Mackinac Island, here we come.

CHAPTER 26

MACKINAW CITY, MICHIGAN.

To say this day was a terrible, horrible, no good, very bad day was the winner of Understatement of the Century.

Not only had Celeste been kidnapped, on top of the continued supernatural and very natural mayhem radiating from Mackinac Island across lower Canada and the Midwest and now East Coast at the hands of seemingly possessed individuals. But every step they had taken to put a stop to it had ended in complete disaster before it had even gotten off the ground.

For starters, their Gulfstream had developed "mechanical problems," leaving them grounded without a set of wings. And the only other Order jet available was half-way across the Atlantic flying some no-name researcher to Rome.

And, of course, every flight to Detroit was booked up and down the East Coast. Even Grand Rapids on the westside of Michigan where Radcliffe and Father D'Amante were still stationed was out of the picture.

Their only bet was to drive to a small private firm out of Buffalo, New York, where the Order Master had arranged a tiny prop plane barely big enough for two, let alone two plus Gapinski. But they made the seven-hour drive in under six hours, lifting off the tarmac just before dinner.

That's when their drop of providence ran dry.

The plan was to fly onto the tiny airstrip anchoring the center of Mackinac Island then go from there, meeting up with Radcliffe and Father D'Amante on the island. But a heavy early evening fog had rolled through the area. One of those freak once in a generation type of deals. Mercifully, they made it to a regional airport within driving distance of docks back on the mainland in Mackinaw City. But still.

It was as if the Universe was conspiring against them.

Or perhaps it was the Devil himself.

Silas shivered at the thought, though with all he had seen he wouldn't put it past the forces of darkness in the interest of self-preservation and in perpetuating its vandalizing violence upon humanity.

Which they sure as heck were going to put a stop to, one way or another. He just hoped he was right about Mackinac being ground zero before it was too late.

Gapinski pulled into the parking lot of Star Line Ferry, blowing past a white welcome booth with a red roof that normally would have been attended. Silas was thankful they didn't have yet another barrier in their way; he was never fond of nosy gatekeepers who were always holding things up. But he feared their absence didn't bode well.

They parked in the back of a gravel lot adjacent to the ferry dock and quickly exited. There was no sign of Radcliffe and Father D'Amante. He texted them as they hustled across the gravel, searching for answers, but he knew the Order Master hated using his mobile beyond your run-of-the-mill phone call. He hoped they made it, because he sensed they might need the expertise with the Devil before the night was out.

People grouped in bunches, mostly older couples and a few middle-agers, all bundled up and armed with bags and luggage, were lumbering down from the long concrete dock that stood past a large ticket booth. Men and women in red parkas were hauling luggage carts piled high and wrapped in cellophane, helping people find their goods and load them for the drive home.

A whiff of nostalgia wafted through Silas as they hustled past the ticket booth on toward a white ship with a dark blue hull anchored at the end. He had always insisted on sitting up top with Dad and Sebastian. Loved feeling the *whoosh* of the wind and summer heat on his back and spray of Lake Huron on his face as he leaned over the sides. Sebastian complained, every time, but Dad indulged. After all, he was the oldest of the two by several seconds.

No summer heat or breeze that fall night, that's for sure. He was having serious doubts they'd make it to the island at the way the lake looked, all concealed and fogged over, and how dark and dead the Mackinac Express catamaran looked. No lights, no people, no nothing.

A bout of hearty laughter at the end of the dock near a blue boarding ramp that had been raised into evening retirement gave him hope.

But just a pinch.

"We need that boat!" Silas said in a rush, coming up fast to the two men he had heard.

"Do you now?" said a large man with a bushy salt-and-pepper beard, wearing brown waders and a brown Carhartt jacket. "Sorry, we're closed."

The man smirked and shook his head, then pushed past Silas.

But he planted a hand firmly on the man's shoulder. "Sir, I'm not sure you understand. We need to get to Mackinac, the three of us, and pronto. And we need you to take us there."

"Johnny, get a load of this guy," Carhartt Guy said to his companion, his face twisting with disbelief. "What part of, we're closed for the night, didn't you understand? Besides, do you see it out there, son?" The man waved an arm toward the fogged over lake. "It's as thick as pea soup out there!"

Gapinski snorted. "That's original…"

"And who are you?"

"Sir," Brit said, stepping forward to play interference, "forgive my friends, here. We mean you no trouble. It's just, we really need to get to that island."

"Take it up with management."

"I thought you were management."

"Look, lady, we ran the last ferry for the evening and I can't go carting three strangers in the dead of night across a foggy strait. We've got rules about these sorts of things!"

Silas closed his eyes and took a breath. Everything within him wanted to whip out his Beretta and train it on that cocky rule follower. But the side that still respected the rule of law won out.

Brit went to respond when Silas intervened.

He said, "Listen, I know you've got your rules. And being former Ranger I get that."

"Rangers, you say?" Carhartt Guy said, folding his arms and leaning back. "I was part of the 75th Infantry Regiment in Nam. Had a real hard-ass of a commander."

Silas laughed. "Yeah. I hear that. Had a commander like that myself who would've whooped my butt from Mosul to DC and back again if I did an end run around his playbook."

The man grunted knowingly, flashing a grin and reaching for his chin.

"But we need your help," Silas went on. "I'm pretty sure my kidnapped girlfriend is on that island. And a whole lot of bad is about to go down unless we get there in the next hour. With the way this fog has rolled in, you're our only hope."

The man rubbed the back of his neck. "I don't know…I don't

wanna get involved, especially not with no kidnappin'. Why don't you just contact the authorities?"

"Sir, we are the authorities," Brit said, whipping out her badge.

The man squinted at it, then recoiled with surprise. Glancing from Brit to Silas, he exclaimed, "FBI? Who's to say that thing is even real, anyhow?"

She put it back in her pocket. "Trust me, it's real. But to be clear, this isn't an FBI investigation, yet. Sort of a freelance gig right now."

Silas sighed and shook his head. Ever the rule follower herself. They needed to kick this into high gear, and fast.

Whipping out his wallet, he took out a wad of cash and fanned it in front of the captain. "Here is six-hundred-and-twenty-three dollars in cash for you and your man if you help us. It's all I have."

"Who the heck carries that much cash on them nowadays?" Gapinski mumbled.

Carhartt Guy glanced at his companion, who shrugged. "Hop in. But you need to get yourselves back. This is a one-way ticket, partner."

Silas scoffed, but relented.

"And I want to be paid upfront. Don't want no funny business."

He frowned, but handed over the wad of cash and told them to get to it.

The captain and his partner lowered the rusty blue boarding ramp and ushered their customers on board.

"You do know they make these things called credit cards, right?" Gapinski said to Silas as the trio slid into benches with slippery blue vinyl.

"Just be grateful I'd had the cash and they took the bait."

He nodded. "For Celeste's sake."

The mention of her name caused Silas's breath to seize in

his chest. Had stuffed the reality of it all deep down, not acknowledging the truth of the matter that his love had been kidnapped and was enduring God knew what.

A guttural gurgling sound erupted from the back of the ship, and it started easing from dock.

He glanced at his watch. Only a few hours until midnight. He prayed they were not too late.

A glimpse of two darting figures caught his attention. Two elderly men wearing black cassocks, hair unkempt and faces drawn with exhaustion.

Radcliffe and Father D'Amante!

"Stop the boat!" Silas yelled, clamoring out of the bench and back to the rear.

He pointed to the men running and persuaded Johnny to lower the boarding ramp for the two newcomers. Blessedly, he obliged.

"You made it!" Silas said, grasping Radcliffe in a bear hug and eyes threatening to erupt with emotion.

"Barely, by the look of it," Radcliffe said.

"Can we get to it now, Mr. Army Rangers?" the captain yelled from above.

Silas shouted his affirmative, and he ushered the two men inside the cabin. Soon, they were shoving off into the black void fogged over, praying to God they made it safely.

IT WAS A ROUGH, slow go of it crossing the strait. The ship was rocked back and forth by wicked whitecaps like it was nobody's business. Like a toddler having a go of tossing a plastic toy around in the tub during bath time. The fog added to their misery, a thick, menacing blanket that portended bad thing to come if it didn't lift.

The captain nearly turned back twice, but Silas threatened to reach into the man's backside himself and take back his money, which was surely more than they made in a week working for the ferry, maybe more, especially during the tourist drought season.

Half an hour later, they caught sight of the lighthouse planted on Round Island, a red and white boxy thing acting as a beacon for passing ships. In Silas's case, it was of hope. Not only because it meant they now had a fighting chance to rescue Celeste, but he was returning to a childhood haunt that had meant the world to him and his brother and Dad.

He took a breath at the memories flooding to the surface as the boat slowed toward the old Arnold Shipping dock Star Line had apparently purchased. Memories of stuffing themselves sick on fudge samples up and down Main Street; of riding three-seater tandem bikes around the eight-point-two miles of coast, nearly careening off into Lake Huron; of playing soldiers as boys up at the fort guarding the straits perched high upon the limestone bluff; of getting caught bike riding in a midsummer rainstorm deep inside the island, only to return to find a mighty disgusting racer stripe of horse crap running up their backs.

Those were the days—when life was simpler, when life was whole, when life was as it should be.

But the docking ship reminded him that life sometimes bites, sometimes relationships fray to the point of giving way, and sometimes it's time to hop on the horse and get to it without looking back on the past, casting those rose-colored glasses we're all prone to wear to the wind.

It was go time.

And Sebastian Grey was squarely in Silas's crosshairs.

The captain wished them luck as the now five-member team disembarked. Silas told them not to spend their new-found fortune in one place. The two men chuckled and said a few Buds had their names on them back on the mainland.

The SEPIO crew hustled across the long dock flanking a

shipping building with a sagging green roof covered in seagull droppings and shedding white paint like it had leprosy.

A cheer arose up ahead through a gaggle of bicycles tied down and locked with cables. During the spring and summer, every one of those two-wheelers would be rented out to tourists coming for the afternoon or needing a ride during their week's stay. After all, cars had been banned since 1898, with the only form of transportation being bikes and—

"Holybamoly, Batman! What's that smell!" Gapinski complained as they walked out onto Main Street.

Horses.

The man planted his hands on his hips and took a step into the road to take in the view straight out of the eighteenth century. When he did, he got the answer he definitely wasn't looking for, his foot sliding on a pile of—

"Crapola!" Gapinski held up his leg and mumbled a curse. Yep, there it was, a light brown patty smeared on the underside of his shoe. "You didn't tell me there were horses on this island resort of yours!"

"That explains the smell," Brit said, holding her nose and stifling a giggle. But one slipped.

"Ha, ha. Very funny…"

Then another. Before long, peals of laughter were roiling through the gang as they stood unaware amidst a throng of Halloween revelers all dressed up for the occasion—with costumes ranging the gamut from your traditional witch and Frankenstein to superheroes and gangsters, even Trump and that freshman politician A.O.C. from New York showed up to the party.

After managing to scrape his shoe moderately clean, Gapinski whipped his nose high up into the air and sniffed.

"Now what's *that* smell?" he asked.

"You mean that lovely sour, over-ripped aroma of hay and dead fish?" Radcliffe asked.

Silas chuckled. "He's talking about the other pile of brown stuff good ol' Mackinac is known for. Fudge."

Mentioning that five letter word was all the man needed to forget about his introduction to the island.

"Take me to your leader," Gapinski said.

"This way, killer."

The team headed right, walking under an overhang with a pink canopy and passing The Pancake House on toward their first stop: Ryba's Fudge Shop. Wasn't his favorite fudge on the island; that was Murdick's, triple chocolate espresso. But this one of four confectionaries that supplied the island with its other brown logs would do the trick.

He was right. They were nearly tossed out after Gapinski asked for a seventh sample, but he was satisfied after buying a slice of dark chocolate caramel sea salt for the road.

"Now where?" he asked, mouth full of the gooey goodness.

Silas shook his head. "Not sure, it's been like two decades since I've been here. Place hasn't changed much, but I need to get my bearings."

They continued walking past a three-story building straight out of history. Bundles of corn stalks hugged white posts propping up the overhang. Pumpkins sat at cherry double doors leading into what looked like a hotel and a restaurant, the Pink Pony. Across the street was Doud's Market, a white-washed building with brown trim and surprisingly still-full flower boxes where Silas and Sebastian would grab bottles of Coke before riding their bikes around the island as boys.

Speaking of which, bicycles lined the road leaning against posts or propped on kickstands, some with baskets (probably the locals), others were mountain bikes (probably the tourists). A dark wood-paneled carriage trotted by, the horses dressed in polished chrome rigging and a man in a top hat and suit riding up top, the words 'Grand Hotel' displayed on the side.

"I dare say, my boy," Radcliffe said, "this is quite the show of things here. Looks like a movie set straight out of the Revolutionary War! Which, as a thoroughly British gent, makes me a little nervous."

Silas laughed. "Well, it was a pivotal fortress for both the British and French, swapping hands through a few battles, one of which was the War of 1812."

"You don't say?"

He nodded as they walked past the Visitor's Center standing next to a harbor still filled with boats and across an expansive lawn nestled at the bottom of a bluff.

"Here," Silas went on, pointing toward the top of the limestone bluff shrouded in fog but still showing the island's crown jewel. "Hard to see tonight, but up there is the massive fortress that guarded the straits, keeping tabs on the fur trade and other affairs. Further down the street are more bed and breakfasts as well as a resort hotel."

"Looks like jolly good fun," Father D'Amante said, leaning to rest against a white fence.

Silas grabbed a map of the island out of a box sitting outside the center.

"Let's see here..." he said, unfolding it and getting his bearings.

A scream erupted followed by an explosion that sent a plum of dark smoke and orange flames high into the foggy night.

Down at the other end of town. Past the fort and on toward the stretch of houses Silas was just pointing out.

An orange and red glow quickly began growing through the fog, and more people were crying out in frightful surprise.

The four looked at one another with the exact same thought.

Nous.

Again.

CHAPTER 27

"Come on!" Silas yelled, motioning the other five toward the foggy void now pulsing orange and red.

Without waiting, he raced down the street past the marina and fortress, rounding past a slow-moving carriage and a gaggle of bicyclists who had stopped in confusion to observe the erupting chaos. The other two agents were close behind, but the two elders took it slow.

Within minutes, he left the harbor in his wake and came up to the leg of hotels and bed and breakfasts that anchored the island's east side, the full measure of the chaos still unclear but the dread of it all too familiar, having found himself in plenty of similar scenarios over the past year at the sudden eruption and interruption of Nous's menacing, violent designs.

The air felt clammy from the fog still rolling through the street. The wetness of it combined with a cool humidity and now smoky spice set every one of his nerves on edge.

People were grouped in bunches along the sidewalks and in the street now under the yellow glow of lamp posts, taking hesitant steps toward the orange and red blooms growing in size and intensity by the second. Cries for help from others further ahead echoed through the corridor of buildings, with a faint whine of sirens from the city now answering their distress.

Passing a yellow two-story bed and breakfast with a white picket fence and neighboring bike rental shop, Silas could tell several buildings were now set ablaze. His mouth went dry at the sight. When he rounded a tall hedgerow, his heart sank and bowels went weak at the realization of what sat at the heart of the inferno.

Saint Anne's Church, one of the original Catholic missions to the island.

Its roof was belching thick black smoke and livid arms of fire were reaching through the fog with menacing intent. Its central spire was already on the verge of collapse from the consuming inferno now overtaking the building. Others on either side and across the road had caught fire as well, threatening to take out the entire block.

A sudden burst of stained glass from the face of the church sent Silas crouching with hands over his head, but he recovered and pressed toward the building for a closer look.

That's when he saw the worst of it.

Leaning against the front deck just outside the church's green double doors was a massive cross, resting upside down and ablaze with a wickedness that made clear the night was doomed to devilish darkness.

Gapinski and Brit came up fast to his side, stopping and heaving desperate breaths then gasping at what Silas himself had seen.

"Nous, then?" Brit said.

"At this point, is there any doubt?" Gapinski asked. "I mean, an upside-down cross at the threshold of a church looking like Dante's Inferno pretty well puts a big, fat cherry on top of all the crazy."

Sirens were wailing from behind now, and rescue vehicles were fast approaching, the only vehicles allowed on the island.

"And it's all a ruse," Silas said, pacing with hands on his head on the sidewalk now, two massive fire trucks with lights ablaze having raced to a halt at the threshold of the inferno.

"What do you mean?" Gapinski asked.

Two firemen shoved the group back farther. The trio stopped at the stoop of a blue four-story building, the Harbor View B&B.

"Think about it," Silas said. "What better way to draw the attention of the entire island than to start a fire that threatened to take out half of Main Street."

"All while what's really going on is, well going on," Brit said. "At least we know they're here then. No way some other nut job burns an upside-down cross at a church on some random resort island the day after Halloween."

Silas nodded. "And we're gonna put the hurt on them something fierce. Come on!"

He stood and started hustling back toward the main city, resolve flooding his veins.

"But how?" Brit called out, hustling after him.

"We meet them at the only place a bunch of pagan witches would congregate the day after Halloween."

"And where is that?"

"The island cemetery!"

"Cemetery?" Gapinski gasped. "Always something..."

Seemed like they had passed the entire town on their way back to downtown. Along the way, they found Radcliffe and Father D'Amante shuffling along the sidewalk and filled them in on what was up ahead. Radcliffe agreed it had Nous written all over it.

They hustled back to the main city and soon reached the corner of Doud's Market. They hung a right, hiking up a hill that flanked the park at the base of the old fort with Silas in the lead.

"Where are we going?" Brit asked as they hung a left down a street that ran parallel to Main Street.

"To get us a ride," Silas said, hustling now without a thought about the others.

"Slow down, would ya," Gapinski complained. "I think I'm getting runner's stitch."

"Here we go…" he finally said, coming up to what looked like a white barn, its big red doors drawn shut, a single fluorescent bulb offering the only light inside beyond small grime-covered windows.

Silas pulled on the doors; they were uncooperative, merely shuddering with locked stubbornness.

"Cindy's Riding Stable?" Brit said.

He pounded on the doors and cupped his hands to look through the windows. Movement caught his attention far back; his heart leaped with hope.

"Riding stable?" Gapinski said. "As in horses?"

"Yeah, as in horses," Silas said, pounding louder.

"Oh, no siree Bob! Uh, uh. Ain't gonna do it."

Silas motioned for the figure to come to the door then pounded again.

He said, "How else do you think we're going to get to the center of the island in the dead of night?"

"I ain't getting my hinny up on no Clydesdale, that's for darn tootin'!"

Silas sighed with relief at the sound of the doors unlocking.

"Well, would you rather peddle your hinny on a Schwinn?" he asked as the doors slid open. "Because those are your two options."

Gapinski folded his arms and said nothing, mumbling a curse under his breath instead.

"What the heck is all this racket?" a squat man asked, wearing overalls stained brown and bearing a pitchfork he looked ready to put to good use. There was alcohol on his breath and in his eyes, and he swayed on unsteady legs.

"We need horses," Silas said in a rush. He turned to his companions. "Five of them, for all of us."

The man twisted up his face, jaw dropping to reveal a wad of chaw nestled under his lower lip. He popped his head out the door to crane outside and take in the pests who had interrupted his evening.

"Sorry, boy, but this here door was closed solid. Which means we're closed for the evening."

The man went to close the door when Silas shoved his hand against it, stopping it with a shudder and sending the man startling back on uncertain feet.

"What the—"

Silas shoved the door open with force and stepped inside the threshold, the back of his neck warming and his face flush with anger.

He felt himself growing out of control, and knew he needed to put a cork in the bottle of rage that was about to come bursting forth at the man. The window to act was quickly closing, and he needed those damn horses.

Lord Jesus Christ, Son of God, make me calm and make my path straight...

"Please, we need your help," he pleaded, his voice softening and face falling. "We need to get to the cemetery and haven't much time. My girlfriend is in danger. Lives are at stake. I know what we're asking, but here..."

He whipped out his wallet again, fishing for more cash.

The man startled but craned his neck for a peek, his eyes seeming to alight at the sight of money.

"Here's five hundred bucks. It's all I got left. A hundred a horse." Silas shoved the cash in the guy's hands. "We won't be long, and when we come back we'll give you more money.

Whatever you think is fair. Now, please, can we get five horses saddled?"

The man eyed the four men and woman. He took a breath and threw back his head, then said, "Five hundred a horse. All upfront. There's an ATM right down the road."

Silas grinned and thanked the man, then ran out to the bank they had just passed. Returning, he handed the man another two-thousand dollars, and thanked him again for his help. He nodded and got to work saddling the horses.

"You know what you're doing? Where you're going?" the man asked as the five mounted their steads.

"We'll manage," Silas said. He clucked and then kicked the underside of his horse, sending it trotting forward. The other four fell in line, Gapinski moaning and groaning with every step.

Soon they were trotting up a boulevard lined down the center with bright lights and festive harvest decorations toward the Grand Hotel, a resort that rivaled a cruise ship gleaming bright white in the gloomy night. The still-raging pandemonium was heard from down below, and the orange-and-red chaos was now bright and visible through the lifting fog.

Silas kicked his horse into higher gear and prayed they were not too late.

Prayed his love was alright.

That Celeste was still alive.

A HARD SLAP jolted Celeste from unconsciousness.

She gasped for air in a desperate panic as if she were drowning, her lungs heavy and searing with each breath. Her head swam with fog and throbbed with lancing pain across her jaw where she had been so rudely brought back to life. And curiously, her left thigh ached something fierce, as if someone had taken an ice pick to it with wild abandon.

Celeste heaved another heavy breath, taking in the musky scent of earth and dry leaves chased by the faint odor of death. A chilly breeze ran across her skin, carrying with it the faint traces of burning wood. She swallowed, her mouth dry and chalky and tasting like copper.

What the...? Where am I? What happened?

All she knew was, she was lying on her back, on a bed of something that was soft yet firm, chilled to the bone.

Then the truth of it slammed into her with revelatory force, sending her heart bolting forward and bowels running watery.

The movie theater massacre and the possessed psychopath; the devilish experience and Nous's raid on the FBI field office; the discoveries at the monastery and second raid by Nous; Salem and the nineteen witches; the car chase and the Beamer missing it's bloomin' face.

The gunshot to the leg, the helicopter, the needle to the neck...

Hence, the ice-pick pain, heavy lungs, and foggy head.

She chanced opening her eyes for a look, but all she saw was a low-lying fog and a few naked branches waving at her from above. Her arms were at her side, blessedly unbound. She squeezed her hands closed, grasping fistfuls of wet leaves and damp earth.

Faint flickering yellow and orange light drew her attention off to the right. Craning her head, she first saw she was wearing a white dress, thin and silky. Then she saw her dressed leg, a round stain of crimson at the center. Then rows of mismatched headstones, tilting and pockmarked with age. Then the torches bearing the flickering light casting wicked shadows across the cemetery.

She eased her body off the ground. "What the bloody—"

"Well, well, well," a voice sounded from behind, "look who decided to rejoin the land of the living."

He came into view, robed in heavy black vestments with red piping along the sleeves and chest.

She gasped and scurried backward on uncertain hands when she saw the rest of him.

The man was masked, the head of a goat fitted around his head with long, devilish horns reaching out.

He chuckled, a low, gurgling laugh that echoed and amplified through the goat's open mouth.

"My, my, my," the man cooed, sounding familiar. "I had no idea Celeste Bourne was such a scaredy-cat!"

He stepped forward; Celeste scurried back further until her head thudded painfully against a tombstone.

Another laugh, and that dreadful goat's head now peering down toward her.

"Here," he said, "maybe this will help."

He reached up to the ghastly mask and wiggled it free from his head, resting it at his side.

Rudolf Borg.

Celeste narrowed her eyes and started forward when a pair of strong arms grabbed her from behind.

"You little bugger..." she said, grunting and struggling with everything she had. Which wasn't much, given the large dosage of tranquilizer she had been given.

She finally collapsed into the man's arms, who turned out to be another familiar face.

Sebastian Grey.

"Hello, dear," he cooed, robed in red with what appeared to be a white clerical collar ringing his neck.

She heaved desperate breaths, her mind swimming with the turn and possibilities of it all.

"What is the meaning of this?" she said breathlessly, swallowing hard and reaching for her leg now welling with pain.

The sound of clomping hooves intercepted a reply.

"Ahh, right on schedule," Borg said, returning the mask to his head and snapping his fingers at Sebastian.

"Soon enough, dear," Sebastian said, throwing her on her stomach and wrenching an arm behind. "Soon enough..."

She screamed and struggled, but it was no use. Sebastian had a strength about him she wouldn't have pegged, and now he had both arms secured behind her and wrists slipping inside rope.

"Please, I beg of you..." she pleaded, her lungs burning from exhaustion and eyes welling with fright. "Please..."

Sebastian giggled, finishing his work binding her arms and then her feet together. He spun her on her back then crouched beside her, picking her up by both arms.

The clomping halted several yards away and a pair of horses gave neighing approval. She turned her head to find two carriages of passengers disembarking, all robed and hooded in black, bearing torches and shuffling toward an iron gate that stood open.

And that's when she saw the extended picture of it. The sight seized her like a pair of cattle prods, jolting her mind into a terrifying flight back to that frightful Halloween back in Britain when she felt the full measure her dabbling with the Devil, taking part in a rite of darkness no human should dare partake.

A structure looking like a marble mausoleum, with a high back and pillars supporting a sloped roof, stood tall and imposing over the vast tract of land serving as the site of last repose for the island. At the center was a stone altar, not high and table-like, but low and more like a circular platform.

And there it was, anchored to the back and on the platform: the pentacle. A talisman used in black magic to invoke and conjure the spirits of darkness and the sigil of Baphomet adopted by Satanists.

The Horned King, the Prince of Beasts, the Lord of Demons. Satan himself.

Sebastian adjusted his hold on Celeste, clenching her bound body closer to his chest. "We have such special plans for you, my dear."

In the near distance, a drum started thrumming a low, steady beat.

Dum-ditty-dum.

Dum-ditty-dum.

The newly arrived guests, their torches ablaze and held aloft, filed toward the ungodly structure.

Celeste could see that each of their necks were ringed by curious white necklaces set starkly against their black robes.

Looking like the one that had ringed Roland's neck.

Were these men and women blood relatives of Salem witches? Bearing the bones of their ancestors to unleash the fires of hell in an unholy rite of darkness?

Celeste strained under Sebastian's grip as panic flooded her.

He giggled and held firm. "Now, now..."

Borg strode forward to meet them, his face shrouded in that dreadful goat mask.

"Did you know," Sebastian said, shuffling forward to follow, "that Mackinac Island is one, vast cemetery? 'Tis true. The aboriginal people used the island as burial grounds, and then hundreds of European colonialists died here as well, during the course of life and in brutal combat. Making these grounds sacred, holy even, for our decidedly unholy purposes."

"What are you playing at?" Celeste said as they arrived at the structure, her body convulsing under the weight of the adrenaline-fueled moment and from the chill of the night.

Sebastian giggled then set her squarely at the center of the platform, her body draped over the pentacle and feeling it almost burn through her with evil intent.

The drumming was picking up pace now, and Borg the Goat Man reappeared, sending a recoiling shudder through Celeste.

"What are we playing at, you ask?" Borg said. "Why, the unleashing of the power of consciousness, Celeste Bourne. With you at the center of it all."

Then he slipped torn cloth around her mouth and tied it into a gag before all hell broke loose.

CHAPTER 28

A wicked wind whipped through the tunnel of trees pressing in against a narrow paved road. An even more wicked fog hid ill intent within the huddled masses of threatening specters lining the road, their naked limbs and imposing trunks mocking the five riders and making it that much darker, that much more menacing for them as they trotted into the unknown.

Silas hoped to God they were heading in the right direction. Because truth be told, he had no clue.

He had been to the island cemetery and Saint Ann's Cemetery a few times as a teenager with Sebastian getting into trouble during the summer at dusk and scaring the crap out of him with ghost stories. But it wasn't pitch black and doused in fog, and it had been over two decades ago. So the odds he could still lead them blindly—literally, given that blasted land cloud—was next to nil.

Couldn't tell the gang that though. Especially the moose still bleating about his backside aching and the island stinking to high heaven. But it had to be out there, somewhere. And it was on him to lead them there.

For Celeste's sake as much as the Church's and the world's...

Silas stood in his saddle, head craning this way and that trying to make sense of their direction, white LED light from their mobile phones shimmering off the miasma of fog that refused to lift and was confusing the heck out of him.

Come on, Lord, throw us a bone here!

After leaving Cindy's Stable Silas had taken the lead, pushing the horses to move faster as they huffed their way to the top of a steep incline climbing past the Grand Hotel that would give most bikers a coronary. Coming up to a four-way junction, he hemmed and hawed which way to go, but then he had remembered taking a hard right as a kid to head to the cemetery. His iPhone map program was zero help, showing bupkis, and he had lost the paper map from the visitor's center in the chaos back in town.

So now they were clomping through the dead of foggy darkness and struggling forward without adequate light.

"Hold it higher, Brit, would you?" Silas complained, directing the agent holding her mobile device as a flashlight.

"Is this better, my liege?"

He frowned. Not really. Even with three mobiles they were struggling to cut through the fog that was, yes, as thick as pea soup. Boy, did the Department of Perpetual Clichés get that one right.

"This was a bad idea," Gapinski complained. "What was that?"

He yelped and nearly jumped out of his saddle as something scampered across the road.

"Thumper, Dumbo," Silas said.

"Now, Silas," Radcliffe said, "let's not let the moment carry us away into disrespect."

"Sorry," he mumbled over his shoulder to Gapinski.

Clompety-clomp, compety-clomp, down the road they went, the sands of time slipping through Silas's hands with each step.

And possibly Celeste's very life.

A hedgerow suddenly spread from the right, and it looked like a two-story building sat on the other side, a trail of smoke rising from a chimney. A house, perhaps.

Come on...where the—

His breath seized in his chest at the sight. The trees parted, the fog was lifting some, and the ground opened up into a grassy lawn, with a street lamp confirming what his gut had realized with dread.

They were not even close to where they should be!

"Is that the fort we saw up top the bluff?" Brit asked.

"Yes, it is," he growled. But at least he knew where they were now, and the good Lord above seemed to be finally answering their prayers.

A breeze, rising high and offering a helping hand, began lifting the fog that had bedeviled them the past few hours. He even thought he could glimpse the full harvest moon riding high on a clear, cloudless sky beyond the menacing miasma.

Silas whistled and clucked his tongue at his stead, then he shouted, "Come on! Git!"

He kicked his horse hard in the ribs. It neighed in protest but obliged, sending them bolting down the stretch to a road he knew was lying past a sizable white building that had served as barracks just past the fort.

A road that would take them straight to Celeste.

THE *DUM-DITTY-DUM-DITTY* of the drums rose into a thumping frenzy, echoing across the island's Elysian Fields and setting the pagan mood for the last remaining hours of All Saints' Day.

Celeste couldn't help but chuckle at the irony through her gagged mouth, since the Christian holiday was a commemoration of the faithfully departed who had entrusted themselves to Christ's care—trusting in his finished work on the cross for rescue from death and the gift of eternal life. A decidedly anti-pagan day, if there ever was one. Appropriately, however, they were observing it in a cemetery. So at least they had that going for them.

But for what pagan, satanic purpose, Celeste could only imagine.

And imagine she did, her own soul feeling frightfully on the brink of bursting under the weight of the sights and sounds swirling around her with witchcrafty memory.

It wasn't only the pentacle that stood behind and below her that set her on edge, or even Borg and his goat mask.

It was the darkly hooded figures lurching back and forth in an ecstatic dance, responding to the continued *dum-ditty-dum-ditty* that was growing in intensity with a religious fervor rivaling more charismatic sects of the Church, their torches waving around in the air like animistic spirits waiting to be unleashed on the night.

It was the censer that a woman in a flowing white robe was waving with rhythmic deliberation around the cemetery, its incense flooding the ground in a miasma of spicy frankincense where the fog had once settled in thick ribbons but was thinning and lifting, a full-harvest moon now peeking high above.

It was the bones ringing those figures' necks. Presumably, the men and women from Salem, convicted of witches, of summoning the spiritual forces of darkness in a rite she feared was being recapitulated that very night.

It was the burnished bronze basin holding some curious pile of white, and a chalice bearing who knew what that sat behind her on a stone table.

All of it was a horrifying collection of highly ritualistic elements that was driving Celeste's soul to the very brink. A rite she feared was poised to summon the darkness she had fought against a day ago.

A darkness she had been fighting the past two decades...

Dum-ditty-dum-ditty the drums continued with rhythmic invitation, the robed figures continuing their ecstatic frenzy.

Dum-ditty-dum-ditty they bellowed, growing louder and faster and more intense, as if issuing a siren cipher call to the Devil himself and his army to rise and rend the world in two, wreaking a ratcheted unholy terror upon a world already under wicked assault since the near-dawn of human existence.

Then all at once it stopped.

No more *dum-ditty-dum-ditty* drumming; no more frenzied dance; no more waving of the censer. All that stood in its place was an eerie silence punctuated by whispering leaves and flapping flames on a breezy, frigid fall breath.

Celeste held her own breath and nearly held her heart's beat—waiting, intuiting, discerning what came next.

Then all at once, the man with the goat head appeared through a parting of the incense and fog, his black robe, edged with crimson swishing with every step, eyes blazing with a demonic fire through the hollowed-out orbs of the dead pagan symbol that set all of Celeste's hairs on end and sent her very soul into a panic.

Following him was Sebastian, dressed in his faux priest garments and wearing a wicked smile that played across his face with ill intent, bleached-white teeth gleaming in the torchlight. He looked vampiric, eyes possessed with thirst as the man took her in, consuming her with his gaze.

Behind him was the woman she had glimpsed casting incense around the ceremonial grounds, playing the part of priestess for this pagan rite of darkness. And then it hit her: the woman Helen from last year, Sebastian's lover whom SEPIO had apprehended in Germany.

There it was, the unholy trinity of Nous: Borg, Sebastian, Helen.

The other figures, robed in black and hooded, formed a semi-circle around the altar area, casting illumination and ungodly, angular shadows from their torches around the cemetery.

Borg strode behind her, flanked by Sebastian and Helen. He rang a bell, signaling the beginning of a ceremony she knew deep in her bones would end in her death.

A FAINT ORANGE light up ahead and the thrumming beat of drums echoing through the darkened forest set Silas's heart jolting forward with fight-or-flight anticipation.

Motion across the road far away but too close for comfort immediately set his brain into Ranger mode with kill-or-be-killed activation.

He cut his phone light and pulled up hard on his reins, hissing a command for Gapinski and Brit to do the same.

Between his horse letting out an irritating whine and the clomping of hooves from the other horses, plus their mobiles' white lights shining like lighthouse spotlights, Silas was petrified the two hostiles on their twelve were sure to have spotted them.

He motioned with his fingers to his eyes and then down the road, the sky opening up now to let in enough of the moonlight above to offer enough visibility.

Gapinski and Brit nodded; Father D'Amante threw a worried look at Radcliffe, who shrugged and danced his horse back a few paces.

Silas dismounted and drew his horse to a large oak inside the woods. Gapinski and Brit did the same, while Silas explained the situation to the two elders.

"We've got two hostiles up ahead. Best if you two stay here."

"You think they've got the place surrounded?" Gapinski asked, weapon already in hand.

Silas nodded. "I'd wager they've got the place pretty well secure. I think I recall another two or three access roads that feed into the two cemeteries. That's at least another six hostiles. Plus, you have to figure another mess of them keeping post around whatever the heck is going on in the property itself, and, well..."

He withdrew his Beretta and chambered a round.

"And those aren't very good odds for the three of us," Brit said, finishing his thought and readying her own weapon.

Gapinski scoffed. "We've had way worse and lived to tell about it."

"Yeah, but a cat only gets nine lives. How many you figure you got left?"

He scrunched up his brow and tilted his head with concentration.

"On second thought, don't answer that."

"You both stay here, on your horses," Silas instructed Radcliffe and Father D'Amante. "After we neutralize the threats down the road, we're going in the rest of the way for Celeste. We don't want you two caught in the crossfire."

Radcliffe acknowledged the plan and told them to be careful.

Under the cover of darkness with barely enough moonlight seeping through the still-rising fog, the three padded forward, drawing up close inside the forest just off the road to confirm what Silas had glimpsed.

Two hostiles, clad in black. And both bearing rifles that would do some serious damage. Not to mention make some serious noise, which would defeat the whole purpose for coming to the rescue on silent feet.

"What's the plan, chief," Gapinski whispered.

Silas sat on his haunches watching the men wander back and forth, crossing paths, then returning to the other side of the road.

Didn't seem all too concerned about concealing themselves, that's for sure.

Then again, with the entire island's attention a mile back in town, they didn't have to.

Silas pointed ahead. "See the way they're walking, back and forth before pivoting and crossing back again. I'd say we give them a bit of a howdy-do from behind."

He explained the plan. Gapinski and Brit nodded their understanding.

Now time to execute.

"With the chaos they brewed down below," Silas said lowly, "I don't expect anyone else to come riding in to save our butts anytime soon. So we've got one shot with this. Any audible response from those two and we're blown, and we're in deep doo-doo."

"That's my worry…" Brit said.

"Not to worry, ma'am," Gapinski said. "We've gotten ourselves out of worse sticky wickets."

"The fact you've gotten yourselves into what sounds like several of them is what troubles me. You sure about this, Sy?"

No, he wasn't. Not really. But what choice did he have? Celeste's life was on the line.

And it was him who was left to lead the charge to save her.

Offering no reply, he motioned for the two to fan out to their spots.

He took his spot in the center of the road, crouching low and padding forward on taut legs ready to respond if need be.

The men had just crossed the center of the road and were heading back to the edges of the road.

His heart was strumming a mean beat now and lungs were keeping pace. His head joined the fun with dizzying fight-or-flight adrenaline.

Steady, Grey…

Each man reached the edge, then spun back toward the center.

He padded forward, continuing to crouch in the shadows and quickly thinning fog, now a few yards away from—

One of the men stopped, pivoting toward him and raising his weapon.

Silas froze. So did the man. The other one slowed his pace and now turned toward his position as well.

Then it happened.

In one motion, Brit and Gapinski came out from the shadows and wrapped their arms around each of the hostiles' necks.

A gagging struggle faintly echoed through the trees.

But importantly, no weapon fire.

Yet.

Silas sprang from his crouch and rushed forward to help, wrenching a menacing snub-nosed assault rifle from Brit's guy. Heckler & Koch by the looks of it. Which was definitely Nous's weapon of choice.

She was the first to put her man down. The hostile slumped like a bathrobe in her arms and she twisted his neck for good measure.

Silas winced, wondering if breaking a man's neck was in the FBI playbook. But whatever. It had done the job.

Gapinski was having a rougher go of it, struggling with a beast-of-a-man who was matching the SEPIO agent. Silas rushed to his aid, wrenching his rifle before he could fire either a deadly shot or warning shot.

Gapinski finally finished his job as Brit came out from the shadows after dragging her man into the forest. Gapinski followed suit, but without the neck-breaking maneuver at the end.

Part of him wanted the man to follow Brit's lead, but Silas was just happy the first round went for SEPIO.

Silas breathed a sigh of relief then rushed to Radcliffe to hand him his Beretta, just in case. Then he quickly scooped up the dead Nousati's Heckler & Koch and followed the two back into the forest under the cover of darkness.

Two down, who knew how many more to go.

The only thing he knew for certain was that they had better kick it into high gear, because the crazy talk bellowing from somewhere inside the cemetery told him a menace far more malevolent than two rentable mercenaries was about to rise.

With Celeste squarely in its crosshairs.

CHAPTER 29

"In nomine *Ha-Satanas*, domino Universi," Borg bellowed through the face of the goat sacrificed for just such an occasion, his voice rising with unrighteous passion and echoing throughout the vast swath of last repose.

In the name of Satan, Lord of the Universe, indeed.

He had dreamt of this moment for years, decades even. Ever since that first taste of the nascent power in the Universe suppressed by the Church, and then the power that struggled to break free in the company of that blasted exorcist as a child.

Little did Mommy and Daddy know that the exorcist they had summoned to their small German town had failed, and so had the Christian orphanage after that to quell the rising tide of darkness that was on the brink of finding completion. Boy, would they be horrified to discover what their sweet little angel had become.

A giggle slipped through Borg's lips, echoing back to him within the head of that goat, the head of Baphomet himself, Lord *Ha-Satan*.

A straining squeal refocused his attention to the moment, drawing his gaze down below at his feet.

That woman, Celeste Bourne, the one whom his precious

Sebastian had captured and whom the cosmic powers of this present darkness had confirmed for him had opened a door to the Angel of Light. He wondered how a high-ranking agent of the Church's defensive arm could bear such a scar from the Ruler of the Power of the Air, the spirit at work among those who are fully enlightened to the full spectrum of human consciousness.

As the woman continued with her useless struggle, her taut muscles bulging with quaint might and twisting against her bindings, a desire began to well within him for what she had tasted. A lustful anticipation began to climax within his belly for what he himself would experience in due time.

Yes, my dear, struggle. Expend yourself trying to break free from the confines of what the Authority has done to you. For I have observed the misery of people, I have heard their cry and know their suffering under the weight of the Authority's consciousness-denying burden. And I have come to set them free.

Soon, she shall find such freedom...

Borg raised his head then lifted his arms. "Brethren! Let us celebrate our consciousness, fully leaning into the enlightened choice presented to all mankind by *Ha-Satan* himself, acknowledging that the flesh prevails and reason will triumph over slavish devotion to the Authority. Intimately knowing good and evil is within our grasp—becoming a god unto ourselves!"

The assembled arrayed in front of him, his congregation, chosen for their ancestral affinity to the bones now wrapped around their necks, raised their arms as one.

"I proclaim to *Ha-Satan*," he continued, "and to the assembled, that I have sinned in ever increasing measure through my thoughts, words, and deeds—by what I have thought in my mind and have done in my flesh."

'We agree,' the assembled intoned.

"Yet I am neither shameful nor repentant. *Never!* For to repent is human, to assert our consciousness is divine!"

'We agree!' they shouted.

"May *Ha-Satan* guide us into full humanity," Borg boomed, his eyes closed and arms outstretched. "May he bless us as we partake of the bountiful pleasures bestowed by the Universe in all of their wondrous glory and open to our imbibing in full conscious awareness!"

As one, the congregants chanted: *'Ha-Satanas nobiscum!'*

Satan is with us, indeed.

"Glory to the Lord of the Universe," Borg went on, "the Angel of Light, the powerful *Ha-Satan*, the One who brings enlightenment, life and freedom, the fullness of consciousness to humankind. We bow in reverence, we give thee worth, and we give thee glory, for thou art the fullness of true Light and true Darkness, the Master of Consciousness who guides us upon the true path of enlightenment, while the religious fools of our enemy flail blindly and babble in their ignorance, following the man from Nazareth who died with pity."

'Veni, exaltatum Ha-Satanas!' the group shouted as one.

O come, exalted Satan!

Borg lowered his arms, ready to offer the invitation. "Let us pray to the one who has delivered us out of ignorance and into the marvelous light of consciousness, inviting the Angel of Light to open the eyes of our full humanity."

He closed his eyes, breathed in deeply, then cleared his throat and began reciting the prayer, the others joining in with echoing memory:

Our Father who art from the depths of enlighten-
ment, glorious be Thy Name,
Thy Republic of Heaven be here, thy truth to bear
On Earth, far-removed from the Kingdom of
Heaven.
Return to us our consciousness, and tempt us with
the fullness of pleasurable humanity.

For ours is the Republic of Heaven, the power, and
the glory, forever and ever!
Ave Ha-Satanas*!*

Hail, Satan, indeed.

Borg went to continue when a rumbling began to course through the cemetery. Something deep within the belly of the earth itself began to well up within, grasping for the surface.

But not just within the earth.

Within Borg as well.

He began to tremble in mighty waves, vibrating with intensity from head to toe. He bent low and brought his arms inside, every limb twisting in at wicked angles. His fingers curled in on his palms with rigidity. His skin was beet red, as if burning a high-grade fever before bubbling into white welts of second-degree burns.

A sudden scream pierced through the night air, shooting up from his belly and out into the night. He threw back his head and arched his back, his face contorting and jaw rending itself this way and that.

And then it came.

The Voice.

Strong and lowly, sure and proud.

"Behold!" the Voice growled with intensity. *"I hath manifested amongst my children to bear witness to thy ignorance. I have come to revel in thy outrages against the Authority, and to hear your pleas for enlightened consciousness this night. Let them be declared in my name and laid at my feet."*

The demonic incarnation scoped the men and women before him, who were erect and all at once trembling in his presence. He licked his lips and flicked his tongue at them with desire.

"May the heavens tremble at thy imprecations!"

The gathered erupted with cheers, and a large gold cauldron was lit on fire by Helen.

Thus beginning the rite of darkness that would usher in the Age of Consciousness.

SILAS SNAPPED his head toward a sector of the cemetery ahead now glowing orange and erupting with cheers, having just put down another Nousati on the backside of Saint Ann's Cemetery.

His mouth went instantly dry, and a fearful tremble began walking up his spine until it burst into a dizzying dread of lancing pain between his eyes.

The Voice.

"Did you hear that?" Brit said, coming up to his side after finishing off her own Nousati with panting breaths.

Silas turned to her and nodded, saying nothing and rushing to Gapinski who was still bent over a man he had put down.

"You alright?" he asked.

"The dude bit me!" Gapinski growled, holding up a hand shimmering black down one side. "Tore a cotton pickin' piece of my flesh right out of my hand, the little—"

"You going to live to tell about it?"

Gapinski stood. "I'm fine."

"Good, because we've got trouble."

"Yeah, I heard. Celeste?"

Silas took a stabling breath and shook his head. "Dunno. But we need to move it. ASAP."

Brit let slip an empty clip from her weapon to the ground. "Alright, where to next? I haven't seen this much action since those armed militant psychos took over the Malheur National Wildlife Refuge in Oregon."

"You were there for that?"

She slid in a fresh clip and nodded. "I wasn't just there. I helped coordinate the interagency response."

"Impressive. But don't get too comfy. The battle is far from over and it sounds like it's heating up."

Gapinski snorted a laugh. "Yeah, literally, if the Big Guy Downstairs is making an appearance."

Silas nodded, then padded forward up Fort Road, hugging a waist-high stone barrier that ran alongside it. The fog was lifted now, and he could see the stone archway entrance to Saint Anne's Cemetery ahead, its wrought iron gate standing open.

The trio slowed, crouching lower and padding with careful deliberation as they came to the intersection of another road. Across the way, a gate between stone pillars to the main island cemetery entrance stood open as well.

They crouched low and glanced up and down the road—waiting, intuiting, discerning under a faint cover of moonlight.

Not one person around.

Too good to be true, but they had already taken out two contingents of Nousati agents. Perhaps that was all they brought along to this shindig.

Silas chanced breathing a sigh of relief and letting his weapon lower.

Until he saw movement farther down the road. Near another intersection along the cemetery's north front that bent toward the orange glow and frenzied eruption of cheers and drums.

He pointed up the road and his companions acknowledged with nodded agreement.

Looked like one last hurrah before the final showdown. Probably with that dreadful Rudolf Borg, who seemed virtually indestructible, having survived past missions like the T-1000.

Definitely with his brother, who seemed to be commanding this devilish plan from the start—whatever it was.

And hopefully—dear Lord, please, hopefully!—to recover the love of his life.

THIS CANNOT BE BLOOMIN' happening...

Celeste strained against her bindings again and struggled for breath through her gag, but it was no use. She was stuck, tied down and prone beneath the incarnation of the Devil himself, and her mouth muzzled.

Her chest felt as if it would explode; her heart was thumping with intensity. Her head was filled with an equally thumping, throbbing pressure, and a heaviness fell over her—as if the weight of the Universe had descended upon her body, holding her and suffocating her with menacing intent.

She closed her eyes and took in a deep breath, then prayed the prayer Jesus Christ himself had taught his people to pray with silent, frenzied petition:

'Our Father in heaven, hallowed be your name. Your kingdom come. Your will be done, on Earth as it is in Heaven. Give us this day our daily bread. And forgive us our sins, as we also forgive those who have sinned against us. And lead us not into temptation and trial, but rescue us from—'

"Witless are the those who deign to submit to the Authority," the Voice thundered through Borg with unholy interruption.

'—the Evil One...'

"Blinded are those who know not the gift given by Ha-Satan. *Two thousand years ago, I offered this gift to the man who would be King of kings and Lord of lords."*

A cold dread flooded Celeste's veins, jolting her heart with a caustic pop and weakening her bowels with watery worry.

The Voice sounded like the one she had vaguely recalled coming from the lad at that fateful Halloween night two decades ago. Low and guttural, masked by an otherworldly garble that smacked of supernatural manifestation.

She was undone. She was done for.

"I deigned to visit with the man from Nazareth, offering him sustenance when he was empty; promising safety when he was imperiled; gifting him all the kingdoms of the world and their splendor when he was but a powerless twat, demanding only that he bend the knee and offer me my due worth."

A tremble ran the length of the altar beneath, as if the very ground were about to erupt with emotion. Instead, it was the man standing over her who erupted.

"And he said 'Noooo'!!" Borg exclaimed, his voice echoing with an amplified, raging disgust. *"Where the First Adam saw that the tree was good for food, and that it was delightful to the eyes, and that it would make one wise, fully opening up the soul to enlightened consciousness, and then partook and ate—this Second Adam, as he was declared by his followers, turned it down."*

The arrayed congregation erupted in laughter, a frenzied giggling that ricocheted across the cemetery lawn and grew a head of otherworldly steam until the trees themselves seemed to be dripping with condescension.

Then Borg roared: *"Quiet!"* And immediately it all ceased. Then he himself began to laugh, erupting in guffawing peals that made Celeste want to scream.

"But I had the last laugh," the Voice said. *"For I entered the man Judas who paved the way for the man from Nazareth's death."*

"Don't you mean Jesus Christ?" Celeste strained through the cloth at his feet.

A screeching like that of a strangled turkey erupted from Borg, and he recoiled as if suddenly being hosed down with boiling water.

"SILENCE!!!" the Voice roared with the trembling intensity of a grizzly—a hot, heavy wind smelling of rot and soured meat erupting from the man's mouth and slapping Celeste in the face before a hand came down and actually did the job.

She cried out from the blow. Her jaw grew numb from the force and she felt faint.

"He-who-shall-not-be-named is never to be mentioned in my PRESENCE!!! He is the man from Nazareth. Nothing more. For he was nothing more than an upstart prophet, put down like a worthless dog."

In that moment, Celeste learned the truth of it: It truly was Satan incarnate standing above her. A power that trembled and recoiled at the name of Christ.

Borg was huffing and puffing and pacing now, back and forth behind the altar, that hot, heavy breath of rot trailing him.

"Perhaps we should prepare the Host, my liege," another voice sounded. It was Sebastian.

My liege? So then he has given himself over like Borg. And Host? What's he playing at?

The pacing stopped. So did the huffing, hot breaths. Then Borg snorted, and the Voice returned.

"Yes, the Host. Prepare the host!!!"

The ground shook, the altar itself quaked so that Celeste thought it would rend in two.

Sebastian walked behind Celeste to the stone table where the burnished bronze basin and gold chalice were kept. He took the basin and walked out in front to present it to the gathered congregants, a few wafers falling to the ground beside her.

Her breath seized in her chest at the sight.

No...

They were thin, round crackers. Flat and unleavened. Like Communion wafers, the sort meant to serve as memory-markers for the Body of Christ, *'my body that is for you,'* as Jesus Christ himself had declared at the Last Supper before his death.

The Host...

Which meant the gold chalice bore crimson liquid, an

unholy desecration of the memory-marker of *'the new covenant in my blood,'* as Jesus had equally declared.

Oh, Silas, where are you?

"O *Ha-Satan*, great and glorious Angel of Light," Sebastian bellowed. "Behold our offering! Give us thy favor, O Glorious One, and may the words on our lips and the tune of our heart be a sweet-smelling savor sacrifice in Thy sight this night!"

A growl erupted from behind. Borg, and the incarnation of Satan within. A growl of desire, not of satisfaction.

"Brethren!" Sebastian went on, his arms bearing the basin now raised yet wavering, the firelight glinting off from its burnished bronze surface with a tremor. "Consciousness prevails and enlightenment runs through us untainted. Blessed is the One who has gone before us, bearing us and nourishing us by the possession of his own consciousness. And accursed are the sacraments that would demand our subjugation to the Authority in all his weakness and slaughter. We reject the so-called Christ and the vessels of his memory!"

'Ave Ha-Satanas!' the gathered roared with frenzied affirmation, surely now possessed.

"I present to you the consecrated Host left over from that burned down island temple to the man from Nazareth!" Sebastian boomed.

He held the basin aloft in front of the gathered, and each of them took turns plucking a wafer until they had all grasped a piece of the Host, including Sebastian himself.

"I deny the body of Christ!" he said. "May it burn in all of its broken promises!"

He threw the wafer into the fire, its hellish flames blackening and consuming it whole.

Each of the other hood figures followed suit, and then Sebastian tipped the leftovers into the fire as well.

The flames rose high with unholy hunger for the memory-marker of Christ's Body, giving off an acrid smell of burnt bread that made Celeste want to retch.

Sebastian tossed the basin to the floor; it thudded and rolled to a stop against a headstone. He walked behind Celeste and snatched the gold chalice from the table, then strode back out front and presented it to the gathered.

"'*The life of the flesh is in the blood*' the retched Scriptures declare, and so is the life. Our ancestors have known this from the start. Which is why they signed themselves over to the Ruler, the Angel of Light with their blood. Now we will form a new pact with him, using the blood of a sacrificial lamb, so to speak, to release the sins of the world back to their rightful place!"

He turned toward Celeste, a Cheshire-cat grin splayed across that pale face of his. "And now, the sacrificial lamb," he boomed, "the one who will bleed for all the ignorant fools who have chained themselves to the Authority!"

A crack of gunfire sounded, echoing with surprising intensity through the cemetery.

Every head twisted toward the road below.

There it was again: *Pop-pop-pop.*

And then a smattering of *rat-a-tat-tat* echoes that recalled what they had encountered in Salem.

Celeste's chest seized with hope, but a fear gripped her as well.

For SEPIO, for Silas.

She prayed fervent prayers of protection and deliverance as the weapon fire intensified.

CHAPTER 30

L*ord Jesus Christ, Son of God, we better make it out of this alive!*

The last time Silas prayed like this was when he was holed up with those Texans and Colton, and under the unrelenting assault of the hornets nest of terrorists.

This was like that, only these hostiles were possessed with a fury that seemed borderline demonic.

Hissing and cackling cries rose above the *rat-a-tat-tat* of the Nousati anchored on either side of the road. Six of them this time, if Silas counted right.

Two-to-one odds ain't the worst in Vegas. Not the worst in SEPIO's world either, considering what he and Gapinski had endured a time or four.

But still.

The darkness combined with the heavy weaponry, plus the fact the three of them had been scattered to the four winds when the trio came up on one of the Nousati agents taking a snooze against the waist-high wall, putting him down cold but sending up a flair announcing their arrival—all of it made for a nightmare.

And horrible odds for coming out of it alive and rescuing Celeste.

A stick cracked with sudden alarm behind Silas, making his bowels go cold.

He whipped his weapon around and nearly popped off a shot, but held off at the last-second pull when he saw a friendly face.

Brit.

He sighed and shook his head. "I'm not sure this thing is big enough for the both of us."

"Speak for yourself," she said, coming low and joining him behind his large maple tree still inflamed with red leaves. "With all of the running we've been doing the past few days and mile-high anxiety, I've dropped at least five pounds."

"Whatever. Where's Gapinski?"

"Lost him when the lug-head tripped over the snoozer and had to put him down."

Silas turned to her with furrowed brow.

"The Nous agent, not Gapinski. Anyway, he ran when we ran. But by the sound of it, he's gotta be on the other side of that road flanking the cemetery, given the direction of the weapon fire."

A frenzied, fanatical cheer arose, and the *dum-ditty-dum-ditty* drumbeat returned again in force as the two held their positions, scoping out their next move.

Which didn't last long.

Rat-a-tat-tat gunfire chewed along the tree's trunk with gluttonous abandon and shredded those leaves into red confetti in an unrelenting assault.

"Now what?" Brit asked, flattening low and aiming through the underbrush toward the gunfire.

"Offer me some cover, that's what."

She nodded and returned fire, interrupting the hostile and sending it back with halting indecision.

Silas launched for a sister maple that had lost its leaves weeks ago a few yards away, falling to his knees and rolling through a cluster of vines with thorns the size of dimes. He stifled pained yelps, but recovered and took aim.

Catching the Nousati square in his sights.

Pop-pop-pop he let loose from his new perch.

Snapping the hostile's head back and sending him slumping to the road.

"Nice shot," Brit said, standing and pressing in against the tree again. "We've just got to do that five more times."

"Always the pessimist."

"No, realist."

More *rat-a-tat-tats* echoed toward them up ahead, followed by a series of *pop-pop-pops.*

"Whatever. We better back up our guy before we find ourselves needing to save two SEPIO agents."

We're coming, Gapinski. Just hold on...

SEBASTIAN RECOILED AT MORE FLARING *rat-a-tat-tat* gunfire followed by several *pop-pop-pop* rejoinders.

This wasn't supposed to happen.

Sebastian had planned it all perfectly. Tracking down and securing his ancestor's bones and lineage, and doing the same with all of those other witches from Salem, the ones who had hung for their crimes and a few more who had escaped—like dear Granny Mary Warren. Securing the Devil's Book and Cotton Mather's work to study and summon the darkness that had arisen from the Massachusetts Bay colony. Leaving his guys to clean up the Silas and SEPIO mess, which was a blessed gift from the Universe after the botched FBI raid. Devising the perfect diversion in the city by setting the resort town's church ablaze.

Yes, there had been hiccups. Their experiments with the

darker arts on the men and women had resulted in the possession clusters getting away from them, leading to the unfortunate events expanding across the country. On the plus side, they had verified what they had thought to be true: The Devil could spread, like an infectious disease let loose in the world to bring about their glorious ends.

Then there was Silas Grey, the man who was supposed to be dead but was clearly firing at his men from the road down below. The one that held quaint memories riding their bikes through summer rainstorms and using it to sneak inside the cemetery to tip over headstones.

No matter. They were so close now. Soon, the transformation would be complete, gifting the influence of the Angel of Light to the world, the One who will open the eyes of the masses to the truth of their consciousness and usher in the Republic of Heaven.

Finally crushing the Church under the weight of its enlightenment.

Another round of gunfire set his teeth on edge, but the congregants arrayed in front of him didn't seem to pay it any mind. They were still too caught up in the ecstasy of it all. The only reply was the whimpering wench tied behind him.

He turned and grinned at her, then caught Rudolf glaring at him, clearly ready to bring it all to a climax.

Here we go....

He turned around to continue the rite.

"As our Angel of Light revolted from up on high in righteous dissent," Sebastian went on, "we too cast aside the shackles of subjugation and the binds of the Authority with this blood of the one who rejected the Light in favor of the Authority. Having cast the Body of Christ into the flaming fires of hell, we will now drink and find sustenance this night in the blood of a different sacrifice, writing the name of *Ha-Satan* upon our hearts in her blood, giving us the strength to repel the

Authority and his minions, rending our foes asunder under our enlightened consciousness."

He lifted the chalice up toward the heavens, a tingling power now coursing through his veins so that he wondered if what had invaded Borg was now seeking another.

"O Children of *Ha-Satan*," he thundered, "by the blood of this reject, I incite thee to rise from tears and come to joy! From suffering, come to pleasure! From injustice, seek restitution! From injury, seek vengeance! Deny and spurn the dominion of the Authority! For thou art thy own, bought and paid by no one!"

The others intoned, *'By our own hand shall we be delivered!'*

His beloved Helen tolled her bell, six times in all. The mark of mankind, of the Beast that was about to be fully unleashed.

Now for the closing act. The sacrifice, that will return the sins of the world in all of its consciousness.

SILAS SNAGGED his pants on another one of those damn pricker bushes, halting his progress and forcing Brit to go around.

They were making too much noise. But given the noise beyond the tree line, it probably didn't matter anyway. And it sounded like Gapinski was having a go of it himself.

He slung his leg around and pressed forward, the scent of dead leaves and rot and burning kerosene making him ill. But he couldn't let it get to him. They had minutes until—

"Arg!" Brit said, falling down and crying out again.

Silas rushed over to her but couldn't see through the darkness and underbrush what had happened.

She was crying again through clenched teeth. "Sprained my ankle. Maybe broke it," she managed to explain.

Not good...

"Alright, here. Let me..." Silas crouched and slung an arm around her, then lifted.

More clenched-teeth crying.

Really, really not good...

Then someone called out, their voice echoing back to them: "Uh, Silas? Brit?"

Silas's heart leaped forward, his bowels dropped to the forest floor.

"Gapinski?!" Silas hissed.

"Oh, no..." Brit said, wincing as he helped her hobble forward.

There he was, silhouetted by the flapping flames of twenty torches in front of a monstrous mausoleum beyond.

Hands over his head and two Nousati goons pointing their weapons at his kidneys.

Silas cursed and held his head; Brit echoed his sentiments.

"Uh, dude? Dudette?" Gapinski said again with a chuckle. "Not getting any younger out here. And not sure how much longer Thing One and Thing Two are gonna hold off—"

Silas and Brit emerged from the forest and hobbled to the road.

The Nousati goons took a step back and adjusted their aim.

Silas put his hands up and slumped to his knees. "Alright, we surrender!"

SEBASTIAN WENT to offer his final benediction to the rite when something startled his attention.

Three figures emerged from the shadows, hands on their heads. Two more of his men trailed behind, weapons aiming with the forceful intent he paid them for.

One end of his mouth curled upward. There he was.

Silas Grey.

On his right was that nosey FBI agent hobbling on a bum leg, and then that loudmouth What's-His-Name.

"CELESTE!!" Silas screamed when he came into view,

lunging forward for that wench at his feet who was squawking like a muzzled goose.

He didn't make it far.

His hired hand grabbed his arms and held him back.

Sebastian chuckled. "Aww, how sweet. Star-crossed lovers at the mercy of forces greater than themselves. A regular Hallmark special. And really, now that I think of it, a true Romeo and Juliet production we have here, don't we. Just like the historical tragedy, one will be offered to the gods as a sacrifice."

Sebastian could see the whites of his pathetic brother's eyes widen before the man bolted to his feet. He lunged forward again with fury, calling for his lover with desperation.

Had to give him credit for trying.

The other well-paid muscle-head quickly earned his quids as well. He jammed the butt of his rifle barrel into Silas's head, throwing him to the ground.

Silas screamed in protest, but it was no use. The Nousati agent was now firmly planted on his back and an arm wrapped around his neck.

Sebastian smirked. "Always one to spoil the fun, Sy. I must say, I'm impressed you put the pieces together that brought you here. Though it hardly took a genius to sort it all out, if you'd been paying attention."

"What in God's name are you doing here, baby brother?" Silas said breathlessly, having been righted by his man back to his knees.

"I told you: magic. Dark magic, you might say. The kind our, how did Dad put it? Great-great-great-great-great-great-great-great grandmother had tapped into."

"Mary Warren."

"Ahh, so you do remember."

"Think you forgot a great or two in there," Silas huffed, catching his breath. "And you're as much as a psychopath as

Roland Vander Molen. Who apparently was a distant ancestor of one of the other Salem witches."

"Alleged..." Brit mumbled behind him.

"Oh, sweetheart," Sebastian said, "there's no allegation about it. Just like our own ancestor, she and others sold their souls to the Devil and opened the doorway for further enlightening."

"And you think their bones, tied around these other psychos, are going to open the door again?"

Sebastian smirked. "Not just the bones, but yes. Our experiments proved it. However, Roland's escape was a slight oopsie, and the ensuing havoc unforeseen."

"Toward what end?" Silas asked, voice rising with exasperated anger.

"Why, knowledge, Sy. Understanding. Consciousness in all of its uninhibited glory! Your religion thinks we need redemption from consciousness, a cleansing from the consequences of knowledge. But what we really need is redemption from the Authority who conceals the truth of it from us in the first place!"

"And you think the Devil is going to do that?"

"He did once before!"

"And look at the consequences you moron! Vandalizing God's good creation, all because Mama Eve and Papa Adam wanted the power to decide right and wrong, good and evil."

"Damn right they did! And so do we, all of us who are sick and tired of the Church's laundry list of dos and don'ts with all of the hypocrisy of a pedophile priest!"

Sebastian was huffing and puffing now and working up a sweaty lather, like any good Southern Baptist preacher worth his salt in the dead of August.

"This guy is seriously coo-coo for Cocoa Puffs..." Gapinski mumbled in a huff.

Sebastian threw him a biting glare, causing Gapinski to look away and shrink behind Silas.

But Silas knew better. Knew the depths of his brother's story after Sebastian revealed his teenage sexual abuse at the hand of their childhood priest. To be sure, Southern Baptists and fundamentalists and others had joined Catholics in such shame. But still—his brother's rage against the Church was personal; it usually is.

A comment from Father D'Amante flashed to the fore, how such abuse often renders a soul wound that opens the door for the Evil One to gain a foothold in their life.

Leading to possession.

Damn that priest...

Sebastian stepped up to just a foot away and bent down with a grin.

"Just you wait, Sy. Just you wait..."

THE *DUM-DITTY-DUM-DITTY* DRUM beat launched a heart-pounding score again that sent Silas's head spinning with delirium—spiritual and existential—with one question on his mind.

How the hell were they going to get out of this one?

Sebastian closed his eyes and held the chalice aloft. Then he quoted from the Book of Revelation, chapter 17, their grade-school catechism classes memorizing the Bible apparently taking and coming in handy:

> And I saw a woman sitting on a scarlet beast that was full of blasphemous names, and it had seven heads and ten horns. The woman was clothed in purple and scarlet, and adorned with gold and jewels and pearls, holding in her hand a golden cup full of abominations and the

> impurities of her fornication; and on her forehead was written a name, a mystery: "Babylon the great, mother of whores and of earth's abominations." And I saw that the woman was drunk with the blood of the saints and the blood of the witnesses to Jesus.

"I am Babylon the Great," Borg intoned from behind, the Voice returning and having become strengthened with power. *"I am the Scarlet One, bejeweled with majesty and adorned with the pearls of wisdom. Beneath my heel and between my ten horns I shall destroy the Church—feasting upon the blood of the martyrs in all of their pitiful weakness. The saints shall tremble before my might and bow before my glory!"*

The man withdrew from his robes a knife, the blade shimmering in the firelight with a handle of ivory encrusted with jewels.

A ceremonial athame blade, used to slay a sacrifice for the gods.

"I have now risen upon the earth in the fullness of humanity," he went on, drawing near, *"and I will not be denied my right to rule! I am the Almighty Cosmic Force, and thou shalt deny me naught! I will no longer lie below, but will ascend on high!"*

The drum beat was beating in a *dum-ditty-dum-ditty* frenzy now, the onlookers dressed in black robs swaying and their arms wrenching this way and that in a state of ecstatic possession.

"Children of enlightenment, unchained from Christian duty," Borg said, voice guttural and growly, *"the blessing of* Ha-Satan *be upon thee. In the full authority and enlightenment of the Angel of Light I release you to unseat the ignorant and superstitious still clinging to the ways of old, and to topple the Church's idol and dance upon their rubble! For verily, give glory to no one but your own*

consciousness—in body, mind, and soul. For you have been freed from the Authority. And whom the Beast has set free, is free indeed!"

A tremble took hold of Silas, the spiritual weight of the Voice pressing in against him in a way he had never before felt. And Borg was now staring straight at him.

Silas felt suddenly exposed, insignificant even, as the eyes bore into him, and he knew he was looking straight into the presence of pure evil.

Refusing to be cowed, he quickly recomposed himself and refused to waver.

I'll be damned if I'm going to let this demon intimidate me!

The demon itself looked away from Silas and fixed his eyes on someone else.

Celeste.

Bowing his head, Borg suddenly held the athame blade aloft, its surface glinting with unholy, murderous intent in the firelight.

Silas's heart seized, his bowels went weak with the wicked reality of it all.

He started forward when an arm clamped around his neck.

"Nooo!" he shouted, struggling to break free. *"Nooo!!!"*

The Voice returned, first with a barkish, sneering laugh. Then he said, *"With this blood, the mighty, full of consciousness and choice, shall inherit the earth, liberated through the power of blood and sacrifice!"*

Stepping back, Borg lifted the knife above to his chest, the drumbeat growing louder, more furious, the *dum-ditty-dum-ditty* rising with a thumping fury.

Then, closing his eyes, the man threw back his head and muttered something before raising the knife high above for the plunge.

Cutting through the night, a series of *pop-pop-pop-pop-pop* shots rang out.

The first one thudded uselessly into a marble column behind Borg.

The second shot hit squarely in his left shoulder, jerking him back before another two planted firmly in his chest.

The final one sealed the deal, striking through the side of his neck and sending a bloom of crimson arcing to the ground.

The man stumbled back and slumped into a heap with a thud, the knife clattering to the ground at his side.

The weapon clicked empty before all eyes turned to uncover the mysterious intrusion.

Radcliffe was holding the Beretta Silas had given him earlier. Standing behind him was Father D'Amante, looking frightfully unarmed and stunned at the events.

The man who had complained about being nothing but an old sack of bones had saved the day!

Then all at once, a melee ensued for control.

Silas pushed off the ground and threw his back into the ogre who had wrapped his arms around his neck, throwing the man backward and loosening his grip in the sudden turn.

Brit kicked the other Nousati in the kneecaps with her good leg, and Gapinski threw himself on the man, driving him into a headstone and sending him into the dark. Maybe for good.

Check.

He grabbed the rifle off the man and fired into the air to bring it all to one climactic halt, but clicked empty after a few shots.

Gapinski tossed the weapon to the ground with a curse. "Always something..."

Silas was having about as good of luck: the Nousati was firmly in control of his own weapon's trigger; Silas was on top and pressing the weapon into the man's throat.

The hostile offered a sudden livid burst of *rat-a-tat-tat* gunfire, sending Brit and the elders ducking for cover on the other side. Even Gapinski yelped before rushing the man and socking him in the temple.

Sending the hostile into another rapid-fire *rat-a-tat-tat* fit.

Gapinski hit him again, then again.

Bringing the man to a halt.

But not before the weapon clicked empty again.

"Really?" he said, plopping down on the ground in a huff. "Empty clips twice over?"

Silas stood to face his brother, narrowing his gaze and clenching his fists to finish it himself the old-fashioned way.

Checkmate.

Until it wasn't.

"Ah, ah, ah, Sy. I wouldn't do that if I were you."

Standing over Celeste's still-bound body was Sebastian, robed in a faux priest's cassock.

And bearing the athame blade inches from Celeste's throat.

Silas swallowed hard, then took a step.

"Nooo....Baby brother, please."

"You ruined it all. Again. I was meant to unleash the full power of the original enlightening consciousness, first offered to our ancestors and then to that man from Nazareth you've given your bloody life too!"

Silas went to offer a reply when a sudden bassy rumble intercepted Sebastian's boasting, echoing with growing intent. A vibration that began crescendoing into a guttural moan and seemed to be coming from just beyond the altar.

From inside Borg's dead body. Just like it had with Roland Vander Molen.

With sudden, supernatural levitation, it began moving with a wicked arch. Its arms stiffened and belly reached dramatically toward the ceiling, heels and goat head firmly planted on the ground while the rest of it bent like a wishbone.

"Not this again..." Gapinski moaned.

Silas went to agree when Sebastian started screaming a

frantic, hysterical howl, his eyes bulging from their sockets and mouth wide with horrifying abandon.

But that wasn't all of it.

For he was still fully in control of the blade. Then, without warning, the hysterics ceased and a wicked grin was splayed across his face.

It wasn't over. Not by a long shot.

CHAPTER 31

There he was again: standing at the crossroads between his brother and Celeste. If he had to choose, hands down it was Celeste. Not even a question. Didn't even have to have a think about it.

Have a think about it.

Man, how he loved that Britishism, where everything Celeste did was something she *had*—had a think, had a look, had a chat. That was his favorite, because it usually meant she was having a chat with him. About all sorts of things.

Grey, focus!

But he couldn't. Not with that blade hovering above Celeste's neck and that snarling twin of his turning into the Devil himself before his very eyes.

Sebastian had been dead to him since last year, a sentiment forged through the choices he had made the past several months joining Nous to destroy the Church.

And there he was, making another choice: cradling his love's neck, the blade now an inch from her throat, to slit it for his rite of darkness.

And he wanted to rip the man's face off for it.

But was it really his choice? Hadn't a darkness come into him, controlling his mind and guiding his hand.

And yet Sebastian had let this demonic possession take hold of him, driving him into darkness and out from the bosom of Christ's light.

The words of Saint Paul struck close to home: '*our struggle is not against enemies of blood and flesh, but against the rulers, against the authorities, against the cosmic powers of this present darkness, against the spiritual forces of evil in the heavenly places.*'

That included his twin brother. Who now seemed to be Satan incarnate and was holding Celeste's life in his hands. Literally.

"Stand back. All of you," Father D'Amante commanded, cutting through his confusion.

Silas swallowed hard and shuffled out of the way, grateful to the good Lord above for the man and his gifting. And praying that he brought the fires of heaven's deliverance down upon the cemetery.

For both Celeste's and Sebastian's sake.

Gapinski inched back with Silas, as did Brit. The only one who didn't was Radcliffe. Apparently, this was a tag-team gig.

Father D'Amante retrieved a gold crucifix from the inside of his garment, the same one he had used on Celeste a few days ago.

Sebastian instantly jolted at the sight. He gripped the blade tighter and held it at Celeste's neck, his tongue now licking his lips and a faint trail of saliva dribbling down his chin.

He bowed his head toward the Christian icon. He fixed it with a penetrating gaze, eyes narrowed and dark and glaring, his lips now curling back with ill intent.

Then a growl emanated from his stomach, the sound of which sounded eerily familiar.

A cross between a strangled sheep and irate mama grizzly.

The same sound heard from the psychopath and from Celeste, and then from Borg moments ago.

Sebastian growled and glared at the exorcist, then gnashed his teeth.

Father D'Amante stepped forward and looked squarely into the man's eyes, taking the full measure of him before voicing a prayer that launched the Rite.

"God, Creator and defender of the human race, look down on this man whom you formed in your own image and now call to be a partaker in your glory."

Silas realized the priest was speaking about Sebastian. Guilt washed over him in that instance, realizing the simple yet forceful truth of it all: His twin was still an image bearer of God, created to display and partake his glory. Regardless of what he had done, what he was doing now.

Even threatening the life of his love.

The Voice rising within the man wasted no time in manifesting.

"You have no power over me!" he growled at Father D'Amante in the guttural voice that had become all too familiar.

The exorcist paid him no mind. Instead, he offered another prayer, echoing throughout the cemetery: "Hear, God, lover of human salvation, the prayer of your apostles Peter and Paul and of all the saints, who by your grace emerged as victors over the Evil one: free this man from every foreign power and keep him safe, so that restored to peaceful devotion, he may return to loving you with his heart and may serve you zealously with his works, may glorify you with praises and may magnify you with his life."

"You don't really believe those children's stories, do you?" the Voice scoffed.

The Voice reminded Silas of the sound a dog might make were it able to speak. It was a deep, dark evil sound that seemed to come from the depths of his brother's stomach.

"I cast you out, old enemy of man," Father D'Amante went on, "Depart from him! Our Lord Jesus Christ commands this of you, the humility of whom conquered your pride, the generosity of whom laid low your envy, the gentleness of whom trampled upon your cruelty."

Again the voice exploded: *"Don't you know that he died on the cross? And you are still following him! We are stronger! We are stronger! We win! We win!"*

"Be silent, father of lies, and do not hinder this man from blessing and praising the Lord. Jesus Christ commands this of you, the wisdom of the Father and the splendor of truth, the words of whom are spirit and life."

Sebastian bared his teeth, warping the image of his brother into a true monster. Thick globs of mucus and saliva oozed from his mouth and ran down his chin now.

"Shut up! Do you know who I am?" the Voice growled with deep, penetrating tones. *"Don't treat me like a pig! Look what I can do to this man, look what I can do!"*

The man gnashed his teeth again and growled, slashing toward the priest with the knife.

Which made Silas's heart leap with ironic hope. Because that meant the blade was no longer contemplating cutting Celeste's throat to ribbons. Now it was outstretched toward Father D'Amante.

"What you are saying is worthless!" the guttural Voice growled again.

The exorcist stood stoic and unmoving. He held the crucifix asunder again, its gold shimmering in the firelight and acting as a repellent with an almost magnetic force.

Suddenly, the abomination howled in pain.

"I am stronger!" the deep Voice bellowed.

Sebastian took several strained breaths that sounded more like screeches: *"Heeeeeeeee! Heeeeeeee! Heeeeeeeee!"*

He bared his teeth and slashed again with the knife.

"I adjure you, accursed dragon," Father D'Amante boomed in the night, "in the name of our Lord Jesus Christ, to eradicate yourself and depart from this creature of God."

Again, the voice exploded: *"Really! Who do you think you are? You can't make me do anything! We are many!"*

Father D'Amante continued, undeterred: "Christ himself commands you who enjoined you to be cast down from the heights of heaven into the lower parts of the earth."

A deep, wicked laugh exploded from Sebastian's being, one that seemed rooted in the earth itself, for the ground trembled and trees swayed in protest.

Then he stepped forward and screamed, *"You think so, priest?"*

Hope surged again through Silas at the change in Sebastian's direction. But Father D'Amante faltered, almost blown back at the force of the man and weakening in the face of his taunts.

Radcliffe stepped forward this time. Now he was holding a gold crucifix, outstretched with purpose and unmoving with defiance.

"Fear that one, who was sacrificed in place of Isaac," he boomed with authority, "who was sold in place of Joseph, who was killed in place of the lamb, who was crucified in place of man, and then was triumphant over hell. Give place to Jesus Christ, in whom you have found nothing of your works."

"ENOUGH!!" the Voice screamed, enraged with snarling pride. *"Don't you know who you are talking to?"*

Father D'Amante recovered and stepped forward, lowering his crucifix and withdrawing a glass tube.

Silas was confused at the tactic, but then it hit him:

Holy water.

Stepping forward to within only a few yards of the abomination, the exorcist uncorked the vial and flung the sacred liquid at the man, saying, "In the name of the Father, and of the Son, and of the Holy Spirit."

Sebastian recoiled and fell to the ground, then immediately thrashed wildly before jumping to his haunches and lunging for the men with supernatural height and strength.

They fell in a jumbled pile of cassocks, so that it was unclear who was who in the darkness and chaos.

Silas ignored the melee, running to Celeste to untie her bindings.

A hideous crunch echoed back, and then another.

He glanced up to find Sebastian on top of one of the portly men, hands wrapped around his head crowned with wispy gray hair and smashing it against a headstone. He couldn't make sense who was under assault, and he was too caught up with helping Celeste to pay any attention anyway.

He recovered the athame knife and slipped it between her bindings then began sawing.

Almost there...

Gapinski climbed on top of the pile attempting to wrench Sebastian off and incapacitate him.

But the man seemed to possess a superhuman, other-worldly strength; he sloughed him off like a bathrobe.

The men down below continued their melee as Silas released Celeste's feet and got to work on her hands.

Gapinski smashed his closed fist into Sebastian's head.

The man roared with a wild, wicked arching of his back, as if a gorilla who had just been hit with a club.

But again, he tossed the SEPIO agent off from him like a rag doll.

Sirens echoed in the distance now and bright red lights flashed faintly through the trees, confirming help was finally on the way.

Sebastian seemed to sense this too. He leaped off from the men and scrambled across the cemetery to freedom.

Silas didn't have it in him to go after his brother. Gapinski made a gamely attempt, taking long strides to try and catch him, but it was no use.

With one giant, otherworldly leap, Sebastian jumped over the cemetery wall and scampered into the dark forest, disappearing into the dead of night.

"Got it!" Silas said as he clipped the last of the bindings before tearing off the restraint from her mouth.

Celeste rolled from the altar on weakened strength and crawled into his arms, hot tears streaming down her face and soaking Silas's collar.

"You came for me," she sobbed. "You came..."

Silas's throat grew thick with emotion, and he couldn't help tearing at her pleas.

"Of course I did, darling. Of course I did!"

Then he gently pushed her off and took her head in his hands. He stared into those wet eyes, his own eyes filling now with emotion, and said the only thing that needed to be said in the moment.

"Celeste Bourne, you are the most intelligent, magnificent, kind-hearted, capable, and hottest woman I have ever met in my life."

She giggled and wiped her eyes and nose. Silas grinned like a schoolboy and sniffed emotion away himself.

He took a breath then asked, "Celeste Bourne, will you marry me?"

She took a breath of her own, and her face fell.

Then it widened into a smile before she burst into more tears and threw her arms around his neck.

"About bloomin' time! Yes, yes, I'll marry you!"

The two fell into one another in the middle of the pagan stone altar, another bout of giddiness overcoming them before it was suffocated under a passionate embrace.

"Silas, Celeste!" someone called out.

It was Gapinski, waving his arms in a panic before pointing down to the ground.

Silas's face fell when he followed the man.

No...

"No, no, no, no, no!" he cried out, scurrying off from the altar toward the body of the man who had given him a new lease on life.

"Rowen..." he said, drawing up to the Order Master.

He shoved Gapinski and Father D'Amante aside, who was mumbling something under his breath.

The man's last rites, by the sound of it.

Silas grabbed Radcliffe's head. It lolled freely, as if unattached, and was whiter than the wispy silver hair matted to his head in slick crimson.

He pulled his hand away; it was covered in blood. Way too much to survive from, especially with the sound of those wicked crunches coming back to memory.

Sebastian...

Celeste came up to his side and held him. He wrapped his arms around her, as did Gapinski and even Brit. Father D'Amante was still kneeling beside his friend, muttering his prayer.

Red lights and sirens swirled around the group in a miasma of impotent help as the man who had given his life to preserving, protecting, saving the Church was whisked away into the safe arms of his Lord, his Savior.

You fought the good fight, Rowen. You finished the race, you kept the faith.

Silas was sobbing, tears flowing freely as the truth of the matter sank deep into his bones now, joined by his friends.

For you, my brother and friend, there is surely reserved the crown of righteousness. Well done, good and faithful servant. Run into the arms of your Savior; enter into the joy of your Lord...

CHAPTER 32

WASHINGTON, DC. ONE WEEK LATER.

Silas arranged the eulogy notes he had scribbled down over the past few days and opened his Bible to the passage he had chosen to memorialize Rowen Radcliffe, Master of the Order of Thaddeus. The man who had given his life to protect the Church and contend for her faith. The man who had given the ultimate sacrifice, laying down his life.

For Celeste.

He was also the man who had radically changed his life, saving it over a year ago and breathing new purpose into it when he was sacked from Princeton.

His eyes began to brim and throat began to constrict with emotion contemplating what the Church had lost, what the Order had lost.

What he himself had lost.

He took a breath and brought a hand up to his mouth to clear his throat. He reached for a small glass sitting on a ledge under the wooden pulpit and took a drink, then another.

Setting the glass back underneath, he paused to scan the room. Gapinski sat in the front at the aisle, face stoic and ready to exact vengeance for what had happened. Behind him sat

Zoe, black mascara smearing beneath those baby blue glasses of hers, along with Abraham who stared solemnly forward. Then Naomi Torres, who had returned just in time to make the funeral from burying her uncle.

Sitting next to Gapinski was Celeste. It was thought that she would give the eulogy, given how closely she had worked with him as his right-hand person over the years. But she had a dreadful case of stage fright and pleaded with Silas to take her place. He agreed without hesitation and got to work preparing one of his most important speeches he would ever give.

Celeste smiled at him with quivering lips, eyes running with emotion that nearly sent him into an emotional heap. She brought a handkerchief to her eyes and dabbed them, and he had to avert his eyes if he was going to make it.

Silas took a deep breath, settled into place, then began.

"You know, a professor of mine from graduate school, a man who also died tragically at the hands of a menacing evil—he would tell us in class that being a Christian means embracing the fact that life sucks until Jesus returns."

He paused as a few chuckles knowingly echoed across the sanctuary, along with several heads nodding with approval.

"I understood all too well what he was saying, because my mother and father tragically passed away far too soon. Rowen Radcliffe passed away far too soon as well. And let's face it: This sucks. None of us want to be here. Yes, we tell ourselves that he's in a better place. He fought the good fight. He's in the arms of the Savior he faithfully served, and the faith he spent his life defending has been made complete. And that's all true."

Silas paused, his throat catching with emotion at his own words.

He glanced at Celeste for support, who edged him onward with a smile that could instill confidence in anyone.

It worked. He smiled back and continued, "But I still want to say that this sucks, because death sucks. Death is not the way it's supposed to be. It is wicked, it is evil. And death simply does not make sense. Death was never what God intended when he created this good world. It stole its way into his very good creation when our ancient ancestors, Adam and Eve, rebelled against God, plunging all of creation into rebellious ruin and opening the door for unrelenting evil to invade. And we've been paying the price ever since."

Silas took another sip of water. "But death didn't have the final word in their story," he went on, "and it doesn't have the final word in our story. He gestured to the closed casket at the front of the sanctuary. "And it doesn't have the final word in Rowen's story, either."

He reached for his Bible. "Listen to these words from Saint Paul, from his first letter to the Corinthians, chapter fifteen."

He read:

> *"Death has been swallowed up in victory."*
> *"Where, O death, is your victory?*
> *Where, O death, is your sting?"*
> *The sting of death is sin, and the power of sin is the law. But thanks be to God, who gives us the victory through our Lord Jesus Christ.*
> *Therefore, my beloved, be steadfast, immovable, always excelling in the work of the Lord, because you know that in the Lord your labor is not in vain.*

"Amen," he said quietly, closing the Bible. Several in the room echoed this sentiment.

"Rowen knew this victory personally, because he knew Jesus personally. As a young man, he had understood that the solution to our human problem of rebellion against God and the wickedness that pervades the world, the fix that God offered humanity was himself. He traded his very own life in the person of Jesus Christ, coming to this world to live our life and ultimately pay our price in our place with his own blood."

Silas scanned the room, feeling a little foolish wearing the role of preacher, but he didn't care. He knew it's what Radcliffe would have wanted, to make it clear what he had lived for all his life.

"But God's solution to our human problem didn't end there. Because what the Christian faith offers, above all other religions, is what these verses spell out: victory over death! Which was made possible through the resurrection of Jesus Christ. Because Jesus lives, we can face tomorrow. Even a tomorrow without Rowen, because we know one day he will be raised to new life, just like Jesus."

His mind jumped to the first mission that had roped him into the Order in the first place: the threatened Shroud of Turin, and his work trying to prove its authenticity and the scientific proof of Jesus' resurrection. And look at where he had come since then...

Silas cleared his throat and refocused back to the moment.

"Rowen Radcliffe lived his life preserving and protecting this faith. But for him, it wasn't just about a set of religious ideas. His devotion was to the person at the center of his faith, Jesus Christ. Because he knew what I eventually discovered myself: that Jesus is who people have been waiting for their whole lives, whether they know it or not. Rowen met Jesus decades ago, and it changed him. He could think of nothing better to do with his life than to hand it back to the One who had given it to him in the first place. His was a life well lived."

Closing, he gathered up his notes and slid them into his Bible. "Yes, this day we mourn the loss of our son and brother and friend. But we do not grieve like the rest of the world, because we have hope. We believe that death has been defeated through Christ's death on the cross and through his resurrection. And Rowen's hope is our hope: along with our dear brother, we will be with the Lord forever. Amen."

The room offered a collective *'Amen'* as Silas made his way down the front stairs. He sat next to Celeste, who took his hand and squeezed it.

He looked into her eyes, beaming with pride and tears streaming down her face. She mouthed, *'Thank you.'*

He nodded and smiled back, squeezing her hand in solidarity, with love.

"Nailed it, bro," Gapinski whispered from behind, giving his shoulders the same encouraging squeeze.

The minister who had been leading the funeral made his way to the front. He announced the conclusion of the service and invited the pallbearers to the front to bring Radcliffe's casket out to the awaiting hearse.

Silas and Gapinski stood, along with Abraham and three other members of the Order. They made their way to the casket and grabbed hold of the handles anchored on the sides.

After the minister made his way to the aisle, the man led the way forward to bury their friend, their colleague—and an era at the Order of Thaddeus.

"BRAVO, LAD, BRAVO," Father D'Amante said, walking up to Silas with outstretched arms. The men embraced. "Radcliffe was truly honored and Christ truly uplifted today."

Gloomy morning clouds had parted to reveal a bright November sun. Though chilly, the sunshine offered enough warmth to bury their friend with proper respect. Silas and Celeste and now Father D'Amante huddled near his grave as others began departing.

Silas offered a smile. "Thank you, Father D'Amante. Appreciate your words, and appreciate your being here. And, well," he glanced at Celeste and smiled again, "for everything."

"I'm just thankful we were able to hold the cosmic powers of this present darkness at bay. For now."

"From what it sounds like, you and your fellow exorcists are making progress with those who've been afflicted."

Father D'Amante nodded. "By the grace of God, we have. Pray that the afflicted will find release from the Prince of Darkness's influence."

Silas nodded and then his face fell. He thought of his brother in his own affliction, escaping while himself under the influence of the Prince of Darkness. Thought of the looming battles ahead contending for the faith, presumably with him at the helm now that Borg was dead. And all without Radcliffe. What would it mean for them? For him?

Recovering with another grin, he said, "Yes, well, the next time we're in need of an exorcist, you'll be at the top of the Rolodex."

Father D'Amante chuckled. "Let's just pray you'll have no need of my services anytime soon!"

The three said their goodbyes, and the man departed.

Waiting in the wings was Brit, dressed in black with eyes surprisingly wet.

"So sorry for your loss, you two," she said, leaning in to embrace them both.

Silas glanced at Celeste and shrugged, not accustomed to seeing her emotional, especially for someone she barely knew.

She withdrew and wiped her nose. "Sorry. I'm not sure what's come over me."

Celeste said, "I'd right imagine the events of the past week would be enough to give most people an emotional wringing. I know I've been through it."

Brit smiled and nodded. "Anyway, just wanted to pay my respects and thank you for your help putting the world back to normal again. As normal as can be expected, I guess, given what we witnessed."

"Our pleasure," Celeste said.

"Let's do it again sometime," Silas said with a wry grin.

Brit chuckled. "No offense, but I don't ever want to see your sorry butt again, Silas Grey. I'd like to avoid the kind of trouble you seem to bring."

"Understand that. But it was nice to see you again. Let's just do it over coffee next time. The three of us," he said, grabbing Celeste's hand.

"That'd be nice. Give us a chance to catch up like normal adults not under fire."

They said their goodbyes and she left, finding Gapinski standing with Torres, who seemed all too eager to cavort with his ex.

Sighing, he mumbled, "Glad that's over."

"I'll drink to that," Celeste said, squeezing his hand. "By the way, Father D'Amante was right, you know."

"About what?"

"About honoring Radcliffe and Christ. It was a proper funeral. He would be proud. He *was* proud."

"I can't believe he's gone, Celeste."

"Tell me about it. He was such a fixture of the Order. Truth be told, I never imagined outliving the bloke, he was such a fighter, so spry. "

"What are we going to do?"

She shook her head. "Dunno. But let's find out together."

He smiled and gave her a peck on the cheek. "I like that."

They went to leave when they were intercepted.

"Pardon me, but it's Ms. Bourne, isn't it?"

They turned to find a trim man in a blue pinstripe suit underneath a heavy charcoal coat, wearing a felt hat and bearing a briefcase.

Celeste nodded. "Yes, I am she."

The man nodded back. "I was told I would find you here."

"And you are?" Silas asked.

The man sized him up and smiled curtly before setting his briefcase on the ground and extending his hand.

"Forgive my lack of courtesy," he said. "Fredrick Gibbs, chief counsel for the Order of Thaddeus."

"Didn't know we had need for such a thing."

Gibbs chuckled and he turned to Celeste for confirmation.

She smiled knowingly. "Radcliffe made mention of you a time or two after helping us sort through a few, shall we say, legal entanglements."

"Yes, well, the Order sometimes has found itself in such...entanglements, as you put it."

His face fell, and then his gaze fell to the ground. He continued with a low voice, "Rowen was a lovely man. A gentleman and a scholar, if there ever was one."

Celeste smiled. "That he was. I don't mean to be rude, but it seemed as though you sought me out."

Gibbs nodded. "Indeed, I did. To give you this."

He reached inside his coat and withdrew a heavy cream-colored envelope. He handed it to Celeste.

She took it and frowned then flipped it over. Red wax sealed the underside flap, stamped with the official imprimatur of the Order. Running diagonal across the seal was Radcliffe's signature in black marker.

"What's this?" she asked.

"Rowen's final orders," Gibbs replied.

Celeste sucked in a startled breath; Silas joined her in the surprise.

"What sort of orders?" Silas asked, folding his arms and eyeing the envelope.

"His succession plan."

"Succession plan?" Wide-eyed, Silas turned to Celeste and added, "Did you know about this?"

She shook her head. "Hadn't a clue."

Gibbs explained, "Master Radcliffe was set to retire at the

end of the year before…" he trailed off, bowing his head and drawing a hand to his mouth. Clearing his throat, he continued, "Excuse me. As I was saying, Rowen was set to retire at the end of the year, and he had outlined his instructions for his successor, the man or woman, as the case may be, to take over for him as Master of the Order of Thaddeus. Traditionally, the Order Master chose his successor through the ages, starting with Jude Thaddeus. Only, well, he never got around to making it public. As director of operations, Ms. Bourne, the only remaining official figurehead after Rowen's passing, I was instructed to deliver this to you."

Gibbs picked up his briefcase. "I trust you will know what to do with these instructions. Pleased to meet you."

The man left, and Gapinski walked up to the pair of SEPIO agents too stunned to move.

"Who was that guy?" he asked.

"Apparently, our attorney," Silas said, eyeing the man as he disappeared. "Dropping off Radcliffe's Last Will and Testament."

"Huh?"

Celeste held up the envelope. "Rowen was set to retire at the end of the year. And he named his successor, tucked away in here."

"Whoa…" Gapinski folded his arms and stroked his chin with contemplation. "So what does it say?"

She shrugged. "Haven't opened it yet."

"Too stunned by it all to check," Silas added.

"Well, now seems as good a time as any," Gapinski said. "You know Radcliffe, not one to waste a second dilly dallying around, especially when the fate of the Church was involved."

Silas offered a weak smile. "No, he wasn't."

Celeste took a breath and eyed her partners, then set about unsealing the envelope. She wiggled a finger in one corner and slid it across the back, the wax seal splintering in red chips and landing on the grass below.

When her finger was free, she peeled back the fold to find similar cream paper peeking out, scrawled with a neat, precise handwriting penned with black ink.

She glanced at Silas then withdrew the paper. Carefully unfolding it, she smoothed its two tri-fold creases and held it between the trio.

The three craned forward to read Radcliffe's final wishes for the Order he had stewarded like a family:

To Whom It May Concern,

For four decades, I have tried to faithfully execute the office of Master of the Order of Thaddeus, relying upon the power of God the Father, the counsel of the Holy Spirit, the example and work of God the Son, and the insights of the great cloud of witnesses who have gone on before to guide me along the way. Though I have certainly failed at times, allowing personal sin to get in the way of Christ's work, I believe I have run as good of a race as the Spirit has enabled me to, both as Christ's child and as Order Master.

However, it is time for me to give it a rest. I fear the Church's hour of darkness is fast approaching, if not nearly here, and I believe someone more suited for the next four decades is in order. For the sake of the Order's mission and the Church's faith, I would like for this to serve as notice of my retirement effective December 31.

In lieu of my absence, I count it a privilege to join the great litany of previous Masters in naming my replacement. Therefore, I hereby name Silas Grey as Master of the Order of Thaddeus, giving him the full rights and privileges of enacting policy, procedures, and precedents for contending, preserving, protecting, and safeguarding the once-for-all faith entrusted to God's holy people.

May the Father, and the Son, and the Holy Spirit gird his loins, joined by the great litany of saints before him.

~Rowen Radcliffe

The trio stood with stunned silence, the crowd of mourners still milling about them with ignorance at the shift that had just occurred, the next chapter in the Order that had unfolded.

Gapinski was the first to break the silence, giving a chuckle and wrapping an arm around Silas's shoulder. Squeezing, he exclaimed, "Yeah, buddy! Or, should I say, Order Master!"

Celeste let the air go out of her nose, as if she were holding her breath for the results. She folded the letter and stuffed it back in its envelope. She looked up at Silas with a smile, but he could detect a hint of disappointment in her eyes, her nostrils flaring slightly. One of Celeste's tells he had memorized over the past year.

"I reckon that makes you my boss, doesn't it?" she said.

Silas offered a weak grin and took the letter. Scanning it, he mumbled, "I guess so..."

"I'll leave you two to sort this all out," Gapinski said, then sauntered off.

He couldn't believe it. The man had passed the torch to him. To preserve and protect and contend for the once-for-all faith entrusted to God's holy people. Silas Grey, of all people.

Silas sighed. "It should be you."

Celeste shook her head. "No way, you've—"

"Celeste, you've got way more experience with the Order than I have."

"Doesn't matter. Besides—"

"And way more experience fighting Nous."

"Alright, can I finish? Perhaps get a word in edge wise?"

Silas raked a hand through his hair then folded his arms and nodded.

"From the beginning," she said, "from Jude Thaddeus even, the Order Master has chosen their successor. Which means Rowen wanted it to be you. He saw something in you that he knew we needed. This wasn't written in the throes of dying. This wasn't the mumblings of a man in and out of consciousness. He wrote this well before this all went down, which means Rowen chose you."

"I don't know why..." he mumbled.

"Well, I do."

One end of his mouth curled upward, and he wrapped his arms around her. "Really? Do tell."

Celeste grinned. "For starters, you're wicked smart."

"Wicked smart?"

She nodded. "And you know your way around a weapon."

"So my brain and brawn, then?"

"Now, I didn't say brawn. You could do for a few more pushups. Maybe add some curls to your routine. I'm kidding!"

They both giggled like those two high schoolers in the movie theater a week ago before it all went to Hades.

"You've got a good head on your shoulders, love. You're a good strategist. You know your Church history like the back of your bloomin' hand, which is exactly what Rowen had been pushing for—helping the Church retrieve the past. And...well, you know the enemy."

Silas's face fell. Indeed, he did.

"So I reckon we'll continue fighting the good fight and contending for the Christian faith together then, won't we?"

He grabbed her hands and grinned, eyes filling with emotion at the next chapter the Lord had in store for him. For them.

Yes, together. Forever. Until death parts us.

ENJOY RITE OF DARKNESS?

A big thanks for joining Silas Grey and the rest of SEPIO on their adventure saving the Church! **Enjoy the story? Here's what you can do next:**

If you're ready for another adventure, you can get a full-length novel in the series for free! All you have to do is join the insider's group to be notified of specials and new releases by going to this link: www.jabouma.com/free

You might also like my apocalyptic sci-fi thriller series, *Ichthus Chronicles*. Set 100 years in the future, the last remnant of Christianity is threatened from forces inside and outside the Church, written in the vein of the *Left Behind* series. Start the adventure today: www.jabouma.com/books/apostasy-rising-1

If you loved the book and have a moment to spare, **a short review is much appreciated.** Nothing fancy, just your honest take. Spreading the word is probably the #1 way you can help independent authors like me and help others enjoy the story.

AUTHOR'S NOTE

THE HISTORY BEHIND THE STORY

We live in wicked times. Not only with the rise of urban violence and recent phenomena of mass shooting events at movie theaters and nightclubs and the like. But also the rise of satanic, racist ideologies that would deny God's glory set within every person by nature of their being image bearers of the Creator. Add to this the toxic display of pride and anger and malice on social media, combined with the rise in the occult and there's no denying it: We live in wicked times.

Why is this?

Part of it is the fact that every one of us is born with a heart primed for such wickedness, having inherited a sinful nature from our original ancestor Adam. Yes, we still bear the image of our Creator. But that image is broken and busted beyond all self-repair; we truly are desperate for a heart transplant, which Christ offers freely through his rescue mission on the cross.

However, there is another reason: the reality of Satan and presence of demonic darkness in the world. We moderns, in all of our sophisticated rationality and demand for naturalistic causes, have generally written off such supernatural manifestations—both outside and the Church, but inside as well. And with disastrous consequences.

I'm not one to find the Devil hiding under every rock, and I am certainly cautious to uncritically ascribe every evil act to demons, but I cannot help but think that much of the wickedness we find in the world has far more demonic and Satanic designs behind it than we give it credit. In America, the rise of white nationalism and mass shooting events come to mind as prime examples. And with the documented rise in witchcraft and the occult in particularly the West, which many excuse as alternative spiritualities, it makes sense there has been a dramatic rise in requests for the Roman Rite.

So I thought, why not write a book that would attempt to clue people into these demonic dimensions and the clear and present dangers that the rulers, the authorities, the cosmic powers of this present darkness, and spiritual forces of evil pose to the world? And why not offer a word of warning for the kinds of doorways that lead to such influences and, yes, possession? Hopefully, the book gave you a bit of inspiration and insight into not only the realities of the Devil and doorways of the occult, but also the healing ministry of exorcism from possession—while thrilling you along the way, of course!

As with all of my books, I like to add a note at the end with some thoughts and research that went into the story. So, if you care to learn more about the foundation of this episode in the Order of Thaddeus, here is some of what I discovered that made its way into SEPIO's latest adventure.

Exorcisms and Possession

As a Protestant, and an evangelical one at that, exorcisms and possession has traditionally been quite outside of my spiritual vision, as well as the vision of my Christian tradition. I have certainly believed in Satan and his minions, and the presence of genuine wickedness and demonic forces in the world—even having personally felt the suffocating weight of spiritual oppression (not *possession*). But until my research, I never gave possession much thought nor the healing ministry of exorcism that clearly traces to Jesus Christ himself.

This is where my Catholic brothers and sisters have a leg up on us Protestants, who have traditionally been far more intentional about naming possession and offering healing. They offer a deliberate process for discerning, identifying, confronting, and releasing people from demonic possession I found inspiring. To inform my story and infuse it with historical fact, I consulted a book by one of the foremost exorcists in the world, Father Gabriele Amorth (*An Exorcist Explains the Demonic*) and another by Matt Baglio outlining the journey one priest took to becoming an exorcist and all that he encountered (*The Rite*).

Both resources were indispensable with outlining the history and theology of the Rite and demonic in chapters 7, 8, and 10—so much so that Father Gabriele D'Amante was inspired by the former, and the exorcism episodes were drawn from the latter. However, the possession clusters theory formulated by D'Amante and Rowen Radcliffe are wholly my own invention.

Celeste's experiences in chapters 12 and 15 are inspired by the actual events of a Catholic nun witnessed by Father Gary Thomas as described in chapter 10 of *The Rite*. I mirrored that episode involving an Italian Sister Janica because I wanted to get the details right of what a person might experience under the influence of a demon, and exactly how an exorcist would ameliorate one's possession. Same for D'Amante and Radcliffe's confrontation of Sebastian in chapter 31, a scene inspired by actual events drawn from chapter 14 in *The Rite*. An article from *The Atlantic*, "American Exorcism" (Dec. 2018), was helpful for some of the background in chapters 7 and 8, as well as informing Rosa's story (name changed) in chapter 5 and some of Celeste's experience in chapter 12.

Which brings me to an important aspect of the story: possession. One of the interesting insights into demonic possession from Father Amorth in his book is the notion of who becomes possessed. Here is how he explains it:

> [People of every faith or none. The Devil does not look in the face of everyone.] No one can consider themselves excluded: they can be young or old, believers or atheists, Christians or those of other religions....Not even consecrated religious are ruled out. I recall the case of Sister Angela, who was obsessed with a cursing that resounded in her mind. In most cases, those who are distant from the Faith are more susceptible to this risk, but this is only an indication of the maxim that says the Devil is more tranquil if he does not have to live with prayer, fasting, the Eucharist, and the other sacramental practices. (67)

So Christians and non-Christians alike can become possessed and influenced by the demonic, which I obviously illustrated with Celeste, and the door she opened in her past dabbling with the occult before she decided to follow Jesus.

Admittedly, I struggled with this idea at first, even doubting and reconsidering this storyline. I wasn't entirely keen on the idea of Christians becoming possessed (and am still considering the notion, to be honest), given my own tradition did not hold this, believing it to be at odds with their becoming filled with the Holy Spirit at salvation. However, another insight from Amorth gave some clarity:

> Without a doubt, diabolical possession, the invincible influence of the Devil on a person, is the most striking

> and serious form of the extraordinary action of the Devil. When the demon is able to take possession of a person, he can make him say and do what he wishes. It is necessary to clarify that the Devil is not able to take possession of the soul of a man (unless the person expressly consents to it), but only his body. (66)

He also goes on to say that cases of vexation, obsession, infestation, and oppression are far more common than actual possession, and is seldom permanent. But again, believers in Jesus Christ possessed?

Clearly Silas wondered the same thing! But I think the dialogue with D'Amante offers some insight. As he explained, Judas Iscariot, one of Jesus' own Twelve Disciples, was possessed by the Devil. The Evangelist Luke makes plain that *'Satan entered into Judas'* before he carried out his wicked deeds. And then the apostle Peter, the rock upon which the Church was founded, was warned by Jesus that *'Satan has demanded to sift all of you as wheat.'* The Devil obtained permission to try and drag them into his dastardly designs, and he succeeded with Peter (who later repented and was restored to relationship with Christ, unlike Judas who hung himself). Then there was Ananias, another disciple of Christ from the Book of Acts whom Luke quotes Peter asking, *'why has Satan filled your heart to lie to the Holy Spirit,'* suggesting a contrast of two 'fillings'—between Satan and the Spirit of God, even within believers.

Like Silas, I've considered the biblical theology of it all, but find these examples of demonic influence compelling. And given that Job seems to make the case that the people of God can be *oppressed* by Satan, and believers are certainly *tempted* by the Evil One, as Jesus Christ himself was and revealed in his prayer, I wonder why the same power can't be exerted on a person from the inside with torturous ends. Experience seems to bear the probability, given the thousands and even millions of Christians who have lived to tell about it, which Amorth and Baglio recounted in their books. And so does the Bible with Judas and Ananias.

Regardless, I hope the story offers some insight into the nature of evil we are up against, whether you're a Christian or not, and inspires you to take the necessary steps to stand your guard against the Devil's schemes. Paul said it best in Ephesians 6, which I quoted, but bears quoting again:

> *For our struggle is not against enemies of blood and flesh, but against the rulers, against the authorities, against the cosmic powers of this present darkness, against the spiritual forces of evil in the heavenly places. Therefore take up the whole armor of God, so that you may be able to withstand on that evil day, and having done everything, to stand firm.*

Given that exorcisms was a major feature of Jesus' ministry, and a ministry function that he passed along to his disciples, I hope that it is something the Church across the spectrum reclaims for these wicked times.

The Salem Witches

First of all, let me be clear: the Salem witch trials and subsequent hangings are a stain not only on America's history, but on American Christianity. The way of Christ and Christian doctrine does not call for killing people no matter how steeped in the occult and witchcraft they might be.

So, no, I am not suggesting we should revive the gallows in the interest of religious purity and protecting the world from evil! However, the deeper truth is that the demonic is real, it has historical precedent, and we should guard ourselves against it since Scripture makes plain that people who practice sorcery, witchcraft, and magic are judged outside the people of God and will not inherit Christ's Kingdom.

The history surrounding the events in Salem that 1692 year are fascinating, and the eyewitness accounts from people like Cotton Mather do seem to point to a diabolical movement by the Devil himself in the region—perhaps even brought on by people opening themselves up to Satan through occult practices and demonic possession. As he opened his book on the events: "I have indeed set myself to countermine the whole plot of the Devil against New England, in every Branch of it, as far as one of my darkness, can comprehend such a Work of Darkness."

Something happened that led to the kinds of experiences—shrieking and babbling, wrenching and contortions of limbs, strange happenings and deaths—that appear to be of demonic origin, even to the point of possession on the part of some Salem citizens. To be sure, I did take liberties with the individuals I named in the prologue and chapters 16, 20, and 26 (all convicted witches, and most hanged). However, the historical record does indicate some were known as dabbling in witchcraft and the occult. Then again, the entire trial process seemed rife with corruption and I imagine many of the fifty-five "confessions" wrenched from it were forced, and the other 144–185 named witches were fake.

But again, my interest in the story was the deeper truth of the doorways witchcraft and the occult open—and what it leads to. The Salem story seemed to be a good historical connecting point for what I wanted to explore. And since the bones were indeed discovered a few years ago at Proctor's Ledge, that seemed like a fortuitous plot point!

Chapter 20 outlines much of the eyewitness account of those events, which I drew from Mather's work and *The Witches*

(Schiff) and *Six Women of Salem* (Roach). Particularly noteworthy was the account written on the underside of the cover, penned in Mather's own hand—a fictional addition of my imagination but one I crafted from his own account of his record from Elizabeth How's trial. As he wrote: "Afterwards there came in the Confessions of several other (penitent) Witches, which affirmed this How to be one of those, who with them had been baptized by the Devil in the River, at Newbury-Falls: before which he made them there kneel down by the Brink of the River and worshiped him."

This nugget led to my prologue envisioning how this might have unfolded, with actual women accused of witchcraft attending a similar ceremony and signing a small, red volume. The Devil's Book, as it was called, was a feature of the trials. Real or not, it was reported that several of the accused (those who hung, others who escaped the noose) had signed their souls over to Satan in a ceremony parodying Christian baptism and the Eucharist.

Mary Warren was a prime witness against the accused, writhing and shrieking herself, even in court. I decided to place my focus on her and her connection with the Grey boys because the truth of her own story is completely unknown after the trials ended. As Marilynne Roach explained in *Six Women of Salem*: "Where Mary went, how long she lived, whether her father and deafened sister still lived—none that is known. The trail of her life evaporates like frost in the sunlight, as insubstantial as a phantom" (397).

Which gave me the opportunity to pick up the trail by writing her as sort of the main orchestrator of the original rite in Newbury-Falls and distant relative of the Greys. For the record, I highly doubt she ended up on Mackinac Island! Like many of those blanks of Warren's life I filled in, that part of the story was completely my invention, because the island has held a special place in my own life (both as a childhood haunt but also a yearly anniversary vacation for my wife and I), and I've wanted to put a story on the island. So I thought, why not!

However, the island is indeed one vast burial plot, for both Native Americans and also French and British settlers. The timing also worked fairly well when the mission by French Catholic missionaries was established. And given the haunted stories that surround the island (the story Dad Grey told Silas and Sebastian about the witch drowning is accurate, as far as I understand it; but again, the Mary Warren bit was my invention) and its remote location for experimenting with possession clusters on the part of Rudolf Borg and Sebastian Grey, I thought it would be a fun part of the story.

The final piece was the so-called Black Mass—yes, that's a thing. It does take the Catholic Mass specifically and Christian Lord's Supper generally and desecrate it. I wondered about adding such a Satanic ceremony to the story, but I stripped it back to focus on key elements that highlight the dangerous nature of the act: primarily the deliberate allegiance of one's soul to Satan. I drew much of the inspiration for the flow of the rite of darkness and some of its accompanying language from an actual ceremony held in Philadelphia. The rest was my invention.

Ultimately, this sort of rite exemplifies what happens when one dabbles in the occult and Satanism: the denial of the authority, sovereignty, and sufficiency of Jesus Christ in favor of an allegiance to the Prince of Darkness. It is also the culmination of the doctrine of consciousness Borg and Sebastian went on about, which twists the stories of human temptation in Genesis and Jesus' temptation in Matthew about human nature and freedom. Because as Father D'Amante made clear: what the Devil offered was not the knowledge of good and evil, but the power to decide what was good and what was evil. A power that inevitably leads to bondage, not freedom, which the whole of history illustrates with perfect 4K-resolution clarity.

The Devil is real, so are his forces that wage war against us. The demonic gains a foothold in the human heart when we open the door through habitual sin, but especially the occult and witchcraft. And while I'm not so sure reading Harry Potter is one of those doorways, the principle is that much in our culture has desensitized us to the realities and plans of the cosmic powers of this present darkness.

May we take deliberate steps to guard ourselves against these forces by taking up the armor of God, standing firm during our hour of oppression and testing. And may we also recognize the forgiveness and healing available to all through the freeing power of Jesus Christ when allow wickedness to take hold in our lives—regardless of its form.

Research is an important part of my process for creating compelling stories that entertain, inform, and inspire. Here are a few of the resources I used to research the history and legacy behind exorcisms, the occult and witchcraft, and the Salem witches:

- Amorth, Gabriele. *An Exorcist Explains the Demonic.* Manchester, NH: Sophia Institute Press, 2016. www.bouma.us/rite1
- Baglio, Matt. *The Rite: The Making of A Modern Exorcist.* New York: Crown Publishing, 2009. www.bouma.us/rite2
- Mather, Cotton. *On Witchcraft.* Mineola, NY: Dover Publications, 2005. www.bouma.us/rite3
- Roach, Marilynne K. *Six Women of Salem.* Boston: Da Capo Press, 2013. www.bouma.us/rite4
- Schiff, Stacy. *The Witches: Salem, 1692.* New York: Little, Brown and Company, 2015. www.bouma.us/rite5

GET YOUR FREE THRILLER

Building a relationship with my readers is one of my all-time favorite joys of writing! Once in a while I like to send out a newsletter with giveaways, free stories, pre-release content, updates on new books, and other bits on my stories.

Join my insider's group for updates, giveaways, and your free novel—a full-length action-adventure story in my *Order of Thaddeus* thriller series. Just tell me where to send it.

Follow this link to subscribe:
www.jabouma.com/free

ALSO BY J. A. BOUMA

Nobody should have to read bad religious fiction—whether it's cheesy plots with pat answers or misrepresentations of the Christian faith and the Bible. So J. A. Bouma tells compelling, propulsive stories that thrill as much as inspire, offering a dose of insight along the way.

***Order of Thaddeus* Action-Adventure Thriller Series**

Holy Shroud • Book 1

The Thirteenth Apostle • Book 2

Hidden Covenant • Book 3

American God • Book 4

Grail of Power • Book 5

Templars Rising • Book 6

Rite of Darkness • Book 7

Gospel Zero • Book 8

The Emperor's Code • Book 9

Deadly Hope • Book 10

Fallen Ones • Book 11

The Eden Legacy • Book 12

Silas Grey Collection 1 (Books 1-3)

Silas Grey Collection 2 (Books 4-6)

Silas Grey Collection 3 (Books 7-9)

Backstories: Short Story Collection 1

Martyrs Bones: Short Story Collection 2

Group X Cases Supernatural Suspense Series

Not of This World • Book 1

The Darkest Valley • Book 2

Against These Powers • Book 3

Luck Be the Ladies • Novelette

End Times Chronicles Sci-Fi Apocalyptic Series

Apostasy Rising / Season 1, Episode 1

Apostasy Rising / Season 1, Episode 2

Apostasy Rising / Season 1, Episode 3

Apostasy Rising / Season 1, Episode 4

Apostasy Rising / Full Season 1 (Episodes 1 to 4)

Apocalypse Rising / Season 2, Episode 1

Apocalypse Rising / Season 2, Episode 2

Apocalypse Rising / Season 2, Episode 3

Apocalypse Rising / Season 2, Episode 4

Apocalypse Rising / Full Season 2 (Episodes 1 to 4)

Faith Reimagined Spiritual Coming-of-Age Series

A Reimagined Faith • Book 1

A Rediscovered Faith • Book 2

Mill Creek Junction Short Story Series

The New Normal • Collection 1

My Name's Johnny Pope • Collection 2

Joy to the Junction! • Collection 3

The Ties that Bind Us • Collection 4

A Matter of Justice • Collection 5

Get all the latest short stories at: www.millcreekjunction.com

Find all of my latest book releases at: www.jabouma.com

ABOUT THE AUTHOR

J. A. Bouma believes nobody should have to read bad religious fiction—whether it's cheesy plots with pat answers or misrepresentations of the Christian faith and the Bible. So he tells compelling, propulsive stories that thrill as much as inspire, while offering a dose of insight along the way.

As a former congressional staffer and pastor, and award-nominated bestselling author of over forty religious fiction and nonfiction books, he blends a love for ideas and adventure, exploration and discovery, thrill and thought. With graduate degrees in Christian thought and the Bible, and armed with a voracious appetite for most mainstream genres, he tells stories you'll read with abandon and recommend with pride—exploring the tension of faith and doubt, spirituality and culture, belief and practice, and the gritty drama that is our pilgrim story.

When not putting fingers to keyboard, he loves vintage jazz vinyl, a glass of Malbec, and an epic read -- preferably together. He lives in Grand Rapids with his wife, two kiddos, and rambunctious boxer-pug-terrier.

www.jabouma.com • jeremy@jabouma.com

facebook.com/jaboumabooks

twitter.com/bouma

amazon.com/author/jabouma

www.ingramcontent.com/pod-product-compliance
Lightning Source LLC
Chambersburg PA
CBHW051007180726
48291CB00006B/2012